DEATH OF
THE
PICKLE KING

A Mary Malone Mystery

Marlene Chabot

Dreams do!
Come true!
Marlene Mcheil Chabot

Other writings by Marlene Chabot

NOVELS
Detecting the Fatal Connection
(Previously listed as *China Connection*)
North Dakota Neighbor
Mayhem With A Capital M
Death At The Bar X Ranch
Death of the Naked Lady

Anthologies
Why Did Santa Leave A Body?
"A Visit From Santa"

Festival of Crime
"The Missing Groom"

Dark Side of the Loon
"More Than Lessons"

SWF Stories and Poems
"The Gulper Eel"

Marco Island Stories and Poems Vol IV
"The Scarf"

DEDICATION

This book is dedicated to my family, fans, and all those who suffer from any form of mental or physical disability. No matter who you are or your station in life, we are all still part of this great world called planet earth.

ACKNOWLEDGEMENTS
I wish to express my gratitude to the following :

Rod Prochaska, VP of Operations for Gedney Foods Company in Chaska, Minnesota, who was so generous with his time during my tour of the plant.

Joyce Young, John Chabot, and Amy Chabot who gave of their time to edit this novel.

Dear Readers,

Ever since the first novel in the Mary Malone Series was released, I've wanted to follow up at some point with Gertie Nash finally persuading Mary to help her Cousin Butch prove his innocence pertaining to the theft of Hickleman Pickle Company's secret pickle recipes. In *Death of the Pickle King* Gertie gets her way after Butch is once again being blamed for something much graver involving the plant, the murder of owner Don Hickleman.

Until I started research on making dill and sweet pickles and relishes out of cucumbers, the only thing I knew about pickles was that I liked eating them and making my own batches of refrigerator pickles from a recipe my Great Aunt Mame shared with me years ago.

Cucumbers, which originally came from Southern Asia, were fed in pickle form to Roman troops many centuries ago. During that time period it was widely believed that eating cucumbers prepared this particular way would give soldiers physical strength. Today, in the 21st century, the benefits of eating pickled vegetables are still touted via the media. It's been said athletes have drunk pickle juice to counteract dehydration. But scientists have also proven pickled vegetables are more nutritious for you and makes food easier to digest.

It's a good thing our country has abundant resources for cucumbers since more than 9 lbs. of pickles are consumed per person annually. Two of the major countries to import cucumbers to the U.S. are Mexico and Canada.

If you haven't checked out the latest pickle-flavored foods and beverages craze yet, here's a sampling of what's in the market place: ice cream, chips, popcorn, candy canes, hard candies, lollipops, almonds, mints, gum, juice, vodka, beer, soda, and sunflower seeds.

For those of you who simply prefer having plenty of bread and butter chips, dill pickles or other pickled veggies and fruit on hand, one of the recipes found at the back of this novel is sure to please your taste buds. Enjoy.

"Have a pickle," she said."
I questioned the offer.
It wasn't exactly chocolate.
"Ah, no thanks, I don't care for any."
"Have a pickle," she insisted more forcefully.
I took one.
Little did I know how significant eating one dill pickle could be.

~1~

Day 1

I flung up my hands. "I've made a royal mess of things," I told a fellow Foley resident while we waited for the elevator to takeoff for the fourth floor where we both reside. Even though it was the Monday after Thanksgiving, the smell of turkey remains still lingered in the stuffy elevator. My stomach growled.

Margaret Grimshaw, a tiny grandmotherly woman with an indestructible donut bun hairstyle was caught off guard when the lazy elevator finally jerked into motion. In order to resume her straight-as-an-arrow stance in her preferred pink Isotoner slippers, the woman drew her feet closer together and pushed one heavily-veined hand against the nearest elevator wall while the other remained clamped around the mail she'd just collected. "How so, Mary?" she politely questioned. "Surely whatever it is it can't be that awful."

My arms dropped. I pressed my shoulder blades against the cold, grey sterile wall opposite the door. "I'm afraid it is." If I had my way, I'd bypass any explanation. But I knew in my heart I couldn't simply slide my remark under the damp black rubber rug resting beneath our feet. It wouldn't be right. You see, Margaret, who has been a resident of the Foley forever, knows the relative from whom I'm subletting the apartment quite well—my brother Matt, a private investigator. "If the huge mess isn't cleared up by the time Matt comes back from Ireland in three weeks, he's going to raise one heck of a stink."

The elderly woman bowed her dainty head. "Oh, dear, what's Zoe done now?"

Margaret was referring to my widowed aunt who has lived with me since I moved into the Foley this past May. She's either redecorating the living room space where she sleeps or destroying the kitchen with strange inedible concoctions she's created. "Actually, Auntie's not totally to blame this time."

"She's not?"

"No. And I can't hide what all Matt might find: his reliable dog Gracie missing, a glitzy-glam Vegas style lounge living room, Aunt Zoe and I still dwelling here, and me probably smackdab in the middle of another case I have no right to be involved with."

The woman of Italian heritage pressed her silver wire-rimmed glasses closer to her face and sighed. "*Che Cosa*? Gracie's missing?"

I nodded.

"Since when?" she inquired.

"Saturday," I replied, inspecting what the thinly-framed, impeccably dressed woman standing next to me wore. Her nicely draped navy-colored cotton pants and matching long-sleeved silk top fit her perfectly. *If only I could be a size eight again.* I tried sucking in my extended tummy; it wouldn't budge. There's no getting around it. I had to stop stuffing my bottomless pit with the wrong foods, especially sweets and snacks. "Okay, okay, pizza, popcorn, and double cheeseburgers belong on the list too, but that's it. Honest."

Margaret's almost invisible eyebrows arched significantly. "Why hadn't you told me about Gracie sooner? I could've asked friends of mine who live near the Foley to keep an eye out for her."

"I meant to, but you weren't around this weekend."

"Well, I can see where the loss of a dog would be a lot to take in for anyone, including your brother." She tapped her arthritic fingers to her wrinkled lips. "Dear, why don't you drop by later after your evening meal. I'm sure we can come up with sensible solutions to your problems while we enjoy a scrumptious dessert I made."

Did she say dessert? It's tough resisting an invitation including sweets. Sugar added to anything entering this gal's stomach soothes jumbled nerves and instantly dissolves problems weighing on my mind, unless, of course, Aunt Zoe's mixed up in it somehow. I licked my chapped lips and tossed aside previous notions of fitting into clothing eight sizes smaller. Well, it wasn't hard to do. With only oddball jobs being offered to me lately, I can't afford a new wardrobe anyway. And besides, I don't like to turn the elderly woman down. She'd feel bad. Accepting the invitation is the best thing for both of us. It's a win-win situation. Not only does Margaret get company, but I get to sample the wonderful things she's made. Hmm? What could she possibly have created this time?

The elevator dinged for our stop sooner than I anticipated; leaving me no time to envision what dilly of a dessert would be served later. I did however manage to give Margaret a quick hug before the door slid open and we went our separate ways. "Thanks for the invite. Just knowing I can use you as a sounding board makes me feel less stressed already."

The ninety-year-old woman stepped off the elevator in slow motion. "Good," she said over her shoulder as she headed towards her door, "I'm glad I can help," and then she slipped into her apartment.

Thunderous steps approached me the second I poked the key in the lock. Only one Foley resident made that much noise. I had to get inside pronto. I struggled with the lock. Nothing happened. Darn! Of all times for me to get stuck in this narrow passageway.

"Mary. Wait," Gertie Nash yelled. "I've got to speak with you. It's an emergency."

What now? I took a deep breath and filled my lungs with stagnant air consisting of heavy cologne, a mixture of perfumes, and hot tamales. Hopefully her emergency isn't about her cousin, Butch the ex-con, again. I'm tired of being told he wants to speak to me. I spun around. "What's happened, Gertie?"

The 200 pound woman with Star Wars' tattoos branching out along every visible part of her body stepped forward. "You've gotta help. Butch is in deep doo doo."

"What's he done?"

She hesitated for a split-second. Her typically ruddy face looked pasty.

Concerned for her welfare, I clutched her arm for a moment. "Are you all right?"

"Yes," Gertie gulped, "I just had to catch my breath. I'm not used to chasing anyone down the hall."

Now that the woman was almost in my face, I prayed her words about Butch's situation would be brief. Unfortunately, my requests aren't always answered the way I want. Before Gertie could share anything, Aunt Zoe flung the apartment door open. "What's all the fuss out there?" she inquired, blocking me from entering with one hand while the other held a half-eaten dill pickle. "I heard shouting."

I pointed to the fifty-something woman standing off to the side, who loves to coordinate her hair color with every outfit in her wardrobe. Magenta appears to be the color pick of the day. Tomorrow it'll probably be tomato.

My aunt looked beyond me and focused on Gertie. "She doesn't look well, Mary. Bring her in," she ordered, "Have her sit a spell."

Not a good idea. I usually regret following my aunt's suggestion, but I did it anyway. I can't help it if I'm a glutton for punishment.

After I brought Gertie into the apartment, Aunt Zoe took a bite of her pickle and then scurried off to the kitchen without any explanation, leaving me high and dry to care for the comfort of our uninvited visitor.

As it turned out, Gertie didn't need any looking after. When she entered the living room, she headed straight to the leather couch Aunt Zoe had painstakingly draped with two yards of neon green colored fabric, having at least six dozen silver sequins sewn to it. With Gertie positioned as she was, I realized all that was left for a genuine Vegas Strip effect was to wrap her with a string of miniature Christmas lights, the clear type.

Since Gertie claimed the Vegas glammed piece of furniture I made do with the uncovered La-Z-Boy, which happened to be the most comfortable furniture in the room according to my garage sale standards.

A few seconds after we settled in, Aunt Zoe returned carrying a glass of water. "Sorry you caught me eating,

Gertie. I'd just gotten my mid-morning snack out when I heard the commotion in the hall."

"No need to explain," she said. "I'm a big pickle lover too."

"Well, right now I think you need liquid more than a pickle, but I can get you one later. We've got plenty." She handed Gertie the glass of water. "Here you go. Dr. Oz says to drink plenty of water when you're dehydrated."

The woman smiled weakly. "Thanks, Zoe." She took a couple sips of the clear liquid offered her. Then she rested the glass on the smooth, dark wood coffee table in front of her, and said, "I'm sorry to be such a pest, Mary, but I don't know who else to turn to. Butch has been arrested."

Aunt Zoe strolled over to the couch, sat, and gave Gertie a sympathetic pat on the hand. "There, there, Gertie. Things will get better."

Great. She'll never leave. "What did he do?" I queried trying to sound like an interested party even though I wasn't.

Gertie slapped her thighs that bulged noticeably due to the too small Skinny jeans she wore. "Nothing at all. Butch is as innocent as a newborn."

Not wanting to insult the woman, I choked back a laugh. Any person who has been convicted of a crime isn't as innocent as a baby in my book and probably not in a cop's either. "Come on, Gertie, you know people don't get locked up for nothing. He had to have done something to warrant his arrest."

The woman remained silent as she fussed with the glass of water she'd set on the table. That worried me. She loved to talk. Could she be spinning a trap?

If I was as lucky as a leprechaun, she'd walk out of here without ever expanding on Butch's problem. Sadly, that's unlikely. I'm extremely unlucky. I can't even win money playing one lousy bingo card at a church event. Besides, previous encounters with Gertie demonstrated she doesn't give up easily. And at this moment she's holding me captive in my own home.

~2~

Our unwanted guest clutched her inked-elbows and leaned forward, signifying her readiness to spill her guts. "Well, this morning," she began, "an employee at Hickleman's Pickle Plant discovered a body floating face down in one of the pickle vats. And of course, rumors started flying at once. Butch had to be the killer. He was seen in the plant a couple nights ago having a heated argument with the dead man."

"Oh, dear! Have they identified the body yet?" Aunt Zoe inquired.

Gertie rested her hand on her flat forehead. "It was old man Hickleman himself."

"What? The pickle king is dead? No. It can't be," Aunt Zoe shook her spiked red head. "It's got to be a mistake. I just saw him in a pickle commercial this morning on TV, the Crunch a Bunch one."

Gertie released a sigh. "Unfortunately he is."

"What's going to happen to my favorite pickles now?" Aunt Zoe whined. "Shelf them? Mr. Hickleman has no heirs to his throne as far as I know."

Who but Aunt Zoe would carry that little tidbit around in her head? A pickle lover since knee-high to a grasshopper, she's vigilant about keeping abreast of any news dealing with the pickling industry.

"I'm not sure if that's true about his not having any heirs," Gertie said.

Aunt Zoe got excited. "You mean there is someone to take over?"

"Well, this is according to Butch of course, but years ago he heard a rumor that Hickleman had an illegitimate child."

"Forget about this so-called illegitimate child," I said. "Back up a bit, Gertie. Didn't you tell me the big shots running the pickle company refused to allow your cousin to step foot in the plant after his last incarceration?"

"That's right." Gertie straightened her large frame on the leather couch. "And Butch didn't intend to go inside the building the other day. When he went to the plant, all he planned to do was catch the marketing manager when he left work for the day, so he could ask him why his prize winning county fair pickles weren't being sold in our community, like winners from previous years.

"I blame the security guard for the mess my cousin is in. Why, if he hadn't spotted Butch and ushered him into old man Hickleman's office, no one would've heard any angry words uttered between Hickleman and Butch."

"That's all the police have to go on, Butch arguing with the dead man? Surely there are other people at the plant who had it in for the owner besides your brother."

"You don't understand. It was old man Hickleman who had Butch arrested the last time."

I drew a finger across my bottom lip. "Hmm? What specific charge did Hickleman bring against Butch then?"

Gertie dug a Kleenex out of her pant pocket and dabbed her sweaty forehead. "He accused him of stealing company recipes."

"Ah, I get it now. Due to Butch's past record, everyone, including the police, is determined to feed him to the lions, disregarding any other possible suspects in Hickleman's death."

"Exactly," Gertie muttered, crumpling the used Kleenex in her shaky hand.

Aunt Zoe scrambled to her feet. "Mary, you've got to help Butch," she pleaded. "He already went to jail once for a crime he says he didn't commit. You can't let him be charged with another."

I pinched my squarish chin. "Gertie, can one of your family members afford to post bail for your cousin?"

"My brother Lawrence, a bachelor, has money up the wazoo. We've been trying to get ahold of him, but no luck yet. I have a feeling he's out of town. His position as vice-president of marketing for a large Twin Cities sporting goods business requires him to travel at least twice a month."

I happened to be working on a case at the moment plus filling in at Singi's Optical, as well as, doing substitute teaching on occasion, I really didn't know if I could shove anything else into my tight schedule, but I was definitely curious about Butch's last incarceration. "Gertie, let me know the minute your cousin gets released. I want to speak with him."

Gertie's pupils grew as large as walnuts. "Oh, Mary, does that mean you're going to help him?" she asked as she pushed her plump body off the couch and stood.

"Ah… I'm not sure I'd have time, but I could at least offer him free advice."

Gertie patted her hands. "Great. Free advice is better than nothing. Butch will be thrilled to hear what you have to say. Well, I'd better skedaddle. Hubby promised he'd dig out the Christmas decorations from storage, and if I'm not there to see he does it, it won't happen in this lifetime."

Aunt Zoe escorted Gertie to the door, leaving me free to hunt for the strongest drink in the kitchen cupboards so I could forget what had just transpired. Hopefully I'd be as lucky as Helen Plum, a fictional character who takes solace in her hidden bottle of brandy when her mother's antics get to be too much for her.

Remember how unlucky I am. Today was no different. No drops of any liquid could be found in the cupboards unless one counted what remained of blue food coloring Aunt Zoe insisted on using in a frosting mix several months ago. At the moment a blue tongue didn't appeal to me. However, another option opened up. I found a package of Kool-Aid I'd carelessly tossed in an upper cabinet this past summer. It would suffice. At least grape flavoring was the color of wine. "Now where did I stash that stupid pitcher?"

~3~

I didn't think Aunt Zoe would ever settle down on the couch with her newly acquired romance novel after helping me clear the supper table and taking care of the day's dirty dishes. But she finally did, which left me free to visit Margaret Grimshaw. Besides discussing the problems I'd already mentioned on the elevator with her an additional one has now cropped up, thanks to my roommate's big mouth.

"Come in, Mary. Don't dawdle at the door acting shy. This isn't your first visit here," the older woman chirped, stylishly dressed in a different wardrobe than earlier in the day: simple tan skirt, long-sleeved cream-colored blouse, and a butcher style apron created from a soft-blue floral print.

I strode across the threshold and went straight to the dining table which took up space in one corner of Margaret's living room. Sitting there seemed the most logical since I'd received an invite for dessert.

The second I caught sight of the oval table I knew I'd made the right decision. Silverware, delicate tea cups, saucers, and cloth napkins decorated the top of a well-pressed ivory colored linen tablecloth, begging to be used. Too bad Miss Manners hadn't been invited. She'd appreciate Margaret's splendid setting as much as me.

"Pretty bird. Pretty Bird."

I glanced around the dining room, expecting to catch a glimpse of Petey, Margaret's twenty-year-old Blue-fronted Amazon parrot perched somewhere studying me, but I didn't see him. All I noticed was the rest of Margaret's warm welcoming living room. I sighed. *This is what Matt's apartment needed to look like in three weeks. But will it?* My mind flashed to the bizarre living room I'd left a few moments prior, requiring super transformation.

The bird sang out once more.

"That's Petey squawking, isn't it?"

My hostess bowed her head slightly. "*Si.* I put him in the back bedroom. He's not happy."

"I hope you didn't put him there on my account. I love birds."

The elderly woman looked down the hallway for a second where her two bedrooms were located. "No, no. Petey always lets off a little steam before he falls asleep in the spare bedroom," she explained, and then she settled her olive-green eyes on me. "Please go ahead and sit, dear. I need to get a few things from the kitchen first."

I ignored the couch and selected one of the four lightly-stained oak chairs arranged around the table. "Don't rush on my account," I said while keeping watch on her slow progress to the kitchen. "I'm not going anywhere else this evening." *No thanks to my male friends.* To kill time until the elderly woman rejoined me I inspected her intricately designed tea cups. They didn't look like ones Margaret had used for entertaining me before.

Hmm? Maybe this set is a recent gift from one of Margaret's male admirers. According to Matt, two men from the elderly woman's church have proposed marriage, but I've never seen any sign of a new ring on her finger since moving into the Foley and I'm certain Aunt Zoe hasn't either. She's got such a big mouth she would've blabbed it to the whole world by now. Actually, hearing the ninety-year-old woman speak as fondly as she does about her late husband, I don't foresee her ever remarrying.

Curious to discover the origination of the cups and saucers, I gently lifted one above eye level: England. Who could've gone there?

I was still holding the dainty cup in mid-air when my cell phone rang unexpectedly, cutting off all thoughts floating around in my cranium pertaining to Margaret's private affairs. Remembering that no good comes from rushing, especially when I'm holding a delicate object not belonging to me, I purposely ignored the ringing until I'd gently set the tea cup back on its saucer and freed up my hands for other uses, including answering the phone. "Hello."

"Mary, have you found Gracie yet?" my mother inquired in a frantic tone. "You know your brother will be home in three weeks."

Really? As if I had forgotten. My free hand instinctively reached for one of the cloth napkins on the table and began to fuss with it. "I know. Believe me I'm working on it, Mom."

"Well, you'd better be. Your brother lost a wife; he doesn't need to lose a dog too."

Way to go, Mom. Adding more stress to my life. "I hear ya."

"What are you and Zoe doing this evening? Please don't tell me you're wasting your time watching NCIS or other such nonsense when you should be putting up posters all over town."

I zoned out the tenseness creeping throughout my body. "I'm visiting with Margaret Grimshaw."

"Oh, is she the elderly lady who lives across the hall from Matt?"

"That's the one."

"Well, I'd better let you go then. Tell her I said hello."

"I will. Good-bye."

The minute the conversation with my mother ended, Margaret reappeared on the scene clutching a fancy teapot. "Did I hear music," she inquired, "or are my old ears deceiving me?"

I took a deep breath and then lifted my head, letting go of the built up stress caused by my mother's phone call before Margaret's kind eyes noticed how upset I was. "Yes. It was coming from my cell phone," I turned the gadget off and stuffed it back in my pocket. "My mother called. She says, 'Hello.'"

Margaret shuffled to the dining room table and gently deposited the beige and dark chocolate glazed teapot near me. I hadn't seen it before and questioned whether it was new too. "You look worried, dear." She pulled a chair next to mine and sat. "What is it? Is everything okay at home? You're father's heart isn't giving him trouble again, is it?"

She was referring to the quadruple bypass surgery my dad had two years ago. "No. He's fine. Mom just wondered if I'd found Gracie yet." Before I said anything

I'd later regret, I tapped the teapot's narrow wooden handle, the safest spot to touch, and switched to a different subject, one that had nothing to do with family. "What type of tea have you brewed this time? I don't recognize the aroma. Is it another new blend you've discovered?"

She smiled. "Yes, it's an herbal one. I'll tell you about it as soon as I get our dessert."

I shoved out the heavy oak chair I'd been perched on. "Stay seated. I'll get it."

"Why, thank you. My legs are rather stiff tonight. You'll find the dessert sitting by the fridge."

"Too much dancing, huh?" I asked as I paraded out to the kitchen.

"Probably, but I'm not giving it up anytime soon."

I entered the kitchen and found a scrumptious pie awaiting me. It happened to be my favorite. The light-as-air pie could be easily damaged though so I'd needed to be extra careful, meaning I'd better take tiny steps back to the dining area.

"Margaret, you're going to have to teach me how you get meringue to sit four inches high. My Mom's eyes would pop out if I showed up with something like this at the next family gathering. The filling is lemon flavored I presume."

"*Si.* It's been way too many years since I've made one. I hope it turned out okay." She placed a hand by her tea cup. "Would you mind pouring the tea for us?"

"Of course not, but I'm still waiting to hear what kind of tea you've prepared." I wrapped a hand around the teapot's smooth handle, filled our cups three-quarters full, and set them back on their saucers.

"Almond Sunset. It has a hint of cinnamon and orange in it."

"Ah, I thought I smelled cinnamon. Did you purchase the tea from Tea 4 Two down the block?"

Margaret grabbed a large smooth knife off the table to cut the pie. "No, I still haven't gotten over there. My friend Tom actually purchased this tea for me as well as the teapot. He recently took a bus trip that included a tour of the Celestial Seasoning's facilities in Boulder, Colorado."

"That would be an interesting place to visit. I hope Tom found the tour worthwhile especially if he likes tea as much as we do." I sat and drew my chair closer to the table.

"*Si*. That's all the man could talk about. He told me an enormous quantity of loose teas are stored in one building and each different tea housed there is kept in its own separate compartment that can be sealed off with a garage style door. Of course, the peppermint tea's door must remain down at all times."

"That makes sense. Peppermint's strong aroma would be absorbed by the other teas before a person managed to snap their fingers."

Margaret placed a spatula under one of the two slices of pie she'd cut, slipped it out of the pan, set it on a dessert plate, and handed me the serving. "You know, Mary, working on more than one problem is like slicing a pie into portions."

"How's that?" I asked, thinking in terms of arithmetic.

"You want to give each person or problem a fair share, but the first always seems the most difficult to tackle."

"And mine would be finding Gracie, right?"

"*Si*. Now eat. Nourishment helps one think better."

I grinned. "Lady, you say such profound things." Thanks to her I have another great excuse for putting off dieting.

The moment I lifted the fork to my lips and tasted the fluffy peaked egg whites along with the thick lemon filling I knew I had died and gone to heaven. "Ooooh, this dessert is fantastic. You must make it more often."

The elderly woman's olive-green eyes twinkled. "*Grazie*, but I think this type of pie should be reserved for special occasions."

"Ah… and what are you celebrating?" Was I off the mark? Could she have gotten engaged to one of her suitors after all? She did say she wasn't home this past weekend.

Margaret's misty eyes drifted to her gold wedding band still worn on her left hand. "Today would've been my seventy-fifth wedding anniversary."

"Wow!" *I'm in my mid-thirties and still haven't found a man interested in committing to me.* "I'm guessing you must've been about sixteen when you and Antonio got married in Sicily."

My words caused undue embarrassment to her. The ninety-year-old's pale complexion turned a brilliant red like a male cardinal. Expecting a rapid contradiction to follow, I waited to hear her comment, but no denial flowed from her mouth. However, she did finally speak. "Pour me another cup of tea and we'll see how you can fix your problems. That's why you came over here, isn't it?"

"Why of course." She didn't need to know including dessert in her invite had something to do with my visit too.

~**4**~

Day 2

Last night Margaret suggested I tack up and pass out
missing dog flyers beyond the few blocks Aunt Zoe and
I'd already covered in our neighborhood this past
weekend. So, before we went to bed, I laid out my plans to
my aunt, including my 7 a.m. rising time.

Unfortunately, she wasn't too keen on the lateness
of the hour. You see most mornings she manages to wake
up around 5:30. But just because she's the early bird
around here doesn't mean she's dressed and ready to go
before I am. "Okay," I said, willing to compromise yet
again, "How about I get up at 6:45." I know I didn't give
her exactly what she wanted, but at least it was better than
nothing. Thankfully she accepted the terms.

At 6:45 on the dot, the clock radio and cell phone
jarred me awake; both were sitting on the nightstand. Not
having set the phone as a backup to the radio wake up, I

assumed the early caller was a teacher from Washington Elementary where I used to work until I got laid off. When I left, I asked to have my name put on the substitute list so the school doesn't forget about me if an opening ever occurs in the lower grades.

I flicked off the radio and grabbed the phone. "Good morning, Mary. I hope I didn't wake you," said the cheery male voice on the other end.

The strong, heavy accent narrowed the possibility to one man, Dr. Raj Singi, and he wasn't a teacher. His livelihood was optometry. He, his wife Kamini, and their three girls aged four, three, and five months live directly below my brother's apartment. "Of course not, Dr. Singi," I fibbed, "I've been up since six like you."

"Good. Good. I don't like to impose on you at the last minute, but if you're not substituting, would you be so kind as to fill in for Kamini at the optical store today. Baby Anika isn't feeling well and Kamini thought she, instead of her parents, should be home with her."

I'd been filling in on and off at Dr. Singi's eyeglass business since Kamini took time off to have little Anika, so it wasn't a job I knew nothing about. And the best thing about this part-time job, I didn't need to fill up Fiona, my VW, with gas every time I went to work; Singi Optical rubbed bricks with the Foley. "Sure, I'd be glad to." Only a fool would turn down income with bills coming in left and right. Besides, the only thing I had lined up for today was finding Gracie.

"What time should I be at your office?"

"One moment please. Kamini should know when the first patient is to arrive." The loud clunk of a landline phone receiver came across the wires instantly. I pressed my ear even tighter to the phone assuming I'd hear the conversation between husband and wife, but didn't. Little

Anika's wails drowned out whatever was shared. Three seconds later Raj came back to the phone. "Our first eye appointment is set for 8:30, so please be at the store by 8:00."

Delighted to have any job thrown my way, I said, "I'll be there with bells on, Mr. Singi."

"What? You're going to wear bells. No. No. That won't do. It's not appropriate attire for an optical store. Kamini only wears those when she performs belly dancing in public or teaches classes."

"Mr. Singi, you misunderstood. I'm not really wearing bells. It's simply an odd American expression from way back when."

"Oh? I see. All right, Mary. I'll expect you to arrive promptly at 8, with bells on." Then Mr. Singi, an extremely serious person, let loose with a thunderous laugh and hung up.

I tossed the cell phone back on the nightstand and flew off the bed. "Holy Smoley. I gotta get rolling."

I scrambled to the bathroom planning to take a quick shower, throw on a dab of makeup, and then select a suitable outfit from the meager wardrobe I owned before heading to the kitchen to fix an uncomplicated breakfast, and pack an edible lunch. And then, after all that was done, I needed to squeeze in a brief talk with Aunt Zoe about flyers.

Unfortunately, things didn't go as planned. The tips of my non-pedicured toes had barely touched the bathrooms cold ceramic floor when a knock at the door dashed shower plans and anything else for the time being. Not wanting Aunt Zoe to wake up before she needed to, I rushed to the door without considering what I was wearing, a tatty purple flannel nightgown that barely dusted my kneecaps.

Could Matt be arriving sooner than he intended? *Don't be silly, Mary. He would've warned you. It's got to be Gertie or Margaret.*

I ignored the possibility that the early visitor might be a criminal and unhooked the door's safety chain without first looking through the peephole. A mistake I'd regret once I flung the door open.

"Wow, Mary, I must say your dressing standards are improving," Rod Thompson, another fourth floor neighbor said, while his wandering eyes continued to check me out. "Nice touch with the nightie by the way."

Acting like I'd gotten caught with my hand in the cookie jar, I grabbed the side seams of my nightie and overlapped the fabric in front as much as possible.

"Ah, don't act so coy with me. That nightie of yours is a far cry from the tee shirt and undies I saw you in six months ago."

Why do people enjoy bringing up embarrassing moments in other's lives?

I kept a straight face, giving the impression I didn't recall what he was referring to. Unfortunately, it didn't help. Clearly Rod enjoyed seeing me squirm.

"Surely you haven't forgotten the day Zoe burnt toast and I popped in to disconnect the kitchen fire alarm, catching you off guard and under dressed. Did you get the pun?" he said, "Under dressed, underwear."

My face heated up dramatically. I clenched my fists. Obviously this man had no concept about what to say and not to a woman. Understandably that's why he hasn't gotten hitched yet. "What are you doing at my door this early in the morning?" I asked, sounding like a mother wolf ready to defend her pup.

"Going to work," the nerdy, Nordic FBI agent replied, lowering his volume to match mine. "Can't you tell?" He held his leather briefcase up for me to inspect.

"With everyone crying for a paperless society, I'm surprised a computer whiz like you would carry any paper around."

He winked. "Can you keep a secret?" I didn't reply. "It's mostly for appearance sake. I hide my lunch in it."

I gazed at the lanky six-foot snappy dresser and tried to guess exactly what he came by to bother me about. I hadn't requested any assistance with a case. I tapped my bare foot. "You still haven't explained what you're doing at my door."

Rod ran a hand through his thick blond hair. "I saw Margaret a few minutes ago."

The tiny tidbit regarding Margaret piqued my interest. "Is she all right?"

"Of course. That woman will outlive us all."

I let go of the flannel nightie and crossed my arms. "Look, Rod, I've got to go to work. If you don't spit out your reason for being here within the next second, I'm shutting the door in your face."

"Oh, she's getting ruffled now. I love seeing your Irish temper flare up, you should display it more." I glared at him. "All right, sweet pea, no more messing with you. Margaret told me Matt would be back in three weeks. Is that true?"

"Yes, but why do you care? Everyone knows you two have never been the best of friends."

He swept his well-manicured hand in front of his face. "Ah, forget Matt. I want to know where you two defenseless women are going to live once your brother kicks you out."

So we're defenseless, huh? Wait till he discovers Aunt Zoe and I've been attending safety classes for women.

"We haven't given it much thought yet, but we will. So don't bother fretting over it." I wrapped my hand around the door knob and started to close the door thinking Rod would get the hint and leave, but he stuck his shiny brown wing tipped shoes across the threshold to block it.

"I… ah…was thinking we should go to Ziggy Piggy's one last time before you move on. What do you think?"

The guy doesn't get it. He'll never be on my A-list of men to date. I stretched my lips to their limits as I prepared to permanently squash any further suggestions of going out together. "Oh, Rod, as much as I love to go to Ziggy Piggy's for their great BBQ offerings, I'm afraid I'm going to be extremely busy the next several weeks. However, if it turns out I'm not, I promise I'll get back to you."

Thankfully my words struck a chord. Not getting the reply he'd anticipated, Rod hastily withdrew his foot, allowing me to finally close the door.

"What… What's going on Mary?" Aunt Zoe inquired from her still prone position on the couch. When she attempted to lift her fiery reddish head, fully decorated with rollers the size of juice cans, she didn't succeed. "Did I oversleep?"

"Uh-huh. By more than an hour, and you missed seeing Rod too. He just left."

"I did?" Aunt Zoe seemed to be energized by the fact that a male visitor dared to see me this early in the morning despite my naked face and disheveled appearance. She tossed Matt's old wool blanket off of her and sat up. "Why did Rod drop by? Did he have information on Gracie?"

"Nope. Gracie was never mentioned." I leaned against the archway between the hallway and living room and chuckled. "It's hard to believe but the geek actually seemed genuinely concerned about where we're going to move when Matt gets back."

"See, haven't I been telling you how nice a fella Rod really is? You just don't want to listen to your Auntie."

"Come on. The guy's full of himself. Besides, I've already got two other men in the wings, David and Trevor." The two cops were located in different parts of Minnesota and had no clue about each other. I'm hoping that's the way it'll stay.

Aunt Zoe stood and folded her bedding. "Yes, I know dear, but there's nothing wrong with having too many law men in the wings." She shook a chubby finger at me. "Remember no one's made a commitment yet. And you keep saying you want to end up with a good guy."

"Look, a discussion on which man I date is getting us nowhere. Besides, I have to be at Singi Optical in an hour."

"What? When did your plans change?"

"About fifteen minutes ago. Raj said Kamini is needed at home. Their little one's sick," I explained as I headed for the bathroom with Aunt Zoe following close behind.

"But... but... we were supposed to hand out missing dog flyers beyond our neighborhood today."

"Sorry. I can't do it. You'll have to be in charge, Auntie." Discussion over, I closed the bathroom door.

Apparently a hunk of wood two inches thick between us didn't faze her. Aunt Zoe kept talking. "I'd rather not be in charge, Mary. I'm no good at it. Edward used to make all the decisions in our household. Hey, what if I call Reed to see what he's up to this morning? He's much better schmoozing with shop owners than I am."

Oh, please. The woman I lived with could talk the ear off a cat if one stayed around long enough to listen. If she wanted her boyfriend Reed Griffin, the owner of Bar X Ranch, for moral support, why didn't she just say so?

I turned on the water for the showerhead. "Go ahead. Finding Gracie is all that matters." I slid back the shower curtain, stepped into the tub, and let the steaming water slither down my five-foot-six framed body, washing away all reminders of Rod Thompson's visit.

~5~

"I'm here, Raj," I announced, gingerly stepping into the optical store's well-lit welcoming waiting room. No one replied.

I continued inward till the three and half foot counter at the far end of the room forced me to reroute myself, causing me to end up in a room a quarter of the size I'd left behind, where Raj Singi had painstakingly set up a tiny lab-one that allowed him to cut, tint, and inspect lenses as well as repair frames. The optometrist wasn't here either which meant he must be in the exam room or the men's room. Either would keep him busy for a bit.

Since I already had plenty of experience fending for myself at the optical store, I removed my black mittens, charcoal-grey wool coat, and matching neck scarf and hung them up where they wouldn't get dirty. Then I strolled out to the waiting room to see what might have been overlooked before the shop was locked up last night. There were a few things I noticed right away.

I tackled what I considered the messiest areas first in the front of the waiting room, one being the left portion of the office where toys for children under four cluttered the brown and gold stripped carpeting instead of resting in the cherry-red storage crate provided for. The cleanup took all of five minutes. Next up—straightening the ten beige-stained wood cushioned chairs, making sure their backs sat directly in front of the two humongous picture windows facing outdoors. The final task required collecting magazines scattered about, examining the date on each one, and tossing outdated copies.

With those menial tasks out of the way, I strolled over to the frame rack displays mounted on the large wall all the way to the right of the office and checked how many empty slots required frames.

While I was on my knees, digging through the cupboards searching for a variety of frames to add to the racks, Raj Singi came out of the exam room with a man I assumed to be a scheduled patient.

"Ah, Mary," the thin five foot three, mid-forties man with thick coal-black hair and medium-brown skin said, "you are here. Good. Sorry, I didn't put a note on the counter to tell you where I was, but Mr. Wolf was in such severe pain when he showed up at the door."

"It's all right. I figured you might be with a patient."

"Ma'am, your boss is a miracle worker," the fifty-something neatly dressed Mr. Wolf said excitedly. "Thanks to him I can see again." His hand shot to his back pocket. "What do I owe you, Doc?"

The eye-doctor's deep set almond eyes settled on the man's round pocked face. "Consider it a freebie."

"Are you sure?"

"Yes."

Mr. Wolf zipped up his crinkled leather jacket. "Okay, but how about giving me a couple business cards. I'm sure you wouldn't mind them being passed out to my coworkers."

"Not at all."

Before Raj Singi could make a move to get the man what he requested, I spoke up. "I'll get them for you Mr. Wolf. Dr. Singi needs to prepare for his nine o'clock appointment."

"Thanks."

Once Mr. Wolf left, I headed to the back room where I found Raj cleaning his silver-colored wire rimmed glasses with a small soft cloth and a clear liquid he had squeezed from a plastic bottle of lens cleaner. "How's baby Anika?" I asked. "If Kamini needs to take her to the doctor, I'm sure my aunt wouldn't mind watching Keya and Charvi for her."

"Anika's problem isn't serious. She's cutting teeth, but I appreciate your interest." Finished with his cleaning project, he rested the bows of his glasses on his narrow ears again. "I'm going to be quite busy in about five minutes, Mary. Since I have patients coming in back to back till six this evening, I would suggest you do what you normally do when Kamini's not here. Help people select frames, answer the phone, and of course let me know when a person arrives for their exam."

"Are you going to have time to go to lunch?"

Raj shook his heart-shaped head, confirming what I'd suspected.

Before I could offer to order lunch in for him around noon, the bell hanging above the entrance door jangled, informing us that a customer had entered the building. Raj and I immediately left the work room behind and went off in different directions, he to the exam room and me to greet the customer.

I stretched my lips to produce a broad smile. "Good morning. How can I help you?"

The elderly woman with silver-blue tinted hair and huge gaudy rings on every finger, except her thumbs, used a slender black cane to lean on. Even with the aid of her cane she still stood at least an inch taller than my five foot neighbor Margaret Grimshaw. "I've come to see Dr. Singi," the woman replied in a no nonsense manner, reminding me of a drill sergeant. She pointed a crooked finger at the back counter. "My name should be in that appointment book of yours. It's Francine Yousup."

I excused myself, strolled over to the book lying opened to today's date, found the woman's name, and checked it off. "Yes, Ms. Yousup, we have you down to see the doctor at nine o'clock."

The old woman ground her shiny brass cane into the carpet. "It Mrs. Yousup, young lady, not Ms. I don't care if my husband's been dead for twenty years."

"Sorry, I didn't mean to upset you, Mrs. Yousup. I only help out occasionally. Please follow me," and then I slowly led her to the exam room at the back of the office.

After I left Mrs. Yousup with Dr. Singi, I strolled to the counter and glanced at the names written in the appointment book. None of the women's names had a Ms. or Mrs. in front of it. It looks like I might be eating humble pie all day and not the type that fuels the tummy.

With the constant flow of traffic in and out of the office this morning, I barely had time to think about lunch until my stomach growled angrily and I glanced at the clock next to the wall on the counter. 11:45. I thought of what I packed to eat thanks to almost bare cupboards, peanut butter and jelly spread on a dried out hotdog bun.

Not what I normally dine on. The simple meal would've been sufficient if I was only staying till one, but I needed something hardier like a double cheeseburger, large order of fries, and a shake to tide me over till supper. Too bad there wasn't one of those meal trucks one sees dotting the streets of downtown Minneapolis stationed outside the optical store.

Raj Singi finally finished up with a contact lens patient and came out to the outer office where I was. Perfect timing. I can ask him if he'd like me to pop out and get him a fast food meal. If the answers "Yes" I can get something for myself as well. Since a few people were waiting for my assistance with minor optical needs, I spoke to him in a whisper. "Raj, I didn't get a chance to ask you earlier but…"

Confounded by Aunt Zoe's sudden appearance my tongue knotted up. Yours would've too if you'd seen her male goldfinch getup: neon-yellow earmuffs and mittens, black boots stretched to her kneecaps, and a black parka over canary-colored jogging pants. Although in defense of this particular bird, the male wouldn't be showing his true colors in winter.

As soon as I got over the initial shock of my aunt's clothing selection, I noted that her hands were weighted down with two Styrofoam food containers. I burst out laughing. *Does the woman have extra sensory perception?*

I mouthed the words, "How did you know?" to her as the three of us swiftly moved to the back room out of the sight of the customers.

Aunt Zoe surveyed the small room, explaining the food delivery as she did so. "It wasn't hard to figure out you needed·food, Mary, after I recalled the measly lunch I watched you packed." Finally honing in on what she must've been looking for all along, an empty spot at the end of a counter, she deposited the food containers and pointed an accusing gloved-finger at Raj. "But I didn't know about you, until Kamini shared you probably wouldn't have time for lunch with your busy schedule. So I decided to feed two with one stone."

Raj scratched his head. "You paid for our food with a stone, not money? I've been in America five years and do not know this. I suppose it takes many, many years for an immigrant to learn everything about a new country."

"Actually, Raj, she was referring to another old saying."

"Like with bells on?" he said, chuckling to himself.

"Exactly." With customers still waiting for me, I figured I didn't need to tell him Aunt Zoe hadn't quoted the saying correctly or explain what it meant. I'd leave that for another time. Instead I switched gears. "Auntie, did you and Reed manage to get the flyers passed out?"

Her head bobbed up and down like a sewing machine needle. "Every last one of them."

"Good."

"I'm sorry you haven't found Gracie yet," Raj said. "I have a large piece of cardboard you can use to make a sign, Mary. When it's ready, I'll post it in one of the front windows."

"That is so kind of you, Raj. Thank you."

"No need to thank me. You help me and I help you." He opened his Styrofoam container now to see what my aunt had brought him. "Ah… you are an amazing woman, Zoe."

That's what he thinks, if he only knew.

The optometrist picked up a forkful of his curried rice and sniffed it. "Mary, is your lunch from the India deli too?"

"Gee, I don't know." I flipped the lid off the container hoping to find a cheeseburger and fries inside. "Yup. I believe it's a kind of chicken dish." *Definitely not what I'd been craving, but I'll eat it.*

Raj leaned over and checked out my meal. "Mmm, you'll like it. Chicken Tandoori with curried rice is very tasty."

"Ah, curried rice. That explains why it's tinted yellow." I quickly resealed the Styrofoam box.

Deep wrinkles spread across Aunt Zoe's brow. "Aren't you pleased with your meal?"

"Sure," I lied, "but we both can't eat at the same time when there are people out front waiting to be helped." I grabbed my aunt's arm and steered her to the waiting room, allowing Raj to eat in peace instead of ending up with a truckload of indigestion.

When we reached the front section of the business, I quickly resumed a position at one of the small tables, thanked my aunt profusely for bringing lunch, and said I'd see her later.

Aunt Zoe didn't budge an inch. "Don't be so quick to push me out the door, Mary. Since I'm here, I'd like you to check the bows on my sunglasses. I think they need tightening." She tucked a hand in her jacket pocket, withdrew an enormous hot pink pair of sunglasses suited for a person traveling incognito, and handed them off to me.

Obviously my aunt thought our relationship gave her priority over anyone else in the room. Too bad. I believe in the *first come first serve* philosophy. I set her sunglasses on the edge of one of the two oak tables I used with customers throughout the day. "Sorry, I can't adjust them right this minute, Auntie. You'll have to wait your turn. Take a seat."

She appeared miffed but quickly chose a chair located between the two picture windows and started an earnest discussion with a middle-aged woman to the left of her.

"Okay, who's next?" I asked as I remained by the table nearest the entrance.

A dark-skinned man around thirty dressed in business suit attire stood and approached me with a spring to his step. His long slender hands held two items: a plastic bow and a frame. "I am," he replied, exposing gleaming white teeth and a Jamaican accent. "The screw fell out. Can you fix it?"

"Sure. It'll just take a second." I excused myself and left to search for the right size screw in the lab where all the repair supplies are kept. Once I found exactly what I needed, I reconnected the bow to the frame and returned to the waiting room to clean the lenses. "Here you go, sir. You may want to try your glasses on to make sure they still fit snug around your ears."

The man lifted his arm and glanced at his expensive watch. "That's all right," he said, taking his glasses back, "I'm sure they're fine. Thanks."

Just as he walked away from the table and the next customer strolled up to it, Gertie Nash charged in, mouth agape, acting as crazy as a bull about to charge a matador. She cooled off fast though once she saw I was busy with a customer. Her mouth clamped shut and she focused her attention on those seated in the chairs by the window, including Aunt Zoe. As soon as Gertie recognized my aunt, her mouth flew open. Then her loud obnoxious voice pierced the air. "Zoe, I didn't expect to see you. I suppose you're here for an eye exam."

Oh great! Just what I need, two wound up women here at the same time. I kept my eyes peeled on them while the lady sitting in front of me paged through our latest frame catalog. She had told me it was easier to point out what she was interested in with the catalog than going through all the frames we had on display.

Aunt Zoe stopped talking to the woman next to her and turned her body in the direction of the door where Gertie still remained planted. "No, it's not time for my eyes to be checked yet," she loudly explained. "I brought Mary and the doctor lunch and decided to have my sunglasses adjusted while I'm at it."

Gertie jerked a thumb in my direction. "Well, I came to tell Mary the good news about Butch, but I see she's busy."

"Yup. Join the—" Aunt Zoe paused a second, then she shot up out of her seat, scrambled over to me, bent over and whispered in my ear. "Keep an eye on that man near the door. I think he's stealing your merchandise."

"What?" Surely Aunt Zoe was mistaken. Who in their right mind would steal anything in front of several pairs of eyes? I rested a hand on the left side of my face. *The customer's merely trying on sunglasses.* A tall three-sided spinning rack loaded with sunglasses sat right next to the man's chair. If I were him, I'd do the same. It helps kills time. *But what if her story is right?*

I moved a hand to the middle of my face and spread the fingers apart ever so slowly, allowing me to peek through an opening without drawing attention to what I was doing. Shoot! Aunt Zoe had it right. The old man with the bushy beard and mustache, who looked like he was on his last leg, was definitely shoving merchandise into the paper shopping bag resting on the floor by the side of his chair faster than I could sneeze.

At some point the guy must've sensed he was being watched. He jerked his Viking cap below his thick eyebrows and looked my way. The second it dawned on him that he'd been caught in the act he grabbed his bag and tore out the door.

Shocked at what had occurred, I tried to remember everything he had on and exactly what had been displayed on the now empty rack. At least fifty pairs of Raj's top of the line sunglasses costing anywhere from two-fifty to four hundred dollars. Why couldn't he have stolen the cheap ones sitting in the window? *There goes my paycheck.* I shoved out my chair and flew towards the door. "Aunt Zoe, hold down the fort. I'm going after that guy."

"But, Mary," she blubbered, "You said you'd fix my glasses."

"And what about Butch?" Gertie whined.

~6~

Adrenaline soared through every pore of my body.
Without giving a thought to subzero weather and icy
sidewalk conditions, I flew out the door wearing nothing
but a short sleeve cotton blouse, klutzy two inch heels, and
a knit pencil skirt reaching slightly below my knees.

By block three my poorly dressed body objected to
the cold it had been submitted to: teeth chattered and
fingers felt numb. Who chases someone down in freezing
weather minus coat and boots? How stupid. Why didn't I
call the cops?

Maybe I could get a little assistance like a person
does when a crime has been committed in a movie. I
arched my back, yelled, "Stop that man!" and pointed
down the street to the man in the Viking cap and dark
brown quilted vest. The few people trudging along the
sidewalk wrapped in a cocoon of winter wear stared at me
like I had just been released from the zoo and then

continued on their way. So much for humankind getting involved.

I rubbed my chilled arms. Despite the cold air filling the lungs and freezing the body, and no one diving in to help, I wasn't going to give up. No store owner deserved to lose their merchandise, especially one who had just become an American citizen and had the good sense to hire this unemployed teacher.

Committed to the task at hand, I increased my running speed, but it didn't seem to make a difference. The old rat who stole Raj Singi's sunglasses kept on going. His feet remained steady as a rock. Why couldn't mine? I was at least thirty years younger. *If only he'd lose his balance.*

Just as I caught myself slipping for the umpteenth time, the man I'd been following ducked into a narrow alleyway that ran between two businesses one block up. I recognized the neighborhood immediately. Gracie's groomer lives on the backside of the street and I knew a shortcut. I swung right, cut across the middle of the yard at the end of the block, made a sharp left turn, and then dashed towards the alleyway, hoping to catch the guy who gave the impression he was preparing for next October's Twin City Marathon.

Hallelujah! I hadn't lost him. Maybe my bad luck was about to change.

Unaware that danger was coming at him, full speed ahead, from the other end of the alley, the thief kept his head bent low and carefully dodged every nuisance in his way as he went.

An imaginary crowd cheered me on. *I've got him now.*

Unfortunately, capturing the thief hadn't been well thought out. When two people, one heading east and the other west, roar through an alleyway like trains mistakenly sharing the same track a collision is inevitable. The two of us smacked into each other head on in the center of the alleyway. When my legs sprang out from under me, I grasped for anything to help reduce injuries to the backside. My hand caught a handle on the old man's bag causing the top of the bag to rip. Sunglasses rained down every which way as I smacked the tarred alleyway.

Before I could even think about getting on my feet from a prone position, the elderly guy stood and tore off with what frames were left in his bag.

Amazing! I couldn't believe the dexterity a man his age had. He should've broken a leg or arm. Either he works out at the YMCA or he pops a ton of vitamins.

"That's it. No more excess weight for me. Tomorrow I'm swearing off candy bars for good." After I raised myself up and brushed off the snow clinging to my body, I wiggled my numb fingers, toes, and legs, making sure they still worked the way God intended them to. They did. The same didn't hold true for my uncooperative butt and head though. The only decent remedy for the tremendous pain radiating from those areas would be to swallow an Excedrin the size of a basketball and they didn't make them that big.

Now that I was standing upright in the alleyway I eyed the sunglasses strewn about and wondered how the heck I was going to get them back to Singi Optical without a bag, pockets, or a purse. It took about a second to figure it out.

I popped the two sunglasses nearest my feet on top of my head and then I moved about a foot, collected two more pairs, layered one on top of the other and set them on my face. The day suddenly turned darker, but I didn't care. There were still ten pairs to gather up and only two hands to carry them in.

Anxious to get back to the comfort of the optical store, I slid five closed frames over the fingers of each hand and then took off in the direction I'd come a few minutes before.

The minute I stepped back into the store Aunt Zoe and Gertie surrounded me. "Oh, Mary," Aunt Zoe said, "You look like something the cat dragged in. I wish I could've seen what the other guy looked like. Did you use a couple of those self-defense moves we learned in class last week?"

"Nope," I replied, releasing my hold on the ten pairs of sunglasses while Aunt Zoe took the ones off my head. "The situation didn't warrant it. The old guy was too slick."

I glanced at the lone customer sitting by the picture window. The girl was about college age. "I'll be with you in just a minute." I removed the two pairs of sunglasses from my face and then attempted to fluff my short cropped hair.

The girl gave me an amused smile. "Don't worry about me," she said. "I'm here for a follow up with my contacts. Although I might take a look at a few of those stylish sunglasses you were wearing when I finish, if you don't mind. A couple caught my eye."

I felt a surge of heat rushing to my cheeks. *If only I could hide somewhere.* I glanced at the carpet. "Of course. I'll leave them on the table."

Raj Singi shook his head when he came out of the exam room, but didn't say a word to me. I've a feeling he wasn't thrilled seeing Gertie and Aunt Zoe, people not scheduled for appointments, occupying his employee's time. After taking in our little threesome, he called to his next patient. "Colleen, please step this way."

The young woman quickly collected her purse and coat and went off with Raj to the exam room.

The second the door closed behind them, I pressed Aunt Zoe for information. "You did tell Raj what happened, didn't you?"

"I… ah, I…ah, never had the opportunity."

My nails dug into the palms of my hand. "I think you and Gertie better leave before Raj comes back out here. I can't afford to be fired."

"Maybe he's just concerned about your appearance," Gertie blurted out. "Have you seen yourself in a mirror since you got back? A huge beet-red mark has formed on your forehead. The skirt you're wearing is twisted and your nylons and shoes are soiled beyond recognition."

"In other words I'm a mess."

Her head wobbled up and down. "That about covers it."

I marched over to the right wall where a huge mirror separated shelves of women's and men's frames and searched for the zipper on my skirt. This particular style of skirt is meant to have the zipper centered on the back panel. Instead it was pressed against my stomach. I hastily straightened it and then spun towards Gertie again. "Okay, my minor flaws have been taken care of thanks to you. Now please leave."

The woman rested a pudgy hand on her hip and stomped her foot. "Not before I tell you why I came to see you."

In no mood for games, I said, "Make it snappy."

"You wanted to speak with Butch, right? I nodded. "Well, he's available whenever you are. He made bail this morning thanks to my brother Lawrence."

I gave her a stiff smile. "Terrific. I'll call him as soon as I can."

~7~

A scary thought fleetingly flicked across my rather fuzzy brain when my exhausted and hungry body returned from Singi Optical to our apartment. Maybe Aunt Zoe took care of supper. I shuddered. Cleaning up another one of her kitchen disasters is not my cup of tea, no matter what time of day it is.

Entering the apartment with trepidation, I sniffed the air. There wasn't the slightest hint food had been recently cooked or scorched. Nor did I hear pots and pans clanging in the kitchen which usually meant Aunt Zoe was about to turn her culinary skills loose. Huh? I wonder what she's up to. Maybe she fell asleep on my bed.

My stomach growled angrily. "I hear ya. Don't worry I'll take care of you after I get out of this filthy outfit."

I charged down to the bedroom expecting to find my aunt, but she wasn't there either. No big deal. It was nice to have a bit of quiet time. I tossed off the clothes I'd worn all day and put on knit jogging pants and the comfy sweatshirt my Washington Elementary students gave me as a good-bye gift the end of school last year.

After changing, I'd intended to march into the kitchen and answer my stomach's pleas for food, but voices coming from the living room caused me to make a quick detour to investigate the situation. Since I'd forgotten to lock the apartment door, anyone could've walked in, even Gertie and Butch.

Aunt Zoe stood near the couch, back to me, holding a laundry basket in her arms while speaking to Kamini Singi, Raj's wife.

The woman wrapped in a turquoise sari reminded me of a royal princess. Her complexion, teeth and figure are picture perfect. And she's always elegantly dressed.

I greeted the third floor resident with a smile. "I suppose you've come by to cancel tomorrow's belly dancing lessons since Anika's teething?" Kamini offers free lessons in the laundry room of the Foley twice a week. I've only made it to her class once, but I swear I felt the pounds shedding with every shimmy I did.

"No," the petite woman with shiny, straight black hair reaching to her waist softly replied. "This has nothing to do with belly dancing."

Aunt Zoe set the laundry basket on the couch and pivoted towards me. "Raj told her what happened at the office today."

"Oh?"

"Yes," Kamini said. "You were so brave, Mary, trying to catch a man who stole merchandise from our store. I told Raj he should've stopped you. You could've been killed."

"Raj didn't know anything about it, Kamini. He was in the exam room when I took off after the thief." I flicked my hand in the air. "Besides, I'm fine. The guy never threatened me with a knife or gun. And the only thing sore on me is my stupid butt."

"Even so," she said, "You did something another employee would've never done for Raj. That's why I want to give you a little gift."

"But Raj already gave me a reward."

Aunt Zoe's heavily colored eyebrows perked up. "He did? What was it?"

"A pen in the shape of eyeglasses."

Kamini shook her head. "It didn't cost him anything. We get free samples of pens all the time."

"That doesn't matter. It's the thought that counts. Your husband knows how much I like to collect unique pens."

"Believe me what I have for you is even better." Kamini reached into the folds of her sari, pulled out a gift card, and presented it to me.

Assuming the card given me had to be used at the optical shop; I turned it over to see how much it was worth. To my surprise the fifty dollar card didn't pertain to anything optical, just food. It was for my favorite hamburger joint in town, Milts. No cooking for this tired gal tonight. I was so excited I felt like doing a Happy dance. "Thank you, Kamini. But you didn't have to do this."

"Yes, yes. You retrieved over a dozen stolen sunglasses, but ruined your clothes. It's the least we can do. The food is good there. When Raj craves a hamburger, that's where he takes us to eat."

"Actually, when my aunt showed up with lunch today, I thought she'd brought me a hamburger."

Aunt Zoe's wrinkles created deeper furrows on her forehead. "You did? Why didn't you say anything?"

Kamini tapped Aunt Zoe's hand as she moved to the door. "It's all right, not everyone likes Indian food. Goodnight."

"Goodnight," Aunt Zoe and I replied.

After Kamini left, my aunt quietly tended to the clothes in the laundry basket. "I feel awful, Mary," she said above a whisper, shaking out a clean towel and folding it. "Did you even touch the Indian food I gave you?"

"Of course I did. You know me I never throw food away if I can help it. That's one of the reasons my hips are getting thicker."

My words perked her up. "I'm sorry I didn't get around to planning supper for us, but between taking calls about Gracie and doing the laundry the afternoon got away from me."

"I understand." I slipped an arm around her shoulders. "You mentioned calls about Gracie. Did someone spot her?"

"No. Once I asked the callers to describe the dog they saw, I knew it wasn't her."

"Darn! I suppose offering a reward will draw plenty of crackpots out of the woodwork, especially druggies." I took another towel out of the basket. "Let's hurry up and get this stuff folded and put away, and then we can go for a ride."

"So we can stock up on groceries?"

"Yeah, but it's not our first stop." I showed her the dollar amount written on the gift card. "That should more than cover meals for two at Milt's tonight, don't you think?"

Aunt Zoe was ecstatic. One would think she'd never ate out. "Oh, yes, and many more."

***

While we lingered in one of the hot pink vinyl padded booths at Milts, an old fashioned diner, enjoying cheeseburgers, heavily salted fries, and thick chocolate malts, Aunt Zoe and I rehashed the bizarre crime that took place at Singi Optical. "I still can't believe that old guy stole Raj's sunglasses," I said, dabbing a couple fries in ketchup. "The value of the items taken is nowhere near the high-end jewelry sold in the shop two doors down from Raj's. If the thief had done his homework, he would've known the jewelry store had less foot traffic and one sales person on duty, making it easier to swipe whatever caught his fancy."

Aunt Zoe tore the paper off her straw, stuck the straw in her malt, and enjoyed a few sips. "Pretty dumb guy, huh?

I nodded. "There's definitely something about him that bothers me, but I'm not sure what it is."

"Maybe his face reminded you of a student's dad."

I pondered my aunt's comment for a second as I got a good grip on my order, a cheeseburger overflowing with extra condiments. "Nah. That's not it. There's something about his dexterity. It seemed a bit off for a man his age. How old would you guess him to be?"

"I'd say around seventy-five."

"That's what I guessed too." I bit into a quarter of the cheeseburger and it quickly disappeared. "The thing is most people in their seventies who get knocked off their feet are usually suffering from a form of arthritis and find it quite difficult to get off the ground without help. The guy I collided with acted more like a young gymnast. He was up and out of the alley before I could even sneeze."

Aunt Zoe pushed her empty malt glass aside and finished eating the four fries left on her plate. "Are you implying the man was wearing a disguise?"

I tapped my lip with a finger. "It's quite possible. If a person wanted to get away with the perfect crime, putting on a disguise would certainly do the trick." I finished with the malt and cheeseburger, tossed on my jacket, and grabbed my purse. "Are you ready to head home, roomie?"

"I guess I'd better be. I don't want to miss seeing *Wheel of Fortune*."

The second we slid out of the booth to pay our bill we bumped into Gertie Nash and her husband Ralph who had just walked in. "Oh, Mary, I can't tell you how delighted Butch is that you're going to talk to him."

"That's good," I said, "Enjoy your meal." Thinking the Nash's had headed for a table, I turned towards the waitress standing on the other side of the counter, dug out the gift card, and handed it to her.

It wasn't until Ralph Nash's deep baritone voice sounded behind me that I became aware the couple from our building hadn't budged an inch after all. "Honey, tell Mary about the interesting field trip coming up."

Gertie smiled at her hubby. "That's right. Thanks for reminding me, dear. I had forgotten all about it." Gertie flipped her hair behind her ears. "Ah… Mary, I planned to call you later, but as long as we've bumped into each other, I might as well spit it out now."

"This isn't about Butch, is it?"

Gertie suddenly grabbed her husband's arm like she needed his moral support. "Nope, nope this doesn't pertain to him. I… ah, signed you up to help chaperone a field trip when I was at Washington Elementary this afternoon. They were short on volunteers and I didn't think you'd mind," she gushed, exposing teeth that clearly needed attention. "It's right up your alley."

She'd some nerve signing me up to chaperone a trip without checking with me first. Normally I'd be madder than a wet hen, but tonight I wasn't. Anytime I can sub or help out with other causes at Washington Elementary I'm more than happy to do so. Ever since the economy went south and I got a pink slip from the school, I've tried to put in as many appearances there as possible to better my chances of getting rehired when the need arises. "Well, it depends. What day of the week is it? Where are they taking the kids?"

"I knew you'd be interested. It's the perfect trip for you and I'm going too."

I rested a hand on my hip and stared at Gertie. *Dear God what did this woman get me into.* "That still doesn't tell me anything. What exactly did you sign me up for, Gertie? And when is this bus trip?"

She squeezed Ralph's arm and stood on her tiptoes, making her closer to my five foot six height. "You're not going to believe this, but the second graders are touring a plant in St. Michael tomorrow."

"Okay. But what's so interesting in St. Michael worth a road trip there?"

"The Hickleman Pickle Plant where Butch used to work. What a coincidence, huh? Please say you can help out."

"Hmm?" I tapped my fingers on my chin. "You're absolutely right, Gertie. Being a chaperone on this specific trip is perfect. Not only can I see what the pickle plant is like without anyone getting suspicious, but I'll also gain knowledge about the company which will be beneficial to me when I speak with Butch."

The woman patted me on the back. "That's the spirit, Mary. See you tomorrow morning at nine sharp."

~8~

Day 3

The six-foot middle-aged man, who was dressed in an ivory colored lab coat, held our group hostage in a cramped lobby while he handed out lime-green hairnets and safety glasses. When his task was finally completed, he shared information specifically directed at the children. "Remember, kids, safety first is our number one priority at the Hickleman Pickle Plant."

The man's name tag read Paul Mason, Shift Supervisor. "It's easy to get lost in a big place like this," he continued, "especially if you've never been here before. So I'm asking that you please remain with your chaperones at all times during the tour today. Chaperones, perhaps you'd like to hold onto the children's special eyewear for a bit. They're not required to wear them outside, where our tour starts, just when walking around indoors."

The second I strung seven pairs of safety glasses on my arm plus my own, two of the girls took ahold of my hands. I knew their game plan by heart. They'd be stuck on me like gum on a shoe until we got back on the bus.

Gertie nudged my elbow. "What do you think, Mary? We're pretty glamourous, huh?"

I shrugged off her comment. I didn't know who she thought she was fooling. I had no idea what I looked like, but the woman standing next to me wearing hairnet and goggles reminded me of a toad on steroids.

"Did you bring your cell phone?" she asked, smiling broadly. "Someone needs to take a picture of us in this getup so we can post it on Facebook."

I'd die before friends of mine caught me in this two-bit costume. "No, I left it at home," I lied, thinking how clever it was of me to shut the phone off and tuck it in my coat pocket before joining everyone on the bus at Washington Elementary.

Gertie sighed. "Oh, well, I guess we don't have time to take a picture anyway. Our tour guide is ready to roll." She pulled off her goggles and slung them on her flabby, heavily tattooed arm with the others. "Talk to you later."

Not if I can help it.

I faced the children assigned to me and made a snappy count, making doubly sure no one had taken off for the bathroom without informing me. Seven kids exactly. "Okay, kids let's move out." I held the exit door open and waited until the last child in my group had trotted past me before joining them in the plant parking lot.

Being outside in November for any amount of time with kids can be risky. If it hadn't been for the mid-thirties temperature and the sun smacking our backsides, there would've been a mutiny on the grownups hands and I would've missed seeing the outdoor open brine vats where cucumbers begin their pickling process journey and where Don Hickleman ended his.

Before we climbed the steps to view the huge vats off to the left of us, Paul shared a bit of background on where the plant's supply of cucumbers comes from and what happens to them the minute they are delivered via truck, summer or winter. "We are proud to share that Hickleman's chooses only handpicked cucumbers for pickle consumption," he said. "Our supply comes from different locations depending on what time of year it is. One truckload may come from Canada or Mexico. At other times they are brought to us from towns in Minnesota, and other Midwest states.

"After the trucks arrive, the cucumbers are unloaded, weighed, and graded a couple feet from where you're standing," he said before pausing to catch his breath.

The instant he stopped talking a hand shot up, belonging to a dark-haired boy from Gertie's group.

Paul acknowledged the child. "Yes?" While waiting for a reply, he shoved his dark-brown plastic eyewear closer to his forehead.

The boy nodded. "Mr. Mason, do the cucumbers get As, Bs, or Cs for grades? That's what we get on our school work."

Our tour guide smiled. "Actually we use the numbers one, two, and three for grading purposes. Cucumbers given a one or two will be made into whole or sliced pickles. Those graded a three will be used for relishes."

The boy squirmed. "Ish. I don't like pickle relish."

"That's all right," Paul replied. "Not everyone likes pickle relish, but it sure tastes good on hotdogs and hamburgers. Are there any other questions?" No one raised their hand. "Okay, everyone, please follow me. You're going to see what happens to cucumbers after they're sorted into the three groups."

The little girl in the baby-blue jacket, who had claimed my left hand, was squeezing the dickens out of it. I opened my mouth to tell her to let up, but she popped a question first. "Miss Malone, why aren't we going inside yet? I came to see how the pickles are made not to listen to that old man talk."

I tried loosening her grip, but didn't succeed. "See those wood vats on that raised platform straight ahead?"

"Ah huh."

"If you want to find out what happens to cucumbers before they end up in jars, we need to go up on the platform and take a peek inside them."

"What are they used for?" she asked.

"I'm not sure. This is my first time touring the pickle plant too."

"Oh?"

"So do you still want to go inside?"

She pumped my hand. "Nooo, that's okay. We can go inside later. I want to see what everyone is looking at."

I led her up the steps and drew us as close to the vats as possible. Being one of the shortest children on the tour, the girl wouldn't see much until the majority of kids moved off the platform, which was fine with me. It meant I'd have more time to think through how Don Hickleman was outsmarted by a murderer and ended up floating in one of the humongous barrels.

Once the adults in our tour group managed to get all the children quieted down, Paul began to explain the vats and what they held. "These seventy wooden barrels lined up along this platform, each twelve feet in diameter, are referred to as holding tanks or vats and must be kept wet at all times so they don't dry out. Right before any sorted cucumbers are hauled up here and dumped in these containers we have to fill the bottom of each one with six to eight inches of salty water or what we call brine."

"What's the reason for putting a bit of brine in first?" Gertie asked.

"You need a cushion for the cucumbers so they don't bruise when they're poured in," Paul replied. He bent over, picked up a bushel basket, and held it over his head. "How many of you kids have seen a bushel basket like this filled with apples?" Half the second graders raised their hands. "Each of these vats on this platform can hold six hundred bushels of cucumbers. That only leaves a foot of space at the top of the vat, but it's enough to add six inches of salt brine again. Incidentally, kids, salt brine plays a big part in the pickling process. It changes the texture and taste of cucumbers and helps kill bacteria."

"How long do the cucumbers sit in the salt brine out here?" one of the parent volunteers inquired.

Paul directed his attention momentarily to the person who asked the question. "Approximately six weeks for fermentation to take place. Kids, up against the vats, would you mind moving back and letting those behind you move forward so they can see what a filled vat looks like too?" The children shifted like he asked. "Thanks. Are there any other questions before we head inside?"

Gertie spoke up. "Yes, how do you make sure the cucumbers that float to the surface don't stay there the whole six weeks?"

"We have long tools to push them down again."

Sensing the tools Paul spoke of could be of importance to the case I now planned to take on, I made a mental note to find out what they looked like.

The girl holding my hand got impatient with me. Anxious to see inside a vat she pulled my arm like it was the handle of a wagon. "Wow, Miss Malone, that's a lot of cucumbers for one barrel."

"It certainly is."

"I wonder if anyone's ever fallen in there?" she said, quickly backing away from the vat. "I wouldn't want to."

"Me neither. It's pretty scary."

She looked around the platform. "I don't see any covers to keep the animals out."

I let go of her hand. "Why don't you ask our tour guide about covers?"

"Okay. Hey, mister, do you ever cover the vats?"

Paul came over and stood by her. "No. The tanks are left open so the sun's rays can prevent the growth of yeast and mold on the brine surface."

"But what about animals?" she whined.

He crossed his arms and sighed. "We haven't had any problem with them."

No, just humans.

I took the little girl's hand and turned her in the direction of the steps. "Come on, I think we've seen enough. Let's get our group together and go inside."

***

The full tour lasted a little over an hour, but our time at the plant hadn't ended yet. The children would now proceed into the employee lunchroom to sample pickles and eat their bagged lunches.

While my group of kids stuffed their faces along with their peers, I strolled around the medium-sized lunchroom and took a look at the corked bulletin board hanging on the far wall by the fridge. The collage tacked to it intrigued me. Someone had actually taken the time to create a huge picture consisting of employee photos. I studied the sixty-some faces staring back at me. *Could one of them have hated Hickleman enough to kill him?*

Fifteen minutes later, the kids and grownups hopped on the bus again, heading to Washington Elementary. While the students chatted among themselves, I relaxed and began to process the world of Hickleman, including the tragedy that had most recently unfolded there and Butch's past problems with the company.

One visit to this company wouldn't suffice. You couldn't possibly draw any conclusions. In order to resolve the serious situation Butch found himself in, a person would have to devote equal time to his last incarceration as well as old man Hickleman's death. I realized I could do that if I applied for a job at the plant. So at lunch break, when everyone thought I'd gone off to use the bathroom facilities, I'd obtained a job application on the sly.

I got out of my seat at the rear of the bus and slowly made my way forward to Gertie who was sitting ten rows ahead of me. As soon as I reached her seat, I rested the palm of my hand against the upper cushion of the forest green seat and leaned in. "Hey, Gertie," I buzzed in her ear, "tell your Cousin Butch I'm ready to talk with him this evening if he's available."

She tilted her head back. "He should be, Mary. His boss doesn't want him anywhere near Tioni's Pizza Parlor until this mess gets cleared up."

"Tioni's? Where's it located?" I asked, thinking I'd check it out sometime soon.

"Two blocks from the pickle factory."

My stomach churned. "Perfect."

~9~

"Butch, I'm glad you were able to drop by on such short notice," I said, resting a hand on the nickel-plated door handle while he carried his beefed up linebacker like frame across the threshold and sauntered into our teeny entryway.

"Heck ma'am," he belted out, "I've got nothing better to do seeing as how the police have branded me a killer."

My ears rang. I hadn't expected Butch's voice to match the size of his body. It threw me off kilter. Although it shouldn't have; he is related to Gertie. "Okay, then let's get to the crux of the matter and clear your name once and for all."

"I'd like that." Butch removed his brown leather jacket and dangled it over his muscular arm. "Gertie's told me you're good at your job. According to her you've already helped put a couple criminals behind bars. She wasn't just blowing hot air, was she?"

"Nope. I've definitely done what she said, but I'm not a PI. You need to know that up front."

He gave me a wink. "Look, whatever you want to label yourself is fine with me as long as I don't end up in the slammer again."

"Good. I wanted you to understand where I was coming from before we went any further." I pointed to his jacket. "Let me take that. I'm afraid there's no chair in the living room to throw it over."

"Sure."

He held out the arm with the jacket draped on it. I scooped it up and put it in the closet behind him, and then ushered him into the living room where Aunt Zoe and I had been killing time until he got here.

When my roommate finally caught a glimpse of the two of us, she scooted off the couch and greeted our visitor like a long lost relative. "Hello, Butch," she said in her naturally, sugary-sweetened tone, offering a pudgy hand whose nails had been painted a sky-blue to match her lipstick only moments before. "It's nice to finally meet you. By the way, I'm Zoe, Mary's aunt."

Butch Bailey permitted a smile to creep across his stony square face as he took my aunt's hand and briefly pumped it. "Her aunt? No way. You can't be. You look so young."

Aunt Zoe's cheeks glowed. "Oh, you're too kind." She dropped her hand to her side and remained frozen in time, except for her thick black eyelashes that continued to wave at the man. "Gertie's told us so much about you," she gushed, lifting the hand Butch had just touched and resting it against her neck. "Why, I feel like I've known you forever."

What's up with her? The last time I caught auntie batting those thick lashes of hers was this past summer when she met Reed Griffin, her boyfriend, for the first time and charmed the pants off him, and as far as I knew they're still on good terms.

Aunt Zoe twisted her upper body slightly, picked up the book she had been reading, and then faced Gertie's cousin and me again. "I, ah, wonder if I can ask you a small favor, Butch. I've never met a real live author before. Well, Mary started a book this year for teenagers but she didn't get very far. Anyway, with my lack of experience I'm not sure if this is inappropriate or not, but would you mind signing your book before you leave?"

Too much info. I gave my aunt an icy stare. I should've known better than to tell her she could stay and listen to what Butch had to say. I invited the guy here to chat but not about the whacky book he wrote, *Ghosts that Haunt the Hennepin County Slammer.* Only the serious issues surrounding Butch are of utmost importance this evening. Who did Butch think was behind his first arrest? And who might be using him for a scapegoat this time? Could it be the same person?

Butch Bailey, a man in his mid-fifties, peered down at Aunt Zoe from his five foot eleven height and lightly fingered his salt and pepper Norse Skipper goatee that required a trimming within the next couple of days. "Of course, I'd be happy to sign it for you, Zoe. You must've gotten a copy from Gertie."

"As a matter of fact, I did."

Hmm. It looks like this gal's going to have to put a stop to idle chatter otherwise I'm going to miss seeing my favorite mystery shows on PBS. And I simply won't allow that. Over the past several months, I've gleaned an enormous amount of info on sleuthing from viewing programs like Father Brown, Miss Fisher, and the Coroner, but I still need to learn much more. Of course, watching a

James Bond movie can be educational too, but being a realist I know there's no way I can get my hands on the futuristic gadgets 007 is supplied with. Besides, I'm not preparing to join the police force, FBI, or the CIA. I cleared my throat. "Ahem, Butch, why don't you sit in the La-Z-Boy. It's not gussied up with layers of fabric and pillows like the couch is."

"Thanks. I'd prefer sitting in a seat not as dramatic," he said with a light chuckle, quickly dropping his roughly 230 pound frame into the beefy chair. "Now this is what I call a chair built for a man, nice and comfy."

Aunt Zoe bobbed her spiked red head. "It should be. This apartment belongs to my nephew, but his current job has taken him outside the U.S."

"Yes, but he'll be returning in a couple weeks and we'll be moving," I hastily added, relying heavily on Butch's alleged exploits. "Butch, can I get you a can of pop or a beer?"

Gertie's cousin ran a hand through his long, thick head of hair that could easily be tied back. "A beer would be fine."

"I'll get it," Aunt Zoe offered. "How about a little snack to go with it? We don't have any nuts, but my oatmeal cookies put Betty Crocker to shame. Every-one says they're to die for."

I shook my head discreetly.

The man decked out in an olive green Fleet Farm shirt, Lee boot-cut jeans, and black Skechers tennis shoes got the hint. He pressed his hand to his bulky stomach. "No thanks, Zoe. I feel like a stuffed pig after eating that huge meal Gertie fixed."

"I understand. Somedays I eat more than I should too. Well, if you'll excuse me I'll go get your beer."

I walked over to the leather sleeper couch, tossed the huge plump glitzy pillows strung out across it on the carpet, and then positioned myself on the end of the couch closest to Butch.

"According to what Gertie told me, you were sent to prison some years ago for a crime you didn't commit, but she never mentioned what for. I think it would help if you walked me through it." I grabbed a pad of paper and the new strawberry milkshake-shaped pen, recently acquired from Milts, off the coffee table.

Butch leaned forward in the La-Z-Boy, pressed his elbows into his upper thighs, knotted his hands together, and then opened his mouth but nothing came out. A behavior that's not unusual, especially when one's train of thought is broken by an interruption, like Aunt Zoe's rapid return with the beer.

"Here you go," she said, handing the Bud Light off to him. "I hope I didn't miss anything."

"You didn't," I said, displeased with her overly zealous return.

Since my roommate had finished her errand, I expected her to sit down by me, but she didn't. She continued to stand next to Butch instead. Her weird behavior tonight was driving me crazy. When a man is ready to open up about his past, he certainly doesn't need Auntie hovering over him like a mother hen.

I tapped the couch cushion like I do when Gracie can't decide where to plop. Aunt Zoe merely rolled her eyes. So I tapped the cushion again. This time she gave in.

Butch had been sipping on his beer while I was trying to get Aunt Zoe to do my bidding. Now that she had finally settled down, he rested his can of beer between his legs and shared his story. "I was working at the plant the first time I got arrested."

"Am I correct in assuming you're referring to Hickleman's?" I inquired.

"Yes."

I shifted my body a tad. "When was that?"

He leaned back in the chair, gripped his chin, and considered what I'd asked. "Roughly eight years ago, I guess."

Aunt Zoe looked at Butch adoringly. "You seem such a nice man. Why on earth did Mr. Hickleman have you arrested?"

Butch vigorously rubbed the palm of his hand as if the pain from that day was still fresh in his memory. "I happened to be working the first shift the day Old man Hickleman discovered a few of his company's top secret pickle recipes missing from his vault. No noise was made about it though. We simply found security guards posted by the time clock when the whistle blew for our shift to end. Being dead on our feet, none of us gave a thought about the guards standing there until they began to inspect our pockets and lunch pails."

"After the three people ahead of me had their things thoroughly searched, my turn came. I wasn't nervous. Why should I be? I knew I hadn't done anything wrong. But when the security guard opened my lunch pail, there sat a few of the missing recipes. I don't know how they got in there and I told Hickleman that when they dragged me into his office. Of course, he didn't buy anything I had to say.

"You see, around 2:30 that day, Paul Mason, my supervisor, informed me Mr. Hickleman wanted me to come to his office to discuss the raise I'd requested the month before."

"Ah, yes, Gertie and I met your supervisor the day we toured the plant with the kids. Go on."

"Well, I was on cloud nine. Nothing could've pleased me more. But the second I showed up at Hickleman's door, he apologized and told me he had to step out for a few minutes. I asked if he wanted me to come back. He said, 'No, just wait here.'" Butch lifted his beer to his lips and took a couple swallows, then set the can back down where he'd been safely storing it.

"Was the vault open when you were in his office?"

"Yup. Wide open."

"Who besides your supervisor knew you went to Hickleman's office?" I asked.

Butch shrugged. "I'm not sure. It's hard to hear or talk over the din of the machinery."

"That's true. I found that out yesterday. I'm surprised OSHA doesn't mandate that the employees wear earplugs."

"If they did," Butch said, "they wouldn't hear the machines beeping when something goes haywire."

I squeezed my chin. "Of course, I didn't think of that. Do you happen to recall anything else out of the ordinary occurring before meeting up with Hickleman that afternoon?"

Butch's thick grayish-black eyebrows shot up, covering half of his forehead. "Like what?"

"Mmm, someone bad-mouthing the company for example."

He rubbed his hands together. "Miss Malone, I've been gone from the factory eight years. That's a long time for a person to remember stuff they didn't give a hoot about one way or the other, even when they were working there."

"Sorry, I had to ask. Everybody's memory plays out differently. Let's take a little detour to the production area. When I toured it, I noticed it takes many hands to pack the pickles. Did you ever have a run-in with anyone while working?"

Butch raked his hair. "If I did, it would've been during the summer months when pickling production is greater, not in the winter."

I glanced at the carpet expecting Gracie's dark piercing eyes to be staring up at me, but she wasn't there. Where did the darn dog run off to? And why did she have to take off now of all times?

"Is that all you needed to know?" Butch inquired.

Aunt Zoe gently poked me. "Mary, Butch asked you a question."

My head jerked. "Sorry, about that. My mind wandered for a second there. A dog we've been caring for disappeared over the weekend and I'm really worried about her."

"Gracie belongs to Mary's brother," my aunt interjected, "And we don't dare tell him about it."

"Dang. That's tough. Dogs are such good critters, aren't they? I sure hope you get her back."

"Thanks." I flicked imaginary lint off my stretch pants. Now, what did you want to know?"

"I wondered if we were finished."

"Not quite. It would help if I knew how many shifts the plant has."

Butch pressed his hands into his upper thighs. "There are three in the summer and two this time of year. The first shift is for production and the other is for plant sanitization."

"So either an employee working sanitization or someone from the first shift snuck into Hickleman's office and stole the recipes, which is going to make it mighty difficult to get at the truth," I said. "Butch, be honest with me, did you ever wonder if your supervisor might have had something to do with the missing recipes?"

"Paul? Nah? He was well-liked by the men."

"Often times the most likeable person can be the most devious," I pointed out.

Butch wrapped his hands around the beer can. "I suppose. But I think if Paul was really nasty underneath, it would've shown through eventually."

Aunt Zoe grew restless. "Edward, my deceased husband used to say, 'There's no such thing as loving everyone you work with.' I'm sure that must've been true for you too, Butch."

Good question, Auntie. It certainly makes up for her earlier behavior.

Butch shifted in his chair, rubbing his heavily-lined forehead as he did so. "Well, yeah. There's always a few who get under your skin, even in prison."

"Care to name those who bothered you at work?" I asked, ready to fill up my writing pad with a long list of people.

Butch didn't have to think that one over. He only shared one name and it rolled off his tongue like a convict ready to sing. "Chip O'Leary."

"A fellow with Irish roots. Is he still at the plant?" I asked.

"Yup. I think he's been made vat manager."

"Then I'll begin with Paul and Chip. Since I already know what Paul looks like, I just need the low down on O'Leary."

Gertie's cousin braced his free hand on the arm of the La-Z-Boy chair, swung his muscular body out of it, and drew closer to the couch. "Sure. You can't miss him," he said. "Chip is short and stocky, about 5 foot 7. He has cold steely eyes, a mighty pocked up face, and a handlebar mustache."

Uncomfortable conversing with anyone towering over me while I'm seated, I got off the couch. "Hmm... a handlebar mustache. Not many people wear those these days. Too much work."

"Exactly, especially when dining with a girlfriend. You got to be wiping it all the time or she'll be staring at the food caught in it instead of thinking about the guy she's with." Butch handed his empty beer can off to me, indicating he was leaving. I took it. "Thanks for your time tonight, Mary. I feel better knowing you're on my side." He turned to face Zoe. "Thanks for the beer. It was a pleasure meeting you, ma'am, also," and then he headed to the door.

"Butch, what about my book?" Aunt Zoe asked, springing up from the couch. "You said you'd sign it for me."

"Right, right. You got a pen handy."

"I most certainly do." She eyed the Milt's pen still in my grip. I didn't offer it. She whipped it out of my hand anyway.

Sensing the two of them would be busy for a bit, I went to the entrance closet and retrieved Butch's coat. When I came back, I caught the tail end of what Aunt Zoe was saying to Butch. Something about how lucky he was. Her comment didn't make any sense. The man certainly wasn't lucky getting arrested twice.

Obviously, Butch had no idea what she was referring to either. "How's that?" he asked. "Do you mean because my book got published?"

Aunt Zoe rested her pudgy hand on his arm. "Well, that too. But I was speaking of what Mary told Gertie when she first learned of your latest arrest. Did Gertie ever mention it?"

He shrugged. "I don't think so."

"She said she had too many irons in the fire and couldn't possibly help."

~10~

That's it! Ever since Aunt Zoe's moved in with me she's repeated stuff she shouldn't. Well, she's embarrassed me for the last time. When I move out of Matt's, I'm going solo. No more sharing an apartment. It's for the birds.

I've been living the life of a nun for far too long. It's time to cut loose. No more crazy interruptions when I'm trying to entertain guy friends. I can get up when I want, eat whatever I desire, and not keep track of anyone but myself. The thought of saying "Hasta la Vista, Auntie," brought a smile to my face.

"What's so amusing, Mary? You look like a cat that swallowed a gold fish. It doesn't have anything to do with Butch's circumstances I hope. That man's problems aren't anything to laugh about."

"It doesn't involve Butch. I just remembered a joke someone shared the other day."

Aunt Zoe opened the sleeper couch and made it up for the night. "Oh? Well, I could use a good laugh.

Another fib that bit me in the butt. I drew serious.
"Oh, I'd totally screw up it up. I'm not in the right frame
of mind tonight. My brain's too taxed with Butch's woes
and worries over Gracie. But I do have something
extremely important to tell you before we go to bed."

My aunt turned her back to the couch and crossed
her arms over her floor-length fuscia-colored flannel
nightie. "Don't tell me you've broken up with that
undercover cop you met working the case at Reed's. I
really liked him."

"This has nothing to do with David Welsh."

"Well, I know Matt's not back in town yet. If he
was, we wouldn't be here." A second later her hands flew
to her freshly scrubbed cheeks. "I know, you've finally got
a teaching job. That's fantastic. I'm really happy for you."

"No, I didn't. Just sit down and stop guessing,
please."

"Okay." She moved her feather pillow and sat. "But
I'm sure I could've figured it out if you'd given me half a
chance." She wagged her finger at me. "I've acquired a
few sleuthing skills of my own you know."

I tipped my head. "You sure have." Well, if you
must know, she did help a smidgen the last two cases I
took on. "I wanted to tell you this earlier but things sort of
got in the way. After I toured the pickle factory this
morning, I asked the receptionist for a job application."

Aunt Zoe's greyish-blue eyes almost popped out of
their sockets. "You're pulling my leg."

I yawned. "I most certainly am not."

"Have you told Gertie?"

I scooted off my aunt's bed. "No, not yet. She
wasn't around when I spoke with the receptionist. The
pickle plant is hiring, but I still have to fax the application
to them and wait for a response." As much as I hated to tell

Aunt Zoe that bit of info the way she blabs, I knew if I didn't tell her about the job, she'd wonder where the heck I was disappearing to everyday. Besides, this was the final time I'd ever share anything with her.

Aunt Zoe kicked off her wedge shaped fuscia-dyed feather slippers created by Vecceli of Italy and slipped under the bed covers. "I don't mean to be negative, but do you really think they'll hire someone with all your credentials, Mary?"

I flicked off the only lamp still lit in the room. "Of course they will. I'm going to lie like heck on my application like everyone else."

Auntie mumbled something under her breath and then bid me and Edward's cremation remains a goodnight.

~11~

Day 4

This morning I'm actually doing something healthy for myself, and food isn't even involved. Ah maybe I'd better retract that disclaimer. While it's true that after returning to the Foley from faxing my filled-out job application form to Hickleman Company, I broke down and took the stairs instead of the elevator, my habits hadn't really changed overnight.

You see, while I chased around town doing errands, temptation struck in the name of Dunkin' Donuts. I just couldn't resist their special of the day, Brownie Batter donuts. Except now, with every new step I take my heart pounds louder and louder, making me feel like death is knocking at my door.

By the time my clammy hand wrapped around the knob of the fourth floor exit door, my body was depleted of energy. I could barely breathe. Sweat poured out of every cell in my body. The only thing that kept me going was the knowledge that I could plop in Matt's La-Z-Boy as soon as I got back to the apartment, unless of course Aunt Zoe happened to be occupying it.

I yanked open the door leading to the hallway and almost knocked Margaret Grimshaw flat on the ugly orange and mud-brown striped carpet as she stepped off the elevator loaded down with bagged groceries from Food to Go. "Sorry, if I scared you. I don't usually rush out of the stairwell like that."

"No need to apologize, dear. As you can see I'm perfectly fine."

I was unconvinced. The woman was definitely struggling to keep the two grocery bags above her waist. "Here, let me take one of those," I offered."

Margaret's thin lips curled up, indicating she was pleased to be rid of some of the load before going any further down the narrow hallway. "Thank you. Has there been any word on Gracie yet?"

"Nope. However, Aunt Zoe might have gotten a call while I was out. By the way, I took your suggestion about posting notices beyond a four block radius and have notified the Hennepin Humane Society. Oh, and Raj Singi offered to put a huge poster in one of his windows at the optical store." We stopped walking now. Our faces were almost touching Margaret's door.

The elderly woman unzipped a small side pocket on her black leather purse, pulled out a key, inserted it in the lock, and pushed the door open. "He and Kamini are so nice. I've never heard anyone in this building speak ill of them."

"Me neither." I handed off the bag of groceries I'd helped carry before I forgot and kept them for myself.

Margaret took the extra bag and shuffled across her threshold without saying her usual goodbye or closing her door. Instead, she left the door open, set both bags down by her hall closet, and turned around. "Mary, you didn't say whether you resolved any of the other problems you shared with me?"

I thought of Tinker Bell with her fairy dust. I know it was for flying but maybe it would work for other things too, like cleaning up messes. "The living room still looks like Vegas," I said, allowing a bit of disgust to flavor my voice, "but I'm about to put a dent in Butch's problems."

"So, you've chosen to help him after all. Good for you. What made you change your mind?"

"I think touring the Hickleman Pickle Plant with Gertie the other day did it."

"You took a tour? How did you manage that? I thought most businesses these days didn't allow non-employees inside their facilities for safety reasons."

I leaned against her doorjamb. "A teacher from Washington Elementary knows someone who works there and they set up the tour for the second graders. When Gertie found out about the trip, she put our names down to help chaperone the students."

"Ah, hah." Margaret's eyes blazed with excitement. "I'd love to hear what you've got up your sleuth sleeve, but I need to get these groceries put away. Can you come in and sit a spell?"

Worried Aunt Zoe may have overheard us talking in the corridor; I scurried into Margaret's apartment and shut the door behind me. "Sure, I've got nothing earth shattering to do today except watch a piece of meat thaw." I bent down, picked up one of the two bags on the floor, and then followed Margaret into her immaculate kitchen where everything has an assigned spot, including the salt and pepper shakers stored on the left-hand side of the upper part of the stove.

As soon as I set the bag down on the table, I offered to help put the groceries away, but Margaret refused my assistance. So I stood by the kitchen sink and silently watched the precision and orderliness she used emptying the first bag containing frozen cans of juice and meat into the fridge's freezer compartment.

Impatient to tell her what I'd done, I finally disturbed the silence in the room. "Guess what? I applied for a job today."

My announcement threw the ninety-year-old woman for a loop. She forgot about the open freezer and clamped her hand over her mouth. "What are you talking about? The other day you said you had too many logs in the fire already."

"I do. But this one will be short-lived, a week at the most." I pulled out a chair and sat at the square butcher block table butted up against the far corner of the 12'x 12' room.

"I suspect this has to do with Butch," she said, finally closing the freezer door.

"Give the little lady a prize," I teased, sounding like a carny barker.

Margaret turned a burner on to heat up an old silver teakettle in which one could still see their reflection if they wanted, and then went back to her task of emptying the other grocery bag. "I don't know how anyone can possibly discover who killed Mr. Hickleman in a week's time. That's an ambitious task even for you."

When the tea kettle finally whistled, Margaret moved over to the stove, poured the hot water into two coffee mugs, dropped a teabag in each, and brought the mugs to the table. "I think you've bit off more than you can chew this time, dear," she said as she sat down with me. "You won't even have me or Zoe for backup."

I picked up a steaming mug of tea, took a couple sips, and set the mug back on the table. "That's what worries me the most, but I don't have any choice. I can't have Matt find out I'm involved in another case."

"Tell me about this job. How exactly does it help Butch?"

"The position is at the pickle plant." I took another sip of tea, hoping Margaret would realize before too long she hadn't offered a sweet to go with it; I'd already burnt off the extra calories I gained from the donuts and my stomach was begging for more. But nothing was said, which was okay. A grown woman like me should know better than to take Margaret's baked goods for granted. It's not like she's my grandmother.

Margaret set her teacup down in front of her and folded her hands. "Ah, you're going undercover. Well, a person can certainly find out a lot working in an office setting with all those file cabinets sitting around and people coming and going all day long."

"No doubt about it. The problem is Hickleman's administration department doesn't have any openings."

"What do you expect to do then?" Margaret unclasped her hands, pressed them into the table, and tapped her arthritic fingers. "Oh, my! Don't tell me you applied for a position on the production line? My dear, you won't last a day."

~12~

Day 5

Torrential rain turned to snow late Thursday night and dropped two feet of powdery white stuff on most of Minnesota, forcing schools at every level to be cancelled, including Washington Elementary where I sub. At least this November storm was nowhere near the Armistice Day blizzard of 1940 old-timers in these parts can't stop talking about. The drastic daytime weather change that November caused forty-nine deaths.

Thankfully, the only thing our winter wonderland caused last night was an excuse for snow lovers everywhere to call in sick on a Friday and take full advantage of the first good snowfall.

Even if I had a job to call in sick to today, this gal wouldn't be joining in the merriment. If you're thinking it's because Mary Colleen Malone's an old fuddy-duddy you're way off target. I'm simply a klutz. Why, I can't even line dance without falling flat on my fanny. But just because I'm not riding a ski lift at Wild Mountain or sliding down a hill at Como Park doesn't mean I can't have a fun-filled day like everyone else. Except, I don't foresee being locked up in the apartment with Aunt Zoe for the next twenty-four hours giving me any pleasure.

As I approached the kitchen still in a state of grogginess wearing my usual winter bed attire of baggy flannel bottoms and an outstretched extra-large long sleeve knit top to fix breakfast, my aunt's cheery voice called out to me. "Mary, did you see how much snow we got?"

Not ready to get into any type of discussion yet, including weather, I simply jiggled my head like a bobble doll.

She tightened the belt on her floor length butterfly print satin kimono. "I can't remember when I've seen streets clogged that bad."

She wouldn't. Aunt Zoe and her rich husband left us poor slobs behind to take winter trips to Jamaica, Bermuda, Grand Cayman, and other hotspots. "As much as I'd like to live in a house," I said, "when winter arrives I'm quite content to be an apartment dweller, not a homeowner."

The comment regarding homeownership drew a blank stare from Aunt Zoe. "Why would you say that?"

A loud yawn escaped my lips. "I don't have to break my back shoveling all that snow. It's hard work." I shuffled my animal knitted slippered feet past my aunt, who was standing by the coffee pot waiting for it to brew, and made my way over to the cupboards to get a box of Cheerios, a cereal bowl, spoon, and juice glass.

The second the coffee machine let out a loud beep Aunt Zoe lifted the coffee pot off its stand, poured steaming java into the mug she won at St. Anne's Church festival in Buffalo this summer, and then placed the pot back where she found it. "Oh, Mary, I forgot to tell you I made French toast earlier this morning if you'd prefer that over cereal. The leftovers are in the fridge." Plucking up her mug now and a folded copy of yesterday's *Star Tribune* newspaper, she trotted over to the table and emptied her hands.

When I pulled out the milk and juice, I looked at the uncovered pile of almost black French toast sitting on a saucer, the perfect meal to kill someone with. A couple swallows and the intended victim would choke to death. I made the right choice. You can't go wrong with a bowl of Cheerios.

I carried the glass of orange juice and bowl of cereal to the table and sat. "Any plans for the day?" I asked, hoping my aunt might want to visit someone in the building, "Other than reading that is," I sneakily added.

My aunt tapped her chin. "I hadn't really thought about it. According to the radio the roads aren't going to be cleared for several hours."

I wrapped my hand around the juice glass. "Well, perhaps we should think about changing out the living room since we can't hunt for Gracie." *Hint. Hint.* "Matt will be home before you know it."

Aunt Zoe set the paper down. "What sort of style might appeal to him? I've been thinking about doing something totally manly for his homecoming gift."

I almost crushed the glass in my hand. *Lord help me!*

A loud knock at the door stopped me from exploding. Wow. The Man Upstairs works mighty fast. Hoping he'd sent Margaret to rescue me, I jumped out of my seat and made a quick turn in the direction of the door, almost tripping over the leg of Aunt Zoe's chair as I did so.

"Rod, what are you doing here?" The man continues to pop up whenever he feels like it. If I understood technology, I'd invent a radar system that wards off unwanted visitors, including Rod Thompson.

He threw up his hands. "Is that anyway to greet a neighbor? I thought you and I were on better terms than Matt and me."

Before I could ask him why he didn't call first, Aunt Zoe shouted, "Tell Rod to come in."

Great. Now I've got two people to contend with.

As I backed away from the door, it dawned on me I must look a fright. "Rod, why don't you head to the kitchen," I suggested. "I'll be there in a second."

"Okay."

I scrambled down the hall to the bedroom, threw on an outdated shorty blue terrycloth robe and ran my hand through my hair. Then I dashed back to the kitchen and joined them at the table. "So, Rod, what brings you here?"

The blond whose genealogy extends back to the homeland of the Vikings had already claimed a cup of coffee for himself. "I figured since there isn't much for any of us to do around town I'd come over and ask if you gals would like to maybe play a friendly game of cards or Monopoly. I've got the Twin Cities version."

I didn't jump in with a reply. Hanging out with Rod wasn't considered fun either. Instead I said, "I'm surprised you aren't out snowmobiling. Matt told me how much you enjoy buzzing around with your buddies."

Rod glanced down at his coffee. "You can't go snowmobiling if the equipment is stored three hours from here and the roads are closed."

"That's for sure," Aunt Zoe said, as she picked up the newspaper and paged through it. "When were you thinking of getting together, after lunch?" Obviously, she was ready to be entertained with or without me.

"Nah, I was thinking more like ten. You can spend a couple days playing the game you know."

I glanced at the hands of the clock mounted on the wall above the kitchen cupboards. They pointed to nine and twelve. There goes any chance of me having fun today. Unless... "Hey, Rod, why don't you ask Margaret if she'd like to play? The game would be more challenging with four players."

"Sure. I haven't sat down with her in a long time."

Aunt Zoe dropped the newspaper. "Mary, you've got to see this."

I shoved my chair out and leaned across the table. "What is it? Did someone post a message about finding Gracie?"

Auntie didn't reply. She merely tapped her plum painted nails on a picture of a male figure. He looked like the spitting image of Don Vito Corleone, the character Marlon Brando played in the movie *Godfather*. The headline above the photo said: Who Killed the Pickle King?

"What's got you so riled up, Zoe?" Rod quizzed. "Did you know Mr. Hickleman personally?"

I pursed my lips together hoping that just once my aunt wouldn't let the skunk out of the hole.

Aunt Zoe didn't catch my facial expression. How could she? Her grayish-blue eyes remained glued on Rod's sapphire ones. "Ah, no, I never met the man. But Mary's planning to go undercover at his pickle factory."

Rod shot out of his chair. "Are you crazy? I thought you weren't taking on cases anymore. You're a teacher. Not a private investigator."

"It's the last case I'm ever taking." I raised my hand. "I swear. Honest. If Matt found out what I've been up to, he'd wring my neck."

"I don't blame him. If you were my sister, I'd do the same."

I went on the defensive. "Thanks a lot. For your information my taking this case is all Gertie Nash's fault."

"Sure, blame it on someone else," the FBI computer geek said, situating himself on the seat of his chair once more.

The dirty look I gave him could've drilled a hole through his skull. "It is too Gertie's fault. Ever since I moved in here she's been bugging me to help prove her Cousin Butch is innocent of a crime he went to jail for."

"And," Aunt Zoe broke in, "Mary continued refusing to help up until recently."

"What pray tell occurred to change her mind?" he quizzed in what sounded like a non-judgmental tone, but I couldn't be sure.

Aunt Zoe reflected for a second. "I believe it was when Gertie showed up at our door, pale as a ghost, all shook-up about poor Butch having been accused of murdering Don Hickleman."

I vehemently denied her statement. "That's not true. After Gertie explained Butch's situation, I simply volunteered to speak with him. Nothing more."

"You're right, Mary," Aunt Zoe replied, resting a hand against her thick short neck. "I got a little confused. She didn't actually make her decision to help Butch until she met him face to face the other evening."

"I don't believe it." Rod brushed a thick lock of blond hair off his forehead, leaned back in his chair, and crossed his arms. "You met a criminal in your apartment? What were you thinking? Even a PI doesn't do that.

You're such a sap. Can't you see you're not meant to solve cases? You lack special training. For all you know this Butch guy filled your head with a bunch of nonsense."

Aunt Zoe waved her hand in front of Rod's perfectly straight nose. "Mary can't help it if she has a heart of gold. Besides, I begged her to help Butch too."

Rod rested his lanky arms on the table. "Oh, so, that makes everything A-Okay. Well, don't expect any help from me when you're in dire straits."

"Don't worry," I snapped, "I wouldn't think of getting your lily white hands dirty."

"That's enough you two," Aunt Zoe demanded. "Save your aggression for the game of Monopoly."

"What? We're still playing?" Rod and I asked in disbelief.

~13~

After Aunt Zoe explained the tiff between Rod Thompson and me, Margaret recommended we play Monopoly on neutral ground, namely her dining room table. I had no qualms about her suggestion and I was certain Rod didn't either. As a matter of fact, I don't know any single person who would pass up a chance to spend time in the home of someone who is known to always have an ample supply of meals, baked goods, and snacks sitting around, simple reminders of when one lived under their parents' roof.

Aunt Zoe had just completed her second play on the board when Rod made a tiny request of her. "Could you please hand me the bowl of shelled peanuts?"

She thrust her open palm under his nose, wiggled her fingers, and smiled. "It would be my pleasure, as soon as you pay me two hundred dollars. I just passed GO again in case you hadn't noticed."

"I shouldn't have volunteered to be banker," he complained as he dug through the play money sitting in the game's box lid to retrieve the fake bills owed Aunt Zoe, "Everyone is keeping me so busy I can't even squeeze a snack in."

Margaret consoled him. "Don't worry, dear. I've got a huge pan of lasagna warming in the oven. It should be ready in half an hour."

"I suppose I can manage till then," he grumbled, "if I don't run out of money."

"A banker running out of money, what a silly notion coming from an FBI agent," I snidely cracked. "As far as I know that hasn't happened since the Great Depression."

He ignored my comment, a first for him.

"I'm a terrible hostess," Margaret declared. "I haven't thanked Rod for bringing peanuts or Mary for the very tasty Cheez-its crackers I can't stop nibbling on."

"I'm glad you're enjoying them. I wanted to bring something kind of healthy and easy to munch on and they fit the bill."

With Aunt Zoe's turn completed, Margaret was up next, but trying to get a good grip on dice with arthritic fingers was proving to be a challenge. The more she tried to get a handle on the slippery dice the further away they slid from her.

Sensing the elderly woman didn't want pity from us or help for that matter, I shoved the dice back to her for a fourth try.

This round Margaret put forth greater effort, got the dice, and was rewarded with doubles when she finally tossed them. "Hot dog! I may be able to purchase another piece of property."

"Darn. No fair, Margaret," I squawked. "That's what I needed. I'm never going to get out of this miserable jail."

"At least you can't land in the cemetery when you're sitting in jail," Rod quietly slid in.

The guy was trying to get my goat and I wasn't going to let him. He did enough collateral damage earlier in our apartment.

"I didn't know there was a cemetery in Monopoly," Aunt Zoe spouted.

"There isn't," Margaret said, moving her iron token forward twelve spaces. "Rod was being witty." After she halted movement of the token and set it on its new location, she adjusted her wire-rimmed glasses and silently read the property she'd landed on. "Does anyone own the Ordway? If not, I'd like to buy it."

No one claimed ownership of the property and Margaret happily parted with one hundred and forty dollars of fake money to receive her newly acquired land. If only things were that cheap, in real life. These days' college students pay more than a hundred dollars for one measly book some professor states is required reading material for his class.

I eyed all the real estate cards Margaret had collected so far. "Boy, lady, you're sure scarfing up the property. The way you're going at it you must've owned a real estate company in your past life."

Margaret giggled. "I'm not telling." She handed me the dice and then rose from the chair she'd been sitting in. "I'd better check the lasagna. Good luck, Mary. Perhaps you'll get more property too."

"One can only hope." I took the dice from her and encased them tightly between both hands, planning to rattle them a bit before tossing them, but I didn't get to follow through. My cell phone rang. "Sorry." I dug the phone out of my pocket. "I think I should take this call. It could be about Gracie,"

"Go ahead," Rod said. "We're not going anywhere."

"Okay. Don't anyone take my turn for me," I warned. Then I rushed to Margaret's kitchen and clicked the ACCEPT button. "Hello."

"Is this Mary Malone?" a thin, reedy voice inquired.

As soon as the caller asked for me by name, I knew this wasn't going to be about Gracie. I never included a name on the flyer, only a phone number. I hesitated a moment. For all I knew the person on the other end could be an annoying sales person. I'd take my chances anyway. It wasn't like the caller was taking me away from a million dollar business deal after all. "Yes, this is she."

"Hello, Mary, this is Sharon Sylvester, head of Hickleman's Human Resource department. I'm calling about your application you faxed us the other day."

"Oh?" I signaled Margaret to move closer to the cell phone so she could hear what the woman had to say too.

Sharon Sylvester went on. "You haven't changed your mind about our advertised position, have you?"

"No, no. I just didn't expect to hear from anyone this soon."

"You probably wouldn't have," she politely stated, "but since I can't go into work today and I had some applications tucked in my briefcase, I thought I'd read through them. I must say I'm very impressed by the thoroughness and neatness of your application. It shows that you care about what you do and are a detailed oriented person."

I laughed. "That's me all right. Unfortunately, my family doesn't appreciate those qualities."

"Well, we at Hickleman's most certainly do. Miss Malone, I wonder if you could come by the plant Monday morning for a short interview and a tour of our facilities."

I displayed a huge grin for Margaret. She pretended to clap.

"Is 10 a.m. too late?" I asked, showing respect for Sharon's position and in the process gaining more brownie points too.

"No, actually that's perfect."

~14~

Day 8

I pounded on the thinly layered bathroom door for the second time in five minutes. "Aunt Zoe, hurry up in there. I don't want to be late for my interview."

"You should've gotten up earlier like I suggested last night," she scolded.

I dug my short fingernails into the palms of my hands. *Grrr.* I hate it when people remind me that if I'd listened to their words of wisdom I wouldn't be acting like a bear. "Just give me an estimate of how much longer you'll be in there," I snapped. I wanted to put my best foot forward for the interview and in order to do that I required the mirror to apply makeup and rehearse the little white lies I'd be telling Sharon Sylvester, Hickleman's Human Resource gal, in a half an hour.

"Probably about five more minutes. Reed's coming by in a little bit to take me Christmas shopping and I want my hair to be just so."

Miffed that it would take her another few minutes to fix her short hairdo, I leaned against the bathroom door and kept my eyes glued to the silver Timex watch decorating my wrist. Five minutes to the second, a loud click announced Aunt Zoe should be exiting the bathroom. Not wanting to knock her flat as she tried to exit the room, I opted to move.

As soon as I backed up, the door swung open and Aunt Zoe's size five black-booted feet paraded off the bathroom's Robin's egg blue tile floor on to the ugly pea soup colored carpet, where with the grace of a spider, she threw back her head and prompted me to react. "Well, what do you think?"

Stunned by the vision in front of me, I was left tongue-tied. I closed my eyes and reopened them hoping what I'd seen had vanished. Sadly it hadn't. Not even the dimly lit hallway fixture could dispel my aunt's appearance. I studied her closely. There wasn't the slightest hint of short fiery-red spiked hair showing atop her roundish head. A black fur hat resembling a Kubanka totally hid it. Even though I had been left speechless, I had to admit the huge hat looked good on her. But she definitely wouldn't be chosen to replace Lara if they ever did a remake of *Doctor Zhivago*. "Where did you get that hat?" I finally managed to ask.

Her thick ruby-red lips quickly parted. She dropped her hands. "Edward picked it up for me on one of his many trips to Moscow. I figured it was the perfect day to dig it out of storage. Please tell me it looks all right."

"Ah, yeah," I replied with a straight face. "It's very practical to wear especially on such an extremely cold day.

I'm afraid Reed won't be able to take his eyes off of you."
Nor will anyone else. Real fur hats are so passé. No one
wears animal furs anymore unless you want a PETA
activist to hunt you down.

Aunt Zoe smiled. "Let's hope so. I don't want his
eyes roving while he's with me."

"Oh, I don't think you have to worry about Reed. He
only has eyes for you."

My roommate dismissed the comment, despite her
cheeks growing rosier. Instead, she investigated the
tightness of the elastic band which held up her snug white
knit pants. Then she moved on to adjusting her bra straps.
Aging gracefully takes great effort. Auntie for instance is
at that spot in her life where everything's shifted south, but
she fights to keep it north. "How long do you think you'll
be gone?" she asked.

"I don't know." I waltzed into the bathroom with my
makeup bag in hand, set it on the top of the toilet tank,
opened it, pulled out an eyebrow pencil, and darkened my
brows to match my jet-black hair. "It takes a good half
hour to drive there. Then the interview and tour will
probably eat up another forty-five minutes. Maybe you'll
see me around noon. Should I give you a call before I head
home?"

"No, that won't be necessary. I don't think I'll be
back that soon from my outing. Knowing Reed he'll want
to eat lunch out."

I tucked the pencil back in the makeup bag and
withdrew a tube of lipstick. "Yup, he probably will. Men
are so predictable, aren't they?"

She nodded. "Have you figured out what fibs you
might be able to use at the interview?"

"Ah huh." I finished swiping the carnation colored lipstick across the upper lip and then proceeded to do the bottom. "I thought I'd practice in front of the mirror."

Aunt Zoe tapped her foot and gave me a stern look. "You've got a real person standing right here who can question you, and you prefer a mirror instead. Sometimes I don't understand you, niece."

Ditto. I smiled smugly at my mirror image and tried to think of a plausible explanation for not asking Auntie for help. Thankfully, I didn't have to come up with one. The ringing of the landline saved the day.

"It's probably Reed," Aunt Zoe gushed, as she rushed to the kitchen phone like a mad scientist trying to escape the police. A few seconds later an exuberant voice floated to me from the other end of the hallway. "I'm leaving. Reed is waiting for me in the lobby."

I poked my head out into the hallway for a second and yelled. "Okay, have fun."

***

I hadn't taken notice of the drive from Northeast Minneapolis to the pickle plant in St. Michael the first time I visited it, too busy calming the kids down. But today I was tooling along, sans passengers, in Fiona on dry streets no less, allowing me to take in sights facing Interstate 94 and beyond without worrying about distractions. Well, okay, there were several really good-looking guys that buzzed by on either side of Fiona that made me forget where I was for a moment or two, but that was it. Honest. When you're driving 70 m.p.h., you've gotta pay attention to the road unless you want to crack up.

Thirty minutes into the drive a sign came into view heralding St. Michael, a bedroom community with a population of 17, 500. I quickly switched lanes and exited off of I-94, reducing the cars speed to the mandated 55 m.p.h. Then I hopped on highway 241 and drove west past businesses such as Marksham Metals, Lucky Pets and Pellco Machines. At this juncture, according to the GPS, I was approximately a half mile south of Oakwood, the turnoff that led to the pickle plant.

As I hung a right onto Oakwood, an orange-flame building housing Tioni's Pizza Parlor caught my attention. It's the place Butch had been working at until his recent arrest. The eatery hadn't joined my long list of restaurants to try until Gertie had mentioned it, but then I usually don't find myself this far north unless I'm heading to a relative's cabin in Brainerd.

The thought of pizza made my mouth water and I promised myself I'd stop there on the way home. While I waited for a pizza to go, I'd do a little detective work on the side. Putting out feelers to see what people really thought of Butch will either strengthen my misgivings about his innocence or lessen them.

I didn't dress flashy for the interview, like my aunt frequently does in her clothing choices, including dashikis bought in Africa, even though the job I applied for would be on the floor of the plant not in the office. Instead I wore a sensible two-piece navy-blue knit suit, the skirt of which stopped just short of the kneecaps. Having prior knowledge that men outnumbered the women 2 to 1 in this plant, I figured the length of my skirt may impress the interviewer if she was say fifty or older.

It wasn't until I opened the door to the office section of Hickleman's that I became concerned the receptionist on duty might recognize me from the day Gertie and I'd chaperoned the kids from Washington Elementary, but I soon discovered I had no reason to worry. The young twenty-something woman gazing up from the front desk definitely wasn't the receptionist I had seen. The other woman was closer to seventy.

Noticing the name badge attached to the receptionist's heavy wool sweater, I used it with confidence. "Hello, Melanie. Sharon Sylvester is expecting me."

"Good-morning," she said with the enthusiasm of a sloth.

The young thing must be suffering from the Monday morning blahs.

Melanie, glanced at the single sheet of typed-paper sitting in front of her. "Your name please?"

"Mary Malone."

"Sorry, I can't seem to find it on this list."

"Mind if I take a look?" I leaned over her desk, swiftly scanned the sheet, and found it. "Here it is." I lightly tapped the spot. "It's the sixth name."

"Oh, so it is." Melanie picked up the phone and made a brief interoffice call to Sharon Sylvester. After informing the head of H.R. that I'd arrived, she instructed me where to hang my coat and then ushered me upstairs to the second floor and the enclosed office labeled HUMAN RESOURCES, having passed a smattering of open cubicles and smiley faces along the way.

"Okay, I'll leave you with Ms. Sylvester," Melanie said, and then spun around on her two inch heels and made a beeline to the stairs.

Sharon Sylvester, a mousey-looking woman of fifty-odd years, pale in complexion with bleach blonde curled hair down to her shoulders and red button earrings secured close to the ears, offered a genuine smile before she scooted her squeaky office chair nearer her rickety desk, that most likely had seen better days more than twenty years ago, and slipped a slim ringless hand out to me. I took it. "Miss Malone, so nice to meet you."

"You too." I took Sharon's soft flimsy hand in mine for a few seconds and then relaxed my grip.

As soon as I released her hand, she pointed to a brown, thinly padded leather chair that had also seen better days. "Please, have a seat."

When I first strolled into Sharon's office I'd assumed she'd offer me a place to put the charcoal-grey wool dress coat I'd worn since the receptionist hadn't, but she didn't. So before I sat, I took off the coat and threw it over the back of a spare chair.

Sharon waited till I sat and then shifted her attention to the neat pile of paperwork in the center of her desk. "I see your application states you've had some experience with canning. Tell me about that."

Here goes nothing. I folded my hands on my lap, presenting what's considered openness. One can never be too sure what people pick up on be it gestures or untruths.

"Well, every summer since I was real little my mother would take me to grandma's farmhouse to help pick vegetables when they were ready. And then I'd sit at grandma's big kitchen table, until I was old enough to help, and watch them can tomatoes, cucumbers, carrots, beets, and such." None of the story was true but it was significant enough for Sharon to verify.

Sharon's face remained expressionless, not even the slightest hint of a wayward smile. "Which vegetable did you like canning the most?"

"I'd have to say cucumbers. The slices were small enough that I could put a few in my mouth before they got canned and no one missed them." I stretched my lips to their limit for her benefit, showing how much I enjoyed doing that.

I noted the interviewer's pupils after my response. They'd grown larger. Usually that's not a good sign. Hopefully it wasn't my fib that jarred her.

Sharon stroked her double chin. "I wonder, Miss Malone if you'd be tempted to swipe a few while working here. Many of our line jobs require hands on work with the cucumbers."

I leaned forward in my chair. "Oh, no, Miss Sylvester, I can assure you I wouldn't dream of nibbling on anything at the plant." Once it dawned on me how my statement sounded, I quickly backpedaled. "I mean anything on the work floor. When you check my references, you'll find I'm an extremely honest person. I don't even sample veggies or fruit while I'm shopping at a grocery store. I firmly believe in purchasing everything before I taste it."

She let my explanation go without comment. Glancing further down my application she said. "I see there's a bit of a gap in here since you worked as a temp for Kelly Services, would you care to explain?"

I raised my clasped hands to my chest. Then I recited a sob story worthy of an Oscar or an Emmy. Only the part about my dad was true. "Two weeks after my father had open heart surgery my mother was diagnosed with breast cancer. Being single and the only daughter, I offered to help out."

Sharon Sylvester squeezed her hands together. "Oh, I'm so sorry. How are they both doing now?"

I bowed my head. "Much better."

The H.R. woman scraped her chair against the wood floor indicating she was about to stand, which she did. "Well, I certainly appreciate your coming in, Miss Malone. Your references will need to be checked out yet, but as long as you're here I'd like to show you the facilities. I feel it's important for an applicant to tour the plant. It gives you a chance to see if the job you've applied for is worth pursuing. You'd be surprised how many people change their minds once they see what the job entails." She turned towards the black metal coat stand a few feet from her desk and grabbed a green lab coat off it.

I stood and smoothed out my skirt. "I'm used to hard work, Miss Sylvester. I'm sure what I see won't scare me off."

The game was over. All I could do now was wait to be shown the plant and hope I passed the test.

Sharon remained silent while she rounded the front of her desk, threw on a lab coat, and buttoned it. When finished, she said, "We'll get safety wear for you on the first floor," and then she marched me out of her office and led me back the way Melanie and I'd come.

~15~

The wonderful aromas of bread, tomato sauce, pepperoni, and sausage played a mean game with my nose and stomach the minute I strolled in to Tioni's Pizza Parlor. I'd come here after finishing the interview at eleven, hoping to see the manager, but the only people standing behind the long dark counter were two workers wearing matching flame-orange shirts, a guy and gal, both roughly in their mid-twenties. Their welcoming grins gave me the impression they were delighted to see anyone come walking through the doors to break up their morning monotony while patiently waiting for the arrival of the early lunch crowd onslaught.

I presented a tiny smile for their benefit before wandering into the parlor's midsection, a basic run-of-the mill bar like interior with dark wood floors, walls and booths.

The slim guy offered a quick nod. Then he slipped off his stool, limped over to the brick oven, opened one of the doors, and took out a pizza. The strong tantalizing smells released in the air almost knocked me senseless.

Ready to devour anything put in front of me now, including a bear, I gazed at the humongous order menu hanging on the wall.

A squeaky voice coming from the woman soon interrupted my decision making. "Are you here to pick up pizzas?" she asked as her thin-as-a-rail frame, bounced off the sturdy wood stool she sat on. "They'll be ready in two seconds."

I rested a hand on my thick hip. "No. I'm here to place an order," I said before I turned my back on her and scoped out the place. "Is Butch going to be around today?" I inquired.

The guy by the ovens shot the young woman a warning look over his shoulder that seemed to imply not to say too much.

She caught the message and smacked her gum. "Do you know Butch very well?"

"Oh, yeah," I lied. "We grew up in the same neighborhood. I just recently moved to this area so I thought I'd check out the pizzas here, and say hi."

"I'm sorry," she carefully stated, "but I'm afraid you missed him."

I shook my head. "Darn. Just my luck he's not working today."

The woman swiped a quick look at her work partner. Probably wondering what she could safely say next. Unfortunately, he was too busy cutting the large pizza he'd taken out of the oven to take an interest in either of us. She faced me again, flipped her long straight bangs to one side, and signaled she was going to jot something down. Then she plucked a pen and notepad off the counter. "So, that's a small personal pizza with sausage and mushrooms, right?" she asked.

I had no clue what she was up to. But since I usually select those exact toppings for my pizza, I agreed to the order. "And a large Coke to go with it, please," I added.

"Sure. To go or eat here?" she quizzed.

I noticed she stressed *GO*. Taking the hint, I replied, "To go I guess."

"Okay. It'll be ready in twenty minutes." She slipped her hand under the counter. When she brought it back up, it held a large paper cup with the pizza parlor's logo on it. "Here you go. The pop is at the back wall." She pointed behind me.

"Thanks." I tried to take the cup from her, but she wouldn't let go. "Oh, I'm sorry, I forgot to pay you. How much do I owe?"

"Just a sec." Then she rang the order up. "That'll be seven dollars and ninety-five cents."

While I took my time digging through my faux Coach purse I'd picked up at Goodwill, the gal scribbled a hasty note and shoved it across the counter. *Meet me out back after you get your order. I'll tell him I need a smoke break.* Then she took my money, strolled over to her co-worker, and gave him my order.

I'd barely left the – 19 °F temperature of the outdoors behind a mere six minutes ago and the heat in this building already made me feel like I was the one being baked. I quickly slipped out of my coat and scrambled to the pop machine with my cup to fill it full of ice and Coke.

Twenty minutes later my pizza was boxed and ready to go. I threw on my coat, slung my purse over my shoulder, grabbed the order, and walked out to the back of the brick building to meet with the gal who helped me. She wasn't there yet, so I had to literally cool my heels since I'd chosen slingback pumps to wear to the interview.

The wait in the extreme cold brought Gracie's welfare to mind, making me feel guilty as hell. Raised as an indoor dog, she wouldn't survive too long in these weather conditions. I still couldn't believe someone hadn't spotted her by now. Hopefully, she was in a warm shelter of some sort and being treated well.

The backdoor of the pizza parlor finally creaked open and out stepped the gal I'd been waiting for. A pale-blue down jacket covered her work shirt. She leaned up against the door, quickly lit up a cigarette, and then introduced herself. "Hi, I'm Ginny."

"And I'm Mary," I said. "Have you worked with Butch very long?"

She took a puff of her cigarette and then blew out smoke. "Yeah, I worked with him for over a year."

"You make it sound like he's no longer here."

"Yup. The boss let him go."

"Geez, that's too bad. Any idea why?"

Ginny cocked her head. "You've heard that the owner of Hickleman's was killed, right?"

I nodded. "Who hasn't? It's big news in Minnesota. What's it got to do with Butch though? He wasn't working there anymore."

"No. But he's being blamed for the guy's death." She brought the cigarette to her mouth again.

I faked surprise. "What? He's such a pussycat. There's no way he could've murdered anyone."

Ginny flicked cigarette ash on the ground. "That's exactly what I said. Butch is the nicest guy around. He couldn't hurt a flea if he tried." She gave a quick glance over her shoulder at the pickle plant and then took another puff on her cigarette. "I'll tell you what I think. Someone over there's got it in for him big time, Mary." She scrutinized me from head to toe. Then she went on. "If I were his lawyer, I'd take a good look at Paul Mason, the first shift supervisor, and another guy everyone calls Chip. They both come off sneaky to me."

She thinks I'm Butch's lawyer. Well, I'm not about to straighten her out. I don't want it getting around someone's doing undercover work at the plant. "I guess we'd better hope Butch has a great lawyer to help him clear his name then," I said, "so he can get back to what he does best, making pizzas."

"Amen." Ginny checked her wristwatch. "Oops. Gotta get back inside." She tossed the partially burned cigarette in the snow. "Nice chatting with you, Mary. Hey, if you bump into Butch, tell him I said hi."

"Sure," and then I headed to the car.

***

I'd just gotten back from St. Michael and was busy jiggling the key in the keyhole of the apartment with one hand and balancing the boxed pizza in the other when there was a commotion behind me. Worried that Rod Thompson, the guy we played Monopoly with the other day, was preparing to launch another sneak attack on me, I promptly withdrew the key and spun around. To my surprise, instead of finding the tall Scandinavian, I caught a petite Italian woman exiting her apartment carrying a fancy metal cage containing one occupant, a parrot.

"Hi, Margaret."

My neighbor slowly backed away from her door and lifted her head, "Mary, I didn't expect to see you until later. Didn't you have a job interview this morning?"

I nodded. "Yup. I'm just getting back from there." I pointed at the cage. "So, where's Petey going this time, to the vet's or to offer his mating services?"

"Neither," she hastily replied.

Having heard his name mentioned, Petey cocked his head and loudly squawked. "Pretty bird. Pretty bird."

"Oops. Sorry, I wasn't thinking. I didn't mean to get him all riled up. Too bad I don't have a towel handy for you to throw over his cage."

"Pretty bird. Pretty bird."

"It's not your fault he reacts so intensely to his name," the elderly woman stated. "I should've put his cover over the cage before disturbing him." She peered through the thin metal bars and scolded its occupant like one would a child. "Hush, Petey. You know better. We're not in our home."

Petey took his owner's words to heart. He immediately bent his head and shut his eyes.

"That's a good bird," Margaret whispered. Then she gave her full attention to me again. "He doesn't know it, but I'm loaning him out to the Veteran's Hospital for a few days. All that attention will do him a whirl of good as well as the veterans suffering from Post-Traumatic Stress Disorder. According to doctors interaction with parrots makes them feel better. And I'm all for that."

"It's nice to hear Petey can be of help. You know last week I caught a news report on that same topic. Apparently, the idea came from a program started in California. Although out there the veterans with PTSD cared for damaged or orphaned parrots and healing occurred for both."

Margaret inhaled deeply as she fought with her arthritic fingers to get a better grip on the cage. "It's too bad it took so long for those people in the field of medicine to realize parrots are just as attuned to peoples' feelings as horses and dogs. I've known it all along. Well, I guess I'd better be off, dear. Someone from the local VFW has volunteered to pick up Petey and me and drive us to the hospital. Why don't you catch me up on your interview later when I get back," she suggested, slowly pivoting her body in the direction of the elevator before continuing on with Petey.

"I will." As I returned to the task of unlocking my door, I was thankful I'd be eating the pizza in solitude. It would give me more time to mull over what Ginny from Tioni's had shared with me in regards to Butch and his two fellow employees.

~16~

Aunt Zoe returned home an hour after I did, all hyped up after spending several hours with Reed, her charming companion, and began interrogating me like she had been handed the role of Perry Mason and me the criminal. I took the Fifth. I wasn't going to spill the beans about my morning until Margaret came over.

True to form, remaining quiet didn't sit well with Auntie. More questions came my way. Not able to contain myself any longer, I held up a hand, signaling she needed to stop talking. It did the trick. Further questions were cut off at the source. "Thanks," I said, without offering an explanation, a dumb mistake on my part. I should've given more thought to leaving things up in the air.

Deep furrows materialized on Aunt Zoe's broad forehead. "What's wrong? Did the interview at Hickleman's go that poorly or do you have a headache? If it's a headache, I'll get you a couple Excedrin out of the medicine cabinet."

"I'm okay. There's nothing to fret about." I pointed to an empty couch cushion. "Kick off your shoes and come join me."

"Well, if you insist. But I think I'll take off my hat and coat too."

While I waited for her to remove her shoes and outdoor clothing in the entrance hallway, I grabbed my cell phone off the elaborately decorated coffee table where I had set it and pressed Margaret's number. She answered on the first ring. "Hi. My aunt just got back from her outing with Reed and I wondered if you could come by for a few minutes."

"*Si*. May I bring coffee cake? It just came out of the oven."

My stomach thrilled to the prospect of eating anything baked from scratch in Margaret's kitchen. "Of course," I responded enthusiastically. "You know me I never turn down food."

By the time I pressed the OFF button on the cell phone, Auntie was getting comfy on the couch. "Is Margaret coming over," she inquired.

I tilted my head towards her. "Yup. I saw her in the hallway briefly when I got back, but we didn't get a chance to chat. She was going to the VA Hospital with Petey."

"Oh, no. What's wrong with Petey?"

Lord, this roommate business won't come to an end soon enough for me. I know our hearing gets worse as we age, but believe me that's not my sixty-five-year-old aunt's case. Things just don't click for her. I squeezed the fingers on my left hand to keep myself from laughing. "The VA isn't a vet hospital."

"It isn't?"

Who actually was confusing whom, I wondered. Semantics, schmantics. I made another stab at it. "See, when I referred to the VA as a **Vet** Hospital I meant the one for veterans."

A tiny light flickered in my aunt's grayish-blue eyes. "Ah, you mean older pets."

I shook my head. *Margaret, please get here soon. My patience is growing thin.* "Nope. I mean guys who joined the army and other branches of service."

"I don't get it. Why would Margaret take Petey to the VA Hospital then if he wasn't sick?"

A noise coming from outside the apartment door kept me from letting my frustrations out of the bag. "Auntie, did you hear something?"

"No, why?"

"I thought I heard what sounded like a knock."

"Oh?" Aunt Zoe tilted her head in the direction of our entrance. "I still don't hear anything. Maybe one of the neighbors is hanging pictures on their wall."

I cupped my ear. "There it goes again. Someone is definitely knocking at our door. It must be Margaret." *Yay.* I jumped to my feet and rushed to the door. I felt like the executioner had just given me a reprieve.

"Margaret," I whispered, "Thank God. You got here in time to save my sanity."

She threw her head back and looked at me through the bifocal part of her lenses. "Is she confusing you again, dear?"

"Yes," I loudly replied. "I can't wait to try a piece of your delicious coffee cake. Come in."

Aunt Zoe stood, smoothed out her gray knit pants and waltzed over to our guest who happened to be wearing the same style and color of pants. "Margaret, what's this about Petey going to the VA Hospital. Why did he get dropped off there?"

Before Margaret could reply, I stepped between her and Aunt Zoe and quickly latched onto their arms. "Let's talk in the kitchen, ladies, over coffee cake and tea," I said, parading them to the kitchen table where I shelled out more orders. "Margaret, have a seat. Aunt Zoe, please put the teakettle on. I'll get the plates, napkins, and other items."

"Certainly," Aunt Zoe chirped, "and I'll grab the tea bags too." Before she wandered over to the cupboards where the box of Lipton's Black Tea was kept though, she collected the teakettle from the stove, filled it with water, and then returned it to the burner it had been on. "I turned the heating knob on high," she informed us, "so the water should be ready in a jiffy."

"Yes, that should do the trick," our ninety-year-old visitor said with no malice intended. "Mary, go ahead and cut the coffee cake. I can see you and Zoe are dying to try it."

I smacked my lips and reached for the knife. "Are we that obvious?"

Margaret smiled. "*Si.* Now cut the cake and tell us about your interview."

After I cut a small wedge of coffee cake for each of us and passed them around like Margaret requested, I said. "Ladies, I'm pretty positive I impressed the woman who interviewed me."

Aunt Zoe sounded skeptical. "How could you tell?"

"Well, for one, I showed up and on time. That ought to have earned me a couple brownie points in this day and age, right?"

"I suppose." She picked up her fork and broke off a bit of coffee cake.

"But there's more to it than that," I continued. "Sharon Sylvester acted genuinely thrilled to receive such a neat, well-filled out application from someone. Although, she did question the gap I had in between jobs."

My aunt almost choked on her snack. "See, that's exactly what I worried about, Mary, you putting stuff on your application that had no business being there."

The teakettle whistled. Nobody noticed.

Always the peacemaker, Margaret tried her best to calm things down. "Zoe, she had to fib about her jobs, she had no choice. Hickleman's wouldn't hire a teacher. They're looking for blue collar workers not white."

The teakettle kept on whistling.

Aunt Zoe's chair scraped the linoleum floor when she pushed it back to stand. "If that's the case, perhaps Mary made a mistake in applying for the job," she said with a snooty tone. "I should've been the one to do it since I have only a high school education." With that said she moved to the stove, picked up the teakettle and a potholder, and brought them to the table.

What can one say without upsetting the applecart? I needed time to think. While I tossed ideas around in my head, I picked the teakettle up off the table and filled each of our cups. "Auntie, this job is too stressful and dangerous for you. If something happened to you, we'd all be at a terrible loss, especially my dad. You're the only sister he has."

Aunt Zoe bowed her fiery-red head. "You're right. I'm sorry I went off like I did. I know you love me and would never want any harm to come to me. Besides, I like being a member of the retirement community and I don't think my feet could handle standing on a cement floor for eight hours."

I sighed. The storm was over. Hopefully the weather in here will remain sunny until move out day. *Wait a minute. Did she say cement floor?* "Oh, boy. I never gave the floors a second thought. I'm so used to working in comfortable environments; cement might bother my feet too. Oh, well, we've got a tub. I guess I can soak my tired feet when I get home." I leaned back in my chair and relaxed.

Margaret shared a smile with me. "Any idea when you'll hear back from Ms. Sylvester about the job?"

"My references still need to be checked, but I have a feeling it could be as soon as this evening."

"Oh, yes. References are terribly important, aren't they?" Margaret wrapped her tiny hands around her teacup. The heat probably made her swollen fingers feel better. "If I remember correctly, a business these days usually wants three names listed. I hope you gave names of people you can depend on to fib for you?"

"I did indeed." I left the table for a short duration to collect something in the bedroom, and then came back. "Here, Margaret, this is what I want you to say when she calls." I handed her a slip of paper with information on it. "And, Auntie, here's your copy."

"I don't like her calling me," she said. "She'll recognize your phone number."

I shook my head. "No, she won't. I put down Matt's landline number."

She lifted her head. "Ah. I suppose Rod Thompson is your other reference."

"Are you kidding?"

"Well, I only thought since he's a neighbor and knows you so well."

My voice shot up. "I don't know what ever gave you that idea, Auntie."

Before battle lines could be drawn, Margaret interrupted. "Zoe, I didn't have a chance to explain about Petey yet."

"That's right. We've been so busy talking about other things. Why did you take Petey to a veteran's hospital if he wasn't sick? It doesn't make sense."

God bless Margaret. If she's not a saint yet, she'll be canonized soon.

***

Margaret had barely left when Matt's landline rang. Since most people contact us via cell phones, I figured the caller had to be Sharon Sylvester. When I last spoke with her, she sounded eager to fill the production positions. I glanced at Aunt Zoe. "You might as well answer it."

"I… I don't know if I can do this, Mary."

The phone continued to ring. "Yes, you can," I prodded. I took the sheet of paper assigned to Aunt Zoe off the coffee table and shoved it in her hand. "Remember the wonderful story you weaved for the jeweler at Padock's in Duluth when you were questioned about the loose gem in your possession and what your plans were for it?"

"Yes."

"This is the same thing. It's all play acting." I led her to the phone, picked up the receiver, and handed it to her. "You'll be fine," I mouthed. Then I prayed she wouldn't screw up.

Aunt Zoe took a deep breath and said, "Hello, this is Zoe Rouge. Who's calling please?" I gave her two thumbs up. She grinned and then dropped her eyes to the paper. "Yes, I've known Miss Malone for roughly ten years. She's a hard worker and very dependable. She'd make a wonderful asset to any company. What's that? Oh, yes, she was willing to take on any assignment Kelly Temps sent her on regardless of how difficult the task sounded. Is there anything else you'd like to know about Ms. Malone's skills? No? Good-day then."

I couldn't believe it. My aunt didn't crack under pressure. Perhaps I expect too much of her. Aunt Zoe was pampered all of her married life. She knows nothing of the real world I've lived in. Maybe it would work out for the two of us to continue living together after all. I studied my aunt who was busy setting the phone receiver back in the cradle as if she was a specimen under a microscope. *Nope. Forget it. The phone call was just one teeny thing she did right.*

"Well, what did you think, Mary? Was I believable enough?"

I gave her a hug. "You bet. Your performance was fantastic. You didn't go off script once. If I get hired, I'll treat you and Margaret to supper at Milts."

Her stomach growled loudly. "Then let's hope you hear before supper. My lunch and the coffee cake have worn off."

~17~

Day 9

Aunt Zoe stood by the kitchen door dressed in morning attire, fluffy slippers, a long flowing neon-pink bathrobe, and her hair wrapped around those humongous foam rollers of hers. "Mary, you'd better get moving or you'll be late for your first day on the job and get canned before you start."

"Don't worry," I said, sounding like a teeny grade schooler as I stuffed the last piece of toast in my mouth and washed it down with orange juice, "I'm watching the time like a hawk. All I have left to do is brush my teeth and redden my lips with lipstick." I stood now and carried the few dishes to the sink to rinse them.

Auntie joined me at the sink, her fancy slippers clacking away as she did so. "You'd better lose these," she said, tugging on one of my earrings. "I overheard a gal in the laundry room tell her friend she can't wear jewelry if she wants a job at a fast food place. I bet the same applies for a pickling plant."

"You're probably right. I hadn't given it any thought. The employees I saw working around the machinery wore hairnets." I set the rinsed dishes on the counter and grabbed a dish towel to dry my hands. "I suppose that's one of the many things Ms. Sylvester will cover during orientation this morning." As much as I hated to remove the two-inch long green beaded pierced earrings perfectly chosen to complement Hinkleman's mandatory work wear, I took them off and tucked them in one of my jean pockets.

"Oh, Mary, I forgot to tell you. Butch called while you were in the shower."

"What did he want?"

"He thought you should know about a trucker gal who used to cozy up to old man Hickleman when she delivered cucumbers."

That bit of info didn't help. Don Hickleman could have a ton of women truckers bringing in cucumbers. I tapped my foot waiting to hear more, but Auntie didn't spit anything else out which is nothing new. Whenever we have what I consider a significant discussion, I end up going into dentist mode. I pull and pull till I extract every last tooth of hers. "Did Butch happen to give you a name?"

"What? A name? Why, yes, of course. Roseanne… Roseanne. Oh, dear, give me a minute. It's on the tip of my tongue." She rubbed her neck as if that would help her remember. "Ah, I have it, Roseanne Harsh."

I quieted my foot. "Thanks." I stored the name in my memory bank and started towards the bathroom, but didn't get far. The insistent ringing of my cell phone detained me.

A quick duck in the bedroom, where I'd left the phone, helped me determine the number displayed wasn't familiar. Since I rarely received sales' calls on it, I instantly thought of David, the undercover cop I'd met while working the case at Reed Griffin's Bar X Ranch. The last time we'd seen or spoken to each other was October, so for all I knew he could be in Alaska.

I plucked the cell phone off the night stand and rested it in the palm of my hand, debating whether to answer or not. If I take it, I could be losing precious drive time. Curiosity eventually won. *The caller better make this conversation sweet and short, even if he's the pope.*

I tapped the ACCEPT button. "Hello."

"Hi, Mary. I hope I didn't catch you on the road. You know how cops feel about people being on the phone while driving." The upbeat male voice didn't belong to David, but to Trevor Fitzwell, a Duluth police officer and a hunk of a guy I'd met this past October when I'd driven to the North Shore to do research for a novel. We didn't hit it off at first, but eventually we warmed up to each other.

Hearing Trevor on the other end of the line made me pleased I'd taken on Butch's case. I'd have something more to share with him the next time we managed to get together besides crying the blues over the lack of long term teaching positions in the metropolitan area. "No, actually your timing is perfect. I planned to leave for work in another five minutes. So, what's going on up your way?"

"Nothing much. It's pretty quiet. Everyone's got Christmas shopping on their mind or skiing."

"I imagine you're planning on coming this way to visit your family at Christmas?"

He hesitated. "Ah, I'm not sure." *Hmm? Could he have possibly met someone?* There's one way to find out.

"I suppose they haven't given you your work schedule yet, huh?"

"No, that's not the reason. I figured since Duke and I are attending K9 drug training classes this week at the Minneapolis Convention Center, I'd visit my folks and you of course. That is if you don't mind the last minute notice. Are you available for lunch?"

I mind? Is he crazy?

"Sorry. Lunch won't work today. I'm starting a new job. Can you swing supper tomorrow night?"

"Sure. I'll call you back this evening and let you know what time to expect me."

"Perfect." I clicked the cell phone off and did a shortened version of an Irish jig. David's out and Trevor is in. What's one man's loss is another's gain so I've been told. The cops don't know about each other and that's the way I planned to keep it.

Before I slipped out of the bedroom and into the bathroom, I glanced at my wristwatch. "Holy cow. I've got two minutes to get down to the garage." I guess I'd better brush the teeth and skip the lipstick.

The second I finished in the bathroom Aunt Zoe rushed up to me with a slim package and pressed it in my hand. "You'll need this, Mary. It's your backup. If there's one thing I learned in that safety class for women, it's you don't go into a hornet's nest without some sort of gizmo for defense."

~18~

My feet felt like lead as I trudged down the hallway to catch the elevator. I hated rising early to drive anywhere this time of year. A coal-black sky, except for a smattering of stars, gives you the false impression you're the only person on the planet. Then **POW** car lights appear out of nowhere and blind you. At least the sun doesn't play games. Speaking of the sun, it's supposed to expose itself later this morning and warm things up to the plus side according to WCCO's bubbly weather gal's forecast last night.

Hmm. I wonder if I'll have a long enough lunch break to even see the sun. If I do, I could eat in the car. I shook my head. "Nope, that won't do. I need to tune into work gossip and I can't do that if I'm not surrounded with employees.

The elevator dinged and I stepped on. While I waited for it to deliver me to the Foley's underground garage where Fiona's parked, I opened the brown paper package from Aunt Zoe and found a camera. I don't know how she expects this to protect me. Curious to hear her explanation, I whipped out the cell phone and dialed the landline number for the apartment. "Auntie, I think there's been a mistake. The package you gave me contained a camera."

"Of course it did. You have one of the hottest items Damsel in Defense carries for women."

"You've got to be kidding." I got off the elevator and walked towards Fiona's parking space "Well, I hope this black box called *Damsel Gotcha* didn't cost too much. Taking a dangerous person's photo is certainly not going to keep me out of harm's way."

A snicker came from my aunt's end. "You've got it all wrong. What I gave you only looks like a camera, Mary. It's actually a stun gun. Look, I've got to go," she said rather rushed, "I left the water running in the tub and I don't want it to overflow."

I pinched the skin at the top of my nose. Things weren't going so well for me since Gracie ran off. I certainly don't need a flooded bathroom too. Aunt Zoe better get the tub water flow under control otherwise her stay at the apartment will be terminated before Matt shows his face.

Once I let myself in the car and settled into the driver seat, I turned the radio off, choosing silence for companionship as I commuted to the pickle plant and reflected on the gadget Aunt Zoe surprised me with.

Despite our safety instructor's amazing sales pitch about the benefits of owning a stun gun, she never had us practice using the stun gun she carried with her, which was okay with me; I never intended to buy one, not as klutzy as I am. Heck, if I didn't accidentally shock myself, Aunt Zoe surely would.

I had to hide the stun gun somewhere, but where? Right now it's tucked in my purse, but it doesn't make sense to leave it there. If I carry my purse in the building, I'll probably be expected to stash it and the phone in a locker, leaving my valuables vulnerable to anyone with a knack for figuring out lock combinations.

I tapped my gloved fingers on the steering wheel. Maybe there's a benefit to having a chunkier body after all. No one will take notice of an extra bulge on one of my hips after it's covered with a knee-length lab coat. Although, someone may want to investigate what a new hire's doing with a camera if they catch it poking out of my pocket before I have a chance to slip the coat on, which means I could end up in a pickle real fast and I'm not referring to the kid's version.

Thirty-five minutes later I pulled into Hickleman's employee parking lot with the problem of the stun gun resolved, and braced myself for what I suspected to be a long hectic day ahead, possibly even dangerous.

With only five minutes remaining on the clock to report to Sharon Sylvester in the H.R. office, I yanked my purse off the passenger seat without retrieving the stun gun from it first. Luckily, Fiona's car doors can be temperamental at times, and this was one of those days.

Finding it difficult to fight with the door latch while holding the huge handbag, I tossed the unzipped purse back on the passenger seat. A mixture of items flew out and spilled to the floor-mat, including Aunt Zoe's present. I ignored everything except for the safety gadget and quickly stuffed it in a jean pocket before tending to the door again.

When I strolled into the lobby entrance of the pickle plant, I found Mandy, the same young gal who helped me last time, sitting at the receptionist desk and informed her I was here for orientation with Sharon Sylvester.

"Do you remember how to get to her office," she inquired.

I pointed to the wooden stairs off to the left. "I think so. Go up that flight of stairs and head straight back."

"You got it." She picked up a plastic badge off her desk and held it out for me. "Welcome to Hickleman Pickle Company, Ms. Malone. Have a great day."

"Thanks." I took the badge with my name typed on it, pinned it to my long sleeve navy turtleneck shirt I'd recently purchased to insulate me better against Minnesota's bitter-cold winters, and headed for the stairs leading to the second floor.

Those who work in Hickleman's business department must have different hours from the plant. When I reached the open cubicles on the second level, there wasn't a sole stirring, but then none of them were expecting me. Sharon Sylvester from H.R. had penciled-me in, not them.

As I trudged on past the rows of cubicles to reach Sharon's enclosed office, I thought perhaps I'd find her waiting by her doorway for me, but that wasn't the case. All that greeted me was a closed door displaying Sharon's brass nameplate. So I did what any sane person would do. I balled up my hand and rapped on the door.

"Come in," the recognizable voice of Ms. Sylvester uttered.

When I entered Sharon's private office, I found a dark-skinned middle-aged woman seated next to the human resources representative and assumed she was there for orientation too, but soon found I was mistaken.

Sharon smiled. "Good morning, Mary. I hope traffic wasn't too heavy for you?" She pointed to an empty chair.

I took it as my cue to sit. "Actually, it was pretty calm. I expected it to be a lot worse."

Sharon Sylvester's honey brown eyes fell upon the gal next to her. "Anita, this is the woman I was telling you about."

Anita's plastic eyewear the shade of eggplant slid down a short distance when her plump face nodded slightly. "Ah?"

Not knowing if I was expected to say anything, I simply said, "Hi."

"Anita Crane is part of our mentor team," Sharon explained, resting her covered elbows on the desk and folding her hands. "She'll be in charge of you for at least a week if not longer."

The thick brightly-painted purple lips belonging to Anita split so wide apart at the mention of her mentoring duties I thought she might have to pick her lips up off the floor.

I beamed right back at the woman with tightly weaved braids the color of a submarine. I had a feeling she and I would get along just fine. There's nothing better than working with a happy person. I abhor crabby people.

"Before Anita takes you over to the plant however," Sharon continued, "I need to cover a few basic rules our employees are expected to follow. We at Hickleman want to ensure that new employees feel comfortable with whatever jobs assigned them."

After Sharon said what she had to say concerning rules, she handed me a personalized copy of Hickleman's employee handbook to take home and read and also mentioned how long I had to be at the plant before health insurance kicked in. Then she wound things up. "Anita, will show you where to clock-in and the location of medical supplies. But if you have any questions concerning your job, Mary, please come up and speak to me directly. A coworker doesn't have the power to change anything."

"Thank you. I'll remember that," I said, remaining seated until Anita indicated we should depart.

Two seconds later Anita Crane stood, giving me a fuller picture of the woman who would be training me. Her body definitely carried more meat than mine and she was at least three inches taller, even though we both wore New Balance tennis shoes. "Well, girl, there's plenty to do before you get on the production floor. So, let's head downstairs, stash your belongings in a locker, and find you the appropriate items to wear. Once that's done, we'll clock you in and get you familiar with the plant."

~19~

Anita Crane's crisp white lab coat softly rustled as she hustled me down the lengthy narrow corridor leading to the back of the plant and the time clock. The speed at which the woman walked made me believe she'd rather be packing pickles than having me shadow her. Of course, I could be reading her wrong.

When we reached our destination, Anita found herself short of breath, forcing her first attempts at breaking the long silence, kept in the hallway, to come in waves of tiny gulps of air, intermittently mixed with words. "Sharon... probably told you... about the cucumber deliveries... and the sorting process when you were interviewed." I nodded. "I thought so."

She plucked a Bic pen and blank time card from a slot directly below the time clock and handed it to me to sign. "You know you look like the kinda gal who'd give her eye-teeth to catch the action up close. Am I right, girl?"

My stomach tightened. Not expecting those particular words thrown at me on my first day of work, I gave Anita's question some serious thought while I signed the time card. Hopefully she wasn't planning to show me how to operate a heavy piece of machinery. "I… ah guess," I finally replied, shoving the pen back in its slot before giving Anita the signed card so she could demonstrate how to stamp it correctly.

The dark-skinned woman with a southern drawl shook her chunky body slightly. "Good. No one's keeping track of my production output today since I'm showing you the ropes, and rumor has it one of our truckers arrived a day early with a load of cucumbers from Baja, Mexico. How about checking it out?"

My troublesome stomach settled down. I wasn't going to be thrown into the lion's den the first day on the job after all. Watching a trucker drop cucumbers off instead of working sounded like a day at the zoo with kids.

"Sure," I cheerfully replied. Besides, Sharon's tour of the plant after my interview never included what goes on outdoors. Probably because she didn't want to talk about the pickling vats and the whole sticky mess the company found themselves in.

Even though my feet hadn't appreciated the speed-walking drill Anita had put us through to get to this side of the plant, at least she had the good sense to explain the rush to get where we landed. Something she didn't have to do. Looking back over the years, most bosses I've worked for never had the decency to tell subordinates what was going on and then wondered why things didn't get done.

After letting Anita know I was okay with her idea, she led me out a side door and we entered the fenced in acreage owned by Hickleman that I quickly dubbed Pickledom. Luckily, there wasn't a moat filled with water anywhere in sight. The only liquid out here was the twenty-two thousand pounds of vinegar placed in each of the 70 vat tanks to ferment the cucumbers for six weeks, which I'd heard about when touring the plant with the second graders.

As the freezing air encircled me and nipped here and there, I held back the need to blink. I wanted to see who climbed out of the cab with the lettering **Tiny's Trucking** stenciled on it, especially with all the restrictions in place regarding illegal immigrants crossing the border.

My mentor didn't skip a beat while we waited for the driver to make his appearance. She went right on chattering about work-related stuff. Maybe talking helps her block out how cold it really is, but it wasn't doing anything for me. "You won't read this in any company brochure, Mary, but none of the people we buy cucumbers from uses machines to gather their crop."

I played ignorant. "Really? Why is that?"

"When Don Hickleman's father started this company up in the early 1900's, he insisted on handpicked only. According to him, handpicked cucumbers provide a better taste and crunch."

I glanced up at the truck's cab. At least five minutes had flown by since we came outside and the darn driver was still perched up in his nice warm enclosure. I don't blame him for not wanting to leave it. Chilled to the bone, I'd already tucked my hands in my shirt sleeves to keep them warm, but I couldn't do the same for my frozen feet or head.

I moved closer to Anita thinking the body heat radiating off of her might transfer to me. "He'd better make a move in the next few minutes," I said, "or my toes are going to fall off." *Keep the blood flowing, Mary.* I gently lifted the ball of the right foot up, tapped it back down, and then lifted the left and repeated the procedure.

Apparently Anita felt the same. She rubbed her arms vigorously. "Hang in there, girl. I think I see movement in the cab."

I stomped my feet. "It's about time."

Remember how I kept my eyes glued to the truck so I could catch a glimpse of the driver. It didn't matter. There wasn't much to see when they opened the cab door and jumped to the plowed blacktop below. If a cop ever asked me to describe what I'd viewed, all I could report seeing was a lanky body clothed in jeans and muddy boots and a face half hidden by a tan cowboy hat with turquoise stones circling the ribbon band.

A few seconds later, a shrill scream pierced my ears. It came from a woman as she rounded the back of the truck I'd been staring at. "Well, I don't believe it," she said, "you're actually standing out here freezing your butt off to see me, Anita." She took her hat off, exposing her shoulder length hair—black with streaks of plum, and swatted Anita on the back. "How you been, lady?"

A sassy laugh poured from Anita Crane's wide mouth. "Keeping myself out of mischief of course, like you."

"Of course," the forty-something woman wearing aviator sunglasses replied. I see you haven't gotten rid of the ugly green hairnets yet."

"Unfortunately, I never got the chance to convey my sentiments to Don Hickleman before, well you know," she said sourly, scraping her foot back and forth. "Maybe the next owner will be open to his employees' suggestions."

Hmm. It sounds like Butch wasn't the only one unhappy with the king.

I studied the woman chatting with Anita. She may have been blessed with an oval face, but the rest of her begged for help. Besides having a body that looked like it suffered from anorexia, she owned a long beaky nose, bushy eyebrows, pencil thin lips, barely a chin, and a bird-like neck. The combination of looks and mannerisms brought to mind one of Cinderella's creepy cruel step-sisters. Yuck. Something tells me I'd better be on my toes whenever she's around. She might be as bad as the stepsisters.

Quickly realizing Anita wasn't by herself the woman pointed a scrawny finger at me. "Who's this?"

"Roseanne Harsh," Anita said, "meet Mary Malone. It's her first day on the job."

Roseanne Harsh? Why, that's the name Butch asked Aunt Zoe to pass on to me.

"Roseanne's been trucking in cucumbers from farms in Minnesota and Mexico for the past twenty years," Anita hurriedly explained.

"Going on twenty-two years to be exact," she corrected, without offering a hint of friendliness to me.

"Hi." I offered a cold hand to her, but her leather-gloved-fingers continued to grip her hat.

A few seconds of awkward silence followed, allowing the trucker to scrutinize me. Could it be she's worried this younger body of mine might draw the attention of men folk away from her?

Roseanne finally shifted her gaze to another spot. "That truckload of cucumbers I'm dropping off ought to keep you gals out of mischief for quite some time," she said, and then she plopped her rodeo-style hat back on her head.

"You're right about that," my mentor answered.

Roseanne pointed to the truck behind her. "Well, I'd better unload these suckers so they can get weighed and sorted. Anita, I'll catch you later for a cup of the plant's watered down version of coffee."

"Okay, see you then." After Roseanne was out of sight, Anita turned to me and said, "I don't know why all the men at work have the hots for her. She's no Miss America. I've seen better looking women at the beauty salon."

"I don't know. I rarely get there. I usually trim my hair."

Anita glanced at my head. "Mmm hmm. I can tell."

My teeth clacked together, making noises only a dentist should hear. "Are we finished out here?"

"Sounds like someone's freezing. Are you sure you're from Minnesota, girl?"

"That's what my birth certificate says."

"Tell you what. The sorting process will start any second. As soon as you understand how it works, will skedaddle and find the coffee machine. Is that a deal?"

I stomped my feet for the umpteenth time. "It's a deal."

~20~

My head felt like mush. Not only had too much cold air passed through it, but it had been filled to the brim with info I already knew about grading pickles, and new stuff. Supposedly, it was Don Hickleman's sole decision this past year to set aside a specific number of vats for fermenting organic cucumbers. According to Anita that decision didn't sit well with all the board members.

The moment we reentered the building I was ready to warm up with a double chai tea latte, but that wasn't going to happen. I was working at a pickle plant, not Starbucks.

Not a big fan of coffee, I was leery of sampling what the company provided. More than likely it was an off-brand that smelled as bad as it tasted. Of course, feeling like an icicle wasn't great either, so I finally succumbed and took a cup of the hot java.

After drinking two free cups of burnt coffee supplied by the plant's outdated electric coffee pot, I had to ask the inevitable question, "Where's the nearest restroom?"

"Straight back, honey, and to the right," Anita said. "You can't miss it. Oh, and remember to wash your hands thoroughly; we don't want to spread germs around here."

No kidding. It's a shame adults have to remind other adults about cleanliness, but I wasn't one of them. People who work with kids know enough about germs they could write a book on the topic, including me. But I didn't dare share that with Anita. I had to keep my previous job a secret.

Roseanne Harsh finally showed her face, but her timing stunk. I'd already committed myself to visiting the ladies room and had put my body in motion.

"Sit down, Mary. You don't have to leave on my account." Roseanne whipped her sunglasses off and exposed her big round hazel eyes with flecks of gold.

Anita lifted her empty Styrofoam cup in the air. "Leave the girl be, she has to pee."

The truck driver snickered. "Well, you'd better hightail it to the powder room then. We don't want you having an accident. Oh, and, Mary, make sure you don't end up in the men's room by mistake. It happens a lot around here, if you get my drift."

Her message came in loud and clear. There's no way this gal intended to end up in the men's room unless I was forced to, which I doubted she was. I wonder how many men she's met up with in the bathroom over the years.

When I reached the door labeled WOMEN, I didn't go in right away. Instead I leaned against the wall, crossed my legs, and listened to the conversation going on between Roseanne and Anita for a few minutes. Recipes and remedies for aches and pains flowed from their lips at first, and then old man Hickleman's name came up. *Yahoo.*

"The police haven't broadcast this yet, Roseanne, so keep it under your hat. When Don's body was pulled out of the pickle vat, the cops found a cucumber lodged in his throat."

That's it? Big deal. Disappointed with the gossip, I succumbed to Mother Nature's complaints.

~21~

When I returned, I found Anita hanging outside the lunchroom door; legs crossed, resting her broad back against the wooden door frame. "I thought you got lost, Mary. Everything okay?"

"Just peachy." I peered in the lunch room. No one was there. "Where's Roseanne?"

Anita fussed with the pocket of her lab coat as if it hid a secret message. "She's gone. That woman flits in and out of here like a ghost. Knowing her she's probably picking up another delivery somewhere nearby." She uncrossed her legs.

Yeah, like one of the men from the plant. "Darn. I wanted to ask her which North American country supplied the U.S. with more cucumbers."

"Roseanne has never brought it up as many times as we've chit chatted over the years, but I do recall one of our sales reps saying the U.S. gets over a million cucumbers a year just from Mexico." She stepped away from the door frame. "Well, girl, I think we've dawdled long enough." I didn't comment. My mentor didn't press it. She simply whisked down the hall to the left and chatted on about the plant again.

"You've already seen the sorting process and the vats where the cucumbers sit in salt brine to ferment for six weeks. But it was too cold outside for me to explain that the fermented cucumbers aren't taken out of the vats the minute the six week period ends. They actually stay in them two extra days so agitation (desalting) can take place."

"Then they're brought into the building," I chirped, while trying to keep up with her long strides, "and made into slices, chips, or relish."

Anita stopped in mid-step and spun around, causing her braids to fly in all directions. "Whoa, girl. You're putting the cart before the horse."

I knew I was, but I did it deliberately. The woman had no idea I'd visited the plant with younger children before taking the job here. She was only aware of the quick walk-through Sharon Sylvester provides for potential employees, which doesn't amount to much. "Oh? Sorry."

"It's all right. People who don't work here usually assume that." She advanced a few more steps, raised her hand, and pointed to the different machinery surrounding us. "After the fermented cucumbers come inside from the vats they spend five more days being desalted in this room."

For the sake of acting interested in the info being fed into my head, I studied the equipment for a full six seconds.

Anita continued on. "The next step in the pickle making process is the washing and rinsing of the cucumbers, which takes place in the wet hopper and brush washer, directly in front of us. Once that's finished, then the cucumbers get cut into chips or slices, depending on the demand, and slide down a chute onto the conveyor belts in front of those employees over there, where they inspect and keep the best to be put in jars for consumption."

Seeing bad cucumbers tossed every which way by the quickness of workers hands gave me serious doubts about my ability to carry out the task if assigned. Sure my mouth moves at motor speed, but the hands don't. The dexterity isn't there. I can't tell you how many times my fingers got stuck between the keys of an Underwood manual before the first computer keyboard came into our house.

Worried that this klutz's undercover future wouldn't last long if it began in the inspection department, I quizzed my mentor. "Is this where I'll be spending my days?"

"No, not this week, honey. We don't throw you into the lion's den that soon. After the sliced cucumbers are inspected, they come along another conveyor belt waiting to be picked up by us and packed in empty jars."

Oh, joy. Trying to squeeze slices of cucumber into a jar is tantamount to me getting a roll of fat in a pair of pantyhose.

~22~

After an eight-hour shift at the pickle plant, every joint in my thirty-five-year-old body screamed bloody murder. Of course, sitting an additional thirty minutes behind Fiona's steering wheel on the stressed-filled drive back home only added to the severe pain.

By the time I arrived home I could barely manage to muster up the energy to rid myself of wet tennis shoes and the enormous purse slung over my shoulder, let alone alert my aunt that a person had entered the apartment.

Despite how I felt, common sense prevailed in the end. Without Gracie here to inform her of another presence, the job fell to me. If I didn't carry it out, I'm afraid Aunt Zoe would leap out of her skin like she did two days ago when I returned from an errand sooner than she expected. Besides that, I didn't want to bear the burden of sending my dad's sister off to greet St. Peter at the pearly gates before her time.

I sucked in stale air and forced the needed words to finally flow. "Aunt Zoe, I'm home."

A swift reply floated my way. "I'm in the kitchen, Mary."

Those weren't the melodious words I wanted to hear after an exhausting day of doing work this teacher had never dreamt of doing.

Instead of conjuring up what a state the kitchen is normally in after Auntie's been let loose in it, like I usually do, I remained calm as a cucumber and sniffed the air. "Hmm? Something smells mighty good." Could my aunt be surprising me with takeout from Mancetti's Italian Restaurant? Although I don't know how she would've gotten there, it isn't a simple hop, skip, and a jump from the Foley. She'd need a car, which she didn't have. And, even if she had a car, I wouldn't want her out on the streets without a license.

Since smoke wasn't pouring out of every crevice in our abode and my aunt wasn't yelling for assistance, I allowed myself a few moments to hang up my coat and put on slippers before proceeding to the kitchen to find out what was cooking.

When I finally came face to face with Aunt Zoe, I found nothing out of place on the stove or counters. Even so, I completely forgot to ask about supper. No, I'm not getting senile. Seeing the intensity of Auntie's bright orange jogging suit dragged me back more than a dozen years to a pumpkin patch and a funny-looking kid called Charlie Brown.

Mystified by my aunt's choice of clothing, I barely heard a soft voice speak to me from another part of the room. "Hello, Mary."

In a flash the memory lane I'd been strolling down disappeared into oblivion. I quickly glanced in the direction the greeting had come from and found Margaret Grimshaw sitting at the kitchen table holding a cup in the air, offering me a warm, motherly smile. Finding her here and the table set for three melted any anxiety felt a few seconds earlier concerning supper. I permitted my lips to curve upward for Margaret's benefit.

The elderly woman took a second to straighten her granny glasses before explaining her presence. "I hope you don't mind, Mary, but I've invited myself to supper. I made enough lasagna this afternoon to feed an army."

I yawned. "Do I mind? Of course not. Not when you've had a hand in the meal."

Aunt Zoe had moved to the stove to set a pot on a burner and turned slightly to speak to me. "Margaret's not exaggerating. She really did make a huge batch of lasagna. By the way, I suggested we invite Rod over to join us."

Oh, God. Rod's the last person I want to see. I smell like pickles. My hair is as flat as a pancake thanks to the hairnet employees at Hickleman's are required to wear. My heart raced. "Did you?" I asked.

My aunt pulled out a couple pot holders from the small drawer next to the stove. "No. Margaret said you might be too worn out to have that much company and suggested I ask you first before calling anyone."

I strolled over to Margaret and gently squeezed her shoulder. "I'm glad you waited. The only people I want to be around tonight are you two."

After hearing my thoughts on additional guests, Aunt Zoe inspected the pot on the burner and retrieved the lasagna from the oven, giving me ample opportunity to let Margaret know with a simple expression how grateful I was for her words of wisdom.

She saluted me with her cup, signifying she understood. "Mary, I know you've had a long day, but I hope you're not too tired to share how it went at the pickle plant. Zoe and I are dying to know."

"No. Just let me get something in my stomach first. What little I packed for lunch didn't stay with me that long." I glanced over my shoulder to check on my aunt. "Do you need any help?"

"Yes," she replied, as she headed to the table with the huge pan of lasagna. "You can turn the burner off and empty the warmed peas into a serving bowl. Oh, and get something for yourself to drink."

After I took care of the peas and got a glass of milk, I joined the women at the table and said a short dinner prayer with them before eating. When we finished, I offered to dish up the lasagna since the pan was too heavy to pass.

When I gave Aunt Zoe her plate back, she opened her mouth as if to share something, but I didn't wait to find out what it was. I jumped right in and asked her about Matt's dog instead. "Has anyone called about Gracie?"

She stared at her brightly polished nails and sighed. "A few people."

The news cheered me up but not for long. "Anything concrete?"

"You mean was it worth answering the phone?" she asked. I nodded. "Nope. It was the same as all the other calls. As soon as they described the dog they'd seen in their yard or along the street, I knew they hadn't spotted Gracie."

I clinched my fist and tapped the table. "Darn. Why do people bother calling if it's not the dog we're looking for?"

"Human nature, dear," Margaret said. "People are so anxious to get the reward, they don't care if the description posted fits the bill or not." She frowned at the plate of food sitting in front of her now as if it wasn't worth eating after all the work she put into it.

"Is anything wrong?" I timidly asked, hoping a strand of my hair hadn't gotten away from me undetected. If there's one thing I can't stand, it's finding something in my food that didn't belong there. That's so gross.

"*Si*, there's too much lasagna on my plate. I'll never eat it all."

Whew. No hair on her plate. "That can be easily remedied." I scooted my chair back. "I'll get you a saucer so you can take off what you don't want."

Margaret waved her fork over her plate. "Don't bother, dear. What I don't eat I'll take home with the rest of the leftovers."

"Are you sure? It's no trouble to get a small plate for you."

She lowered her fork to her food. "I'm quite sure. Eat your lasagna before it gets cold."

"Yes, ma'am." I moved my chair closer to the table and took several bites of our supper before setting down the fork and wiping my messy lips with a paper napkin. "This is delicious. I wish I could cook as well as you, Margaret."

Margaret's pale cheeks looked like she recently added rouge. "You can, dear. All it takes is many years of practice."

Aunt Zoe's eyes widened. "Yes, Mary, remember the old saying 'practice makes perfect.'"

This from a person who doesn't have a penchant for tackling anything more than once.

I lowered my eyelids. "I certainly do. I use those words on a daily basis when I'm teaching."

"Oh, but of course," my aunt replied. "Someone in education would, wouldn't they?"

With this particular discourse ended, my aunt picked up her fork and pressed down hard on her serving of lasagna causing the flavorful tomato sauce, mixed with cheeses, noodles, and meat to ooze out so fast I thought it was going to spill off the plate and on to her lap. Lucky for her it didn't occur. Her jogging suit couldn't afford any more color added to it.

Once Aunt Zoe's fork held enough for her to eat, she looked up from her plate and directed the conversation my way again. "Mary, you haven't offered any details on how your day went yet. Did you get to use the stun gun?"

At the mention of a stun gun Margaret's fork slipped through her delicate hand and fell to the plate in front of her. "A stun gun? Whatever possessed you two to purchase such an item?" she nervously inquired. "I've seen police demonstrate those on TV. They're dangerous."

Not wanting to discuss the stun gun or the pickle plant until I had more food in my stomach, I shoveled it in as fast as I could.

Margaret wagged a bent finger at me, reminding me of Sister Luigi, a nun who stood watch over me and my elementary classmates during the lunch hour. "Better slow down, Mary, or you'll need Tums." At least she didn't tell me I'd choke to death. That's what Sister Luigi said.

I looked at the food on my plate, only an eighth of a cup of peas remained. Holy cow! Slowing down wasn't going to help. I needed a break. I laid the fork across the plate, took a couple sips of milk from my glass to counteract any indigestion that might be brewing, and finally followed through on telling my dining companions what they were dying to hear.

"Margaret, I'm sorry I ignored your inquiry about the stun gun, but there isn't much to tell. I only found out about the purchase this morning when Aunt Zoe put it in my hands and insisted I take it with me for protection."

"Mary's stun gun looks exactly like a camera," Aunt Zoe boasted. "She'll have to show it to you before you go home."

"I don't need to see it," Margaret insisted, quickly shifting her focus from my aunt to me. "Please tell me you didn't take the stun gun into the building with you."

"Ah… it wasn't that simple. Believe me, I waved the pros and cons. One minute I thought I should, and the next I didn't."

Aunt Zoe's grayish-blue eyes lit up. "Knowing you, the pros won out, am I right?

I threw my head back. "Yup. I tossed it in my purse."

Margaret's thin eyebrows inched upward, making her eyes appear much larger. "Weren't you afraid it might fall out of your purse?"

"I gave that careful consideration…"

"And?" she prodded me on.

I leaned back in the chair and crossed my arms. "Well, since employees have to put their belongings in lockers, which are easy to break into, I figured the safest place to hide the stun gun was on me."

Margaret shook her head in disbelief. "Dear, I understand your dilemma this morning regarding the stun gun, but if you continue bringing it to the plant, the person who killed Don Hickleman could very well use it on you."

"I've thought about that." I uncrossed my arms and rested my hands on my knees. "But with no one to back me up, I have to have some sort of defense weapon. Surely you don't want me to carry one of Matt's hunting knives?"

Margaret's mouth made a maddening clicking noise. "Absolutely not. A person could slice you in two in no time."

Aunt Zoe's hands shook. "I abhor blood and gore. Can we please drop this type of talk?" Such a strange request coming from one who finds great pleasure in describing her African hunting expeditions.

Our neighbor readily apologized and swept talk of defense tools under the rug. "Mary, I noticed you haven't mentioned if anything came up at work that might be helpful to Butch."

"Well, as a matter of fact, I heard two interesting things today. Both made a dilly of a mess that can't be ignored, but whether either might help Butch I can't say. The first involves hanky-panky at the plant. The other deals with a business owner who didn't relish suggestions from his lowly employees."

Aunt Zoe smoothed her deep furrowed forehead. "Do you mind repeating what you said in plain English? I can't make sense out of what I heard."

There's always one in the crowd that doesn't understand. "Sure. I have two hot items for you to chew on. First, a certain woman truck driver has been fooling around with men at the plant for years, including one Don Hickleman. And second, the woman training me in complained about Don Hickleman's not listening to employees' suggestions."

Margaret lifted her cup of tea. "My, my, Mary, it sounds like your first day of sleuthing at the plant went splendidly. Don't you agree, Zoe?"

Zoe supported her chin with her hand. "I guess so. But I still wish I was working with her."

Not me, I thought as I finished the peas, and went for round two of lasagna.

~23~

Day 10

Matt's clock radio went off at 6 a.m. on the dot, signaling me to get out of bed, but my achy body refused to budge. Knowing I couldn't possibly solve the murder of the Pickle King from a supine position, even if I wanted to, I flicked the alarm off and tried convincing myself there was a plateful of blueberry pancakes warming in the oven, waiting to be devoured. Unfortunately, my head wasn't in the mood for playing games, not even the pinky toe itched to get up, so I continued to lay on my backside.

Not too long after choosing to stay put, a faint rustling noise came from the other side of the bedroom door, and then the door knob jiggled. Expecting the door to crack open any second, I slowly counted to three, and it did. "Just checking to see if you're awake, Mary," Aunt Zoe said in her cheery, early-riser tone, "and to let you know I've already used the bathroom so you can spend as much time in there as you wish."

I lifted my head off the pillow and turned a smidgen in her direction. "I appreciate your checking on me," I croaked, "but as you can see I'm awake. It's my body that has a problem."

"Oh, you poor thing," she said, flinging the door wide open. "Are you still sore from what you did yesterday?"

Begging for as much sympathy as I could milk, I said, "Ah huh," and then pressed my elbows into the overly-firm mattress, forcing the upper body up a tad.

Without waiting for an invite from me, Aunt Zoe marched over to the edge of the bed and settled her warm pudgy hands on my shoulders. "What you need is a massage and a good soak in a hot tub. Sit up tall," she ordered, "and let my fingers work their magic."

My aunt does lots of crazy stuff, but one thing she's terribly good at is giving massages and I wasn't about to let her offer go to waste. I drew up my hunched shoulders and stretched the neck.

"Much better," she said and then threw herself into her work.

"Ooo. My muscles are relaxing already. Why didn't I ask you for a massage last night? After you get those kinks out, can you please rub the middle of my back too?"

"Yes, but I can't stand here all morning otherwise you won't be able to soak in the tub." She lifted her hands off my shoulders and gently laid them near the center of my back now.

"By the way, I appreciate your leaving the bathroom open for me."

"Well, I thought it might be nice to give you a few extra minutes to pretty yourself up before going to work."

She pressed her thumbs into my skin, slowly rotating over a single knot until it disappeared, and then moved on to another location.

"What for?" I asked, taking a deep breath when she hit an extremely touchy area. "No one at the pickle plant cares how I look."

"Ah, but that charming policeman friend of yours from Duluth might want you looking special for him. And you can't very well put makeup on when you get back here tonight. There won't be time. Trevor's picking you up for dinner the instant you walk through the door. At least that's what you told me last night."

"Trevor? Yikes! I forgot about our date?" I jumped out of bed, totally forgetting about my sore, over-worked body and glanced at the person staring back at me from the mirror on the dresser. "What am I going to do with my hair? It already looks like it's taken off for Jupiter. Wearing a dumb hairnet for eight hours is only going to make it worse. Too bad I don't have a cute hat to cover this hair. I would've had one by now if I didn't keep convincing myself I can make it through winter without one."

Aunt Zoe chuckled. "I should've mentioned Trevor sooner. Relax. I'll think of something while you're at work." She strolled to the door and rested her fingers on the handle for a second. "Say, I bet Gertie would lend you a hat. She has oodles of them. I'll check with her later."

I'd rather be six feet under than wear one of her wild creations.

Before I could tell Aunt Zoe to skip her quest for a hat, especially from one of my least favorite people, she slipped out of the bedroom and pulled the door shut behind her. Oh, well. It's easy enough to fib my way out of using one of Gertie's Goodwill finds. I'll tell her it doesn't fit right. Since I started sleuthing, I've become quite proficient at telling little white lies beyond my home turf.

Wondering how much time I'd left to work with, I glanced at the clock radio. The hour was dwindling rapidly. Thirty minutes had already elapsed and I still had a ton do before returning to the pickle plant and sleuthing again.

I paraded over to the open closet and gave my thoughts over today's work wardrobe. Even though the plant job didn't require anything other than casual clothing I wanted to pull out all the stops for Trevor this evening. A nice pair of black jeans and the black sweatshirt with an embroidered cardinal on it that I got from Mom last birthday ought to fill the bill.

After grabbing what I needed, including black dress shoes I'd set by the entrance door to conveniently slip into the moment I got home, I opened the bedroom door and walked the few steps to the bathroom.

Aunt Zoe had suggested a soak in the tub, but plucking eyebrows and putting on layers of makeup required a considerable amount of time which would cut into this gal's breakfast nourishment for the hard day ahead, so I opted for the shower instead.

~24~

Finally ready to go, I slid my black, thermal-sock-covered-feet into the only pair of tennis shoes sitting by the door, tied them, and stood. Then I zipped up my ski jacket, put on a pair of wool gloves, and loudly proclaimed, "I'm leaving, Aunt Zoe," hoping my message carried all the way to the kitchen.

An unexpected reply came as my hand hit the door knob. "Wait, I'll be right there."

"Okay." I turned my back to the door and leaned against it, wondering what Aunt Zoe wanted to speak to me about that couldn't wait till tonight.

Despite the fact my aunt bent over to catch her breath the second she reached the entryway, I managed to understand her somehow. "Mary, you must be extremely careful today. I don't want a policeman showing up at our door to tell me you're in the hospital or worse."

She didn't have to explain to me what she meant by worse. All one had to do was see the beautifully carved wooden bowl on the coffee table that still held a small amount of Uncle Edward's cremation remains. "I promise. And if you run any errands today, make sure you're back here by four. I don't want Trevor showing up early and no one here to greet him."

"Don't fret. I should be here all day."

"Good. I'll see you tonight, then," I said, in a state of calmness. But when I walked out the door, fear gripped my chest cavity. Aunt Zoe wasn't to blame. Not knowing what to expect the first few weeks of a new job is known to cause anxiety for a worker bee, including me. Some seasonal positions I've worked promised fourteen days of training, in reality it boiled down to one.

The minute my tennis shoes settled on the carpet shared by the other residents of the fourth floor hallway a familiar male voice hailed me from behind. "Hey, Mary, hold up. We can ride the elevator together."

Leave it to Rod to catch me off guard. Well, I'm not about to share an elevator with him. I'll take the stairs.

"What are you doing up so early? Trying to get the apartment cleaned before big brother gets back home and boots you out?"

I spun around, forgetting about my highly made up face, and stared at the well-groomed FBI agent. Even though I wasn't interested in Rod, I couldn't deny he looked mighty handsome dressed to the nines like James Bond in his charcoal colored Brooks Brothers' suit. "No. I'm going to work."

He grinned. "Looks more like you're getting off work to me."

"What's that supposed to mean?" I snapped.

"Did you take a close look at yourself in the mirror this morning?"

Why did he have to draw attention to my hair? I patted the top of my short cropped do where static usually makes loose strands stand up like toothpicks. "Of course I did. I know my hair looks frightful, but I didn't expect to run into anyone on the way out."

"I'm not referring to your hairdo, although I have to agree with you it does look scary." He touched his face. "I'm talking about this. Don't you think it's a little early to be wearing so much greasepaint?"

Slow on the uptake, it suddenly dawned on me what Rod meant when he mentioned coming off of work. "Whoa! Hold on a minute, buster. Let's back up a little, shall we?"

"What for?"

The guy might know how to dress to impress a woman, but he didn't know the first thing about talking to one. At this point I didn't care if I woke the dead at Stein's Mortuary, two buildings down from here, or not. "For your information, mister, you insinuated I look like a call girl."

Rod put his hand on his hip. "Don't frame me for wording I used. I merely hinted at it. There's a difference."

"Oh, yeah?" Before I could throw out a quick barb, Margaret Grimshaw opened her door. She was nicely covered in a long white terrycloth bathrobe and her pink Isotoner slippers. "What in the world's the fuss out here? Has someone stolen someone else's newspaper?"

Rod's face turned red as a poinsettia. "No. Mary and I are simply having a tiny misunderstanding, that's all."

"You call what you said 'a tiny misunderstanding?' Boy, you've got lot to learn about women."

"Is that so?" The tall blond shoved his hand in a pocket and took out a cell phone. "Oh, look at the time. I gotta go. I was expected at work ten minutes ago. Bye."

"Sure, leave it to him to rush out when the pressure builds," I mumbled.

Margaret remained confused as she watched Rod beat it to the stairwell. "What happened out here?"

"I'll fill you in later. It would take too much time and effort, and I haven't got either this morning."

"Of course not, you're heading off to work like Rod." Margaret wrung her arthritic hands like she was about to share a juicy tidbit, but the words that spilled out were anything but. "Before you go, dear, do you mind telling me who you plan to spy on today? I'm pretty sure you won't have time this evening. If I'm not mistaken, you have a date tonight with that young cop you met in Duluth."

Thinking of Trevor made me smile. "That's right, Margaret. We're going out to dinner. But in reference to the investigation, I haven't a clue who I'll seek out today. I'm too frazzled about the job I might get stuck with. I guess it boils down to which man is available. Cozying up to Chip O'Leary might be hard to swing since he manages the outdoor vats. However, I did notice Paul Mason, the first shift supervisor, ate lunch at the same time as I did yesterday. So, if he sticks to a routine, I could tackle him at least."

"I see. Well, good luck, dear. And remember, whatever you do, watch your backside and try not to use that stun gun."

***

"Come on, girl," Anita Crane said, "Time's a-wastin'. Those pickles aren't going to bottle themselves."

"I know. I know." I kept my eyes glued on the mirror over the sink in the women's bathroom, hoping my uncooperative do would give in. "I knew I shouldn't have worn a stocking cap to work. My hair is so full of static I can't control it. When I get one side situated under the hairnet the other side pops out."

Anita snatched the hairnet from me and stuffed it under an arm. "I'll fix that. Pay attention." She wet her hands under the cold water faucet, wiped them off in my hair, and then set the hairnet back on my head. "See, you're good to go."

"I certainly am. Thanks for the help." As much as I hated my crappy appearance this morning, I soon realized how much worse my headgear might be tonight if Aunt Zoe followed through and borrowed one of Gertie's hats for me.

"No problem." She held the door open. "Just get your butt out there and get to work."

I saluted her. "Yes, ma'am."

Even though Anita was anxious to get where we needed to be, I stole a few seconds to don the required safety goggles I hadn't been wearing as of yet. No need to have both of us chewed out because I hadn't followed orders my second day on the job.

Anita grinned. "Good to see you putting those on. We can't afford to have your eyes damaged. And remember, no schmoozing while working. We want to keep our production numbers up. Chatting can wait till break time.

Not if I run into Chip or Paul before then.

When we finally entered the production section we worked in yesterday, Anita still hadn't said if I'd be staying with this group or not. So I boldly inquired.

Anita peered over the top of her plastic glasses. "Girl, don't tell me you're already bored with stuffing pickles in the jars? You've put in less than eight hours on that job."

I thrust out my hand. "No. No. I just wondered how many days a new hire spends in each area of the plant before they're assigned a specific task."

My mentor placed her dark, rough-looking hands on her hips. "It kinda depends on you. If you demonstrate you've got the hang of pickle packing this morning, we can wrap it up and I'll take you over to help inspect the jars after brines been added. The jars can't be sealed unless the pickles are completely immersed in brine."

The chance to move on to another area and get chummy with other employees energized my sore body immensely. I stepped up to the conveyor belt where space had been left for another worker and tried to stuff loose cucumber slices into the jars as fast as my fingers could without shorting a jar of product.

Fifteen minutes into the job the conveyor belt shut down abruptly. "What happened," I quietly quizzed the gal from Mexico standing to the right of me. She shrugged her slim shoulders.

I glanced at Anita, standing on the other side of me. Her eyes looked like they were ready to pop out of their sockets. I threw up my hands. "I didn't do anything, honest."

"I know." She rested one hand on her hip and with the other pointed to the end of the conveyor belt. "We've got a serious situation."

"Oh, my, God. That guy's hand is stuck in a jar of pickles. Will they break the jar to free it?" I asked.

"Beats me. I've never witnessed anyone doing that before."

I felt sorry for the little fellow from Honduras. I'm so clumsy it could've been me. Forgetting my surroundings for a second I went into instant teacher mode.

I wasn't going to stand by and watch a jar get busted especially one with a hand tucked in it.

A year ago a similar incident occurred in my classroom when two boys stuck their hands in a jar containing crayons at the same time. It took grease and cold water to resolve the problem. Thinking of the baloney and mayo sandwich I'd packed and the ice cube maker in the lunchroom freezer, I yelled, "Don't break that jar yet. I'll be right back," and I ran off to gather what I needed.

~25~

Getting Jose's hand out of the pickle jar paid off big time. Not only did my quick thinking get high fives from the employees working alongside me, but Paul Mason, the first shift supervisor, whom I had hoped to bump into during lunch, showed up after the fact to pat me on the back.

"Mary, I heard what you did for Jose. If we'd resorted to smashing the jar with a hammer, his hand could've been cut severely and this year's perfect safety record would've gone down the tubes as well." His thick brows rose when he glanced over at my mentor standing about a foot away. "According to Anita this is only your second day here. Is that right?"

Pretending to be embarrassed about all the attention drawn my way, I cast my eyes downward. "Yes."

"Well, I appreciate your fast reaction. I only wish Don Hickleman would've been around to witness it."

"It was no big deal. I'm sure someone else would've behaved the same way."

Paul's gentle tone suddenly turned cold. "Afraid not. Don was pretty set in his ways. He liked everything the way it was, including safety procedures. Breaking a jar to release a hand has always been the way to go."

As I nonchalantly brushed off his comment and stored it in the old memory bank for later recall, I noticed employees slowly snaking their way towards the conveyor belt, hinting that the show was over.

The minute the conveyor belt kicked in Anita leaped into action and squeezed her plump body between Paul and me. Working around women as I have in the teaching field, I got the feeling Anita split Paul and me apart to convey some sort of hidden message. But what was it? Was she simply showing me she didn't like my spending time with our shift supervisor, merely demonstrating she was in charge of this new hire, or something entirely different? Her tone was authoritative and coarse when she spoke. "Sorry, Paul, but pickle packing needs all hands on deck, including Mary," and then she hooked her hand around my forearm for emphasis.

Paul gave us a wink and stepped aside. "Of course. Catch you later, ladies."

"Not if I can help it," Anita murmured.

Anita's sharp words quickly brought to mind the "Old Boy's" network she'd spoken of yesterday. Clearly she did not like Paul. Did the gals at the plant have trouble with him too? What if my mentor's words referred to something deeper, more sinister? Could Paul possibly be the murderer? Womanizer or murderer didn't matter, both spelled trouble, which meant I'd better remain on guard when he's around.

***

When lunch break came, there was no need to seek out Paul Mason. He caught my eye the second I stepped into the lunchroom with Anita, nodding at me with his sultry, pale blue eyes. I politely smiled back at him, knowing full well what was coming next.

Paul swooped his jet-black bangs lightly sprinkled with gray off his eyewear and signaled me over to his table. Talk about making it easy for me. Safety wasn't a concern here, not while I was surrounded by other employees. How could I refuse? Unless Anita throws a hissy fit and prevents me from chowing down with him. I guess I'll tempt fate.

"Hey, girl, where are you headed?" she questioned sharply, wrapping her thick hand around my wrist. "Are you sure you want to mess with him? He's like a wolf in sheep's clothing. You never know what's going on in that thick head of his."

"I'll be fine. I think he just wants me to fill in the details regarding what I did earlier. But if not, my two brothers showed me a couple moves I can use where the sun don't shine." They hadn't, but my safety instructor did.

Anita rested her hands on her wide hips and shook her head from side to side. "I sure didn't expect that coming from you. You're one tough cookie. I'm glad I don't have to worry about you. Enjoy your lunch."

"Thanks. I'll try."

When I reached Paul Mason's table, he shoved out a metal chair for me and then picked up his half-eaten sub sandwich filled with an abundance of toppings and various meats. "I'm glad I caught you, Mary. I still can't believe your quick thinking this morning. I hope you don't mind rehashing what you did."

"Not at all, but like I said, it was nothing," and then I sat and proceeded to empty my lunch bag on the small round table, which now only consisted of a slice of bologna and a cut up apple.

Paul set his sandwich down and stared at my meager lunch. "I hope that's not a new diet fad. If it is, you're going to fade away before the end of the day. At least get something to drink for cry'n out loud."

"I will in a bit." I unwrapped the wax paper holding the single bologna slice, still peppered with mayo here and there, broke it into bite size pieces, and ate a few. "By the way, I don't usually eat like this, but I promise it'll make sense to you once I explain what I did for Jose." Now, I stacked a few more pieces of bologna together and ate them too.

"Go ahead, I'm all ears."

You heard him. He wants to know what I did for Jose. Well, that's going to include a whopper of a story.

I cleared my mouth and began. "The minute I saw Jose's hand in the jar, a newspaper article from a while back came to mind. It concerned a four-year-old who'd gotten his hand stuck in a baby jar. The mother said when she saw her son's dilemma she immediately went for the jar of mayo, took a handful, and rubbed it on the part of his hand that was exposed, but nothing happened. So then she put ice and water in a bowl and submerged the jar in it. Presto. The cold reduced the swelling in the hand and it slid out."

Paul chuckled. "So that's what happened to your sandwich."

"Yup."

"Hmm. After hearing your story, I think you deserve a dessert." A huge piece of apple pie ala mode came to mind. My mouth watered. But when Paul reached in his back pocket, whipped out his wallet, and handed me a dollar I wasn't impressed. You can't get anything with a dollar these days. "Here, treat yourself to something chocolaty from the candy machine."

"Thanks. That's very kind of you," I lied. "Don Hickleman must've instilled the generous spirit in his employees or you learned it from the cradle. Which was it?"

Paul's mood changed considerably as he leaned back in his chair. "I don't like to speak ill of the dead, but old man Hickleman was a penny pincher. Any raise you got around here you had to fight tooth and nail for. He never even threw a company picnic or a Christmas party for us." He shifted his body and sat forward again. "But things are going to be quite different from now on. Wait and see. By the way, I've already arranged an employee Christmas luncheon for next week, so come hungry."

"That I can do." *If his luncheon is as cheap as my dessert, the employees will probably be served canned tuna.*

While I chewed on a piece of apple, I pondered what Paul had said and what I dared ask next. His words clearly indicated to me that he didn't like Don Hickleman. But did he dislike the man enough to destroy him, by means of murder or theft. If I wanted to find out about Butch's first arrest, I'd have to circle around to it by way of another story.

"A major news broadcast company, I forget which one, recently covered a story about a big food company, similar to General Mills, suing an employee for stealing company secrets. Does stealing secrets in the food industry actually happen as frequently as it does in Silicon Valley?" Thinking Paul required a couple seconds to produce an adequate response I munched on another piece of apple.

The first shift supervisor slid his half empty Styrofoam cup closer to him and fidgeted with it. Bingo: The first sign of hitting a nerve. Tiny bits of Styrofoam fell to the table within seconds. A minute later Paul's words drifted my way. "I really wouldn't know, Mary. I've been working here since high school."

"How about at this particular plant? Anyone you ever worked with get their hand caught in the cookie jar?"

His face grew grim. Obviously, he hadn't expected me to shoot him another serious question dealing with a subject closer to home.

I took my eyes off the man for an instant and glanced at the clock on the wall above the coffee machine. "Geez, lunch breaks almost over," I said, acting as if I hadn't noticed the change in his facial features. "I'd better grab that candy bar and beverage before I have to clock-in. Thanks again for the dessert." When I stood, the chair dug into the floor making an ear-splitting noise. No one seemed to care.

"Sure," Paul replied. "Hope your afternoon goes well."

"You too." Anxious to get away from the man, I took a couple steps in the opposite direction, but didn't get far.

Paul called out to me. "Hey, Mary."

Oh, oh. Did he put two and two together already.

I spun around and braced myself for what might come. "Yes?"

"You dropped something."

What could've possibly fallen out of my pockets? *The stun gun, dummy.* I rested my hand on the section of lab coat covering my pant pocket. It felt lumpy. Phew. What else could I've dropped? I scanned the floor surrounding the chair I had sat in. Nothing. Hmm? I put my palms face up indicating I needed a little help from Paul.

He pointed to an object near his shoes.

Thinking it was food, I said, "I must've missed some apple, huh."

"No. I don't think it's from an apple."

Clueless, I treaded over to the table, stooped down, and picked up what Paul had pointed to, a green earring. It perfectly matched the ones I'd put on this morning, but had chosen not to wear them after Aunt Zoe suggested I didn't. In a hurry to get going, I stuffed them in a pant pocket instead of the jewelry box.

Paul Mason's thick brows arched when he caught a glimpse of the earring I plucked off the floor. "You didn't have earrings on earlier did you?"

"No. I planned to put them on at the end of the day. I'm glad you noticed it." I opened my hand wider, allowing him a better view of the earring. "It's one of my favorite pair of earrings," I explained. "I would've been devastated if I'd lost it. My grandmother gave me them." With that said, I scurried off with the knowledge I hadn't blown my cover.

~26~

"Mary, I'm so glad you're home," Aunt Zoe said, rushing to greet me.

"What's the problem?" I asked, taking my jacket off and hanging it up. "You look like you're ready to burst at the seams."

"I am, but not because of the outfit I'm wearing."

"That wasn't what I meant. Oh, never mind."

Since my aunt mentioned clothing, I thought I'd better examine what she had on before interrogating her further. I knew for a fact a particular Dashiki she brought back from West Africa, the one with a lion's head painted on the front, could easily scare the crap out of anyone, including a cop. *All right! She passed inspection.* The magenta and black outfit she's wearing from Lands' End is perfect. "So, what's going on, Aunt Zoe? Has Trevor phoned? Did he cancel the date?"

"No, dear."

Pleased to hear he hadn't, I said, "Good. Then I'll change into my dressy shoes while you tell me what's going on." I grabbed the shoes from the hallway where I'd left them this morning and found a spot on the couch to sit and change out the tennis shoes for the nice pair.

"We ran out of milk," she slowly began, standing in front of the coffee table now. "So I walked to the corner grocery store three blocks down. You know the one."

I straightened up. "Yeah, what happened? Did Marty's get robbed while you were there?" I teased, sincerely hoping that wasn't the case. Although I could picture Aunt Zoe getting in the middle of something dicey going down and taking things into her own hands, like clobbering a robber over the head with the humongous purse she carried around town.

"It's best if I show you, Mary," she said, more excited than I've ever seen her. She hastened to the other end of the couch and picked up her purse.

Oh, oh. I hope she's not going to demonstrate on me.

Luckily, it wasn't the purse Aunt Zoe wanted after all, it's what it contained, her cell phone. As soon as she retrieved the phone and clicked it on, she carried it over to me and pressed the phone's photo icon. "Take a look at this picture, Mary. Do you recognize the guy?"

Receiving the shock of my life, I left my mouth agape, leaving room for any little critter to waltz in. "Of course, I do. He's the one who stole the sunglasses from Singi Optical. What was he doing? Buying groceries with his old timers' gang?"

She smiled. "You're not going to believe this. He was selling sunglasses."

"Outside the grocery store in this sub-zero weather? Is he crazy?" Aunt Zoe's mouth cracked open. "Don't waste your breath," I said, slipping on the good shoes and tucking the tennis shoes under the coffee table. "One has to be a little nutty to take what doesn't belong to them in any kind of weather, hot or cold. You didn't talk to the thief, did you?"

"Sure," she replied like it was an everyday occurrence. "Did you ever catch the show *Golden Girls?*"

"Yup. I've seen reruns."

"Well, I pretended I was Maude's roommate Rose. You know the one who asked umpteen questions and everything had to be spelled out for her." *Hmm. Sounds like you.* "Step 1: I explained to him how I was interested in a pair of sunglasses for my ninety-year-old mother. Step 2: I wore the guy down by asking him to repeat the benefits of each pair of sunglasses over and over. Step 3: I hit while the iron was hot. I asked where I could find him after getting sufficient funds together. Unfortunately, he didn't offer an address. But the dumb guy told me to take a picture of him. 'That way,' he said, 'you'll have an easier time finding me around here again.'"

"Auntie, you're a genius. I take back all the crummy thoughts I've ever had about your idiosyncrasies. Not only do we know where to find the guy, but we have a photo of him to give the cops."

She fluffed the decorative pillows resting in the middle of the couch and then sat. "At least you understand why I was busting at the seams."

"Ah, huh." Before I could say more, there was a knock at the door.

Aunt Zoe clasped her hands. "Mary, I believe that's the charming fellow you've been waiting for. Should I let him in or do you want to?"

I jumped up. "Stay put. I'll get it," and I scrambled to the door. The moment I opened it, Trevor and his K9

Duke bounded in. They both looked the same since I last saw them; neither ones girth had changed a fraction of an inch. *See that, Mary. Working out does payoff.*

Trevor continued to hold the bag of dog food he'd brought with while he stood in the archway between the living room and hallway and gave our apartment a serious once over before greeting us. I figured the examination was due to the cop side of him kicking in, being aware of his surroundings at all times, but it wasn't. It turned out he was concerned about something else. "Gracie must be putting on the shy act. Say, she won't mind if Duke relaxes here while you and I go to dinner, will she? He needs a break from working."

I choked up at the mere mention of Gracie's name. "Well, I, ah. It's like this, Trevor. My brother's dog's not here, but if she were I'm sure she wouldn't mind. She's pretty laid back."

Aunt Zoe tapped my arm, her way of giving comfort without speaking.

My date picked up on her gesture. "Obviously, something's going on here, and I've put my foot in my mouth. I'm terribly sorry."

"No need to be," Aunt Zoe replied. "I'm sure Mary will explain everything over supper."

"I certainly will. I could use an expert's input." Now I reached out and patted Duke's head without asking first if he was off duty yet. When I realized my mistake, I asked Trevor if it was okay that I'd given the K9 attention.

Trevor ran a hand through his thick, wavy cinnamon-colored hair. "Sure. He loves his down time as much as us cops. By the way, where would you ladies like me to set this dog food, in the kitchen?"

"Yes," Aunt Zoe replied, "We can put it next to Gracie's dishes. Mary, why don't you get your hat and coat on while I show Trevor to the kitchen, then you two can get going."

"Thanks, I'll do that." *Wait a minute, did she say hat? Oh, my God. Not one of Gertie's.* "What hat Aunt Zoe?"

"You'll see it. It's on the shelf in the entryway closet."

I opened the door reluctantly afraid of what I might find. To my dismay I discovered one lousy hat on the shelf, Aunt Zoe's black Kubanka of course. Here's hoping Duke doesn't attack me when he sees it. I slipped the wool coat on first and then reached for the hat.

While I stood in front of the hallway mirror fussing with my aunt's thick hat, I overheard Trevor say, "Zoe, I love the Vegas look you two have got going on here."

Oh, my, God. Major mistake. Now my aunt will never want to change the décor back to its original appearance.

***

When Trevor explained on the elevator how he'd found a spot for his Toyota Corolla close to the Foley, I had to wonder how close. For a policeman who works a set beat in Duluth it could mean anywhere from three to twenty blocks. Having been raised in Minnesota, I found the longer walking distance doesn't usually deter me this time of year either if I'm wearing the proper clothing and the temperature is above freezing, but the temp was below zero and I wasn't wearing boots, I had dress pumps on and a considerable amount of snow still covered the walkways from the last storm, so staying vertical for even a block could be a bit of a challenge.

Always thinking ahead, like any woman with a grain of smarts should, I immediately latched onto my date's arm on the way out the lobby door and hung on tight. Surely an off duty cop would keep me upright, right? Besides, I couldn't think of a better excuse to stay this close to him.

Trevor tilted his smooth-featured face down a bit and looked into my eyes with his gray heavy set ones. "So, where do you think you'd like to eat?"

My shoes slipped a little on the snow halfway down the first block and I automatically gripped Trevor's arm tighter. "There's a great little place a couple blocks from here called Ziggy Piggy's. The buildings divided into two parts. One side holds the restaurant and the other a dance floor."

"What kind of place is it?" he asked as he walked us across a lighted intersection and onto street two where he finally pressed his key fob. "You know, are they known for anything special?"

"Yup. It's the best darn barbecue joint in the Midwest. I'm surprised no one has told you about it. Their hottest item is the Dagwood, a barbecue sandwich."

Yay. Three more cars to walk past and I'm home free. No klutzy incident landing me flat on my back. Of course there's still plenty of opportunity to do so, if Trevor chooses to line dance with me. The grapevine step can do anyone in.

As soon as we reached Trevor's Toyota, I let go of his arm and patiently waited while he opened the front passenger door, and then slipped in. "I bet I know what your favorite sandwich is," he said as he closed the car door for me.

I laughed. "Any good cop should be able to figure it out."

Four minutes later we were seated in one of Ziggy Piggy's scarlet-colored vinyl booths, sipping on mugs of hot buttered rum, being warmed by the building's only brick fireplace from the late 1800's. "I can see why you like this place, Mary. The people here are friendly, overly generous with the food, and don't gouge the customer."

After Trevor had another taste of his drink, his eyes drifted to the six foot bar across from us. "Hey, did you see the tower of onion rings our waitress delivered to that guy at the end of the bar?" I nodded. "I think I should've ordered that instead. I bet there's at least twenty onion rings on his plate."

Thirty to be exact, but who's counting. The menu gives it away, but I'm not about to disclose that info and embarrass Trevor. Instead, I said, "I wouldn't doubt it." I set my mug aside and stared at Trevor's dimpled chin. "I'm sure glad you had to come down for K9 drug training."

He smiled, exposing perfectly straight white teeth. "Me too." I wonder if he wore braces during his teen years, like me. Probably not.

My hands encircled my drink. "What do you think of the training so far?"

"It's been good. I had already trained Duke to find marijuana and methamphetamine this past October so he's on to cocaine, and heroin."

"That's right. I remember you two were working together when Aunt Zoe and I ran into you at Park Point."

Our slim, middle-aged waitress appeared with our orders and placed them in front of us. "Do you two need anything else before I leave? Another hot buttered rum or perhaps a beer?"

"Not that we can think of," Trevor and I replied in unison.

"Okay, enjoy."

Trevor looked at his plate. "This meal is unbelievable, but I haven't a clue how to tackle it. Any suggestions?"

"First protect your clothes. Watch." I shook out one of the thick paper napkins provided and tucked it into the opening of my blouse. Then I picked up another one and laid it on my lap.

"Ah, I see." Trevor followed suit to the letter and then bit into his vinegar laced pulled pork sandwich aptly named On Top of Old Smokey. When his first taste finally came, a large quantity of barbecue sauce oozed out of his sandwich and drizzled unto his chin and fingers, making him look like a victim of a crime scene. "Messy but good," he announced, before setting his sandwich back on the plate and wiping his face with a napkin. "Mary, I noticed you've been avoiding the subject of Gracie. What's going on there?"

I tried to nibble on a fry, but stopped when the tears took over. "She ran away eleven days ago. Neither my folks nor the humane society has seen her. And the posters and flyers Aunt Zoe and I've spread around town aren't doing the trick."

Trevor pressed the palm of his hands against the table and leaned back. "I wish you would've told me sooner. Would you like me to ask the cops in your area to be on the lookout for her?"

I pulled the napkin off my lap and dried my face. "I guess. I've put off asking the police force around here since they're so busy, but I need all the help I can get. My brother Matt arrives home from Ireland in eleven days."

"Wow, you haven't got much time to find her." He reached across the table and took her hand. "I meant what I said. I'll spread the word for you."

"Thanks. Now that we've discussed Gracie, perhaps you wouldn't mind lending an ear to a few other things going on in my life too."

"Sure. Let me guess. One wouldn't be your roommate would it?"

I shook my head. "Actually, no. My problems involve sunglasses and my work."

Trevor cocked his head and grinned. "You're pulling my leg, right?"

"Nope. See—"

"Hey, Mary, I didn't expect to see you here?" Rod Thompson said, maneuvering his way to our table with a bottle of Coors beer in hand. "A working girl like you should be at home in bed already, unless, of course, you weren't heading to work when I saw you early this morning."

I slammed my hand on the wooden table, rattling my plate as I did so. "Save your smart remarks for another time." I took a deep breath and then introduced Trevor to Rod. "Rod lives at the Foley too," I explained.

Rod nudged Trevor. "Yeah, we share a common wall on the fourth floor," the Nordic geek brazenly added. "I'm surprised you managed to get her here for a meal, Trevor. She keeps telling me she's busy. Isn't that right, Mary?"

At that Trevor's face tightened. "It was nice meeting you, Rod," he said in a brusque tone, "but Mary and I have been looking forward to this evening for a long time. Perhaps you can chat with her another day."

Rod lifted his beer in the air. "Sure. Sure. Nice meeting you." He backed up a couple steps and plowed into a waitress who was right in the middle of serving drinks to the booth directly behind us.

Drinks went flying. Trevor and I got doused. And that was the end of what was supposed to be a quiet dinner out.

~27~

Aunt Zoe dropped her romance novel on the coffee table the second she caught a glimpse of us. "What on earth? What happened? You two look like drowned rats. I know it started to snow after you left, but I didn't think that much had accumulated yet." She pressed her hand to her cheek. "Oh, dear," she continued, don't tell me the sprinkler system went off at Ziggy Piggy's? Wait right there. I'll go get a couple towels," and then she dashed to the linen closet.

"Thanks but I don't need one," I called out too late.

Duke got up from his prone positon by the coffee table, paraded over to us, and sniffed his master and me like crazy.

"Don't worry, Mary. It's not the food he's interested in," Trevor explained, setting the small black gym bag on the floor he'd brought in from his car. "It's the alcohol."

He gave Duke the command to follow him into the living room and then squatted next to the dog. "It's okay, boy. There's nothing worth wasting your sniffer on. Save it for tomorrow."

"Wuff. Wuff."

"Well, look at you, Trevor," I said, standing over Duke's master. "You're looking pretty darn cozy despite being wet."

"Yeah, it's not too bad down here. You're welcome to join us."

"No, thanks. I'd better hang up the coats before my aunt returns from the linen closet," and then I marched back to the entrance closet a few feet away.

No sooner had I mentioned Aunt Zoe and she breezed into the living room carrying a couple bath towels. "Sorry, Mary, I didn't quite catch what you said. My ears seem to be blocked. All I heard was a bunch of gibberish."

I took one of the towels. "It's no big deal. I'm going to get out of these wet clothes."

"Oh?"

"Me too," my date candidly announced, not realizing his statement was taken to heart by Aunt Zoe. Her wide eyes suddenly appeared too narrow for their sockets.

Trevor's face turned crimson the instant he realized his faux pas. "I…ah, mean I'll change after, Mary."

"Of course you will," I teased.

Aunt Zoe immediately tried to eliminate the pitchforks we'd seen in her eyes. "I knew he wasn't going to change at the same time as you, Mary. He's a policeman and a gentleman. Now go get changed," she ordered, "and I'll warm up whatever's in those containers you brought home."

"Thanks. We're starving."

I waltzed out of the living room, took a slight detour to drop the Styrofoam containers off in the kitchen, and then continued down the hallway to change into a comfy, outdated sweatshirt and a pair of old jeans.

When I returned, I found Trevor still on the floor next to Duke playing tug-a-war with a rag tied into knots. Even though I hated to cut their fun short, I knew Trevor had to be as miserable in his wet clothes as I had been, and hastily advised him the bathroom was available.

Upon hearing the news, Trevor grabbed his gym bag and left Duke to fend for himself, which he did.

The German Shepherd immediately flattened his fury body by my feet and treated me to a soulful look. "It's not the end of the world, Duke, although it might be for my aunt if she's nuked your master's sandwich and fries to death. Maybe we'll give her a treat if she didn't. What do you think?"

Duke scrambled to attention. "Wuff. Wuff." I patted his head "Don't worry she won't get any of yours. She'd choke on them."

When I entered the kitchen with Duke, I found my aunt peeling carrots. "What are you doing with Trevor's dog?" she inquired.

"I figured he was probably ready for a snack. Did Trevor bring any treats for him?"

She nodded. "You'll find the bag on the counter next to your food."

Oh, great. That's all I need. Doggie treats added to what should've been a delicious barbecue sandwich, sans beer.

Duke watched my every move as I traipsed over by the microwave where the already warmed sandwiches and fries and doggie treats sat. I poked my hand in the bag of treats and came out with two large Milkbones. I dropped them to the floor. "Here you go, boy. Don't chew them up too fast." Done with handing out dog snacks, I plopped in one of the chairs and watched Aunt Zoe work at her task. "What's with the carrots?"

"I figured you'd like to eat something else besides soggy French fries with your sandwiches. Would you like celery too?" She peeked over her shoulder for a second. "Someone stocked up on it for midnight snacks and 'dieting purposes.'"

I noted dieting purposes was stressed more than snacks, but didn't react. "Nah. That's plenty."

Aunt Zoe tossed her pile of peelings in the trash. Then she grabbed a sharp knife and cut the cleaned carrots into smaller pieces. "Mary, did you have a chance to tell Trevor about Gracie?"

"Yup. He offered to contact the police in the neighborhood for me."

"Wonderful. Every little bit helps."

"What helps?" Trevor asked, pulling out a chair and sitting. I thought maybe he'd have changed into gym clothes, but he had slipped into another blue cotton dress shirt and black pants, looking sharper than ever.

"I told Aunt Zoe you offered to contact police in the area and make them aware of our missing dog." I shoved my chair back so I could get up and collect our warmed up supper from the counter.

"It's the least I can do."

Aunt Zoe put her knife down and rinsed her hands. Then she brought a plate of raw carrots to the table. "Would either of you like water, pop, or coffee?"

"No thanks." I handed Trevor his meal and sat back down with mine.

Trevor picked up his sandwich. "I could use a cup of coffee later, Zoe."

"Okay," she replied, backing away from the table as if we wanted complete privacy.

Noticing what she was up to, Trevor said, "You don't need to leave. Mary had hoped to discuss a few more things with me concerning sleuthing, while at supper, but then we got doused with liquor and that took care of our evening,"

My aunt pressed her fingers to her red painted lips. "For heaven's sake, who would do such a thing?"

Trevor glanced down at his food. "Your neighbor Rod."

"What? I can't believe it." Aunt Zoe pulled out a chair and sat. "I knew Rod had a crush on Mary but I didn't know it was that bad. It's hard to picture him being so jealous he'd ruin your evening."

My date opened his mouth. "Ah, actually that's not—"

I tapped his hand. "Save it for another time. Did I tell you about a customer at Singi Optical who stole a ton of sunglasses while I was working?"

I caught Trevor at the wrong time; he had a mouth full of food. All he could do was shake his head.

Aunt Zoe blatantly interrupted before I could share. "Mary wants to catch the thief."

The man finally had a chance to swallow. "Oh? Why? Is your boss blaming you for the loss of merchandise and threatening to subtract the amount from your wages?"

I took a bite of my barbecue sandwich. "Absolutely not. Raj Singi is one of the kindest men around. He knows I tried to apprehend the old guy after he left the building and doesn't hold it against me. Besides, the thief was simply too darn agile for his years."

"But get this, Aunt Zoe recently ran into this guy outside of a local store. Care to guess what he was doing?"

"Selling stolen sunglasses," Trevor replied.

"Yes, and I actually chatted with him," she said, tapping her painted nails on the kitchen table for emphasis. "That man may be fast on his feet, but he has a screw loose upstairs. He told me I could take a photo of him in case I wanted to track him down to purchase a pair of sunglasses."

Trevor laughed. "I'd say he has more than a screw loose." He turned his head slightly and gazed at me. "I suppose you'd like to catch the man in the act?"

"You got it," I said, "but what method of capture would you advise? Corner him at his dwelling or stake out his place of business? Remember it's not summer."

He held his half eaten sandwich in midair. "Normally, I'd recommend passing the information on to your local police department, but in your case I'll bypass that. I know you wouldn't follow through, Mary."

"You got that right, Trevor. She was born stubborn."

I held my head up high. "I can't help it. When it comes to seeing justice prevail, I'm like a bulldog."

"More like a Rottweiler," Aunt Zoe said.

Trevor rested his elbows on the table and leaned in. "Zoe, I think it sounds better if you say she has tenacity."

"Hmm, tenacity? I guess it does have a nice ring to it."

"You bet. Okay, Mary, here is my input for what it's worth. First and foremost, play it safe." He dropped his arms to his sides and sat up tall. "Don't follow the thief home. Too dangerous. He might have weapons stashed there. Instead, take a trip to the store every other day. When you find the guy, one of you keep him busy playing customer while the other contacts the cops. Got it?"

"Loud and clear," Aunt Zoe and I chanted.

When I picked up a napkin to wipe my messy chin and lips, I inspected Trevor's plate. Not a crumb of supper evidence remained. "What did you think of your sandwich?" I asked.

"Great, even though the bread was a bit soggy."

Aunt Zoe's hand flopped on the table. "This darn brain isn't what it used to be. I forgot to put something else out for you two?"

Thrilled that she might be speaking of an after dinner sweet, I said, "What? Did Margaret bake a pie for us?"

"No. I forgot to put the pickles out."

I shook my head. "You and your darn pickles."

"You should talk. When you come home from that job of yours, you reek of pickles."

Trevor tilted his head to the right. "You sure you aren't sisters? You certainly sound like it the way you go on about stuff."

His comment stopped Aunt Zoe and I cold. We shot a glance at each other. The poor guy. He was probably looking forward to a quiet evening and instead he ended up with Lady Mary and Lady Edith, from Downton Abbey, going at it minus boxing gloves. "Sorry about that Trevor, but pickles are a segue into my other problem."

Trevor's jaw dropped. "Where do you work that your clothes are absorbing the smell of pickles? I thought you were still subbing."

"I was, but after I got the job at the pickle plant two days ago, I put subbing on hold indefinitely."

"Oh? Well, I bet with your qualifications you got hired to train employees, am I right?"

"Nope."

He scratched his head. "What then?"

Aunt Zoe giggled. "She's stuffing pickles in jars."

Trevor's grey eyes widened. "I have a feeling this is going to be a long night. Can I have that cup of coffee now?

"You certainly may," I said.

~28~

Day 11

I had a rough night. Barely slept. It was the worst night of my life as far as I was concerned, except for possibly the night in fourth grade when I had flu like symptoms and the appendix almost ruptured. But then how does one compare an appendix to a budding relationship on a scale from zero to twenty, especially when a man gladly spends the night, but not where one would expect.

You see, last night when whiteout conditions prevented Trevor from driving back to his hotel, super gracious Aunt Zoe readily offered the sleeper couch to him. Yes, yes. At least I kept my virginity intact. Yay. But did Aunt Zoe really have to stay and act as chaperone, sharing the full size bed with me when Margaret has a spare bed at her place.

I glanced at my aunt who was snoring away. I guess last night's arrangements were for the best. I'd no idea where the brief dating Trevor and I'd done thus far was headed. It could be trivial or end up being grand—with wedding bells, flower girls, and a six-tiered cake. Of course, I keep thinking the same about David and me.

I listened for the roar of snowplows, but heard not a peep. I suppose I should get out of bed and make Trevor a gourmet breakfast, wearing apron and all and play Martha Stewart, but there wasn't much in the way of breakfast foods except, cereal, bread, juice, and coffee. Besides, as soon as the roads get cleared we'd both be hustling out and heading in different directions, him to classes and me to work.

A knock at the entrance door finally jarred me into action. Before I charged down the hallway, I grabbed the ratty-looking terry bathrobe I'd left at the end of the bed last night and tossed it on. The attire wasn't glamorous, but I didn't care. It was more important to stop the knocking.

I won't be receiving the medal for the ten yard dash after all. Trevor, dressed in exercise pants and short sleeve shirt, was already handling the early morning visitor with his K9 dog. If that scene didn't invoke danger for the person on the other side of the door nothing would. Feeling safe, I eased up behind him.

"Hi, can I help you?" Trevor asked amiably in a relaxed stance.

"What the heck are you doing here? Rod Thompson said in a quarrelsome mood. "I didn't expect to run into you." Duke growled.

Oh, boy. Here we go again.

"Where's Mary?" he asked. "I came by to talk to her."

I stuck my hand out from behind Trevor's back and waved. "Right here," and then I stepped next to Trevor. "Whatever you have to say, Rod, you can say in front of

Trevor." I planned to make the man sweat bullets. He deserved it after wrecking Trevor's and my perfect evening at Ziggy Piggy's.

Rod pouted. "Fine," he said, "but could you at least get the dog to back off? He's making me nervous."

I braced my hands on my hips. "You're nervous?" I laughed. "That's a good one coming from an FBI agent. What could you possibly be nervous about? Is there something stashed in your pockets that shouldn't be?"

Rod shifted his foot. "Are you telling me this dog is part of a K9 team?"

"Yup."

"That must mean Trevor here is the service handler."

I grinned. "Two for two, Rod, that's an accomplishment for you."

My visitor's pale face turned a rosy pink. He pulled himself to full height. "Look, I came by to apologize to Mary for my behavior last night. Since you're here, Trevor, I might as well apologize to you too. I've known Mary's brother for a long time. With him overseas, I feel the need to protect her, but obviously I've overstepped my bounds. I'm sorry. It won't happen again." Rod shook Trevor's hand and gave me a hug." Have a good morning," he said and off he went.

I closed the door. "Phew. I didn't expect that. Did you, Trevor?"

"Not really. The guy's got class. Your brother is lucky to have him as a neighbor."

"Hmm? I'll have to chew on that one. In the meantime, what do you say we have cereal and toast for breakfast?"

"Sounds good. You want me to make the toast?"

I grinned. "Yes, please. My aunt can't seem to get the hang of it."

"Is that an inside joke?"

"Nope."

***

News reports this morning said Minnesota's heavily traveled Interstate corridors, including Interstate 94, had been plowed during the night while we slept. Our neighborhood though didn't see the big machinery until 7 a.m., making me wonder about conditions in St. Michael. It all boiled down to how much snow fell in that vicinity and which roads the Department of Transportation considered important enough to be taken care of first.

So before heading out, I dialed Hickleman's employee hotline number listed in the company handbook. If the roads were bad, a recording would state a later start time. As it turned out, the first shift would be up and running within the hour.

With no time to spare, I tossed on boots and coat, offered a hasty good-bye to Aunt Zoe and Trevor, and buzzed out the door.

"Mary, it's nice to see you showed up," Anita said with a wide grin when I arrived. "I didn't know if you'd make it, seeing as how you live near downtown and the news last night said the freeways were mighty dangerous." She buttoned up her lab coat.

"They were." I hung up my coat and purse in the locker before tossing on the lab coat and ugly hairnet. "But the Interstate snowplow drivers were out in full force while we slept."

Anita closed her locker. "Good to hear. It's going to be interesting to see how many people don't show today. Are you ready?"

"Yup."

"Okay, let's go clock-in, girl."

After the time cards got stamped, Anita took us on a short side trip and announced she had chosen me to be the dill pickle packing section's designated runner for the day, like the task was right up there with rock star status. I knew better. She figured the new hire was lowest on the totem pole and wouldn't make a fuss. Well, she was right. I didn't dare create havoc. I had to be as quiet as a mouse in order to stay where I was and dig holes in all the Don Hickleman stories I heard.

Anita stopped abruptly, planting her feet by the door of the huge walk-in cooler. "When I say we need supplies, this is where you'll come." The second she opened the door cold air smacked me in the face, making me feel like an ice cube. If it'd been summer, I wouldn't have minded. "The shelves are all labeled," she continued, "so only grab spices and garlic, nothing else."

Oh, joy. A chance to exercise and get high on garlic too.

~29~

By eight the dill pickle machine was humming away and we, the tightly knit band of six employees, diligently began the long tedious task of packing jar after jar with slices of cucumber.

I couldn't believe I'd been working in this same section going on three days and still felt like Lucille Ball in the candy factory scene. Overwhelmed with all the unwrapped candy coming at her on the conveyor belt, the woman didn't admit defeat. She simply stuffed the extra pieces inside her blouse, her mouth, and anywhere else she could think of.

No one around here can deny I'm having trouble with what's passing in front of me too. But the cucumber slices I'm supposed to be squeezing into jars aren't ending up in any lab coat pockets, hairnet, or mouth. No siree. When those green slices slip through my fingers, they slide to the floor and create a disastrous design instead. However, I may have to admit defeat regarding the case before too many more hours pass by. Trying to solve Hickleman's murder and clearing Butch of any crime in a plant this size is shear folly, especially with no sidekick to watch my back.

My major beef right now is hanging around the same faces for three straight days. It kinda hinders this sleuth's modus operandi. With snooping at a standstill, I can't pump other employees for info. *What can I possibly do short of resorting to an injury to get out of this department?*

My mind was still in the clouds when Anita motioned for the gal next to me to go on break. "So, how's it going, Mary? Your eyes look droopy. I hope this works not putting you to sleep cuz we'd have a major problem on our hands."

"Nah, I was up late with company that's all."

She nudged my elbow. "Uh-huh. Your company didn't happen to be a guy did it?"

I pretended to zip my lips.

"I get it," Anita said, continuing to pop the long, slim slices of cucumbers in the jars at top speed. "You don't know me well enough yet to share. It's probably for the best. Some secrets are hard for me to keep."

"I know how that goes." *Maybe the end isn't as near as I think. I bet she has tons of work related secrets stored in that thick noggin of hers. I just have to press the right button, but when and where?*

"I've been keeping a close eye on you, Mary." *I hope not too closely.* "You seem to have packing cucumber slices down pat. I think we can forget about your experiencing packing chip cucumbers since there's less of a demand for the sweet ones this time of year. How about going to the brine section after lunch?"

I acted blasé. It's better to be indifferent than overly excited, right?

Not getting a reaction out of me, Anita examined my face for clues. "Look, I know exactly how you're feeling. It would be a whole lot easier staying with this job, but the thing is the company wants to find the perfect fit for you. Believe me we don't like losing good employees."

"It's nice to hear that," I said, finally managing to add cucumber to a jar, "especially since I'm on probation for another twenty-seven days."

Anita laughed. "Girl, you've got nothing to sweat about. You're a shoo in. We don't kick out those who show up on time and are drug free."

First shift supervisor Paul Mason strolled by just then. "Everything okay here, ladies?"

"Yup," Anita's thick hands dropped to her sides. "I just informed Mary it's time to move to a different section."

Paul's eyebrows lifted sharply. "Oh? Where are you moving her to next, Anita? You haven't forgotten that I like to keep track of the new employees."

Anita's smooth facial features hardened. "Nope. Now if you don't mind, I need to get busy," and she turned her back on him.

Despite Anita's snippy attitude our supervisor remained glued to his spot, which made me wonder again whether she had something hanging over his head, like a death maybe. I hated the fact that Paul's eyes were still focused on us and tried wishing him away. Like that would work. It didn't.

The man inched closer to the conveyor belt instead of further away. "Mary, I'm going to be in the lunchroom at noon. Stop by my table. I'd like to continue our discussion from the other day."

"But I…I don't really have anything else to add."
He winked. "Sure you do."

***

Ten minutes to twelve Anita pulled me aside and told me
I'd better make a run to the walk-in cooler for supplies
since the crew we'd been working with would be short two
people this afternoon, meaning us. "We'll cut out to lunch
as soon as you get back here, Mary. So don't be pokey
about it."

Lunch? I hadn't given it any thought until Anita
mentioned it. My stomach growled so loudly forklift
drivers in the shipping section probably heard it despite
wearing ear protection. I tapped my belly. "Hush, you'll be
fed soon."

As I trotted into the walk-in to collect spices and
garlic, I was distracted momentarily by visions of Trevor
Fitzwell parading around in my apartment this morning. I
would've loved spending more time with him. Right this
minute he and Duke are probably chowing down at the
Local or Hell's Kitchen.

If only I could've gotten away to join them
downtown instead of having to sit with Paul Mason and
discuss who knows what. I haven't been around the man
long enough to know if he really is a womanizer or not.
His wanting to talk to me didn't necessarily mean he
wanted to set a date for us to connect at an undisclosed bar
later tonight. Maybe I accidently blew my cover the other
day when I saved Jose's hand from destruction.

When I finally pulled my head up and glanced
around, I noticed a few changes in the walk-in since Anita
had me check it out several hours ago, namely boxes and
clipboards scattered on the floor and shelf items disturbed.
I didn't give it too much thought at first. Human nature

being what it is one doesn't expect to always find things put back the way they were originally. It wasn't until I saw the heavy plastic sheeting covering the entire spices and garlic section that I questioned what was truly going on.

Why would someone block off that particular area? Were they stealing stuff? I strolled over to the section where my supplies should be, pulled the thick plastic away from the shelving units, and was greeted by a familiar body. "Well, Paul, this is the first time I've had a dead man cancel a date. I hope it wasn't something I said."

~30~

Anita Crane's deep-booming voice came across like it was reaching me from the deep beyond. In reality it only traveled a mere four feet. "Girl, what's taking you so long? I expected you back before thi—" Her large calloused hands flew to her face. "Oh, Lordy! What've you gone and done, girl? Didn't you believe me when I said your job was secure?" She shook her head. "Paul was a supervisor, but he never had much say in who stays and who goes. At least tell me you were defending yourself. You're too young to spend the rest of your life in the slammer."

I grabbed Anita's trembling arm and calmly assured her I'd nothing to do with Paul's death. "I barely knew the man. What motive would I have for killing him?"

Anita looked confused. She leaned forward and glanced at Paul's body one more time. "There's… there's a cucumber stuffed in his mouth," she said, placing her hand against her neck. "When the police found Don Hickleman in the vat, he had one in his mouth too. Of course, you wouldn't have known about the cucumber. The information hadn't been released to the news media."

I studied her face. "Well, there you go. I'm not guilty of anything. I wasn't around when Don died."

She took a deep breath and straightened her posture. "That's right. You weren't. Then who could've killed Paul?"

I shrugged. "I'm the wrong person to ask. I've only been here three days, remember?"

Anita's body continued to shake, one of the many signs of severe shock. "I've... I've never seen a dead person up close, except in a funeral home, how... how about you, Mary?"

I shook my head. Even though I'd already worked two cases involving death this year, I had no qualms about telling Anita I hadn't either. You see, in the previous two cases I wasn't around when the people were actually murdered. I wish we were in a bar though instead of a walk-in. We could use a shot of Tequila or whiskey to settle our nerves.

I released Anita's arm and tried to get a handle on the messy situation in front of us. "I know we're both trying to come to grips with what happened here," I stated in a soothing tone," but one of us needs to get help and the other remain with the body. Which do you prefer?"

Anita's dark-hazel eyes drifted downward as if the floor would magically help her decide. "I guess I'd better be the bearer of bad news since you haven't been with the company that long."

Yes. I was hoping she'd say that. I didn't relish being alone with a dead man any more than she did, but being a sleuth I knew how to make the best of it.

"Should I send one of the men to join you, Mary?"

The gist of what Anita implied wasn't wasted on me. Nothing more needed to be said. I would be safer if a man was posted with me, especially if the killer was still lurking about.

"No. I think this situation better be kept under wraps till the police arrive."

"Good idea," she said. "But whatever you do, don't touch the body," and then she charged out the door.

She certainly didn't need to be concerned about me touching Paul's body. All I planned to do was take photos of the crime scene before police and medical personnel swarmed in and pushed me aside.

My stomach growled angrily knowing there'd be no noon lunch. The death of Paul Mason took priority over that. Although, a late lunch would be the perfect excuse for getting Anita over to Tioni's Pizza Parlor to have a private chat concerning Paul and other work related subjects.

With not even a crumb to satisfy the stomach for the moment, I cautiously scanned every inch of the walk-in searching for hidden cameras used in deterring theft. Once the brain informed me it was all clear, I swiftly plunged into action. I lifted up the bottom of my lab coat to retrieve the cell phone I'd stashed in a pocket, selected camera feature, and snapped away.

When finished, I checked the time. Three minutes had passed since Anita blew out of here. *Better hide the phone, Mary, and search a bit.*

"Hmm." The pickle designed pen attached to the clipboard on the floor begged to be released. And why not? I didn't intend to touch Paul's skin, only his pockets where many a secret has been discovered between those two tiny pieces of cloth, like a key to a hotel room or a safety deposit box.

Knowing how important it is not to leave prints behind for the cops, I carefully plucked the pen off the floor with the front flap of my lab coat and gently poked it in Paul's shirt and pant side-pockets, searching for answers. The first pocket held a few coins, the second a scrap of paper the color of tangerine with a brief message—*Meet me the same place as yesterday.*

"Who set up the meeting with you, Paul? And why?" That's the million dollar question. The sounds of shoes smacking the concrete in the hallway outside the walk-in grew louder. It's got to be the cops.

Lucky me, I'd freed the pen from the lab coat in the nick of time; Sharon Sylvester stepped in first, wearing a well-fitted black two piece suit and high-heels that looked like they'd been copied directly from a CIA magazine. She was soon followed by two police officers. Anita had returned too, but remained outside the walk-in. Maybe so she could keep an eye out for the expected EMT crew.

"Mary," Sharon said, drawing closer to me, "would you please show Officers Lloyd and Henderson where you found Paul Mason's body?"

I moved forward about ten paces, stopped, pointed at the thick plastic sheeting hanging in front of the existing shelving unit, and got out of the their way.

Before they pulled the heavy sheeting aside, Officer Lloyd turned to face me. "Ma'am, don't go anywhere," he ordered with a firm tone. "We'll need to question you and the gal out in the hallway."

~31~

Anita unzipped her heavy parka and put it alongside her in the booth. "Girl, I'm glad you suggested eating lunch here. I couldn't have digested anything over there the way the police and everyone else tried squeezing information from us like we were rotten tomatoes. That older cop, Officer Lloyd, tried to con me into pleading guilty with his scare tactics, but I saw right through him. What happened to being innocent until proven guilty anyway? Tell me the truth. Do I look like a killer? Never mind. Don't answer. I probably do before our morning coffee break."

"I didn't like the way he treated me either, but it's his job to get at the truth." I set my can of Sprite aside and plucked a slice of thin crust sausage pizza off the large metal pan delivered to us only seconds before. Heavy steam escaped into the air as I did so, warding me off from tasting it yet. Instead, I held the slice in front of my lips and blew on it for a while.

"That may be," Anita said, "but I think he could've gone about it differently." She took a quick sip of her Diet Coke and then dived into our shared pizza. "Well, at least we can take as long as we want for lunch, thanks to Sharon."

"I was surprised she gave us the option to take the rest of the day off though, weren't you?"

Anita had been gearing up to eat the slice of pizza she'd just picked up but held off long enough to respond to me. "Nope. How often does a person find a dead body?" Noticing the cheese and sausage slowly sliding off the crust, she quickly leaned over her plate to catch it. Unfortunately, the woman's wide hand caught more of it than the plate.

I handed her one of the extra napkins I'd taken from the napkin dispenser when we'd first walked in. "But this isn't the first death at the plant, Anita."

She wiped her hand off. "You're right. But I wasn't around when they found Don Hickleman." Anita stared at what was left of the pizza she still held. "You know this pizza sure is mighty tasty. I haven't had any in a while," she revealed. "Not since the doctor said I was supposed to watch my girlish figure."

I grinned. "I should be too." I swallowed what remained in my mouth and then went on. "Do you mind if I ask you something?"

Anita's mouth too occupied with chomping, gave her consent with a flick of the hand instead.

"Did any women on the day shift ever complain to HR about Paul Mason's overly zealous flirtations?"

"Not that I know of. Even though he came off awful edgy to the female workforce, I think the new hires realized rather quickly he was more blow than show. Personally, I never figured out what made him tick. He just got under my skin," she said, and shoveled what remained of her pizza in her mouth.

I eyed the two slices of pizza still left on the pan and hoped Anita would save one for me. "What motive could there possibly be for someone to knock Paul off then?"

"Honey, you're beginning to sound like a crime fighter. If I knew that, I would've shared it with the cops."

Ah, the heck with it. I couldn't put off eating a slice of the remaining pizza any longer. I grabbed one and took a couple bites. Then I inquired of Anita how long she'd been at the pickle plant.

"Oh, my goodness. You would have to ask." She shut her eyes for a moment. "Going on thirty years already I reckon."

"Wow. You were barely out of high school."

She grinned. "Not quite. More like a decade."

I scarfed up what was left on my plate and immediately began to fidget with the can of Sprite I'd ordered. Anita and I seemed to be comfortable enough with each other after all we'd experienced earlier, but I questioned whether I dared push the envelope further, and ask about Butch, fearing she might become suspicious. After much internal debate, I took a stab at it. "Do you remember a guy by the name of Butch Bailey? Paul Mason was his shift supervisor."

Anita's submarine-colored cornbraids bounced up and down. "Sure. Sure. A nice, quiet fellow. He ended up in the can over the theft of Hickleman pickle recipes. I was so shocked when I'd heard what he'd done. Is he a relative of yours?"

"No. He's related to a neighbor of mine."

"Ooo? Did she tell you he was arrested for old man Hickleman's murder?"

"Yup. He's out on bail."

"Really?" She plopped both hands on the table and wiped them with a napkin. "Hmm. Maybe he snuck into the plant and killed Paul too. I shouldn't be telling you this, Mary, but for years tension has been building up among the higher ups at the plant. I've just never been able to put my finger on it."

Could Don Hickleman have found out Paul Mason stole the recipes and when he threatened to throw him in jail, Paul killed him? I shook my head. That theory only works up to a point. What about who killed Paul and why? Was there an accomplice? If so, was that person blackmailing Paul? The pot was stirring but not anywhere near enough to declare what was in it. I just hoped to heck I could prove Butch's innocence.

For now Paul Mason would stay in the mix, but there's still another person I need to check out, Chip O'Leary. Butch mentioned Chip liked making other's the butt of his jokes. "Anita, could you introduce me to the vat manager when we go back to the plant? I think he's the only one I haven't met."

"That's a good idea. There's no rush to get back to our work. Besides, Chip rarely comes inside the plant. This way if you ever do run into him you'll know he's an employee not one of our suppliers."

~32~

The sun came out long enough during lunch to warm the temperature to ten above, making our visit to the outdoor vats at the pickle plant bearable. "Hey, Chip, you got a minute?" Anita inquired as she whipped her hairnet off and rubbed her hands vigorously. "I've got a new employee I'd like you to meet."

Chip and another guy were busy tending to the vats with long handled rakes. "Just a sec," he hollered.

Anita shifted her body a smidgen, giving her a view of the street while we waited. "Look at those people cruising by, Mary." She smacked her lips "They've no idea it takes six hundred bushels of cucumbers to fill one of those crazy vats."

"Nope. And when you say it in terms of pounds, holey smoley, fifty thousand is really hard to wrap one's head around."

"You got that right." Anita replied, continuing to keep one eye on Chip. "That man better come down here soon my fingers are getting numb."

"What's he doing up there, anyway?" I asked, even though Paul explained the procedures out here during the school tour.

"Stirring the salt brine to keep the cucumbers from surfacing."

I stared at the vats for a few seconds and tried to picture someone knocking Don Hickleman, a hundred and ninety-five pound man, into one of them and then holding him under with the long handled rake until his body gave out. A woman or man could've easily done it.

I shifted my gaze from the vats to Anita. "You'd think OSHA would require the vats to be covered," I said, wanting to hear Anita's explanation versus the one Paul gave.

Anita's cornrow braids bounced back and forth. "Don't start fretting about occupational safety out here, girl. These vats have to be left open. The sun's ultraviolet and infrared rays stop yeast and mold from growing on the surface."

"Oh? Sharon must've forgotten to pass that on to me." I rubbed my arms and turned slightly to see if Chip O'Leary was ready to leave the vat platform yet. He was.

Chip's open jacket flapped in the wind as his short, stocky fortyish body traipsed down the steps two at a time. When he reached the ground, he parked his hands on his hips and focused on Anita. "What's this about a new employee?" Then his cold eyes shifted to me. The eyes were two different colors, one blue the other brown, a rarity known as complete heterochromia. "Say," he said, "don't I know you from somewhere?"

"I doubt it." *Crap. He must remember me from the Washington School tour. Or perhaps he saw my photo in the paper this summer when I solved the crimes at the Bar X Ranch.* "I don't live in the area." I continued. "Maybe you've run into one of my many look-a likes over the years. I've been told they're plenty of them out there."

"That could be." He pinched one end of his stiff black handlebar mustache that reached up to his cheeks. "So you must be the new employee?"

"Yup."

"Chip, this is Mary Malone. She started here three days ago."

"Oh, yeah?" He slipped his hands in the pockets of his ill-fitted down jacket. "Where have they got her working, in the office?"

Anita grimaced. "No. I'm training her in on the floor. This afternoon I'm introducing her to the brine section."

"Ah?"

I found it surprising that neither Anita nor Chip mentioned Paul Mason's body being found in the walk-in earlier. I understood Anita's reluctance to bring it up again, but why wouldn't Chip inquire about the carnival like atmosphere of cop cars, ambulance, and firetruck. Didn't he care what went on inside the plant? Or did he have something to do with Paul's death?

Chip's mouth cracked open for a split-second like he was about to add more to the conversation, but then the employee up by the vats signaled he needed him. "Sorry, ladies, but work requires my attention. Maybe I'll have more time to chat next time."

Anita rubbed her thick lips. "Well, that went down better than I expected," she said as we tramped through the remaining snow in the lot and headed inside to the locker room to rid ourselves of our coats and purses. "One never knows what Chip's going to spit out. He can be downright blunt at times."

"I understand Don Hickleman was like that too."

"Uh-huh, but I'd rather not speak of the dead at the moment." She tore off her parka that had seen better days and tossed it in her locker. "Come on, Mary, the brine section waits for no one."

***

"Take a good look at the example on the wall behind you," Anita instructed. "It shows what the jar of sliced cucumbers should look like after we've patted down the cucumbers."

I marched over to the large photo on the wall and stared at it for a few seconds.

"Got it stuck in your head, girl?"

I nodded. If this ex-teacher couldn't remember one little picture, I'd be in deep do doo.

Anita swung her arm out. "Good. Move up to the conveyor belt so you can see what's actually happening." She pointed to the left of us. "That gal's job at the very end is to fill the jars of sliced cucumbers with brine. When her jars come your way you lightly tap down on the slices, making room for a bit more brine. After you're done, the guy at the opposite end adds more brine to the filled jars and weighs them. Okay. I'm going to step back and let you get to it. Too many hands only add more confusion in this section like it does in the kitchen."

I wouldn't know about that. Aunt Zoe's hands create enough confusion in our kitchen.

~33~

As soon as I got home, I kicked off the Sorel snow boots and headed straight for the La-Z-Boy. After the wild day I had at work, I didn't plan to lift as much as a pinky finger unless Aunt Zoe did something nutty like setting the apartment on fire. Which, thankfully, as far as my nose could tell she hadn't.

"Oh, Mary? I didn't hear you come in," Aunt Zoe said as she ambled into the living room, scooped up the TV's remote control from the coffee table, and selected a station. An ad for Tums popped up on the screen.

"Were you preparing supper?"

She sat on the couch and continued to hold the remote. "No. I hadn't realized it was that late. I dozed off about an hour ago," she explained. "When I awoke, I had so much energy I decided to rearrange the kitchen cupboards. We'll be moving out soon you know."

No kidding. "How did it go? Were you able to remember where Matt kept everything before we moved our stuff in?"

She shook her head. "I'm afraid my memory can be a bit stale at times."

Stale? I hate to tell her but at her age refreshing it ain't going to help. If she'd only tackled the living room instead and gotten rid of the Vegas look before Matt shows up. I can't imagine why she's stalling.

I faked a smile. "Don't worry. Matt's been gone six months. He won't notice if his dishes aren't exactly where they used to be. So, did anything interesting happen around here today?"

The question seemed to confuse my aunt, her brows lifted considerably. "Like what for instance?"

"Oh, I don't know. I thought maybe you received a call about Gracie or," I mumbled, "you heard somebody was murdered?"

She leaned forward on the couch and threw her meticulously manicured hands in the air. "What? Someone got murdered in our building. I never heard any sirens. I must've been sleeping when the cops showed up. What floor did it happen on? Did the cops mark off the apartment door with yellow tape or did they decorate the whole hallway?"

Aunt Zoe stared blankly at the TV and released a heavy sigh. "The poor residents on that floor must be scared out of their wits. How are they ever going to sleep tonight, Mary?" she asked as she rested her back against the couch again.

"Don't fret about them," I said with a firm tone. If I didn't set my aunt straight, she'd worry herself to death and then my father would never speak to me again. "Auntie, there's something I need to tell you."

"Yes?"

"I—"A loud knock at the door stopped me cold. I tensed up. "When Trevor left this morning did he mention coming back here this evening?"

"No. All he said when he left was he had a great time and looked forward to seeing us again soon."

Crap. "Soon could've meant tonight. I look a fright. What am I going to do? There's no time to throw makeup on or fluff my hair."

"I'll get the door, Mary. If its Trevor, I can hold him off till you make yourself presentable."

I took a deep breath and released it. "That's all right. I'll go. Whoever is there will have to accept me the way I am." *Hopefully I won't find a man on the other side.* On the way to the door, I ran my fingers through my hair. It couldn't hurt.

Margaret Grimshaw's olive-green eyes lit up when I opened the door. "Good evening, Mary. I hope you don't mind that we stopped by without calling first. I told Gertie you're probably worn out after such a long day at the pickle plant and didn't feel like visitors, but she insisted."

"Well, I—"

"Of course she doesn't mind," Gertie said as she pushed her way past me and immediately plopped her abundant body on the couch next to Aunt Zoe's, not giving any consideration to the woman in her nineties who came with her.

Poor Margaret. Missing her chance to have a seat on the couch meant the petite woman would be swallowed up by Matt's La-Z-Boy. The only other choice though would've been a kitchen chair and I figured she'd prefer something cushiony over hard as a rock. I on the other hand had a well-padded butt and could put up with a solid wood chair and went to fetch one for myself.

"What brings you two here," I asked, after returning with the heavy chair and setting it near Margaret. "Are we having some sort of meeting?"

"No, dear," Margaret replied. "Gertie came by and asked if I'd heard anything new concerning your undercover work at the plant."

Gertie's newly dyed hair the color of plum bounced with enthusiasm. "Yes, and since Margaret said she hadn't spoken to you recently, I suggested we catch you when you got home from work. So, here we are." The huge grin on Gertie's face nearly exploded.

Aunt Zoe, who usually wants to know everything I'm doing to help Butch, totally ignored us. "I don't believe it. The local news is cutting into the last half hour of Ellen's show," she said in disgust. "It better be something serious or I'm going to go down to that station and give them a piece of my mind."

Not if I don't drive her. "Aunt Zoe, turn the volume up," I ordered. "I'm sure we'd all like to know what the 'Special Report' is about."

She quickly obliged.

"Good evening. WCCO has just learned the name of the victim found murdered today in St. Michael. The body of Paul Mason, first shift supervisor at Hickleman Pickle Plant was found shortly before noon. At this time the police have no suspect in custody. When asked if Mason's death could be related to that of Don Hickleman's, the police chief said 'no comment.' Stay tuned. More news is sure to follow on our 10 o'clock newscast."

Aunt Zoe didn't wait for the Ellen show to return. She got up and turned the TV off by hand. "A murder at the plant? Is that what you were hinting at, Mary?" I nodded. "Why didn't you tell me straight out? You didn't witness the murder, did you?"

"Well, no, but…."

"I hope you had your stun gun on you."

I rolled my eyes.

"What's this about a stun gun?" Gertie asked. "I've been thinking about getting one."

"Ladies, let's forget the stun gun," Margaret said in her soft, hypnotizing voice. "I want to find out what Mary knows about Mr. Mason's death. Where did they find his body? Were there any witnesses?"

I turned slightly to face Margaret. "I don't know anything about witnesses," and then I lifted one of the hands that had been resting on my lap and stroked my forehead several times. All this talk of death this evening made me feel light-headed.

Obviously, the reality of finding Paul Mason's body earlier was finally taking its toll on me. An 1800's quote by French novelist Eugene Sue's came to mind. It was used in the *Father Brown* series last week, so apropos to this crime. Without realizing it, I repeated it aloud. 'Revenge is a dish best served cold.'

Margaret stretched her arm out and grasped my shoulder. "Dear, are you all right? You look paler than usual, as if you've seen a ghost."

I rubbed my arms. "I haven't seen a ghost just Paul Mason served up cold."

"What do you mean?" Gertie spouted. "How the devil could a man have been served up cold? Was he found outdoors like Don Hickleman?"

"No. I discovered him on a shelf in the cold storage walk-in when I went to collect supplies. It was so surreal. One minute the man's alive and requesting that I speak with him about God knows what and a few hours later he's dead."

I folded my arms and tucked them under my breast. "I keep thinking if I'd arrived five minutes earlier somebody would've found my body stowed on the shelf along with Paul's."

Margaret let go of my shoulder. "It sounds like one of the employees is worried their secret is going to surface. Who suggested you go to the walk-in?"

"The woman who is training me in, Anita Crane."

"Hmm?" Margaret tapped her thin lips, but didn't say anything further.

Gertie shook her head. "I don't know, Mary. Maybe I shouldn't have begged you to take on this case. It's getting way out of hand. Cousin Butch would understand if you threw in the towel. I'll call him and soften the blow if you want."

Aunt Zoe chimed in. "You don't know my niece very well, Gertie. She doesn't give up that easily. Once she's got her hooks in something, watch out. She's like a mother tiger." Dad's sister formed her fingers like claws. "Mary will shred her foe up and spit him out like she did with a neighbor boy when he told her she'd never be able to do a pop a wheelie on her bike."

"You remember that?" I asked.

Aunt Zoe laughed. "Of course I do, Mary. Not much got past me when you were a tyke. I recall the nickname your friends had chosen for you too, Kitten. I never told you, but I had the lion tattoo put on my arm just to remind me of you."

Whoa. She doesn't realize it but her light-hearted and touching remarks just restored my state of mind. Usually, it's Gracie who helps me feel better.

Gertie tilted her head in my direction. "I bet when the cops showed up at the plant they dragged you over the coals, didn't they?"

"Yup. They treated the woman training me in and myself like they do any other suspects. Luckily, we were questioned in separate rooms. The minute I told the cop interviewing me that Matt's friend, Sgt. Murchinak at the downtown sub-station, would be more than happy to vouch for me if he wanted to dig deeper into my background, he was thrown off balance and let me go."

"Mary, dear, I'm not trying to be morbid," Margaret said, "but would you be so kind as to describe exactly what you saw when you discovered the deceased in the walk-in."

~34~

Day 12

Anita Crane caught sight of me strolling into the locker room and immediately got in my face. "Girl, I don't know whatya did, but Sharon Sylvester's been asking for you. She said the second you clock-in you're to report to her."

Oh, oh. Who let the cat out of the bag? The only reason Sharon would want to see me is if the cop who interrogated me yesterday shared my personal data he acquired from Sgt. Murchinak. If that's the case, there'd be no more sleuthing for me in pickledom. Sharon Sylvester wielded all the power here. With the stroke of a pickle pen, she could cut me off at the knees and toss me out on the street all because this gal lied on the application about her so-called work experience.

It took me all of ten minutes to stash my personal stuff, toss on work apparel, and clock-in before my size nine tennis shoes tackled the well-tread stairs leading to H.R. on the second floor.

When I reached Sharon's office, I found the door ajar and poked my head in to make sure she was there. She was. "Anita said you wanted to see me."

"Yes," the H.R. administrator replied, signaling me to come in with her flimsy hand.

Surprise, surprise. The woman's complexion hadn't been transformed overnight. Someone needs to inform her that she desperately requires a serious makeup job especially during the winter months; her paler than pale heart-shaped face today did nothing for her honey brown eyes or the snug, dark-chocolate two piece suit she wore. Although, I did note her exposed auburn roots had been taken care of since I last saw her. Of course, most women do tend to fuss with their hair more than makeup these days, including me.

"Have a seat, Miss Malone," Sharon said in her thin, reedy voice.

After I selected the straight-back leather chair closest to Sharon Sylvester's desk, she swiveled her squeaky office chair halfway around to face the black metal credenza behind her on which sat an antiquated coffeemaker and a fresh package of Styrofoam cups. "Would you care for a cup of coffee?"

If her intention was to call me up here to give me the axe, she was certainly taking the gentle route to announce it. I crossed my legs and tried to display calmness. "Ah, no thank you."

After Sharon poured a generous cup of coffee for one, she slowly swiveled her chair back around being careful not to spill a drop of java on herself. "I'm sorry to call you up here, Miss Malone, considering the circumstances, but I feel a serious issue regarding yourself needs to be addressed." She took a couple sips of the hot liquid and then set the cup on her rickety desk. I really regret..."

Here it comes

"Sharon, are you busy?" A high-pitched brash female voice asked. "Oh, sorry. I thought you were by yourself."

Even though there was no mistaking the speaker, I kept my back to the door and waited for the conversation to playout.

Sharon tilted her head up and glanced at the person in the doorway. "Oh, Roseanne, I thought you weren't bringing a delivery till tomorrow. I'll be free in about ten minutes. Can you come back then?"

"Sure, I'm in no rush."

Sharon moved her coffee cup over a few inches and folded her hands. "Sorry about the interruption. What I wanted to say was I regret that you were put through such an ordeal yesterday. No, one should have to go through that. Anita Crane told me how well you're catching on having been here only three days. And your handling of two major incidents here during that time has certainly impressed me. Not everyone would've acted as calmly as you did with Jose's accident or Paul's death."

She opened her thin hands and flattened them on the desk. "As the head of H.R., I'm authorized to bump up a person's pay scale whenever I see fit. And I've decided you definitely deserve one after all you've been through. So I've added a quarter more to your hourly wages. Is that all right with you?"

Hmm? Sharon must think I'm pretty gullible if she's offering me a raise. What's in it for her? Is she afraid I might sell my story to the newspaper? I bubbled over with enthusiasm. "Sure. Of course it is. Extra money is always

nice especially with Christmas just around the bend."
Figuring that was all she wanted to hear from my lips, I
prepared to leave.

"Please don't go. I'm not through yet."

"Oh, sorry."

Sharon stretched her hands across the wide desk. "I
know the police questioned you yesterday, Miss Malone,
but after having time away from the plant, are you still
positive you didn't see anyone near the walk-in when you
entered it?"

I nodded. "I'm positive."

"All right then. That's all I wanted to know. You
may go back to work."

***

Even though Anita never mentioned where we'd be
working today, I assumed I'd be expected to help in the
brine area for at least two days since I worked that many in
the sliced pickle section before moving on, so after I left
Sharon Sylvester's office that's where I headed.

My mentor's plump face broke out in a smile similar
to a chimpanzee's the moment she laid eyes on me. "Mary,
am I glad to see you. I was afraid Sharon thought you'd
killed Paul and gave you the old heave ho. Then I got to
thinking if she thinks Mary's guilty, what's to stop her
from canning me too since we were both in the walk-in
near the time of Paul's death."

I stepped up to the conveyor belt and began to pat
the pickles down in the open jars "Nah, I'm still here.
Sharon was just concerned about how I was doing since
discovering Paul's body," I lied. "Hey, was your trucker
friend supposed to be delivering cucumbers today?"

Anita lifted her broad shoulders. "You mean
Roseanne? I don't know. Why?"

"I thought one of the women upstairs mentioned she was in the building."

"Hmm? I wonder if anyone has told her about Paul yet." Anita muttered. "Probably not. I guess I'd better be the bearer of bad news."

~35~

Anita yanked me away from the conveyor belt for a second. "If anyone asks, I've gone over to the capping and pasteurization area for a few minutes." Then she zipped out of our section.

I didn't believe her story. Knowing Anita she was determined to find Roseanne Harsh and the most logical place for her to look would be the breakroom. But she won't find her there. Any second now the trucker should be coming down the backstairs near the first floor bathrooms and wouldn't you know it my bladder is conveniently screaming for attention. So I headed in that direction.

Thanks to a tennis shoe coming untied at the perfect moment, I saw Chip O'Leary hustle Roseanne off the steps to a corner safe from prying eyes. Wondering what they could be up to, I snuck up as close as I dared, within the boundaries of the women's bathroom, and eavesdropped on their conversation.

"What gives, Roseanne? I thought we had a pact."

"Let go of me, Chip, or I'll scream."

"Go ahead. I dare you."

Roseanne didn't say anything.

"That's what I thought. You don't dare cause a ruckus." He snapped his fingers. "I'd blow the whistle on you."

Ooo. This gets more intriguing as it goes along.

"For what? Having had an affair with the owner of the company?" she asked.

"Don't forget Paul. The police would be mighty interested in hearing about your romances with the men around here."

"You're just jealous I never gave you a second look. At least the old man got one thing right before he died, Chip."

"What's that?"

Roseanne leaned closer to Chip's pocked square-shaped face before blowing off more steam. "He tossed you aside like a bad cucumber before you could stir up trouble within."

Chip's face reddened. "When exactly did you arrive in town, Roseanne," he inquired.

"None of your business," she snapped.

My ears perked up. Heavy steps were approaching from the direction I'd come. Not wanting to get caught in the hallway, I ducked in the bathroom to take care of legitimate needs. At least my appearance will look normal when I popped back out.

When I cracked open the bathroom door to enter the hallway again, I heard Anita's southern drawl. "There you are Roseanne. I've been looking all over for you. I should've figured you'd be busy with other things."

Roseanne laughed. "Hush up. Chip and I crossed paths on the stairs. That's all."

"Yeah, yeah."

"Hey, you don't believe me, go ask him."

"Calm down. I believe you."

"So why were you looking for me?" Roseanne asked. "It's not break time for you yet, is it?"

"Nah. I heard you were in the building and I thought you'd want to know about Paul Mason since you two had a thing going."

"Oh? Thanks. But Sharon broke the news a few minutes ago."

The bathroom door closed loudly behind me, startling the two women. They glanced in my direction. "Nice to see you again, Roseanne. Sorry, if I scared you gals, I didn't mean to. I had to make an emergency pit stop," I explained. "Forgot to watch how many cups of coffee I had before leaving home." I slowly pivoted in the direction of the work area and began to head that way.

Wait, Mary," Anita said, "I'm coming with you. Catch you next time, Roseanne."

"You bet."

~36~

Day 13

"Mary, I'm making banana pancakes if you're interested," Aunt Zoe announced through the tightly closed bedroom door.

Halfway between reality and dreamland, I mumbled, "Okay," and yawned. Then I slowly rose to a sitting position, dangled my legs over the edge of the bed, stretched my arms overhead, and wiggled my fingers at the off-white ceiling. "Ow. Ow." *Dumb move.* The arms hadn't recovered sufficiently from yesterday's work load at the plant. Looks like the housework I wanted to get done before Matt got back will have to wait another day.

I gently lowered the sore arms and automatically grabbed for the bathrobe lying at the foot of the bed. Ever since I'd been made fun of by an early morning visitor, namely Rod Thompson, I didn't dare march to the kitchen wearing nothing but holey PJ's.

My aunt's brief words regarding breakfast didn't really sink in until I reached the archway dividing the small kitchen from the hallway. "Pancakes?" The last time she attempted to make them they got so charred even the birds at the park refused to eat them.

Aunt Zoe greeted me with a cheery, "Good morning sleepy head," while keeping her focus on the stove and a frying pan. Even though her hair was still in those humongous rollers she likes to use, she'd already changed from her bed wear to a wardrobe consisting of a fire-engine-red two-piece sweat suit and matching tennis shoes.

Good Lord! The woman's ready for Christmas and I haven't even purchased one gift yet. I forced myself to come back with a cheery greeting before I inched my way to the table, even though my body wasn't about to take part in fake enthusiasm.

"I figured the banana pancakes would get you moving on a Saturday morning," she said over her shoulder. "You seemed to like them as a kid."

I bit my lower lip. *That's because I instructed you on how to make them.* "Oh, yum. I can't wait." I pulled out the nearest chair and plopped down. While patiently waiting for Mrs. Claus to surprise me with what I'd hoped would be edible pancakes at least six inches in diameter, thoughts soon surfaced concerning the possibility of gagging on the food soon to be served.

A few seconds later Aunt Zoe left the stove behind and waltzed over to the table with two coffee mugs, one filled and the other not, and what looked like an empty plate. The plate was for me. I'd no idea who the empty second mug was for. "Enjoy."

As hungry as I was, I couldn't possibly put anything in my mouth yet. I had to know what the extra coffee mug meant. Would someone be joining us or had my aunt simply assumed I wanted coffee? I stabbed the mug with a finger. "What's with this? I didn't request one."

"It's for Margaret," she said, sitting in the chair opposite me where she'd set one of her latest collections of coffee mugs purchased from a Goodwill store. "She asked to stop by."

"When did you see her?"

Her hand shot to the cup of coffee sitting in front of her. "I ran into her about a half hour ago when I went to dump the trash down the chute."

"Ah?" I stared at the two tanned circles the size of silver dollars lying on my plate, expecting them to expand any second. Surely she doesn't plan to offer our neighbor breakfast too. "Looks like the pancakes shrunk. What happened?"

"Every time I tried flipping a regular size pancake it fell apart." She embraced her arms. "So I decided to stick to a smaller version. Hope you don't mind."

My stomach demanded a larger breakfast, but I didn't care. The pancakes were made and my aunt expected me to scarf them down, so I would. I grabbed the maple syrup and drizzled it over the tiny pancakes. Then I tasted one. Despite the fact that there wasn't much to munch on, the pancake got lodged in the roof of my mouth.

"Well, what do you think? Do they taste as good as you remember?"

Still fighting with the doughy substance, I simply nodded.

My aunt sighed. "Good. I was hoping I'd put enough bananas in it. When you're ready for more, let me know. There's plenty of batter left."

Oh, Gracie, if only you were here. Maybe I can drop the other one on the floor by accident.

"*Buongiorno*," Margaret sang out in her usual charming way as she shuffled her light body across the kitchen floor while toting a pan of caramel rolls. Her green and red apron edged with white ruffles worn over a long-sleeved hunter-green knit top and pants went well with Aunt Zoe's choice of outfits. "These baked rolls are fresh out of the oven. Would anyone like one?"

"Would I ever," I said.

"But, Mary," Aunt Zoe whined, "you didn't clean your plate yet."

I crossed my feet. "I will."

As soon as my aunt got up to get plates and forks for her and Margaret, I took a roll and stowed the remaining pancake in the paper napkin on my lap.

Having noticed what I'd done, our neighbor saluted me with her cup of coffee like she was in on the conspiracy. Maybe she was. After all, she did bring a pan of rolls. "I suppose the two of you have tons to do today," she said, "Like wash clothes and clean."

"Actually, Mary and I haven't had a chance to discuss what needs to be done around here yet," Aunt Zoe replied candidly. "I've been busy cooking and she just got up. But I thought if she wasn't too busy this morning maybe we could hunt for Gracie as well as the sunglass thief."

"I haven't any pressing plans," I stated, still holding on to my partially eaten caramel roll, "but I don't feel like running around outside if it's not any warmer than yesterday."

Margaret readily replied, "I believe the newspaper reported sunny and a balmy 28 for today."

"Great, a spring like day, perfect weather for finding a lost dog and a thief who is trying to unload stolen merchandise. I glanced at the wall clock by the fridge.

"We can hit the streets in an hour if you want. But before we go, Aunt Zoe, remind me to call Hennepin Humane Society one more time. No sense in hunting for Gracie if someone has already turned her in."

Aunt Zoe rubbed her hands together. "Boy, wouldn't that be a weight off our shoulders. Then all we'd have to concentrate on is catching that darn thief." With the rest of the morning mapped out for us, my aunt gladly gave her full attention to our guest once more. "Would you care for more coffee, Margaret?"

When our neighbor shook her head, a few strands of hair broke loose from the bound bun positioned on the top of it. "I'm fine," she replied, cutting a caramel roll in half and taking a portion for herself. "How's your case coming along, Mary? Anything new to report since you found Mr. Mason?"

"Plenty." I licked the remaining caramel residue off my fingers before elaborating. "When I got to the plant yesterday morning, I was told the gal in charge of H.R. wanted to see me. I assumed she'd found out I'd lied on my application and expected the worst. Talk about being surprised. I got a raise instead. Sharon explained it was because of how well I'd handled myself in a couple serious incidents over the past three days, but I didn't buy her story for a second. The lady has a hidden agenda."

"That being what?" Margaret softly questioned.

"She fears I'm going to sell the story about finding Paul Mason dead in the walk-in."

Margaret remained quiet for a second. "Yes, indeed that would be motive enough for keeping anyone quiet, wouldn't it?"

Wanting to be included in the discussion, Aunt Zoe promptly injected her misgivings regarding the salary increase. "Mary, if what you suspect is true, that H.R. lady is using hush money to keep you quiet like gangsters do. You shouldn't accept it. Besides, it's probably tainted."

The wrinkles on our neighbor's forehead sloped downward. "Zoe, bad publicity of any sort for a well-known company, such as Hickleman's, could ruin them. Mary doesn't have a choice. If she's to remain undercover at the plant, the H.R. woman needs to think she's on her side."

"Hmm. I hadn't thought of that."

Margaret adjusted her glasses and then peered at her dainty wristwatch. "Well, I guess I'd better get back to Petey, make sure he hasn't gotten into any mischief. One of the ladies from the garden club is stopping by to visit in an hour and I don't want her sitting on cracker crumbs."

I grabbed Margaret's frail hand. "Wait, don't you want to hear what else occurred yesterday morning? It's a humdinger."

The elderly woman's eyes grew wide like a baby's when given a new toy. "Ooo, that sounds intriguing. I guess I can stay a few more minutes." Ready to listen, she braced her elbows on the table and steepled her hands.

"On the way to the bathroom later that morning, I spotted Roseanne, one of the truckers, and Chip, the vat manager going off to a secluded area past the men's room to have a chat, and knew I had to listen in." I paused just long enough to take the half of roll Margaret had left in the pan.

"Go on, Mary," Aunt Zoe commanded. "Don't keep us hanging. What did the two of them talk about?"

I took a bite of roll and continued. "According to the flow of conversation, Roseanne and Chip had made some sort of pact and Chip was furious that she'd broken it. He also brought up her affairs with the men at the plant, including Don Hickleman and Paul Mason."

Margaret's face lit up. "I wonder what their pact was about."

"That's what I keep asking myself."

Aunt Zoe pushed out her chair and stood. "Well, I guess our life can finally get back to normal."

"What are you talking about?" I asked.

"You don't have to work at the plant anymore. You've found the killer."

"And who would that be, Zoe?" Margaret somberly quizzed.

"Why, Roseanne of course. She had affairs with both men. When they tossed her aside, she decided to get even."

I glanced at the ceiling. *Oh, Boy. More nonsense gleaned from her books.* "Aunt Zoe, we're discussing real life here, not some stupid romance novel. Just because the woman had an affair with both men doesn't make her a killer. Remember when looking for a murderer three important things need to be looked at: means, motive, and opportunity. Chip could just as easily be blamed for the murders. As a vat manager he comes and goes as he pleases. He definitely didn't like Don. And Don's body was found floating in a vat."

Margaret scooted her chair away from the table and stood. "I really must go now. But if you intend to prove Chip did commit the murders, Mary, you'll have to find some way to discover whether he stole the recipes and planted them on Butch."

"You're right." I pressed an index finger against my sticky lips. "According to Butch, Chip worked indoors at the time of the theft, didn't he?"

"*Si.*"

***

My cell phone rang just as Aunt Zoe and I'd finished donning our outdoor clothing and were about to lock up. "You'd better answer it, Mary. It's probably your mother wondering if we found Gracie yet."

I stomped my booted foot. "Darn. I don't feel like dealing with her questions right this minute." I tossed my mittens aside, dug the phone out of my pant pocket where I'd stashed it, and read the words displayed across the tiny screen. "It's not my mom."

"Okay, then let's go."

"No."

"Why not?"

My hand wavered over the ACCEPT button while I explained. "It's Trevor. He might be calling to tell me one of the cops around here found Gracie."

She flicked her hand at me. "Go ahead. Find out what he wants."

I walked over to the couch and sat. "Hi, I didn't expect to hear back from you so soon. Are you still in town?"

"Yeah," Trevor's voice sounded upbeat. "I decided to visit my folks while I had the time."

"I'm sure they were glad that you did. Any word on Gracie yet? I could use some good news."

"Sorry, I haven't heard back from any of the cops I spoke with. Listen, when I was there the other night you mentioned you're working at the pickle plant in St. Michael, right?"

"Yup. What about it?"

When I told my dad where you work, he informed me that another fellow's body had been carted out of the plant the other day. Is that true?"

"Afraid so."

Trevor's tone changed dramatically. "You should've called me, Mary."

"Way too much going on after the body was discovered. I'm the one who found it."

"Really? Man, I bet you were shaking in your boots."

"Actually, I had tennis shoes on," I lightly joked, something I wouldn't have been able to do two days ago.

Trevor grew more serious. "Well, whatever you had on your feet, I wish I could've been there to comfort you."

"It's all right. It's water under the dam. Besides someone from Duluth, I can't remember his name, told me I have nerves of steel."

"Ah, yes, a young cop not long out of the academy if I recall. So what's your take on the latest victim at the plant? Was he connected to Don Hickleman's death somehow?"

"No idea, but it's getting crazier by the minute."

"I don't like the sound of that and there's not a darn thing I can do about it." He let out a loud sigh. "I wish your brother was back in town."

"Why?" I watched Aunt Zoe unzip her jacket. She must be getting overheated. I probably should do the same. I yanked on my zipper.

"It's getting too dangerous. He'd tell you to back off

"Is that your opinion too?"

"You're darn right. I don't want to see your name splashed across the paper next."

How sweet. I guess the guy really does have a thing for me. "Don't worry about me, Trevor. I'm a big girl. I've been carrying a stun gun ever since I started working at the plant."

"Except Thursday," Aunt Zoe whispered.

"Shush," I said.

"Are you talking to me or Zoe?" he asked.

"Neither." I fibbed. "I felt a sneeze coming on."

"You can't depend on a stun gun like the one your aunt showed me the other day. It doesn't pack enough power. Even a cop's Taser only immobilizes a person for five seconds."

"Five seconds?" *Oh, oh. I'd better figure out some other means of defense.*

Aunt Zoe signaled for me to windup the call. I took the suggestion to heart. Who knew how long we'd be hitting the pavement in search of a dog and a thief.

~37~

Trevor didn't let our conversation end that easily. Before I could disconnect, he made me swear to keep him in the loop, the loop being the strange activities at the plant since I hadn't revealed this morning's plans. Keeping silent about them meant Auntie and I could follow through without interference from anyone.

The second Aunt Zoe and I traipsed out into the sun's warmth and onto the sidewalk that runs in front of the Foley we stuck together like two peas in a pod, marching merrily down the street, glancing every which way, giving the illusion to anyone watching we must be up to no good. The last part made me a bit nervous though. But I told myself as long as I don't end up in the clinker, why should I care what they think.

After hoofing ten blocks both east and west of the Foley and not sighting any dog resembling Gracie, I suggested we take our search north and south where we might find the sunglass' thief as well if we're lucky.

By this time though, Aunt Zoe was short of breath and complained of her bunions hurting. With the shape she was in, I knew she'd be no good to me if we ran up against a problem and told her so. Thankfully, she agreed with me. "I guess I'll go back to the Foley then and soak my feet in the tub. Buzz me if you run into any trouble. Either Reed or Rod should be home if you need assistance."

I doubted if I'd need any help. Besides, by the time anyone got to me it would probably be too late.

After my aunt abandoned me on the west side of the Foley, I debated which direction to go next. Since the grocery store was to the south and the Saturday crowd had increased rapidly within the last half hour, my instinct nudged me to head for the food. Of course, the message might have been coming from my stomach with all the calories I'd already burned.

The sun was rising higher in the sky with each step I took, but it did nothing for the slippery sidewalks which were getting trickier to maneuver.

Two blocks short of my destination my butt skimmed the ground, forcing me to ask why I was so determined to carry on the hunt when housework back home was beckoning. The only answer I received was to save face with Matt and Raj Singi.

When I reached the grocery store, I wasn't the least bit surprised to find no one trying to make a sale near its entrance. Either the thief thought it was foolish to stay in one spot too long or he'd sold all his merchandise. I hoped I was wrong on both accounts. Perhaps the thief just got a late start. With that in mind, I strolled inside to check out the freebies, including a sample of the newest flavor of hot chocolate the store advertised.

Bingo! The man I hoped to find was strolling around the store as if he hadn't a care in the world, sampling food with one hand while the other held a large fully expanded cloth bag, the same as he'd brought to the optical store.

Not wanting to scare off the guy with the Viking cap and dark-brown quilted vest, I decided to follow his route through a couple aisles before approaching him.

I don't know exactly when he became suspicious of me, but the moment I stepped up to the next sample stand and took the pizza offering, he tore into me. "Why are you following me, lady? Are you the store security? The only things I've got in this bag are my sunglasses." He flung the bag open. "See, no food. So there's no reason to follow me around. Now scram."

"You're right. There's no food in there. But those sunglasses belong to Singi Optical, and I'm here to claim them."

"No you're not." He kicked me in the shin. It hurt like heck but I ignored it. Instead, I grabbed his leg before he could put it down. He tried to yank out of my hold but didn't succeed. I fell on top of him.

When I looked up, I discovered Mr. Oscar, the store manager towering over us. "I don't know what you two are up to," he said, "but the cops will be collecting you any minute and they can sort it out. In the meantime you're going to wait in my office. Is that understood?"

I said, "Yup." The little weasel who started it didn't reply.

~38~

Talk about dumb luck. When the cops collected the sunglass thief and me from the office of the grocery manager, they hauled us off to the downtown police substation, a place I'm very familiar with since Matt's buddy Sgt. Murchinak works there. If he's on today's duty roster, he'll square things for me in a jiffy and this gal won't even have to utter a single word. If not, well, I've been told orange doesn't look too bad on me.

The second I settled my rump on one of the many hard chairs situated between two empty rooms, a significant distance from the traffic flow surrounding the main entrance, I made a hasty inquiry of one of the freshly scrubbed cops passing by. "Excuse me, but is Sgt. Murchinak here today?"

His thick light-brown brows lifted. "Who wants to know?"

I swept my short bangs to one side, trying to flaunt the attitude of a movie star. "Why, Mary Malone of course."

He shook his head. "Never heard of ya. But to answer your question, Sgt. Murchinak should be in shortly," and then he strode off.

A few minutes later, a cop around my age came by carrying a clipboard. As soon as he caught sight of me, he signaled that I should step into the empty room with him. "What about this guy?" I said referring to the thief.

He gave a gruff reply. "Just worry about yourself, lady."

Not wanting to be construed as a problem for the already overworked police department, I followed him into the interrogation room as quietly as a timid cat and took a seat across the table from him with a view to the hallway, hoping I'd catch the eye of Sgt. Murchinak when he arrived.

The cop I was with allowed two seconds of silence to slip by and then questioned me in deadly earnest. "Have you ever been arrested before Miss Malone?"

"No, never. Not even for a traffic violation."

The cop grilling me checked off a box. "Are you employed? If so, where?"

That question was tricky. At present I worked at the pickle plant, but I don't want it listed since I'm there on official business. Instead I said, "Yes, Singi Optical," which should make my case about ownership of the sunglasses even stronger. After I shared the info, I caught a glimpse of movement in the hallway and patiently waited for someone to reveal themselves.

Two seconds later Sgt. Murchinak marched in front of the window where I was occupied. He gave a quick glance into the room. Thankfully the cop questioning me didn't notice. He had his eyes glued to the clipboard. Taking advantage of his ignorance, I gave a short wave.

"Ma'am, I asked you a question."

I turned my attention back to the cop across the table from me. "Hmm? Oh, sorry, I got distracted by all the activity out in the hall."

The interrogation door suddenly swung open and Sgt. Murchinak walked in. "Okay, I'll take it from here, Al," he stated with authority, "I've been brought up to speed."

"Yes, sir." Al left the clipboard behind and strode out.

"I'm surprised to see you here, Mary," the cop in his mid-fifties stated with an awkward grin. "What's going on?"

I laughed. "I thought you knew."

He pulled out a chair and sat. "Sometimes it pays to fib. You should know that by now. But don't try it on me. I can't help you if you don't lay it on the line. Do you understand?"

"Yup. There's no way I'm spending the night here."

Murchinak briefly examined the info on the clipboard. "According to this report, the manager of Marty's grocery store claims you and another person were found fighting over a bag of sunglasses in aisle two. Is this accurate?"

I nodded. "The guy was selling sunglasses he'd stolen from Singi Optical."

"I see." He pinched his square chin. "And how do you know this?"

"I was working there when he stole them. The minute I realized what he'd done I chased after him, but he was too quick on his feet for me."

The cops green eyes gave nothing away. "I hope you haven't been trying to track him down ever since the incident happened.

"No. Today is the first day I've had a chance to do so. I wouldn't have even known where to look for him if it wasn't for my aunt."

Sgt. Murchinak scratched his head. "Your aunt?"

"Yes, on my dad' side. She shares Matt's apartment with me. A couple days ago that guy out in the hall wearing a Viking's cap tried selling her a pair of sunglasses outside of Marty's store."

"All right, Mary, sit tight. I'm going to have a chat with the thief. I've got to get his side of the story even though I know what comes out of his mouth won't be as interesting as having heard the truth. Is there anyone you'd like to call while you're waiting?"

I nodded. "Yeah, my aunt. She needs to arrange a ride for me."

***

"You're darn lucky I was home, Mary," my nerdy Nordic neighbor Rod Thompson said when he collected me from the police station. "I had planned to go cross country skiing with a buddy of mine this afternoon."

I claimed my belongings and then followed him out onto the street. "You shouldn't have changed your plans for me, Rod. I could've found another ride."

He laughed. "And miss seeing you squirm. Not on your life. I warned you about taking things into your own hands." He unlocked the passenger door for me. "So, what exactly did you get brought in for?"

"Can you wait till we return to the Foley? I'm not up to rehashing everything again for my aunt's sake." I stared at the passenger seat before climbing in. No room for my butt. The seat was ladened with empty food wrappers from Arby's and Milt's. I shoved the garbage unto the floor mat and slid in.

"Sure."

~39~

Aunt Zoe smothered me in her arms the second Rod and I walked in the door. "Mary, thank goodness you're out of jail. I've been sitting here fretting ever since you called, imaging what sort of hoodlums you were locked up with in that building. " Finally relinquishing her hold on me, she then claimed Rod Thompson's hands. "Rod, you don't know how much I appreciate your going to get my niece. I didn't know who else to call. I tried Reed and family members first, but no one picked up."

"Christmas is just around the corner," I reminded her, "They're probably out shopping."

Rod dismissed my aunt's concerns with a wave of the hand. "No problem, Zoe. I was glad to help out," he added with a smirk targeted at me.

My aunt shook her head. "Its times like this that I wish I'd followed through with those driving lessons I'd signed up for in November. I don't know why I chickened out."

I do. I talked her out of it. She'd be a danger on four wheels.

Aunt Zoe's short fingers pointed to the living room. "Rod, can you chat for a few minutes, or have you got plans?"

"Sure. I'm in no rush." His towering military-poised body followed her into the living room. "My buddy cancelled our cross country ski date."

What? That's not the version he gave me. You mean I apologized for nothing. All right I'm taking the La-Z-Boy and he can have the stupid decked out couch along with the humongous tossed pillows Aunt Zoe hasn't taken care of yet.

Not wanting my aunt to continue believing she can persuade Rod to do anything she requests, I gently broke the news. "Actually, there was no need to invite Rod to stay. The spiel I gave him when we left the police station convinced him to sit with us for a spell."

Her eyes widened like an owls. "Oh?"

The undercurrent of my aunt's comment slowly caught up to me. She thinks more is going on between Rod and me than we let on. Well, she's in for a rude awakening. I've told her over and over again the only two men I'd even accept a marriage proposal from is Trevor or David.

"Yup, it's true," Rod chimed in. "She promised to explain why she got arrested when we got back here." The guy was having a devil of a time trying to get comfortable on the glitzy, slippery fabric still covering the leather couch and boy was I enjoying his dilemma.

"I still can't believe you got arrested," Aunt Zoe stated.

I pressed my hands to my cheeks. "Me neither. You can't imagine how embarrassing it was sitting around with all those criminals waiting to be processed."

"I bet they made you change into an orange jump suit," she said.

"No, thank God. Orange is not my color."

Rod leaned forward on the couch and pressed his elbows into his knees. "So how did you end up in the slammer? Did you get caught stealing something or sass back to a cop?"

"You really think I would do either of those things?"

He slapped his knees. "Nah, I guess not. You're too uptight, but that's good, right, Zoe."

She fiddled with her hands. "Why, ah, yes. Absolutely."

I felt like a spoiled child. I crossed my arms and shot them an icy stare. "Do you want to hear what really happened to me or not?"

"Of course," they replied.

"Okay, but no more comments from the peanut gallery. Got it?"

Aunt Zoe answered for the both of them, "Yup."

I relaxed my arms. "My dilemma all began with a simple suggestion from you auntie."

"She's right. I wanted us to walk around the neighborhood and see if we could find Gracie. Oh, and look for the guy who stole sunglasses from Raj Singi's shop while we were at it too," she blurted out. "But I never thought we'd be in any danger."

Great. I can always depend on her to share information I don't want her to.

Rod shook his head in disbelief. "You two were looking for a criminal? Whatever happened to common sense? Cops are supposed to hunt for a thief, not you. That's their job."

"We know. But Aunt Zoe happened to spot him outside Marty's grocery store a few days ago, so we thought why not see if the thief was still hanging around there. If he was, we'd notify the cops."

"But my feet were killing me after the little bit of walking we did," Aunt Zoe explained, "so Mary told me she'd go on without me."

I'd been stiffly poised on the edge of the La-Z-Boy, but soon gave my back over to the comfy chair and gently rocked, hoping the motion would calm my nerves. Dredging up what happened over an hour ago bothered me more than I thought it would.

I picked up Aunt Zoe's story thread and went on. "When I got to Marty's, there was no sign of activity outside the store, so I went inside to warm up for a bit and sample some freebies. I sure didn't expect to see that little thief wandering around inside with the bag of sunglasses. I confronted him. Then wham, we both fell to the floor, me on top of him, and the manager informed us he'd called the cops."

"That's hilarious," Rod said, having a hard time keeping himself upright.

"It's not that funny. If you keep it up, you're going to break a blood vessel in one of your eyes," I warned, "and then that pretty face of yours won't look so appealing."

The nerd ignored me and kept on laughing.

"Please, Rod, settle down," Aunt Zoe begged, "I want to find out how Mary convinced the police to let her go."

Rod pressed his large muscular hand to his chest. "Forgive me, Zoe, but picturing a woman on the floor wrestling with a man is something one usually only sees in slapstick comedy. Mary, do you know if anyone captured you on video for YouTube?"

"I hope not." I felt a smile rising to the surface. "I have to admit the situation does sound like it would be hilarious if one was watching the scene unfold from the sidelines. Anyway, after ending up at the substation, I was taken to a room and questioned by one of the cops."

"Just like on TV," Aunt Zoe interrupted.

I nodded. "I'm darn lucky the cop didn't get to grill me as long as he would've liked."

"What stopped him," she asked, "an emergency call?"

"Nope. It was Matt's friend Sgt. Murchinak. When he learned that I'd been arrested, he told the other cop to take a break and he'd finish up with the people brought in from the grocery store. He only spoke with me for five minutes or so before he released me. After he escorted me to the nearest phone, he took the sunglass thief back to the same room and raked him over the coals.

"Oh, Auntie, I almost forgot to tell you something Sgt. Murchinak shared with me as I was leaving the police station?"

"What?"

"Stanley Foghorn, the thief, wasn't an old man after all. He was a twenty-year-old wearing an expensive disguise he'd stolen from the Guthrie costume department."

Aunt Zoe poked Rod with her elbow. "Mary kept saying the guy was too agile to be an old man and she was right. How about that?"

Rod glanced down at his feet. "Yeah, how about that," he softly repeated.

I cleared my throat. "If you don't mind, I'd like to finish up sometime today."

"Of course," Aunt Zoe replied. "I thought you'd told us everything."

"Not quite." I clasped my hands together and rested them in my lap. "It turns out the cops in the area have been looking for Stanley for over three years. As soon as someone reported sighting him he'd disappear under a rock."

"Did Sgt. Murchinak ever mention how much stuff he's stolen or if there was a reward for finding him?" she asked excitedly.

"Nope."

"What an ingenious thief," Rod commented before moving into FBI mode. "Most are not that smart you know. Hmm? I wonder if he was involved with an underground group."

I pushed myself out of the La-Z-Boy. "I don't know and I don't really care, Rod. My mind's been on overload too long already. All I want to do is take a shower and then have a stiff drink. Now, if you'll excuse me...."

Rod stood. "Is that my hint to leave?"

I turned to face him. "You'd better believe it."

~40~

Day 14

Sunday. A day of rest. And I'm taking full advantage of it, including keeping my mind off the case. But before I permit myself to lounge around the house in sweats, stuff myself with Lay's potato chips, and binge out on classic movies from the forties, there's something I want to take care of first, church obligations.

Most Sunday's my aunt and I join my parents at their church in Spring Lake Park, but today I've decided on a change of venue. We'd attend services at the Basilica of St. Mary in Minneapolis which opened in the early 1900's and is listed on the National Register of Historic Places. I'd never been there before nor had Aunt Zoe, as far as I knew. So she probably wouldn't fuss about the break in routine.

I climbed out of bed and rummaged through the closet trying to select the proper clothing for church. A black knit pantsuit and long-sleeved white blouse seemed a good combination. I set them on the bed and then returned to the closet to hunt for the dressy black boots I wore almost a year ago.

Within seconds I found the boots at the back of the closet. As I picked them up and got off my knees, I wondered if Margaret Grimshaw would like to go to the basilica as well. I glanced at the clock radio on the nightstand. It's 7:30. I'd better act fast if I'm going to catch her. She'll be taking off soon for St. Olaf's, the church she usually attends.

An hour and forty-five minutes later the three of us rode the elevator down to the Foley's garage level and slipped into the car ready to attend church services.

The second I backed the VW out of its allotted parking spot my two chatty companions simultaneously went into silent mode as if they'd made a mutual agreement not to break my concentration, which I appreciated. Too much talk in the car and I could easily miss a turn. I've done it before.

Once I hooked up to Interstate 94 going north though, things changed. Margaret broke through the quiet interlude, smoothing out a few wrinkles in her wool coat at the same time. "I want to thank you for inviting me to go to the basilica," she said. "I've lived in Minneapolis for over forty years and have never set foot in there yet."

"Neither have we," Aunt Zoe informed her from the back seat, "But I understand the stained glass windows are worth seeing as well as the carved marble altar that came from Italy."

With a minute to spare before exiting off the freeway for the basilica, I felt I owed my passengers a brief explanation for our special trip since seeing the structure of the building and its art work was only a minor reason for going there. "A friend of mine from college, Cindy, suggested I come by sometime. She's been in charge of the lectors and servers at the basilica since this past September."

Ah," Margaret said. "I wondered if this visit involved the case you're working on."

"Definitely not," I replied as I pulled into the basilica's parking lot ten minutes before mass.

After Aunt Zoe stepped out of the car, she offered her arm to our neighbor and helped her get a steady footing on the blacktop. "It's so peaceful here, isn't it Margaret? I'm glad there's nothing surrounding the church services that will stress Mary or me out. You wouldn't believe the terrible ordeal we went through yesterday."

The ninety-year-old's almost transparent eyebrows arched considerably. "What are you talking about, Zoe?"

Here we go again. I slipped an arm around Margaret's free arm and leisurely guided my companions towards one of the eight double bronze doors. "Nothing that can't wait till we get home to divulge," I said, and then slid in talk about the basilica's active church community and their annual Block Party, a two day music festival.

Once we settled into a pew near the front, Margaret and Zoe pulled out their rosaries and joined others in the recitation of Hail Mary's and Our Father's.

While they prayed devotedly, I gazed around the church and watched for any sign of my friend Cindy. If she was at this mass, I intended to ask her to join us for breakfast at the French Meadow Bakery and Cafe on Lyndale Avenue. Even though I hadn't mentioned my breakfast plans with my companions, I was positive they'd like the idea.

The recitation of the rosary finally ended and prelude music began, but there was still no sign of my friend. *Perhaps I'll spot her after mass.*

And I did. But her morning wasn't free. It was her turn to give a tour of the basilica after the 9:30 mass. "Darn," I said, "I'd hoped my friend could've joined us for breakfast at the French Meadow Bakery and Café."

"Mary, dear, we don't need to go out to breakfast," Margaret said as we walked back to the car. "I've fixed a delicious egg sausage dish. It just needs to be warmed. Besides, a restaurant is not the proper place to discuss private things like the case you're working on or the terrible ordeal you went through yesterday."

"You're right. I guess we're off to the Foley for breakfast then."

***

After I helped Margaret get the breakfast ready, including toast and coffee, the three of us dished up generous portions of warmed egg-sausage bake on our plates and carried them into the dining area to enjoy.

Unfortunately, I didn't get to partake of the delicious meal Margaret had prepared quite yet. I'd forgotten to collect the steamy dark morning refreshment the older women so dearly loved when I left the kitchen. So I traipsed back there to collect the coffee pot and filled their cups upon my return.

"I suppose you'd like to hear about yesterday first," I said to our hostess as I sat and picked up a knife to dip into the jar of strawberry jam sitting in front of me.

Margaret nodded, continuing to chew as she did so.

"Okay, but it's going to be brief. The breakfast you prepared is too tempting."

"Go ahead and eat, dear, whenever the urge strikes. I don't mind."

I took Margaret at her word, ate half of my toast first and then cleared my palate to speak. "I went to Marty's yesterday."

Margaret rested her fork on her plate. "You mean the grocery store?"

"Yup."

"That's right. Zoe mentioned she wanted to hunt down the sunglass thief. Did you catch him?"

"I sure did."

Aunt Zoe stopped eating long enough to add what she knew. "Mary found him in the store. They had a scuffle. The manager called the police. And then she and the thief got hauled off to jail."

"Oh, my. You poor thing," Margaret said, pressing her hands against her chest. "How many hours did they keep you behind bars, Mary?"

"None," I said, as I sampled the egg bake. "Matt's police friend made sure of that."

"You're lucky Matt has a good connection with the police in this area."

"I know. I hope he'll continue to be as friendly with me when I ask him if he's heard any new scuttlebutt concerning Don Hickleman's death or Paul Mason's. Of course, he may want me to offer what I've learned too."

"But what could you possibly tell him?" Aunt Zoe asked as she refilled Margaret's and her cup with hot coffee.

"When I found the body of Paul Mason with an unsigned note stuffed in his pocket, I began to secretly check time card signatures against the photo copy I'd made. Something I'm sure the police haven't thought of. The note spoke of an arranged meeting place both knew of.

But that's not all. After the police questioned Anita and me, she confided that tension among the plant managers and higher ups had been brewing for years."

"Well, you've certainly been a busy bee at the plant," Margaret said, as she scooted her chair out and collected the dirty dishes. "If you don't mind my saying so, your sleuthing is equal to Miss Marple's, dear. Too bad she's a fictional character. She'd be extremely pleased with you."

I studied the light-green lace tablecloth covering the table. Receiving undue praise from Margaret was embarrassing. I didn't deserve it. "The case is a long way from being solved," I said. "A lot can happen before then."

~41~

Day 15

"Aunt Zoe, have you seen my red sweatshirt? It's not in the closet and I wanted to wear it to work."

She pulled her roller-covered head out of the morning newspaper where it had been buried ever since I got up, and removed her new wild-rose and plum reading glasses to get a better look at me. "I must've brought it up. I remember putting it in the wash load with the other clothes on Saturday. Have you looked in the front closet, yet? I might have stuck it in there."

"Yup. I've already checked every spot I can think of."

"Hmm? My aunt rubbed her lightly-grooved forehead. "Oh, oh. You know what? I bet I left it in the dryer by mistake. Ten minutes before the dryer was supposed to go off, I checked the clothes to see if they needed to continue drying. The only damp garment in the bunch was your sweatshirt, so I let it go the full length. Of course, a few residents came and went during that time, even Sally Fuse. And you know how she can yak up a storm when she has something juicy to share about another Foley resident."

Leave it to her not to stay on track.

Aunt Zoe could probably tell from my facial expression I wasn't a happy camper. She pushed her chair back and stood. "Look, I know how short you are on time. Why don't you pack your lunch, Mary, and I'll go down and see if I can find your sweatshirt. I'm sure who ever found it set it aside."

"Stay put," I calmly stated. "I'll check out the laundry room." But I didn't leave immediately. I was too private a person to proceed there while still wearing a flannel pajama top, especially one covered in cartoon characters. What if I should run into one of the guys who lived in the building like Mr. Edward's the caretaker or Rod Thompson? Not wanting to chance any scenario like that, I rushed to the bedroom and threw on the first tee shirt I could find. It happened to be an old one from college days emblazoned with what I thought at the time was a nifty quote, "Everything happens for a reason." But after my parents' used those exact words on me when I got laid off, the saying didn't impress me anymore. Believe me, if I could've afforded to gag, I would've.

Once I got down to the laundry room, I checked the insides of all four dryers and the space between them. Unfortunately I came up with nada. While I remained glued to the spot I was in, wondering where I should look next, who should grace my presence, but Gertie Nash loaded down with a basket of dirty clothes. *Crap.* Knowing her, she'll probably grill me about what's getting done concerning Butch, and I have nada to report.

The second Gertie saw me her eyebrows shot up so high I thought they were preparing to blast off. "What's Foley's famous sleuth doing down here?" she asked as she set her basket of laundry on top of the nearest wash machine. "Shouldn't you be at work already?"

I braced my hands on my hips. "I'm leaving in about five minutes. Hey, Gertie, you didn't find a red sweatshirt down here over the weekend, did you? My aunt washed it on Saturday and thinks she forgot to bring it up with the rest of our wash."

"Talk about perfect timing. I didn't find anything down here then, but when I finally got around to folding the clothes last night I discovered an item that didn't belong to us. That's why I'm down here so early, to return the sweatshirt in case someone's been looking for it."

Gertie shoved her hand to the bottom of the laundry basket, pulled out the red sweatshirt, and handed it to me. "Here you go. I don't think it's had enough time to absorb the body odor from our clothes yet."

"Thanks. Say, what's this nonsense about 'famous sleuth' you mentioned?" *I sure hope it's nothing to do with my being arrested.*

Gertie dropped her soiled clothes in a wash machine and then measured out the amount of Gain laundry detergent needed for her wash load. "Why, don't be so modest, Mary. Everyone around here is talking about the way you single-handedly captured that eyeglass thief."

The second Gertie finished her patter, she closed the wash machine lid with such determination I thought she'd damaged the machine's internal mechanisms. But when she pushed the START button, the machine roared to life.

I flapped my hand. "Oh, that." I glanced at my wristwatch. According to the position of the hands on it, I had only a few precious minutes left to return to the apartment, put on a different top, and gather up my purse and lunch before heading to work. I twirled towards the door to leave, but Gertie was determined to keep me captive.

"I sure hope you can find out who killed Don Hickleman soon. Butch is climbing the walls."

He's not the only one.

After I shut the door behind me, I held the sweatshirt to my nose and took a whiff. I'm not too keen on wearing clothing that will cause people at the pickle plant to back away from me. No, no. If I'm going to find out the secrets floating around that place, I have to smell so good they'll want to share their personal space with me. Good news, the sweatshirt passed the stringent test taught me as a tot. It still smelled like Tide.

***

"Right on time, Mary," Anita said as she finished fastening the last button on her lab coat. "That's what I like about you, you're consistent, girl."

"That's me, consistent Mary," I said tongue in cheek, "I've never had the chance to find out what it's like not to be." I hung my jacket and purse in the locker and then donned the required uniform: lab coat, goggles, and hairnet. "So what department am I experiencing today?"

Anita yawned. "I thought we'd by-pass pickle packing and go straight to the pasteurization and labeling area. That's the final stage before we box up the products and ship them off to our customers. Everyone likes working there. You're not as exhausted by the end of the day."

"Sounds like the perfect place to be. I've been falling asleep as soon as I get home at night."

Since I began working here, Anita and I have gotten into the habit of chit chatting on the way to wherever she wants me to be and today was no exception. The minute we strolled out of the employee locker room and headed to my new task at the far end of the building, I inquired whether she had a memorable weekend.

Anita's lips parted considerably as she shared a broad grin. "I sure did. I won a hundred bucks playing the slot machines at Mystic Lake Casino. Can you believe it? It'll come in handy for Christmas shopping. Oh, my!" Her hands suddenly flew out in front of her. Her smile evaporated.

Could she be having a heart attack?

"Are you okay?"

She gripped my arm. "Yes, yes. I'm fine. But I just remembered you haven't heard the latest company news. It occurred over the weekend."

"What happened?"

"Chip got injured Saturday night."

"Oh? Was he involved in a car accident?"

Anita shook her head. "No, honey. Apparently he received a call late Saturday night that there was a problem with one of the vats so he came out to check on it. According to what I heard he slipped on the platform and fell down the steps."

"Whoa. There must've been a hunk of ice on the platform. I imagine he broke a few bones taking a tumble like that."

"Yup, we won't be seeing him around here for a while. I just wonder who's going to have something happen to them next." Anita pulled a wadded up hairnet out from a pocket attached to her lab coat and attempted to tuck her cornrow braids inside it, but her hands shook so badly it didn't look like she'd ever complete the small task.

"All this stuff going on here has got me scared silly. I come from a long line of people who believe in curses, Mary, and I'm not afraid to say someone's put a big hex on this plant."

Well, well. Another golden opportunity concerning crimes comes knocking at your door, Mary. You might as well take advantage of it. "Anita, are you saying you don't think Chip's fall was an accident?"

"Girl, if that's the only thing that had happened around here lately, I might've swallowed his story, but you and I both know it ain't."

Did I dare share the thoughts that had been rambling around in my head lately? I chose to chance it. Speaking softly I said, "I've been thinking, Anita, about the cucumbers that were lodged in Don Hickleman's throat and Paul's. Is there any way a person could find out what country they came from or at least the grade?" If she said 'yes,' I might be able to narrow the suspects down.

She leaned towards me. "What've you got up your sleeve?" she asked, keeping her voice to a minimum like mine.

Since I didn't dare let her know I was trying to solve Don's and Paul's death in case she was involved somehow, even though I thought it unlikely, I said, "I was thinking if the police knew where the cucumbers came from or the grade, they might be able to narrow down their list of suspects."

Anita's thick hand slapped me on the back. "I like your line of thinking. Those cops aren't getting anywhere, Why not help them? But how would we go about it?"

"I've got a few ideas up my sleeve, but let's chat after work in the parking lot."

"All right. It's safer to speak of things we shouldn't outside the building than in. Too many people can eavesdrop in this confined area."

I jiggled my head up and down. "I agree."

~42~

When we reached the section where filled jars of pickles arrive via conveyor belt to receive lids, be vacuumed sealed, pasteurized, and then labeled, we found there were too many hands on deck already in a department that mostly required automation. So Anita suggested we help with something else I hadn't done yet, like unpacking new jars which would be stuffed with cucumbers destined to be dill or bread and butter pickles.

"It's kind of a boring job, Mary, but once we take our morning break, I'll try to convince a couple old-timers to trade off with us so I can train you in on their job, otherwise we'll have to put that section off until tomorrow."

I shrugged. "No big deal. Today or tomorrow doesn't matter to me as long as I don't have to stand around all day twiddling my thumbs."

Anita chuckled. "Believe me, you won't be. As soon as we empty out all the unopened boxes of jars already sitting near the conveyor belt and do what needs to be done with them, we'll be retrieving more of the same from the packaging department."

Great. Memories of finding Paul lying dead in the walk-in fridge made me apprehensive about chasing for any supplies again. Who knew what might turn up next. I swallowed hard. I'd have to make the best of it. "Sounds like a good workout plan, Anita. I indulged in way too many donuts at breakfast."

"Well, I didn't have any donuts," she complained, "but I sure hope I don't regret the ton of coffee I drank."

It turned out Anita's prediction that I wouldn't be standing around waiting for a job was right. When a person works in this area, they don't have time to stare at chipped fingernails or think about their flattened out hair. Their mind is too focused on staying awake. Once we sliced open a box, we had to check that the jars removed from it remained in the upside down position and were securely positioned on the conveyor belt. After that we focused our attention on the jars whizzing past the metal detector, keeping track of the rejected ones and making certain the accepted ones went on to be sterilized.

Two hours later when I heard the magic words, "break time," flow from Anita's thick purple painted lips, I was thrilled. Quite honestly I don't know how many more days I can keep up with the charade of being a devoted employee of Pickledom. Working in a plant like this is hard work, not child's play.

Since Anita had mentioned earlier that she'd be schmoozing with old-timers from the capping, pasteurization, and labeling department when she took this ten minute break, I decided to do some schmoozing of my own with various employees, asking a question here and there that wouldn't create any suspicion. At least I hoped not.

The minute I strolled into the lunchroom I purchased a can of Pepsi and then joined five other gals already sitting down at a table. "Do you mind if I pull up a chair and join you?" I asked with an air of shyness.

"Go right ahead," Yukiko, a young Asian woman I'd worked alongside of my first week here replied for the rest of them. "We're just hashing over what happened to Chip this past weekend. Had you met him yet?"

I nodded and then pulled the tab on the Pepsi can. "Anita introduced me to him last Thursday. It sounds like he won't be back for a while." I set the metal tab on the table and then took a drink from the opened can.

"That's what we heard too," a dark-skinned woman near retirement age said.

Yukiko picked up her steaming cup of coffee and then set it back down. "It doesn't make sense what's been going on here. If I didn't know better, I'd swear someone was out to destroy the plant. Fortunately none of us women have been harmed yet."

"Yes, thank goodness," the rest of the women quietly agreed.

Hmm? *That's true only men have been harmed. But what woman involved with the company had a strong enough motive to harm all three men?*

Only one name came to mind, Roseanne Harsh. It had been said the woman had scored a touchdown with Don and possibly even Paul. And I did catch her arguing with Chip on Friday. But was she capable of killing?

Being a teacher I had to remind myself two and two don't always add up to four. Roseanne certainly doesn't come off as the type who would care one way or the other if she was jilted or not. Shoot, I don't know what to think.

I guess the next logical step any good crime fighter on TV would take is to confront Roseanne, ask if she'd stayed in town over the weekend, and go from there. But who knows when that opportunity will come around again.

I'd been so deep in thought concerning the three men and their involvement with Roseanne I'd barely caught one of the gal's reference to a funeral. "Was this a friend of yours who died?" I quizzed.

The middle-aged woman gave me a strange look. "No, I was talking about Paul Mason. I saw his name listed in the *Star Tribune's* obituary section this morning. The funeral service is on Thursday morning."

Wow. I wonder if Anita's heard the news yet.

"Obviously we won't be attending that," Yukiko said with a sharp edge to her voice. Before continuing on she took a quick sip of coffee. "If the big shots didn't shut down the plant for Don Hickleman's funeral, they certainly aren't going to do it for a shift supervisor." After expressing her feelings on attendance at the funeral, she turned to the woman who told us about seeing Paul Mason's name in the obituary column. "Sarah, was there any mention of a viewing the night before?"

"Yes," she replied in a hushed voice. "Bromley Funeral Home in Maple Grove, chapel three from six to eight."

Yukiko propped her tiny head on her hand. "I think we should all make an effort to go Wednesday night since we can't take time off Thursday. I'm sure Paul's wife would appreciate meeting people who worked with her husband, don't you?" The other women merely nodded.

Yeah, right, especially anyone who might have had an affair with him.

Anita suddenly appeared at our table with a sour expression on her face. "It's a no go, Mary. I thought I could charm them but I didn't succeed. We might as well get back to the boxes." She put her hand on my shoulder. "Come on."

I pushed out my chair and thanked the gals for letting me sit with them.

"Anytime," Yukiko said.

When we had moved far enough from the table I'd been sitting at, Anita inquired whether the gals had been talking about anything interesting.

"Yup. At least I think so."

"Well, cough it up, girl. What did they have to say?"

"Paul Mason's name was listed in the *Star Tribune's* obituary column this morning."

Anita stopped abruptly causing her large glasses to slide down her nose. She pushed them back up before they fell to the floor. "Did anyone say they were going to the funeral?"

"Nope. They figured they wouldn't be allowed the time off so they've decided to go to Wednesday night's viewing instead."

She rubbed her thick forehead. "I suppose it would look funny if I didn't show up since I've known Paul longer than most of the employees. You wouldn't care to attend the viewing with me would you? I don't feel like showing up by myself."

I was hoping she'd say that. It'll give me a chance to see who makes an appearance and how they react when they see Paul's body lying in a casket. "I only spoke to Paul twice, Anita, but if you really want me to go I'll be there for you."

She squeezed my hand. "Thanks, Mary. If you ever need a favor, you know where to come."

I sure do and believe me I won't forget.

~43~

Anita kept her word. After work, she joined me in the parking lot as planned. Unfortunately, the weather outside had changed drastically since this morning. Besides being greeted by a howling wind, the temperature had dropped almost twenty degrees and snowflakes were collecting on our shoes the size of Jacks, a game many young children play.

My upper body didn't like the impact the combination of the lower temperature and wind were having on it. Pulling up my jacket collar instantly cutoff any chance for the unkind weather to slip in undetected, but there was still another area that required a warm barrier: the face. So I gathered a small portion of the wool neck scarf hanging over the shoulders of my jacket and created a winter face mask.

Having a scarf cover most of my face was awful. I felt claustrophobic. Not only that, but every time I tried to speak the wool scarf got caught in my mouth. In order for

Anita and me to do any serious chatting without freezing to death we required a warm enclosure near the plant. And I had just the spot in mind. "Let's sit in my car with the heater running," I suggested.

Anita stopped patting her gloved hands. "No problem. The further away we are from spying eyes the better. So where's your car?"

As I turned to point a little to the left of the building, I was stunned to find Butch Bailey at the end of the parking lot holding a huge sign proclaiming his innocence in the death of Don Hickleman. I couldn't believe he'd shown up here. What a stupid move. Not only could he get hauled off by the police again, he could blow my cover. I've got to get him out of here pronto, but what about Anita?

Since I'm getting to be an expert at fabricating tales, I chose to pursue that route until I realized I don't need to worry about Anita. She wouldn't question my motives unless she'd forgotten I'd mentioned Butch was related to a neighbor of mine.

To my surprise I didn't have to warn Butch to get off the premises after all. Anita beat me to it. "Butch, are you crazy?" she hollered, running towards him full speed ahead despite the snow-covered parking lot. When she finally stood toe to toe with him, she tried to grab the sign out of his firm grip. "Get rid of that sign and leave before someone calls the police."

I backed Anita up. "She's right, Butch. You don't want to end up in the slammer again. Your relatives would be devastated, especially Gertie's brother who put up your bail."

Butch's white moistened mustache twitched. He disengaged his fingers from the cigarette he'd been holding, watched it fall to the wet parking lot, and then stomped on it. "You gals don't understand."

"What don't we understand?" I quizzed, as I spit out the damp scarf along with my words. "That you're going to get in trouble spelled JAIL?"

"Nope. Chip called me yesterday," he explained. "I don't have to worry about that any more. I can stay on this property as long as I want."

Anita hid her hands in her jacket pockets. "So, Chip called. Big deal. He has no authority here. Besides, he can't help you from a hospital bed. Did he even mention that teeny fact?"

"Of course, that's why I'm here. Chip said he realizes now that I didn't steal the recipes or kill Don."

I didn't know what to think about Chip reaching out to Butch. Could it be he was responsible for Paul Mason's death and wanted the police to finger Butch instead? I shook my head. I'd have to analyze Chip's motives later. All I knew was the guy standing in front of me could be in grave danger showing his face around here, and the only way I could protect him was to get him as far away from the plant as possible.

"Look, Anita and I were heading to my car to discuss a few things. Why, don't you join us? We'd like to hear what else Chip shared with you."

Anita must've thought I was trying to pacify him. She supported my idea whole-heartedly. "Yah, Butch, come to Mary's car for a few minutes. We don't want to continue talking out here. It's too cold. Besides, we don't know who's watching us."

Butch slicked his long wet hair behind his ears. "You're right. I didn't really think this through." Then he pointed to me. "So where you got your car stashed?"

I dug my cars keys out of my purse and pointed to the left of the lot. "See the navy VW two rows back?"

Chip nodded. "Ah huh."

"That's the one."

As soon as the three of us got in the car and closed the doors, I turned the fan up in the VW as high as it would go to warm us up. I didn't want anyone whining about blue lips; although, I couldn't picture a big guy like Butch, sitting up front with me, complaining about being cold. Anita, on the other hand, who sat directly behind him, her idea not his, probably wished that she'd gotten first chance at feeling the heat the way her teeth chattered. If I didn't know better, I'd swear a squirrel had taken up residence in the back seat.

Since Anita and I had planned to discuss possible ways of catching the person or persons who killed Don Hickleman and Paul Mason without interference from anyone, I chose to pump Gertie's cousin first and send him on his merry way.

Before the drilling proceeded though, I shifted my body from it's straight on position overlooking the other cars to a sideways one facing Butch, making it easier for Anita to hear me. "Okay, Butch, why don't you finish telling us gals about the conversation you had with Chip."

Butch tried to copy me and situate his large frame sideways too, but his legs wouldn't cooperate and he finally gave up. "Like I said Chip contacted me. He mentioned having an accident at work and that he ended up in the hospital. When I asked what happened, he said he got a call Saturday night saying he needed to get to the plant. There was some problem dealing with one of the vats. But when he got there, he couldn't find anything wrong."

So far his story confirmed what Anita and I already knew. I adjusted the car fan to low speed. Then I threw off my neck scarf and opened my jacket.

Anita leaned between the two front seats. I noticed she'd already removed her gold-toned well-worn Down Parka. "Did he say he recognized the caller's voice?" she hastily inquired.

"Nope." Butch unzipped his bulky jacket as well. "But he did tell me his feet didn't give out near the steps, someone shoved him from behind."

Anita's voice rang out. "I knew it. I knew it. There's a curse on the plant. Maybe old man Hickleman has come back from the dead to get his revenge."

The woman's beginning to sound like my aunt. "That's a bunch of malarkey," I said. "No one's come back from anywhere. A real live person is rattling cages. But the question is who? Butch, are you free Wednesday night?"

"You betcha. Why, you got a ticket for the Viking's game you can't use?

"Afraid not. But there's going to be a huge gathering I think you might want to check out."

"Oh, yeah. Is it even better than watching a Viking's game?"

I nodded. "It could be. Bromley Funeral Home is holding a viewing of Paul Mason's body. You should be on hand for it, don't you think, Anita?"

"Oh, girl," Anita hooted, "you must really love fireworks."

~44~

Day 16

The hinges on the bedroom door creaked, giving me fair warning that Aunt Zoe was about to enter without permission. Usually I'd complain, but not today.

I didn't sleep a wink last night. It started around one with a fever and eventually morphed into frequent calls of nature mixed with dizziness and an achy body that felt like a ten ton truck had rolled over it.

"Mary, honey, you're going to be late for work if you don't get up," my aunt said with a syrupy tone, totally ignorant of my condition.

I tried to roll over to face the door so she could see me, but couldn't manage it. "I'm too sick to care," I moaned. "I just want to curl up in a ball and die."

"Don't talk like that," she grumbled. "You may get your wish the longer you stay at that pickle plant."

"Pickles!" *Yuk. Why did she have to mention that?* My stomach rumbled again. I don't know how long I can hold off before, well, you know. "I didn't intend to upset you, Auntie. Could you…could you do me a favor?" I asked, as my voice trailed off.

She opened the door wider. "What is it? Do you want a glass of water? Should I call a doctor?"

"No doctor. No water. Both are pointless," I forced myself to say. "Just call the pickle plant. Ask for Sharon Sylvester. Tell her I've been bit by the flu bug."

"Is Sharon the head honcho over there?"

I tried to nod but was too racked with pain. "Yes. She's been running the show since Don Hickleman's death."

"Where's the number, on your phone or written down?"

Good grief. Why would anyone play a game of twenty questions with a sick person? I laid a hand on my feverish forehead and tried to recall what I did with the number. "Look for a small blue piece of paper by the kitchen phone."

Instead of zipping off to take care of my request, Aunt Zoe questioned the veracity of my statement. "Are you sure? I don't remember seeing anything on the counter by the phone that remotely resembles a note."

My stomach turned nasty. I took the warning to heart. The discussion concerning the phone number had to be tabled.

"Quick, move out of the way," I warned my aunt, giving her ample time to comply while I forced my weak body out of the position it had been in.

Aunt Zoe heeded the message. She scooted out of the doorway before my feet even had a chance to make it past the bedding. Having never seen her move so swiftly before, even when Reed Griffin, her boyfriend, picks her up for a date, I couldn't help wondering if the expensive slippers covering her feet were what motivated her to respond in such a way.

When I finally dragged my wobbly self into the hall for the short trek to the bathroom, I expected Aunt Zoe to be gone, but she was still firmly planted outside the bedroom door, and boy did she let loose with a tactless comment. "I kept telling you to get your flu shot, Mary. See what happens when you don't listen."

I wrung my hands. *If they found me standing over her dead body someday, I could always claim self-defense.*

***

By mid-day I felt much better and let Aunt Zoe know via the cell phone that I was accepting any charitable contributions of food, especially a bowl of Campbell's Chicken soup, something I knew her cooking skills couldn't destroy, and plenty of saltine crackers.

"Coming right up," she replied, "I've been keeping the soup warm on the stove. All I have to do is ladle it up."

A few minutes later my aunt stiffly entered the bedroom in full sweat gear, carrying the tray of food so tightly her knuckles had turned a ghostly white. At least the honeydew colored outfit she wore wasn't as outlandish as the eggplant colored negligee she appeared at my door in this morning.

After she set the tray on my lap, she studied my face for a moment. "I think the coloring in your face has greatly improved since this morning, Mary. Would you like me to grab a hand mirror so you can see for yourself?"

Is she crazy? Every morning this gal is greeted by matted hair, baggy eyes, and a blank colorless face before getting ready for work. I certainly don't need a dose of it today. "No, thanks," I said, crushing a cracker over the soup and then mixing it in with the noodles and broth. "I'll take your word for it."

"Well, then, how about I get a magazine for you to read or maybe invite someone to keep you company?" she asked with the enthusiasm of a well-trained nurse determined to do whatever it took to make her patient's stay in bed more pleasant.

Even though I'd rather chat with a person than read, I knew I had to mention who would be off limits. "I certainly hope you're not referring to Rod Thompson or Reed. I'd be too embarrassed to have them see me like this." I picked up the soup spoon and dipped it in the bowl to gather up broth, noodles and cracker crumbs.

"Actually I didn't have any man in mind," she replied, taking a napkin off the tray and tucking it into the opening of my pajama top. "I haven't told Reed or Rod that you're sick. And I certainly don't know how to contact David or Trevor. I was thinking of Margaret. She's inquired about you several times already."

I swallowed the tasty liquid and then rested the spoon in the bowl. "Margaret's so sweet. I imagine she's up-to-date with her shots like you, but I still don't think she should sit in this bedroom. Why don't you call and tell her I'm feeling better. And if she insists on coming over, put a kitchen chair outside my door and she can visit from a safe distance."

"All right. I'll give her a jingle and see what she says," and then she buzzed out the door leaving me alone to finish my meal.

Margaret must've been mighty antsy to get over here to check on me. The second the soup in my bowl disappeared I heard a knock at the door. It was followed by a quick question presented to Aunt Zoe. "Is Mary still in bed?"

"Yes," she answered, "but she asked me to set a chair outside her room for you."

"Whatever for?" Margaret inquired, sounding a bit testy. "I've had a flu shot."

"Mary thought you might've, but she wants to play it safe. She says it's possible she could have a different flu strain than what this year's shot protects us from."

"Well, there is always a chance of that."

The conversation between the two women ended. The next thing I heard was feet shuffling down the hall towards the bedroom. It had to be our neighbor. Aunt Zoe makes more noise with her feet than the light-weight Margaret ever could.

"Mary, dear, I'm here," Margaret quietly announced, briefly poking her head in the doorway."

"I appreciate your coming over on such short notice. I'm bored to death."

"I understand that's always a good sign, dear, when a person who has been ill mentions boredom. Did Zoe call Hinkleman's to tell them you wouldn't be in?"

I moved the tray to the end of the bed where I'd have less chance of knocking it on the floor and scaring the woman in her nineties who came to keep me company. "Yes, I made sure she did that this morning. Say, Margaret, do you remember my telling you about the note I found on Paul Mason?"

"*Si.* I do. Did you conclude who wrote it?"

"Not yet. But another guy, Butch mentioned to me before I started working at Hickleman's, got injured late Saturday evening."

"Did this happen at the plant?" she quizzed.

"Yes. Chip, the one who got hurt, says he would never have gone there if it hadn't been for a call he received concerning problems with a vat."

"Hmm? I suppose you couldn't very well visit Chip in the hospital and question him further about that night, without him guessing what you're up to, could you."

I yawned. Evidently I wasn't feeling as chipper as I thought or the lunch that Aunt Zoe prepared was weighing too heavily on my stomach, making me desire a good snooze instead of chatting with Margaret. "No," I replied, "but he did reach out to Butch." I released another yawn.

"Butch?" When Margaret spit his name out, she sounded like a mother whale giving birth. "Why would he contact him? According to Gertie he hasn't worked at the plant since being tossed in jail for the theft of company recipes."

My eyelids flickered. "I know it sounded odd when I heard about the call too."

I'd been sitting up so long the strain on my back and butt needed to be relieved. I stretched and then slid further under the covers, being careful not to kick the tray off the bed. *Ah.* The supine position felt good. All I could think of was going to sleep. "Can't stay awake," I mumbled. "Explain tomorrow. Butch is going to a fun... funeral". Then I conked out.

~45~

Day 17

"Sorry I had to put you back on the pickle packing line again, Mary," Anita said as we slid into a newly emptied booth at 3 Squares, a restaurant at Arbor Lakes in Maple Grove, the eatery we'd chosen to meet for supper before going to view Paul Mason's body at Bromley Funeral Home. "But I had no choice. Several people from that particular section called in this morning saying the flu bug had caught up with them."

"Sounds like I'm not the only one who puts off shots as long as they can." I unbuttoned my wool dress coat and studied one of the two menus the waitress had left on the table.

"I hate shots too," Anita declared, "but I decided to get one the beginning of November after all the warnings they'd announced on TV about this flu season being bad for older people. Not that I'm that old," she snickered, "but I am burning up in this jacket."

After removing the bulky jacket she complained about, Anita plucked off her large glasses next and quickly propped a pair of fire-engine red readers on the edge of her nose, a much needed item that would allow her to examine the other copy of the restaurant's lengthy menu.

"So what do you think?" I asked, continuing to peruse the menu.

Anita peered over the top of the readers and lowered her menu. "What do you mean? Are you referring to the meals or the viewing?"

I glanced around the section we were sitting in curious to see if other employees had stopped in here too, but didn't see any familiar faces. "Well, food is definitely on my mind of course, but I'm actually more interested in how many people you think will show up at the funeral home."

Anita rubbed her wide forehead. "Lordy, I haven't a clue. I know a lot of people talked about it over the lunch hour, but no one actually shared that they'd show up."

The young waitress finally finished up at the booth behind us and returned to ours. "Are you two ready to order?"

I glanced at my watch: 5:00. Paul Mason's viewing starts at six. "I am," I replied, "How about you, Anita?"

"Yup." She pressed her fingers to her plump face. "We don't have a lot of time to sit and gab," she informed the waitress, "so how about bringing me a pulled pork sandwich, sweet potato fries and a Pepsi. Your turn, Mary."

I passed on the pulled pork even though it was tempting and went for the crunchy shrimp, a small salad, and water instead.

"Is that all for you gals?"

"Yup," we replied in unison as if we were twins.

"Okay. I'll check back later to see if you want a dessert."

When the waitress walked away, I told Anita I planned to control my sweet tooth urges. "No dessert for me, at least not here."

"I feel the same way. We'll be too rushed with our meal as it is without adding a few more minutes to shovel down a slice of cake or pie. But I gotta admit, when the restaurant hostess walked by a couple seconds ago with a dessert tray, I almost followed her to the kitchen. Shoot! Maybe I should order a dessert to go. I could wrap cake or a bar in a napkin and toss it in my clunky purse I brought." She held up her purse so I could see how big it was.

It reminded me of the hot-pink and purple-splotched purse Aunt Zoe owned. I swear everything but the kitchen sink could fits in hers. "It looks like you've got room in there for a couple meals, plus dessert."

She set the purse down and wagged her finger. "That's why I bought the darn thing. My nosy neighbors don't need to know how often I go out to eat."

With the discussion concerning Anita's purse ended, we now rehashed the demise of Don Hickleman and Paul Mason. Unfortunately, we didn't come to any conclusion regarding who wanted the men out of the way or why.

I slid my glass of water closer to me and took a sip. "Maybe we'll get some answers at Bromley's tonight, Anita."

"I hope so." She tore the paper wrapper off her straw and poked it in her Pepsi. "I can't handle any more deaths at the plant. My nerves are shot. And the blood pressure meds I'm on aren't helping."

"That's not good," I said.

Anita sipped the Pepsi. "You're telling me."

Having run out of topics to chat about for the moment, I was pleased when the waitress suddenly appeared and handed us our meals.

By the time quarter to six rolled around we left 3 Squares bundled up in our winter paraphernalia fully fueled for the night, prepared to drive to Bromley's Funeral Home next, a mere six blocks away.

When we eventually reconnected in the mortuary parking lot, Anita swiftly inquired whether I thought Butch was here yet. "I don't know," I replied, not bothering to glance around the mortuary's parking lot to seek out his car like one normally does when meeting up with a friend or family member; it would've been a waste of time. But Anita didn't realize that. So I kindly reminded her we hadn't seen what car Butch drove to the plant. "Remember, he parked outside of the plant's gates the other day."

"That's right," she said. "He parked on Oakwood somewhere. No reason to stand out here freezing then. Let's go inside, thaw out, and see who's come for the viewing."

Eager to get in a building that should be well-heated, I hastily agreed with Anita. So the two of us walked briskly up the shoveled path to Bromley's main doors, brushed off the snow that had accumulated on our outerwear the best we could, and then entered the mid-sized mortuary where we found a tastefully decorated gathering area or lobby to be extremely subdued. No people were present however, only ornate vases overflowing with highly-scented flowers filled the huge space.

Ready to move on, Anita peeked in the first room to our left, shook her damp cornrow styled hair, and shrugged. "Funny, I don't recognize a living soul in there, Mary."

Most people say they feel uncomfortable in a mortuary's somber surroundings, including myself, so I attempted to lighten the mood. "You shouldn't. Only God can see souls, Anita."

She tucked her lips in. "Girl, you know I mean people like you and me."

I nodded. "You're looking in the wrong chapel. That's Chapel 1," I said and steered her to the sign-in book for Chapel 3 where we could easily find out if anyone from Hickleman's had arrived yet.

Anita studied the open book resting on the podium before signing it. "Butch is here," she whispered. Then she stepped back and made room for me.

I moved up, quickly added my name to the book, and then followed Anita into the chapel to find Butch.

We'd barely entered the viewing room assigned to Paul Mason when a tall slender woman, early fifties, wearing a black dress and heels, with cinnamon colored shoulder-length hair greeted us. "Hello, I'm Gloria Mason, Paul's wife. Thank you for coming.

Anita hurriedly explained who we were. Then both of us offered our deepest sympathy and continued into the already packed chapel.

Trying to remain close to Anita was impossible. She got swallowed up in the crowd like one does upon leaving the Guthrie Theater or a sporting event. One minute she was there and the next gone.

Not really seeing anyone else I knew, I thought about returning to the gathering area until the chapel cleared a bit. Thankfully, I didn't have to choose that option. A female I didn't recognize loudly hailed Anita, just as a movie screen unfurled next to them at the front of the chapel and began sharing photos of Paul Mason throughout his life.

Curious to see how much fifty-five year-old Paul had changed over the years, I viewed the screen for several seconds before picking up my feet and choosing the path of least resistance to Anita.

When I finally caught up to her, the woman she'd been talking to vanished into the crowd, never to be seen again by me.

"There you are, Mary," Anita said. "I thought maybe you'd left."

"You needn't have worried. I told you I'd stick by you tonight and I meant it."

Anita flapped her hand. "Sorry, I get nervous when things don't go the way I planned. Have you found Butch yet?"

I shook my head. "No." I stood on my tiptoes to get a decent view of the men near Paul's casket, hoping to spot Butch among them. If he was here, he certainly wasn't visible to me. Eventually my toes got tired of holding me up and after I resumed what I considered a normal stance I considered the possibility that he may have stepped out for a smoke.

"Well, did you find him?"

"Afraid not."

"Do you think he backed out?" Anita asked as she unzipped her jacket.

"I hope not."

"You never know. I've seen plenty at viewings one wouldn't expect," she said.

"Like what?"

"Well, I've watched people come in, sign the book, not speak to anyone, and then leave. Hey, maybe Butch got cold feet."

"Nah. He doesn't come across as that type of person." I raised my heels one more time and looked from one side of the room to the other. "You know, Anita, after meeting Paul's wife Gloria, I can't imagine him fooling around on her."

"Me neither."

As I continued to search for someone resembling Butch, a person tapped my shoulder. It wasn't a heavy, firm one like a man's, but soft like a woman's. Knowing I'd better not ignore whoever it was, especially if they were from the plant, I relaxed my feet and turned around. "Zoe!"

~46~

"What are you doing here?" I asked. All it takes is one ounce of Aunt Zoe's blabbering and its good-bye pickle job, good-bye case, good-bye extra income.

Even though my aunt's presence made me seethe inwardly, I had to admit she had the good sense at least to react as if we weren't roommates or related in anyway. "Why, Mary, what an odd place for us to run into one another. It's been ages since I last saw you."

As much as I wanted to ignore her I couldn't, not with Anita almost hitched to my hip. "It certainly has been," I cordially replied and then turned to Anita and explained about Zoe. "She used to live in my apartment complex."

"Ah, nice to meet you, Zoe," Anita said, offering a hand to her. "Are you a relative or friend of Paul's family?"

Aunt Zoe cast her eyes downward as if reflecting upon the kind words she should share concerning her connection to the departed. "Actually, neither. Butch Bailey, an apartment neighbor of mine, asked me to accompany him tonight. He's having a hard time accepting the death of his old boss and didn't want to drive out here alone."

"Why, Zoe, that's so thoughtful of you" I said. "You haven't changed a bit."

Anita remained riveted to where she stood not saying a word. She didn't need to. The blank look registered on her face said it all. She was clueless to the comment I just expressed. Having been in her shoes many times, I felt compelled to fill her in. "When Zoe lived where I do, she always went out of her way to help residents in need."

Anita released a smile. "Good for you. My Baptist minister is always saying we need to be more concerned about the downtrodden around us."

Zoe blushed. "I can't take credit for what I do. That's my mother's doing. 'Live by the Golden Rule,' she forever drummed into our little heads. Even though I miss her, I'm glad she's passed on. She'd be upset to see how today's society is so lacking in that philosophy."

Anita's brief smile disappeared. She nervously rocked her body from side to side. "Zoe, you did say you came with Butch?"

Zoe nodded. "That's right."

"So where did you leave him?" Anita quizzed. "Mary and I have been waiting to talk to him."

Aunt Zoe motioned towards the door. "Right after he viewed Mr. Mason's body, he told me he needed to use the restroom. He should be back any second. Oh, I see him. He's standing in the doorway." She arched her hand over her head and waved.

Being five foot eleven, Butch easily spotted her and weaved his way towards us. "So you two ladies made it. I wondered if you were here yet. Did you view the body?" He didn't wait for a reply. His eyes had settled on the huge screen. "Well, look at that. Paul hasn't left us after all. The guy's up there bigger than life. He was kind of a handsome dude; every strand of hair always in place just like it is tonight. No wonder women were drawn to him like bees to nectar. I suppose he still had plenty of them buzzing around him before he got the life knocked out of him, huh?"

"I wouldn't know," I said, "I haven't worked at the plant that long."

Anita squeezed between Aunt Zoe and me. "Where have you been, Butch?" she asked, sounding irritated. "We've been looking for you for at least fifteen minutes." The sudden change in her mood made me wonder if it was Butch she was actually upset with or having to remain in a funeral home any longer than necessary.

He leaned on the empty folding chair in front of him and grinned. "I've been busy schmoozing with a few pals from the plant who stuck by me after I got arrested the first time."

"Were you able to weasel anything out of them concerning the plant?" I asked, hoping to blow the case wide open within the next couple of days.

Butch loosened his grip on the chair and relaxed. "Like what?"

With his arms now dangling at his sides, Anita took advantage of them. She yanked on a sleeve of Butch's leather jacket and pulled him down close to her height. "Like who might have hated Paul enough to knock him off for instance?"

"Nah. All those guys wanted to talk about was Chip's accident."

"Did I hear someone mention Chip's accident," a reedy voice asked, coming from a slight distance away.

"Butch, scram," I said. "Whatever you do don't let Sharon see you."

Instead of taking my advice seriously, Butch simply turned his back on us and pretended to be chatting with people not from the plant.

Sharon left the tiny group of employees she'd been conversing with and strolled over to where we were. She was cloaked in a long royal-blue coat which added a tinge of color to her pale complexion tonight. "Gal's, I don't think we should be discussing Chip at the viewing. We're here tonight to share our memories of Paul."

At that precise moment, Butch spun around to face Sharon.

Shocked at seeing him, her jaw almost came unhinged. She pressed a hand to her bare neck. "What... What are you doing here? I thought they had you behind bars by now."

"Apparently not. Someone believed in me enough to pay my bail," Butch said, sharing a broad smile. "Aren't I the lucky guy?"

Sharon ignored him. "If... if you'll excuse me, ladies," she stammered, "I need to speak with Paul's wife. I haven't had a chance to offer my condolences yet."

If the head of Hickleman's HR was searching for attention tonight, she got it in spades. Her bright colored coat caught everyone's eyes as she whisked past them to find Gloria Mason.

"Tsk. Tsk," Aunt Zoe uttered. "Somebody isn't happy Butch is here. By the way, did anyone notice Sharon's coat?"

"Why?" I asked. "The coat's no big deal. It's just a different style than I'm used to seeing in my neck of the woods."

Anita pinched the rough edges of her jacket. "Mine too."

"I bet you liked it though?" Aunt Zoe's question was directed at me.

"Well, maybe a little."

She beamed. "It's okay to admit it, Mary. Most women would look good in a coat like that. Unfortunately, it's a pricey one. My personal income couldn't touch it. The Canada Goose PBI Expedition coat Sharon is wearing was listed in the current Neiman Marcus catalog for over a thousand dollars."

Butch blew air through his crooked smoked-stained teeth, creating a subdued whistle.

Anita bent her head and stared at her jacket. "Apparently I've been working on the wrong floor at the plant all these years. How else do you explain Sharon's ability to purchase an expensive coat like the one on her back?"

Not waiting for a reply she proceeded to process more thoughts aloud on the subject, her head continuing to bob as she did so. "Okay, sure, she's a single woman, she doesn't have anyone else to share her dough with like me but still, Don Hickleman was never noted for being generous with the payroll."

Several thoughts sprung to mind, but I'd keep them under wraps for a while longer. "Maybe Sharon's been squirreling away money for years or a relative left her a huge inheritance. Either is plausible," I said.

I expected a rebuttal from Anita, but none came.

Since I figured there was nothing more to gain remaining here at the mortuary and I was becoming more uncomfortable the longer I stayed, I decided to slip away. "I'm going home," I announced.

Anita had been in a fairly decent mood when dissing Sharon, but now that she realized I was departing, she grimaced like she'd eaten a mud pie. "You can't go yet, Mary," she scolded. "You promised to hang out here with me."

"I did. We're done. You can go home any time."

She crossed her arms. "But I didn't view Paul's body yet. And aren't you going to share what you learned tonight?"

"Not here," I whispered in her ear. "We'll talk privately tomorrow." I turned to Butch. "Well, you definitely stirred the pot like we hoped. I wish you all the best. Maybe someday soon you'll be able to work at the plant again."

He nodded. "I sure hope so," and then his eyes drifted to something more interesting, not Paul's photos flashing by on the screen again but rather a person standing at the entrance of the chapel where we'd all be heading soon. "I don't believe my eyes. Can it be Miss Roseanne Harsh in the flesh? I hope she didn't come here to create trouble for Paul's grieving widow. You never know what she'll say or do."

Anita unzipped her jacket again. "I think I'll stay a while longer," she announced. "Roseanne needs watching and I really should view Paul's body."

"Smart move," I said. "While you're at it, find out if Roseanne's dropping off a load of cucumbers tomorrow." *Swiping a cucumber from Roseanne's delivery truck is just what this gal needs to narrow the list of suspects even more.*

~47~

I ran into Margaret as I stepped off the elevator on our floor at the Foley. She wasn't her perky self. The additional creases that lined her narrow furrowed forehead made me wonder if health issues were to blame. Hopefully it's nothing serious.

"Mary, it's about time you got home," she said, clasping and unclasping her gnarled hands. "Do you know where Zoe is? She mentioned going to a mortuary with Butch but she's not back yet."

"Yes. She was with me and Butch at Bromley Funeral Home. They should be back any minute. Why are you asking about her?"

Margaret bowed her head, focusing her olive-green eyes on the hall carpet instead of me. "Mr. Edward's, our caretaker, and two officers of the law were standing outside your apartment door about a half an hour ago."

Oh, boy. My roommate must've instigated the visit. "What did Aunt Zoe do?" I asked, drumming my fingers on my coat. Did she leave a burner on and forget to remove a pan of cooked food from it?"

Her shoulders drooped. "I don't think so, dear. The hallway would still be reeking of smoke and I'd be coughing up a storm. I do remember that after Mr. Edward's knocked on your door and no one answered one of the policemen, I think the older one, said it was extremely important to get ahold of Mary Malone."

My back stiffened. "Me?" I pressed my hands against my cold cheeks. "Oh, my, God. Something happened to my dad." I whipped my phone out of my purse and checked for messages. "No calls from anyone in the family," I said aloud, "and my phone still has plenty of energy."

I inhaled deeply to clear my head and then analyzed the situation. If my father had ended up back in the hospital, a member of my immediate family would've called and left a message. "I can't figure out why the police showed up here, Margaret. It doesn't make sense. Even if something serious happened to another family member, they wouldn't have tried to locate me. The spouses are always notified first. So what else did they want?"

"I've no idea. They didn't say much. But since they came to see you I presumed it had to do with Zoe," She pulled out a hankie from a pocket sewed to her butcher-style apron and wiped the tears away that had settled in her hollow cheeks. "I'd heard the weather man on TV report that the roads were icy, so I thought Zoe might've been in a car accident."

I clutched the elderly woman's thin shoulder. "There's no need for tears. I know the police officers visit couldn't have been about my aunt. When I left the mortuary in Maple Grove thirty minutes ago, she and Butch were still there."

"They were?" She returned the hankie to the pocket it had been in and relaxed her shoulders.

"Ah, huh." Seeing there was no further need for my comforting hand to be resting on her shoulder, I dropped it to my side. "I suppose the police cleared out once they realized I wasn't home."

"No, but I certainly expected them to."

I pressed a finger to my lips. "What reason would there be for them to linger longer than necessary?"

"I heard the police tell Mr. Edward's they'd like to leave a couple messages for you since he had a master key for the apartments."

I shoved my hand in a coat pocket, dug out my apartment key, and stuck it in the keyhole. "You said 'notes,' Margaret. Did Mr. Edward's say if the two policemen came together?"

She shook her head. "I never spoke with him. Once he stuck the notes in your apartment, he and the policemen hopped on the elevator."

I turned the key in the lock, but didn't step into my apartment quite yet. With two unexpected messages from policemen awaiting me, I wanted someone to lean on if need be when I read them. "Margaret, would you mind joining me for a couple minutes? I'm concerned how I'll react to the messages."

"I'd be happy to, dear. And when you finish with them, I'd like you to explain why Zoe went off to a funeral home with Butch, and what you were doing there as well. Last night, right before you fell asleep you tried to tell me something, but I didn't understand a word. It sounded like gibberish."

~48~

Margaret stepped across the threshold of my apartment, but didn't proceed into the living room immediately; something on the slim entryway table had caught her eye. "Ah, I see Mr. Edwards set the policemen's notes on the first piece of furniture he could find."

"A smart man," I said, closing the door behind me. "One needs to avoid our kitchen at all costs when I'm not home."

"Oh, dear, then Zoe's skills around the kitchen still haven't improved much."

"Nope." I plucked the folded notes off the entryway table and joined the elderly woman on the couch where she normally sits when she visits.

Poor Margaret. As soon as I sat, the petite woman was swallowed up by the many layers of fabric still engulfing the couch that Aunt Zoe had personally put there and was supposed to remove.

With all the free time on my aunt's hands, I can't believe she hasn't found one single minute to restore the gaudy Vegas appearance of the queen-size sleeper sofa back to its original look, bare bones basic black.

Luckily it doesn't take much to remedy the situation. I reached for a couple toss pillows at my end of the couch and handed them off to Margaret. "Here you go. Put these behind your back. They'll keep that stupid material away from you."

Margaret's thin lips produced a generous smile. "*Si.* That should do the trick." She took the pillows and set them aside for a moment while she adjusted her wire-framed glasses that had gone askew when the fabric tumbled down upon her. "Ah, that's much better. I don't know why any child would want to dress like a ghost at Halloween. Having layers of material cover you is quite spooky."

I rested the messages on my lap for a second. "I totally agree. In winter, my siblings and I hung out in the basement a lot, which I didn't mind unless it was wash day. That's when the boys would gather up the dirty sheets and throw them over us girls so they could hear us howl like banshees."

"I imagine you girls had terrible nightmares afterwards."

"I did," I said as I gathered the notes off my lap. "But I don't know about my sister."

The elderly woman's aged-eyes swiftly shifted from me to the notes. "Why, Mary. I can't believe you missed this." She tapped a stiff arthritic finger on the top note. "Sgt. Murchinak's signature is on it. Isn't that Matt's police friend, the same person who helped you out when you were arrested?"

"Yes. But why drive over here to talk to me? It doesn't make any sense. He could've saved himself a trip and left me a message on Matt's answer machine. He has that phone number. Unless…"

"What is it, dear?"

"Unless his visit pertained to something urgent concerning that ornery sunglass thief I caught." My hands shook. "Shoot. I was hoping his trial wouldn't come up for a while yet there's so much going on in my life at the moment, including moving out of the apartment and the upcoming holidays."

"Why does the note have to be about you, Mary?" Margaret's ever calming voice questioned. "Couldn't it concern one of Matt's old cases?"

I waved Sgt. Murchinak's note under my nose "Of course it could. I should've thought of that. This coming New Year's I'm going to make a resolution to surround myself with more positive thoughts."

Margaret grinned. "Good for you. The more positive thoughts floating around in this universe the better off everyone will be."

"You know if Sgt. Murchinak left this note for me to hand off to Matt, maybe it's a warning concerning a criminal Matt's put behind bars—like the jailbird is being released from prison earlier than anticipated. The last conversation I had with Murchinak I mentioned Matt would be home in a couple weeks."

"Dear, instead of trying to convince yourself what the message might be about, perhaps you should open it and find out," she kindly suggested.

"Sorry, I just can't get it out of my head that it's bad news of some sort, but you're right, I'll never know what it's about if I don't read it." Trying to display nerves of steel like Superman is for the birds. I couldn't do it. My hands shook, causing the note to rattle.

Margaret grasped the bottom of the paper to still it, making it easier for both of us to read. "Hmm. Oh, my! Why, this is exciting news, dear. I can't believe both of us were wrong about its contents. This note has nothing to do with you or Matt." Margaret patted my hand. "But one of your three problems has been solved. You must be so relieved."

"You better believe it."

"Believe what?" Aunt Zoe quizzed as she strolled into the living room and set her Russian Kubanka hat and coat on an arm of the La-Z-Boy.

I glanced up at her, surprised to see her standing there. "You must've been as quiet as a mouse when you came in, we didn't hear a thing."

"Well, I did close our door as softly as I could in case you were snoozing after the long day you had."

"Thanks for your consideration, but as you can see I'm still awake."

"Oh, Zoe," Margaret said eager to share what occurred while she was out of the building, "You missed a bit of excitement."

"Really? What happened?"

"Would you like the long or short version?" I asked.

Aunt Zoe yawned. "After attending a viewing at a funeral home for over an hour and hanging out with wall to wall people I didn't know, I'd prefer the short one."

"Sgt. Murchinak left a message. Guess what? Gracie's been found."

Aunt Zoe covered her eyes. "Oh, no," she wailed, "Please don't tell me she's dead. Matt will be devastated."

"You needn't get so melodramatic," I scolded. "He never mentioned the word *dead*."

"Well, where is she then?"

"I don't know." I handed her the note Margaret and I just read. "All Sgt. Murchinak said was to come by the police station tomorrow morning and he'll explain."

"That won't work," Aunt Zoe croaked. "You have to show up at the pickle plant before the sun rises."

I ran my fingers through my hair. "Darn, I was so excited that Gracie had been found I forgot about work. I'd better call the station and explain that I can't come by until around 5 p.m."

I dug out my cell phone and searched for Sgt. Murchinak's private number. The minute I found it Aunt Zoe placed her freshly-manicured nails on my phone. "Stop, Mary. Don't call him yet. I want to get Matt's mutt back just as much as you. Let me talk to Reed first. If he can take me to the station, I'll go meet with Sgt. Murchinak and find out where Gracie is. Who knows, maybe by the time you get home from work, Gracie will be here waiting for you."

Margaret pointed to the second message still sitting in my lap. "Dear, don't forget about your other note. Since it's from a policeman, it's probably as important as the first one. Who knows, maybe it contains even more good news."

Aunt Zoe's eyebrows arched. "I don't understand about these notes. When exactly did they arrive? No one tried to deliver anything before I left at 5:30."

"You were at the funeral home when they were dropped off," Margaret shared, as she struggled to pull her tiny frame up straighter. "What I'm still waiting to find out is what you both were doing there with Butch. Mary said she'd explain after reading the notes. That's why I'm pressing her to get on with it."

"I'll read it, Margaret," Aunt Zoe said, grabbing the second note off Mary's lap.

"Good grief. What's with you gals? I've never seen you this antsy before." I took the note from my aunt and opened it. "Ah?"

"Well, are you going to tell us what it says or not?" the two women quizzed.

I shrugged. "It's no big deal." I dropped the note back in my lap.

"Good news at least I hope," Margaret said.

"It depends. David Welsh wanted me to know he'll be finishing up an undercover case he's been working on next week, freeing him up to see me before Christmas."

Forever the incurable romantic Aunt Zoe said, "I don't see a problem with that unless you're worried his timing will interfere with the welcome home party your mother has planned for Matt and his fiancée.

I sighed. "My feelings on the subject have nothing to do with Matt."

Margaret fidgeted with her double-banded wedding ring. "What is it, dear? Don't you like David anymore?"

"I like him but I don't know if I enjoy his company more than Trevor's, although David is closer to my age." I rubbed my forehead. Things weren't working out the way I planned. The two men don't know about each other and I wanted to keep it that way.

The women looked as bewildered as I felt. "Okay, okay, there's more to the story than that. Trevor sent me a text the other day and mentioned coming down next week too if the snow holds off."

Aunt Zoe wagged her pudgy finger at me. "I told you it doesn't work out dating two men at once, but you didn't want to hear it. Things always go awry."

Margaret went on the defensive for me yet again. "Yes, Zoe, but if you recall David's out of the picture for long stretches of time. Your niece is too young to sit around and twiddle her thumbs waiting for a man like that to come back into her life. She needs to get out and do fun things not sit by the phone night after night."

At the conclusion of the ninety-year-old woman's speech, she leaned forward and tucked a hand in mine. "Don't fuss so much, dear. Like my mother always preached to me 'things will work out for the best.' And they always do."

I put my free hand on top of hers. "Thanks, Margaret. I appreciate your support."

"No need to thank me, dear. Now, what in the world were you, Butch, and Zoe doing at a funeral home in Maple Grove tonight?"

~49~

"I honestly don't know how Aunt Zoe got snagged into coming to Bromley's with Butch," I said. "She wasn't around when I approached him about the viewing."

"It's easy enough to explain," Aunt Zoe said. "There's not much to the story. Gertie told me Butch was nervous about going there by himself, so I offered to go with him."

Margaret steepled her hands as if she was contemplating prayer. "Forgive me Mary for being critical of your decision, but why ask Butch to attend a viewing for someone who worked at Hickleman's, a business that's caused him nothing but grief?"

"May I comment on that?" Aunt Zoe asked as she strolled over to the La-Z-Boy and finally got off her feet.

Curious to hear her explanation, I said, "Go right ahead."

"Mary thought Butch's presence at the mortuary might rattle whoever stole the recipes, killed Don Hickleman and Paul Mason, and injured Chip."

"I see. And did your plan work, Mary?"

I nodded. "Perfectly. Thanks to Aunt Zoe's keen skills of observation at the mortuary, the field of suspects can be narrowed to two individuals. One has fooled around with several of the men at the plant. The other seems to have money to burn. For all I know, the two could be in cahoots with each other."

Margaret peered at her wristwatch. "My, my, where has the time gone? I'd like to know more about your two suspects, Mary, but I'm afraid I must check on Petey. Who knows what that parrots been up to."

After making several attempts at scooting her thinly-framed body off the heavily draped couch, Margaret finally managed it, sidestepping the coffee table parked in front of her feet as she did so. "By the way," she said, "have you two found a place to move yet?"

"Afraid not," I replied, getting up to escort her to the door. "I've been too busy."

Margaret patted my hand. "Of course you have, dear. I feel bad that I haven't been able to assist you on this big case, but I don't think the Hickleman Pickle Plant would want a ninety-year-old woman wandering around their production line."

I chuckled. "Probably not. But you've offered me a ton of support along the way, especially tonight. I shouldn't have let my imagination go hog wild when I heard a couple cops left notes for me. Everything turned out all right, didn't it?"

"*Si*, it did on the home front, but I'd advise you to be extremely cautious at work," she warned. "It could be quite dangerous for you especially if the killer or killers knew you were on to them."

"Don't fret. I'm sure neither person does. Besides, without solid proof I'm not a threat to anyone yet."

"'Yet' being the operative word," she said. "Remember things can change in an instant. You'd better carry that stun gun on you at all times."

"But… but you said it wasn't a good idea for me to carry it."

"Well, this old woman has changed her mind."

~50~

Day 18

I awoke to a dark dreary day. One that warned of imminent danger, but I didn't take it seriously. Why should I? To me, the heavy clouds hanging over Minneapolis only represented the possibility of rain or snow, depending on the rise or fall of the day's temperature, nothing more.

After I made the bed and ate my usual breakfast of Cheerios and orange juice, I dug through the scant wardrobe I owned and selected a pair of casual pants with deep enough pockets to hide the camera style stun gun Aunt Zoe gave me to carry the first day on the job, an important safety item I'd been leaving at home the past couple days. Thankfully I hadn't needed to use it yet.

Once I gathered my clothes, I hopped in the shower and plotted out my strategy for the day. The first thing on my agenda was to ask Anita if Roseanne was dropping off a load of cucumbers this morning. If she was, I'd hint that the three of us should have a cup of coffee in the breakroom together.

Shower done, I quickly dressed, put on a smattering of makeup, and ran a comb through my wet hair. While staring at my reflection in the mirror, I came to realize I looked kind of blah without earrings dangling from my lobes and thought about the many pairs sitting idly by in my jewelry box waiting for the job at the plant to be over so I could show them off again. Hopefully they won't have to be kept out of sight much longer.

After I left the bathroom, I strolled down to the kitchen again to pack a lunch and seek out Aunt Zoe, whom I figured would be dying to get her hands on her first cup of java by this time.

"Ah, there you are," my aunt said as I appeared in the kitchen doorway. She was standing by the coffee maker pouring a cup of coffee, like I presumed, dressed in a fancy silk slide robe and gown I didn't recognize. My memory bank may be stashed with a lot of unnecessary clutter but it never forgets the brilliantly colored outfits she wears that easily, especially sleepwear that clashes with her red head. The gown was dyed solid fuchsia while the robe contained hues of green, gold, turquoise and hot pink. "I thought perhaps you'd left. I found breakfast dishes in the sink and hadn't heard you making any noise for a while."

"It's me in the flesh," I assured her.

"Yes, I can see that." She picked up her filled coffee mug and took a sip before moving to the table where she'd left the paper. "What brings you back to the kitchen?"

"I wanted to prepare a bag lunch and give you a message to pass on to Sgt. Murchinak since you and Reed are meeting with him this morning." I marched to the fridge, took out a few carrots, and also the fixings for a sandwich: baloney, bread, cheese, and mustard.

My aunt folded up her newspaper, making room for me to make my sandwich there. "What exactly did you want me to tell Matt's friend?"

I got a knife out of the silverware drawer and spread mustard on both pieces of bread. "Tell him I'll call him over the lunch hour. It's about the two deaths at the plant."

"Wait a second." She left the table, grabbed pen and paper sitting by the landline, and opted to use the counter as her desk. "Okay, just repeat everything but a bit slower. I don't what to mess up your message."

Good grief. A first grader could remember what I said.

As I slapped the baloney and slices of cheddar cheese on the bread, I chided myself for feeling the way I did. Instead of being upset with her I should be thankful she recognizes her occasional memory lapses and wants certain things in writing. I sealed the sandwich in a plastic bag along with six baby carrots and then told her what she wanted to hear one more time.

After she finished writing, she drew closer to me and said, "Mary, I've been thinking as long as Reed is coming out this way to get me, perhaps I should check out a couple apartment rental properties that were listed in today's newspaper, don't you agree?"

"Sure, I haven't got time to run around town. Just don't put any money down until you discuss it with me." I didn't have the guts to tell my aunt she's put a damper on my life style long enough and that I'd been contemplating going solo.

Aunt Zoe shared a smile that could melt even a chimpanzee's heart. "Good, I'm glad you approve of my plan. I was afraid you might not," and then she inquired whether I had my stun gun on me and if I'd be home at my usual time.

I patted my pocket. "Got it. And as for being home around 5 p.m., I can't imagine why I wouldn't be, unless of course tons of snow gets dumped on the city between now and then. You probably haven't glanced outside yet, but the sky appears undecided at the moment."

"No, I haven't." She gave me a hug. "But whatever the day brings, Mary, please remember to be on your guard. I don't want to hear you've flipped your car or ended up another pickle vat victim."

"I will," I promised.

***

Anita looked at me strangely when I trotted into the employee locker room. "What's going on with you, girl? Looks like you're carrying the weight of the world on your shoulders."

I wasn't. But the serious countenance seen on my face could be easily explained. On the hike in here, from where I parked the car in the employee lot, I'd been strongly focusing on what to say to Anita in reference to Roseanne. Unfortunately, it's too late to undo what's already been seen. The situation will have to be handled appropriately. "I feel like it," I said, trying to sound depressed.

Not ready to disclose what was actually on my mind, I tried to formulate a feasible explanation while I struggled with the combination lock on my locker. PMS came to mind, an excuse many women use. But since I'd just come from the Foley, I decided an apartment dilemma would be a good one to tackle instead.

I inhaled deeply and then let loose. "I've been living in my brother's digs with a roommate while he's been out of the country, but he comes back next week and we still haven't found a place to stay in our price range."

Anita flipped the top of her lab coat back to release the cornrow braids stuck inside it. "Boy you've got it rough, Mary. Finding a place to live in December can be a bummer, especially if the city gets socked with several snowstorms. If I hear of anything, I'll let you know."

The lock finally gave way. "Thanks. I appreciate that. Maybe I should spread the word at lunch time too."

"It couldn't hurt," she said, dabbing her lips with more burgundy colored lipstick.

After I hung my coat and purse in the locker, I snatched my lab coat and hunted for the ugly green hairnet stashed in one of its three pockets. When I found it, I stretched it to its limit and tried to settle it over my short hair, but its staticky condition fought back.

My problem amused Anita. "I'm glad my hair isn't that hard to manage in the winter."

"Some people have all the luck," I complained. "So what's on the agenda for me today? Opening boxes of new jars again?"

Anita shook her head. "Nope. You're a quick learner, Mary. Sharon's been looking at the daily reports I've given her regarding your work and she says you've graduated to the final step here at the plant."

Taken aback by the news, I said, "Really? So soon? Does that mean I'll be spending the whole day shipping pickles out?"

"Don't worry, girl. You're not working in the distribution departments of Amazon or Walmart. Our boxes don't travel down a conveyor belt at speeds up to sixty miles an hour. Most of the work here is done by machines." Anita glanced up at the huge clock centered on the wall above the lockers. "Oops. Looks like you and I have been dallying too long. We'd better hustle to get our time cards stamped if we don't want to see a smaller paycheck."

Even though we rushed down the hall like fox hounds were in hot pursuit of us, I still managed to squeeze out an inquiry regarding Roseanne's behavior. "Anita, you haven't mentioned your time spent with Roseanne last night. Did she behave respectfully or did she embarrass everyone?"

Anita stopped jogging for a second and rested her hands on her wide hips. "You've never seen her in action have you?"

"Nope. Can't say I have."

"Well, be thankful," she said, continuing down the hall at an even faster pace.

When we finally reached the time card room, we had exactly two minutes to go before we showed our shiny faces in Distribution. I grabbed my card and then waited while Anita's got marked.

As soon as Anita's card was taken care of, she said, "Sorry, I didn't really answer your question about Roseanne's behavior last night. Are you still interested?"

"Of course."

"It's kinda hard for me to explain, but I reckon I can try seeing as how you weren't there. That hussy brazenly moved among the men from work, clinging to each one like she was scoping out a place for target practice." She shook her head. "Nothing new for her, but it's a good thing their wives weren't around to witness the show. On the flip side, the she-wolf had enough sense to hold shenanigans to a minimum and didn't express one iota of nastiness towards Paul's wife, Gloria."

"Glad to hear it." I moved up to the machine, stamped my card, and jammed it back where it belonged.

"Did you ever find out if she's delivering a load of cucumbers this morning?"

Anita escaped into the hallway once again and I followed. "Roseanne said she'd see me today so I assume it's to make a delivery. Why did you want to know?"

"I thought if she came by I might join you two for coffee again. I didn't get a chance to really chat with her before."

"Girl, I think you've got something up your sleeve. Are you planning on weaseling info out of her about certain men she's had in her life?"

"Nah. Why would I want to do that? I just thought I'd like to get to know her better. The woman's traveled the road for many years by herself and I'm curious about the experiences she's had."

"Uh-huh. Just as curious as I am to know how many beans of coffee it takes to fill a can."

~51~

"You gals caught me on the right day," Roseanne said, leaning into one of the tables in the lunchroom and lifting a cup of coffee to her uneven lips. "I don't have to hustle out of town for at least another four days."

"I bet you appreciate your down time," I said, with a hint of sarcasm.

Not catching the gist of my words, Roseanne touched the brim of her tan cowboy hat and nodded. "You bet your boots I do. I get to spend time at my house like any other homeowner: cook meals, shovel snow, cut down trees, fix leaky plumbing."

"Ah, yes," I replied. "The thrills of owning a home, something my roommate and I'd recently discussed. Say, Anita told me she ran into you at Bromley's Mortuary last night. What did you think of the gathering?"

Roseanne scratched her forehead. "I try to stay away from funeral homes as much as I can. I don't like the vibes they give off, kind of creepy. But I gotta say Paul's viewing was topnotch. When I walked in the chapel and saw the big screen showing off his life, I thought I'd entered a movie theater by mistake and expected an usher to ask for my ticket." She tilted her head slightly in Anita's direction. "Do they use those screens a lot?"

"Honey, I couldn't say," Anita replied. "None of my friends or family have dropped dead recently." She bowed her head. "Thanks to the good Lord."

Roseanne took a sip of coffee and then wrapped her rough hands around her Styrofoam cup. "How about you, Mary? Have you been in attendance at other funeral chapels that use huge screens to display photos of the departed?"

"Ah, yeah, twice last year when relatives died." I set my cup down and then scooted my chair back so I could stand. "Darn weak bladder," I explained. "Gotta take a potty break." I don't need to go, but I couldn't think of a better excuse to leave the two women behind and swipe one of the cucumbers Roseanne just delivered.

Matching a cucumber of Roseanne's with cucumbers the cops found shoved down Paul Mason's and Don Hickleman's should be easy. Analysis was the problem. It could take days to be completed once Sgt. Murchinak received it. And even after tests results show conclusively that the cucumbers came from Roseanne's deliveries, the case can't be neatly tied up with a bright red bow until three questions are answered. Who stole the pickle recipes? Who caused Chip's injuries? And, who wrote the note I found in Paul's pocket?

As far as I could tell, Roseanne had no motive for stealing the recipes, but the quarrel I witnessed between her and Chip may have been significant enough to do him bodily harm.

I sped down the hall at a fast clip to reach the outdoors, hoping my trip didn't get caught on camera. If Sharon Sylvester saw what I was doing, this gig would be up. You see, the exit I was racing towards led to the location where deliveries were made and is officially off limits to an employee needing a smoke.

The delivery Roseanne dropped off over a half hour ago was still piled on the blacktop in an eight-foot tent like formation waiting to be sorted and graded. I immediately went into overdrive not knowing when workers might show up to handle those chores. After checking to make certain no one was in the vicinity, I squatted down, grabbed a cucumber, stuffed it in a pant pocket, and then dashed back inside.

My luck had held out. No one was standing guard by the door, waiting to haul my butt off to either HR or the police station.

Even though things couldn't be running more smoothly for this sleuth, I still had enough sense to rub my cold hands to warm them in case Anita or Roseanne accidentally touched them. Hands that felt like they'd been playing with ice cubes rather than being held under warm water would definitely raise a red flag.

I'd been gone from the lunchroom five minutes at the most, but it seemed like eternity. As far as I could tell, Anita and Roseanne hadn't budged from their chairs, but the one I'd sat in and another had been filled by women who worked with the plant's dill slicing machines.

When Anita caught sight of me, she broke with the serious pow-wow she was having with Roseanne and the other women. "Mary, get off your feet. Grab a chair."

I snuck a peek at my watch, pretending to be concerned about the time. "Oh, all right. I thought for sure our break had ended." I swiped a chair from another table and dragged it over by Anita and sat.

Since I hadn't anticipated additional employees being around when I questioned Roseanne, I wondered how the heck I was going to get info out of her without her going on the defensive. Then it dawned on me. When I returned to the lunchroom I'd passed in front of the board that displayed photos of all the employees. So the second I sat, I pointed to the photos. "Great photo of Chip, isn't it? Speaking of him has anyone heard how he's doing?"

Anita and the two other gals from the plant shook their heads.

Roseanne simply remained aloof at first, looking like a deer frozen in its tracks when a car's headlights illuminate the road where it's feeding, but her bushy eyebrows certainly made a go at responding as they jetted upwards higher than humanly possible. When she finally came around, she said, "What's this about Chip? Was he in a car accident or something?"

The woman's response made me think she was either a darn good actress or she truly doesn't know about Chip's close call. Which was it?

Anita lifted her coffee cup. "That's right. You haven't been around for a while, have you? Chip wasn't in any car accident. He got hurt out by the vats this past Saturday."

I noticed Anita didn't bother mentioning that Chip was pushed down the steps. Perhaps she too believed Roseanne had a part in his injuries.

"Oh, that's awful," Roseanne remarked, laying on the sympathy. "How long will he be out on sick leave?"

Anita shrugged. "No idea. Hey, Mary, as long as these two gals are here why not ask them for help."

"You mean about my apartment situation?"

"Yeah."

I briefly glimpsed at the wall clock. "Too late," I said. "We have to go."

Anita adjusted her glasses and then stared up at the clock. "You're right. The people in Distribution probably think we've bailed on them." She hopped out of her seat. "Catch you gals later. Well, not you Roseanne."

She rubbed her chin. "You never know you might. I've got some catching up to do with Sharon Sylvester."

~52~

Anita had explained a bit about what went on in the distribution department before we went to break, but she never shared why row upon row of stacked pickle products, securely bound by clear wrapping tape, were still waiting to leave the plant, despite the orders that had been filled. So I questioned her about it.

The woman squeezed her round chin firmly between her fingers. "Company policy states that we hold the filled orders for a two week period for safety reasons, one being spoilage. This way if anything bad does show up within our time frame it's here and we don't have to post a recall." She shook her head. "You never want a bad product ending up in the customer's hands. It ain't good for business. You know what I'm saying?"

"Yup, the company doesn't want a big law suit messing things up."

"Exactly." Anita pulled a clipboard off a shelf and handed it to me. Several sheets of paper were attached to it. "I want you to keep this with you," she said. "What you've got is a running list of all the shipments that are wrapped and sitting on pallets waiting to be trucked out of here. The list is in chronological order. You're going to verify that the shipments listed are sitting there and that the release date posted on each one coincides with this list. Only make notations if something isn't right. If the shipment date is for today and the product looks good to go, I'll slap one of these green ship labels on it, letting the forklift driver know to move the pallet to the pickup station for the truckers."

"Sounds like a simple enough process," I said, as I examined the long list I'd been provided with. The pickle orders weren't just going to grocery stores and restaurants familiar to me in Minnesota like Cub and Mc Donald's. They were being shipped to stores and restaurants I'd never heard of throughout the Midwest.

As soon as I finished studying the information given to me, I held the clipboard down by my side, glanced at Anita, and inquired where the first shipments listed were situated.

"Closest to the pickup area," she said, indicating the spot with a jerk of her head.

I nodded. "Of course, I should've thought of that."

Anita made light of what I said as she followed me to the back of the packaging department. "Girl, don't go all serious on me now. Take it from me it's impossible to know everything that goes on at this plant even if you've worked here thirty years or more."

"Even though you might not know what all happens here, Anita, you must have some inkling who might be capable of murder."

"Shh," she warned, "keep your voice down. There are too many ears around here." Before saying anything more, Anita pointed to the aisle we needed to begin our task in and pushed me forward. "Okay," she whispered, "I think it's safe to talk here. Ever since Don and Paul's death, I've been looking at the people around here differently, even Roseanne. I gotta tell you its hard imagining any of them as a murderer, but someone has to be, right?"

I didn't say anything. All Anita needed was a few more minutes to seriously consider who the killer might be. In the meantime, I kept busy comparing the list of dates on the clipboard against the dates on the shipments standing in front of me.

After a brief interlude of silence between the two of us, Anita finally announced in a definitive manner what she'd been mulling over. "Sharon's been running the show since Don died, but my gut says Chip has to be the one who killed the men and stole the recipes. It makes the most sense. The man worked inside and then suddenly he's dumped outside with the vats. A switcheroo like that would anger anyone, including Chip. He must've felt like it was a demotion."

I stopped what I was doing. "I understand how it feels to lose a job one's been doing for a while, but that doesn't make the person a killer," I said, thinking of my own circumstances. "If Chip killed the men, why tell Butch someone pushed him down the steps?"

Anita rested a hand on her hip. "Oh, honey, no mystery there. Chip created a phantom. He wanted to throw everyone off the scent. I bet he stole the recipes too, otherwise why bother telling Butch he knew he was innocent."

As much as I'd like to agree with Anita, her theory didn't jive. A scorned woman could just as easily take a man out and steal the recipes. The way I see it, one of the gals stole the recipes after being jilted and things continued to snowball until the Hickleman Pickledom came tumbling down.

~53~

I can't imagine what Sharon Sylvester and Roseanne Harsh talked about for two whole hours this morning. But that's how much time had elapsed when Roseanne hunted Anita and I down to ask if we wanted to join her for lunch at Tioni's Pizza Parlor.

Anita was all for it, but I didn't jump on the bandwagon that quickly even though my stomach was begging to go and I'd been given another chance to loosen Roseanne's tongue. Another matter of grave importance took top priority, setting up a time this evening to meet with Sgt. Murchiank. I couldn't do it with them around. "I'll go," I said, "on one condition. I have to get back here at least ten minutes before we have to clock-in. My mom hasn't been feeling well and I promised to check on her over the lunch hour."

Roseanne tugged on the brim of her cowgirl hat. "There shouldn't be a problem with that."

"So whose vehicle are we using?" Anita inquired as we wandered into the locker room so she and I could dump our lab coats and retrieve our coats.

"No need to ask," Roseanne replied, locking her eyes on Anita whose locker was situated to the left of me and a generous distance away. "I invited you gals to join me, unless someone objects to riding in the truck?"

"It doesn't bother me," Anita said as she took her lab coat off and slipped into her jacket.

I had been putzing with the fasteners on my lab coat, waiting for the perfect chance to get the cucumber intended for Sgt. Murchinak out of my pant pocket and hide it somewhere else. Now, thanks to Roseanne's focus on Anita, the time had arrived. I took the lab coat off and draped it over my arm, hiding the pant pocket with the cucumber. Then, leaning partially into the locker, I hung up the lab coat, stashed the cucumber in the bottom of my purse, grabbed my coat, and closed the locker.

Roseanne questioned me now as we headed for the same exit I used during morning break. "Mary, you haven't voiced your opinion yet. How do you feel about riding in my truck?"

I raised my hand to fluff my hair and discovered I still had my hairnet on. I whipped it off and stuffed it in my ski jacket. "I guess I'm fine with that."

I sense some hesitation," Roseanne said, looking back at me over her shoulder. Are you positive you don't mind riding in the cab of the truck?"

I tilted my head back and stared up at the cab. I wasn't concerned about riding with her on the way to the pizza parlor, but after I finished drilling her about who might have had it in for the three men she may leave me stranded. "Nah. It looks like there's plenty of room."

"Roseanne, you don't get it," Anita said. "The girl doesn't give a rip about how much space we've got for our rumps. She's still thinking about that phone call, aren't you, Mary?"

Not able to share my real thoughts, I merely nodded.

The trucker unlocked her cab doors and hopped in. "Stop worrying. There's no need for you to drive separately. I'll get you back on time." She shoved the key in the ignition and then allowed the truck to idle for a bit before taking off.

After making sure Anita had enough elbow space, I settled back in the mid-section of the truck's cushy seat, looking forward to the view of St. Michael from almost 14 feet off the ground for the next five minutes, knowing this would probably be the only time I'd have the opportunity.

When I caught sight of Tioni's Pizza Parlor sign, I couldn't believe I'd never been there before this year. This was my third visit since the interview with Sharon Sylvester, but I have a hunch today's trip is going to be the most memorable.

Ginny, who served me the first time I stopped by, wasn't working the day Anita and I came in, but I was afraid today might be different. If she's there, hopefully she has enough sense not to mention our conversation about Butch otherwise my cover will be blown. Of course, several days ago I worried about Butch ruining things too when he showed up at the plant. Luckily, it worked out just fine.

I thought about my elderly neighbor for a second. If Margaret was here, she'd advise me to focus on what I can handle and forget the rest. That's probably for the best. You can't change the course of events, but you can always work around them.

***

Ginny sat perched on one of the stools behind the counter at Tioni's eager to greet customers. She flashed us a broad smile. Then she reverted back to chewing her gum and patiently waited for us to stamp our snow-packed shoes on the mat by the entrance. The second we finished the task, she jumped up and rested her elbows on the counter. "Hi, ladies, welcome to Tioni's Pizza Parlor. How can I help y'all?"

Roseanne acted as spokesperson. "We haven't a clue what we want yet. Can you give us a sec to study the menu?"

Ginny nodded. "Sure. Just let me know when you're ready." She went back to her stool and waited.

"Will do," Roseanne said, as she looked around the crowded room "Wow. I sue didn't expect it to be this busy. We'd better get crack'n if Mary's going to squeeze that phone call in."

"I know what I want," I said, moving to the counter, "How about you two?"

Anita slipped her mittens off and placed her hands on her hips. "I was kinda hoping someone would want to share a pizza."

"Don't look at me," Roseanne said, "I've got a girlish figure to maintain. I'm sticking to one slice of pepperoni."

Anita faced me and batted her thick eyelashes. My aunt does the same thing when she wants to butter someone up. Of course I gave in. "Okay, I'll go in with you. How about getting a large sausage with mushrooms?"

"Mmmm. Sounds good, but do you mind adding green peppers," Anita said, as she stepped off to the side. "Oh, and a Coke."

Once Roseanne and I got the orders out of the way, we filled our beverage cups and slid into one of the two remaining booths.

So far so good—Ginny, didn't acknowledge knowing me when I gave her my order. Of course, I had worn a nice outfit and dress coat when I showed up that first time, giving her the impression I was Butch's lawyer. With the clothes I had on today and my short hair shooting up in every direction, the young worker probably took me for a slob. Wouldn't she be shocked to know what I've actually been up to.

I didn't get much out of Roseanne regarding Chip at my morning break, so I planned to approach things from a different angle. As tactfully as possible, I said, "Roseanne, you've gotten to know many of the plant employees. Who do you think had the most to gain from Don and Paul's deaths?"

She wrapped her fingers around her straw and poked it up and down in the cup of pop she purchased. "Geez, I don't know. It could be almost anyone."

Anita offered a suggestion, "How about Chip? That's the way I'm leaning."

Not expecting Chip's name to be brought up quite so soon, my eyes and ears paid close attention to the trucker's response.

Roseanne cleared her throat. Her hazel eyes widened like an owls. The fair skin she was born with gained a bit of color. "I suppose it could've been him. There was no love lost between him and Don."

I tried to add a little confusion to the discussion to see if I could succeed in riling Roseanne more. "When we chatted this morning, did I hear you say you were in town the Saturday Chip got hurt?"

"I don't believe so," she calmly replied.

Shoot. The woman's a tough nut to crack. Obviously she's had a ton of practice skirting issues.

Before I could proceed with another inquiry, Ginny delivered our orders. As she set the large pizza in front of me, I noticed a glimmer of recognition skim across her face. Would she give me away? She opened her mouth to say something directly to me, but I shut her down with a heavily stressed, "Thank you," hoping she got the message.

She did. The only word that passed her lips was, "Enjoy," and then she went back to the counter.

I slipped a slice of pizza on my plate to let it cool a bit and then I threw out the question I'd been holding on to. "Is it possible someone at the plant might have been having affairs with Don, Paul, and maybe even Chip?"

Roseanne almost choked on her straw. "Where would you come up with such a foolish notion? Has someone at the plant been spinning yarns?"

"Nope. It's just something I've been pondering on my own."

"Roseanne, honey," Anita said, lifting a piece of pizza to her mouth, "As much as you want to hide it, we all know you had the hots for Don and Paul, why not just admit it and we can figure out if someone else might have felt the same."

Roseanne bowed her head and began tapping her fingers on the table. "Oh, my, God. Isn't anything kept private around that darn plant? Sure Don and I had a thing going after his wife died, but it didn't last long."

Anita bit into her pizza. "What about Paul?"

"Paul?" Roseanne cackled. "I don't sleep with married men, Anita. I just mess with their heads. You know how flirtatious I can be."

I pushed the envelope. "Where does Chip fit into the picture?"

"What kind of question is that?" Roseanne asked, accidentally knocking her empty plate to the floor, causing all eyes to look our way. "Ladies, I didn't invite you to lunch so you could interrogate me. That's the job of the police. And so far they haven't requested that I come to their station. So if you don't mind, let's drop the twenty questions. Okay?"

"Fair enough," Anita said, grabbing another slice of pizza. "It's almost time to get back anyway."

It's fine with me if she wants to throw in the towel, but I'm not giving up that easily. I'm going to find out what's going on one way or another. Paul was murdered on the sixth of December. Roseanne delivered a truckload of cucumbers on the seventh, a day earlier than expected, which means she could've killed Paul. The woman knows her way around the plant, seamlessly evades questions regarding Chip, and is keeping a secret under wraps.

~54~

The minute Roseanne dropped us off at the door designated for Hickleman's employees, I rushed down the corridor to the locker room and rid myself of the ski jacket. Once that task was done, I grabbed my lab coat and cell phone.

Not feeling the need to hurry like me, Anita arrived in the room shortly afterwards and watched as I finished fastening my lab coat. "Mary, I hope you don't believe that hogwash I spit out at Tioni's. You know about being fine where things were left with Roseanne. I'm not sure she's so innocent after all."

"I don't have time to discuss her or anyone else right now." I flashed the cell phone in front of Anita, hoping it would remind her of the call I needed to make. Then I charged out the door and down the hall a ways to what I considered a safe spot to call Sgt. Murchinak, not realizing an air vent overhead carried my voice somewhere in the building it shouldn't.

"Hi, this is Mary Malone. Sgt. Murchinak is expecting a call from me."

"Just a minute please."

"Mary, good timing. I have to be at the courthouse in fifteen minutes. When your aunt stopped by this morning, she mentioned you wanted to talk about the death of the two men at the pickle plant. Sorry, but I'm afraid I don't know much about the cases. The Wright County Sheriff's Office is handling those."

Amazing. Aunt Zoe actually got something right. "I realize that Sgt." Before I went on, I glanced down the hall in both directions. The coast was still clear. "I have an item that could possibly crack the cases wide open. Of course, it's going to require lab work which I know your team is equipped to do."

Murchinak's voice became heavy. "What exactly are we talking about here?"

"Cucumbers. Both dead men had cucumbers stuffed in their throats."

"That I actually did know about," he shared.

"Good. I want to drop off a cucumber at your station tonight on my way home. I got my hands on one from a fresh batch delivered today."

He released a sigh. "What do you expect me to do with it, eat it?"

Matt always said the guy had a good sense of humor. I suppose you have to in his line of work when facing such harsh realities day after day. "No, Sgt., I was hoping you'd have it analyzed and see if it comes from the same region as the one's found in the throats of the deceased."

"Ah, I see where you're going. If we find out the cucumber is from the same area as the others, you can narrow down your list of suspects. By the way, how long is your list?"

"It's growing shorter by the minute."

"Oh? In that case swing by tonight and I'll see what we can do for you."

"Thanks. I appreciate it." I checked the time on the phone as I clicked it off. With only a minute to spare before I was expected back in the distribution department, I couldn't possibly run to the locker room to stash the phone and clock-in too. Those areas were too far apart. Breaking company policy in regards to carrying around cell phones during work time wasn't high on my agenda, but with no other option left, l shoved it in a pocket of my lab coat and went to take care of the time card.

***

"Mary, did you get ahold of your mother?" Anita asked as I rejoined her in the distribution department.

"Yup."

"How's she doing?"

I flashed a smile her way. "Better. She thinks it's probably because the meds the doctor prescribed for her have finally kicked in."

I moved over to the desk, which held information of all sorts for this department, and picked up the clipboard holding the shipping info and examined it. Obviously, no one had felt the urge to complete the task while we were at lunch: the company I'd left off with was still on top of the others. I guess I should've expected that. At least I had an inkling of what I'd be doing this afternoon.

I waited for Anita to confirm what I'd suspected before returning to this morning's task. She didn't comply.

Instead she babbled on about my mother's health condition. "What's wrong with your mom? Is she down with the flu or pneumonia? I hope it's not pneumonia. That's a tough one for the elderly to get over. I remember when my granny got it. She was so doped up she acted like she'd hit the moonshine too hard."

I may not have learned everything about the pickling industry yet, but I'd gleaned enough about Anita. If she wanted certain information, she'd persist until she got it. So I tossed her a bone lacking any substance. "She doesn't have pneumonia. Her ulcers have flared up again."

Anita's mouth formed a perfect circle. "Ooo. That's pretty painful. Ulcers aren't something I'd want to suffer with especially in December. Uh-uh. No siree. Not with all the free goodies friends and family load me down with."

Now she put her hands behind her back and clasped them. "Well, girl, I suppose we'd better stop standing around before someone complains we're not doing our share of the workload." She pointed to the clipboard I was holding. "But you won't need that yet. I've got something else to show you first. Follow me."

"Where are we going?"

"You'll see."

After we walked about twenty-five feet from where we were standing, Anita stopped near a huge piece of equipment I hadn't been shown before. Sitting with the machinery were several layers of finished pickle products stacked on top of each other with only a pallet in between to separate the layers.

"You're about to see the pallet wrapper machine in action," Anita said. "I wanted to show it to you this morning before we started verifying shipment dates, but there wasn't anything ready to be wrapped yet."

Without thinking of my safety, I stepped away from Anita the second the machine came on and inched nearer to it.

"Girl, don't get too close," Anita lightheartedly warned, "otherwise you're gonna get sealed with the product and be shipped out of here. We can't have that. Uh-uh. Think of how upset our customers would be when they found an item not pickled in their delivery."

Even though Anita was joking, I soon realized how mesmerizing a pallet wrapper machine presentation could be and took a few steps back. The stretch wrap didn't miss a beat. It continued to twirl and twirl around the stacked product in an upward motion and wouldn't stop until it completed the mission. I've used plenty of three-inch wide tape to wrap packages to be mailed, but the size of this wrap was unbelievable. Only comic book crime fighters like Superman or the Hulk could manage to use it. And when they did they'd have their have their foes wrapped up in a mega-second.

After watching the merry-go-round show for a couple minutes, I had to break the spell. I didn't want to puke on my tennis shoes.

"Seen enough?" Anita asked. When I didn't reply, she drew closer to me. "Good grief, girl. You look like you've been scared silly." She took ahold of my arm. "I'd better get you out of here before someone calls a medic."

"Good idea," I said as I quickly covered my mouth.

~55~

My stomach calmed down somewhat once Anita removed me from the area causing the nausea. I just didn't know where she planned to take me. As far as I knew there wasn't a room designated for First Aid, so that left the bathroom unless she was going to escort me up to HR. Although, I couldn't picture Anita taking on steps while assisting a person of my weight up them.

Anita halted the second she came upon a desk in Distribution, the one where I'd left the clipboard. "Here," she said, "lean up against the front of the desk while I get one of those folding chairs stacked by the doorway." After retrieving the chair, she placed it next to where I was standing and ordered me to sit and lean over.

I didn't argue. The stomach was still scrambled. I simply plopped down and hung my head like a hound dog.

The woman in charge of me slowly lowered her body to my level. "I'm going to go get you some water. Are you okay with that?"

I nodded briefly.

She patted my back. "Good. I'll be right back."

Even though I sat in a chair near the flow of foot traffic, no one questioned my behavior the whole time Anita was gone. That was fine with me. I would've been too embarrassed to explain.

Anita must've run all the way to the lunchroom and back. She returned huffing and puffing. As soon as her breathing flowed more evenly, she set the bottle of water she'd retrieved for me on the desk and unscrewed its cap. "There you go, girl. Drink as much of that water as you can. I can't have you collapsing on the job. We've got to finish what we started this morning."

"I'll be fine," I said after downing half a bottle of water. "I just needed to get away from that machine. I didn't realize how much it was affecting me."

She flapped her hand. "Honey, believe me I understand. When I was pregnant with my kids, everything bothered my stomach, including the Ferris wheel at Como Zoo."

I set my bottle of water on the desk. "But... but I'm not pregnant, Anita."

She stared at my mid-section. "Are you sure?"

"Positive." I stood up.

"Well, okay then," she said, swooping up the clipboard I'd used earlier. "Let's get back at it."

***

When we finished work for the day, Anita dragged up Roseanne again and her possible connection in the deaths of Don Hickleman and Paul Mason. Perhaps it was time to share with her about the note I found in Paul's pocket. I'd been keeping that bottled up long enough. Besides, there's always the possibility Anita may have been privy to something I wasn't.

Like before, when we ran into Butch after work, I suggested we talk away from the building, meaning in my car or hers. "But I can't chat too long," I said. "I have to be at a meeting by five."

"That's fine," Anita replied as she knotted her wool neck scarf and slipped on mittens. "I've gotta make a few stops on the way home myself. Christmas will be here before you know it." Looking like she just arrived from the Arctic Circle, she left her locker behind and made her way to the doorway to wait for me.

"Yup," I concurred, having struggled for the last five minutes to get my jacket zipper past my stomach. Somehow I'd outgrown my ski jacket since lunch. "According to my math, there's only twelve days left before Santa comes down the chimney and all the good boys and girls gather around their stockings to find out what the old man left." Determined to get the zipper up, I played with it yet again.

"It looks like you're fighting a losing battle," Anita said. "Do you want some help?"

"Nope." I took a deep breath and pulled in my stomach. "I just ate too many free sweets in the breakroom this afternoon." I tugged on the zipper one more time. It finally went up. "Okay, I'm ready to go if you are."

"Any idea what it's doing outside?" Anita asked as we headed towards the exit.

"No clue. I never checked my phone."

"That's all right. We'll find out soon enough."

When I pushed opened the door, my stocking cap blew off. Strong wind mixed with heavy snow was to blame. I picked it up off the ground before it took flight again. "Crap. I thought the weatherman said not to expect a shift in weather till this weekend. You can barely tell which car is which."

"Who ordered this anyway?" Anita complained, yanking her wool scarf loose and pulling it up over her head. "Girl, I'm thinking we'd better forget hanging around here, don't you?"

I nodded. "I'll come in a little earlier tomorrow before the rest of the crew. We can talk then."

"All right. Drive safely," Anita said, tightening her grip on her scarf. "I want to see you in one piece tomorrow."

"You too," and then I stomped off to find the VW, knowing I'd be out of the parking lot long before Anita found her snow covered car since she owned a mid-sized sedan and half the vehicles peppering the parking lot were similar to hers.

However, when I reached the car, I was in for a surprise and it had nothing to do with the battery. The two tires on the passenger side were flat. I guess Anita will make it out of the parking lot before me. Who knows how long it'll take a tow truck to get here. I unlocked the car and slipped inside.

As I sat behind the steering wheel watching the snow wrap its angry claws around everything in sight, two persistent questions pricked the recesses of my mind. Did I have a current VISA card? And, what were the chances of having two flat tires on the same day? Since the money situation ranked higher in importance than the other, I immediately dug through my purse, whipped out my wallet, and found I did indeed have a valid card to pay towing expenses.

No longer concerned about paying a bill, I moved on to the second question which required Google's services. Recalling how treacherous the freeway could be leading into downtown Minneapolis on a night like this, I quickly vetoed any unnecessary use of cell phone energy that might be needed later and simply stated the obvious. "Not likely. Something fishy was going on here."

I flipped the cell phone open, researched the nearest tow truck company, made the call, and then waited and waited. Fifteen minutes later a real human spoke and told me with the crazy road conditions I'd be lucky if I saw anyone in an hour. I drummed my fingers on the steering wheel. I might as well wait in the building instead of wasting gas.

I shoved the phone and car key in my purse and trudged back to the plant with no regard to being in the building by myself. Why should I? Hadn't several people informed me that the clean-up crew comes in after we leave?

~56~

Expecting to bump elbows with the clean-up crew when I stepped in the building, I was surprised to find the bright lights I worked under on the first shift had been dimmed considerably and no employees were roaming around. It freaked me out. That is until I realized the cleaners had probably been told to stay home due to the snowstorm. But then, why wasn't the building locked up?

Despite the eeriness surrounding me, I ventured forth, taking the path that led to the lunchroom where I could at least feed my fears. My stomach growled noisily. I took it as a sign it agreed with my decision.

As soon as I got to the lunchroom, I took off my jacket, opened my purse, and whipped out the phone along with a few bucks. The money was for treats: Snicker bar and Coke. The phone to let people know I'd be late, namely Aunt Zoe and Sgt. Murchinak.

After my stomach enjoyed a huge piece of the Snickers bar, I picked up the phone and punched in the number for the apartment. Once again, I was forced to waste precious phone usage, waiting for the dumb answer machine to kick in. Aunt Zoe, it's Mary," I finally said. "I wanted to let you know —" Shoot! Either the tape ran out, I lost cell power, or the phone battery died.

Before I bothered trying the apartment number again, I glanced at the top of the screen. Verizon was doing its part, but the battery displayed RED. Not good. It cut out even though it had shown half used when I called the towing company. This wasn't the first time the battery had let me down. I guess that's what I get for putting off updating the phone, but a new one is so dang expensive it would cut off my Christmas shopping before I even started, and I certainly didn't want to be thought of as Mary Scrooge.

Hoping I might have stashed the portable charger in my purse when I left for work that I share with Aunt Zoe, I dug through it once more. The only object I found that dealt with power was the stun gun. Aunt Zoe and Sgt. Murchinak would not be hearing from me after all.

Frustrated, I dropped my butt in a cold chair, chomped on the rest of the candy bar, and contemplated who was behind the cruel joke played on me. If the weather hadn't been so crummy to hinder the activity of a person on crutches, I'd have been inclined to rethink my thoughts on Chip's innocence.

Roseanne Harsh, on the other hand, still floated to the top of my suspect list. The trucker's timely arrival this morning and delayed departure had given her the perfect opportunity to damage my car tires. I'm such an idiot, letting her persuade me to ride with her to Tioni's. She probably came up with that scheme to keep me from discovering the flat tires too soon.

I'd just finished off the Snickers bar and had popped open the Coke can when I heard the clicking of high heels in the hallway, traveling my way at a rapid pace. Perhaps an office person stayed late to lock up. But what if it was the killer?

The minute the heels went silent I panicked. Was the wearer of the shoes merely weighing snack options, changing their route, or deciding how to deal with me? With nowhere to hide, I stuck my hand in my purse and wrapped it around the stun gun.

"Mary?" Sharon Sylvester said, flattening her hand against her chest as she burst through the doorway. "What are you doing here?"

"Two flat tires," I said, tensing up as I recalled the extremely expensive coat Sharon wore at Paul Mason's viewing and her so called friendship with Roseanne. "I already called a roadside service. They said it'll take at least an hour or more before they can tow my car out of here." There. Making sure Sharon knew someone expected to find me at the plant should be enough to safeguard me from any devious plans she might have had.

She dropped her hand to her side, acting as though the news didn't faze her. "Well, you certainly don't need to sit in these uncomfortable chairs. Grab your Coke and join me up in my office. It's warmer up there and I've got plenty of magazines for you to peruse while you wait."

I released the stun gun. Noticing Sharon didn't make a move towards the snack machines as I collected my jacket and purse, I said, "Did you come down here to get something to eat?"

"Ah, yes, but I changed my mind. The food in those machines can kill you."

Or someone at the plant. As I trudged up the steps behind Sharon, I wondered who else might be waiting for me and hoped I wasn't like a lamb being led to the slaughter.

***

The moment I entered the HR office I scanned every inch of it, looking for any indication that another individual had been keeping company with Sharon. I didn't find anything. Even so, every bone in my body told me to stay on guard.

As the mousey-looking woman breezed past the front of her cluttered desk to claim her swivel chair situated behind it, loose papers the size of spreadsheets fluttered in the air. Her hand shot out to catch them before they floated to the floor and then she sat.

"Hang up your belongings," Sharon's reedy voice suggested once she settled in. "And when you're done, check out one of the new leather chairs I purchased." She pointed to the ones she'd passed getting to her chair.

I hung the ski jacket on the coat rack, but not the purse. I'd keep that close by my side in case things suddenly turned ugly.

A gallon jar of whole pickles caught my eye when I sat. Probably because it seemed out of place in this particular work space, the corner of Sharon's desk. Not exactly a safe spot to store it. The pickles must be a new addition to her minimalist decorating scheme. Surely I'd have remembered seeing those six days ago when she told me I'd be getting a raise.

Catching my interest in the jar, Sharon said, "It was a birthday present."

"Oh?" I clasped my hands around the Coke can and rested it on my lap, patiently waiting for the woman to hand over the reading material she mentioned. As it turned out she never did. Apparently the offer of reading material was a ploy to snare me.

"Have a pickle," she said."

I questioned the offer. It wasn't exactly chocolate. "Ah, no thanks, I don't care for any."

"Have a pickle," she insisted more forcefully.

I took one. Little did I know how significant eating one dill pickle could be.

Sharon's honey-brown eyes lit up. "Taste it. You'll find it's quite delicious."

I bit into the huge pickle, hoping it hadn't been soaking in poison all day.

"My friend makes them especially for me."

Funny, hearing those words didn't make me feel warm and fuzzy all over. Although, after the huge pickle's slimy juice dribbled from my hand to the elbow, leaving the arm smelling vinegary, soaking in a bath crossed my mind. I rested the half-empty can of Coke on Sharon's desk and then I dug in my pant pockets for a Kleenex.

Sharon leaned her heart-shaped face over the desk and shared a wicked grin. "I hate cleaning up messes, don't you?"

I thought I knew where Sharon was going with talk of messes, but I wasn't in any hurry to get there. Instead, I pretended to be on a different page than her. "I definitely do. Especially the ones my roommate makes. Some nights when I get home after work the kitchen looks like a tornado whipped through it."

"That's not what I'm referring to," she snapped. "I know you've been snooping around, but who convinced you to do it? According to your resume, you haven't got the right background to be a PI."

I pretended her accusations shocked me. "I'm not. Whatever gave you that idea?"

"Let's just say I've heard things from others, but walls have ears too. And video cams come in mighty handy also."

"I don't know what walls can tell you, but you know how easy it is for jealous people to ruin someone's reputation. What exactly have you heard or seen?" I asked, noting Sharon's handwriting on a form lying on her desk. Another important piece of evidence I could use to prove who killed Paul.

Sharon rested her narrow chin on her hands. "Fine, have it your way. It's not going to matter in a few minutes anyway. Paul and Roseanne mentioned how uncomfortable they felt around you. According to them the new hire was asking way too many questions about the deceased, which gave me plenty of cause for concern. So I gave you a little rope to see what you'd come up with.

"This morning one of the video cams caught you using a door off limits. The only people I've ever seen using that exit door are smokers. But you're not a smoker, are you? Why would you go out that door, I wondered? Thanks to a certain air vent in the hallway on the main floor, it didn't take long to get the answer. I heard every word you spoke on your phone. You got a cucumber and wanted it analyzed. Too bad you told some cop your list of suspects was extremely short. You're a good worker, Mary. I would've liked to have kept you around longer, but you gave me no choice. I'm going to have to kill you."

I screwed up royally. Why didn't I transfer the stun gun from my purse to a pant pocket when Sharon led the way upstairs? I glanced at my purse on the floor. Could I get it to my lap in time? My hand tingled as I slyly slid my hand to the floor to retrieve the purse. What did Sharon add to the pickle brine? I have to get to the heart of the matter before I collapse.

"I didn't need to quiz you about Don and Paul's deaths," I said, as my purse flopped over on the carpet and the stun gun fell out. "Sure you had the means and opportunity, but I couldn't put a finger on your motive until recently. This all started with the theft of the pickle recipes, didn't it?"

Sharon glared at me. "How did you figure that out?"

I yawned. "Selling company recipes would give you enough money to do whatever you wanted. Buy an expensive coat or even a pickle company. Before you could take over Pickledom though, you'd have to get rid of Don Hickleman first and his illegitimate son." I leaned over the arm of the chair, but couldn't quite scoop up the stun gun. Thank goodness Aunt Zoe bought me one that looks like a camera. At least there's no chance Sharon will use it on me.

"If you're reaching for your phone," Sharon said, "don't bother. It's too late." She got out of her chair and came around to the front of her desk.

My tongue was growing heavier as the seconds ticked by, but I wasn't going to let that stop me from talking. When the bad guy corners the good guy, the good guy always stalls for time until help can arrive. Not that it's going to make a difference for me. No one knows where I am. "Paul Mason was blackmailing you, but not just over the theft of the recipes. What else did you find in the vault that day?"

"The new will Don had recently drawn up." When Sharon leaned over to help my ragdoll-like body out of the chair, she spotted the object that had fallen out of my purse. "Is there any incriminating evidence on that camera of yours?" she quizzed before kicking it under her desk.

"Maybe."

"Well, you'll love where I'm taking you then." She pulled twine out of her pant pocket, tied my hands together, and led me towards the stairs.

~57~

Chills ran through my body as I remembered where Don and Paul's bodies had been dumped, a vat and a walk-in fridge. One had to walk towards the other end of the building to get to those locations. So when Sharon dragged me down the dimly lit hallway towards the distribution area, I was caught totally off guard. What could she possibly have in mind? There was no place to hide a body there.

When we reached our destination, Sharon turned up the overhead lights and set my sluggish frame down. Sitting here in this particular spot by the desk brought to mind the nausea I experienced this afternoon after watching the pallet wrapper in action. I never wanted to feel that way again.

In my weakened condition, I was finding it hard to remain upright. Sharon clutched my shoulder to keep me from falling. "I understand a certain machine in this department has left an indelible impression on you. Lucky for you, Mary, I've put in enough time at this plant to know exactly how every machine operates and can offer you the same thrilling experience again tonight." She helped me out of the chair and brought me over to the pallet wrapper machine.

"Look at that," Sharon's voice shrilled in the range of High C. She plucked up a long piece of wire that hadn't been tossed in the trash. "How thoughtful of the men to leave me something to wrap you up in. Shall we get to it?" she asked not waiting for a reply.

Holding me and the wire with one hand, Sharon used the other to push a movable ladder up to the wrapper machine where a customer's order sat waiting to get wrapped in the morning. "I'm so tired of cleaning up messes," Sharon sighed. "If only Don had kept his promises to me. But no, he'd rather be a chameleon, changing his tune whenever he saw fit. He was supposed to marry me after his wife died. Do you see a ring on my finger?" She flashed her left hand in my face. "Of course not."

Sharon forced me up the steps and unto the platform. After she wrapped the wire around me and the jars of pickles, she climbed off the platform and flipped the switch to run the pallet wrapper.

The stretch wrap whizzed past my feet and kept going. There was no stopping it.

This is it. Death was knocking at my door. I didn't expect to pass over to the next world this soon. Incredible as it may sound, my life didn't flash before my eyes, like I've heard it's supposed to. I also didn't feel the need to make things right with my Maker. Which one could take as a good sign or not, depending on how you looked at it. What did cross my brain waves then? I'll tell you. *What a way to go out, wrapped up as a Christmas present. Won't the company receiving this order be surprised.*

The wrap was gaining ground on my upper torso. It was only a matter of minutes before it suffocated me. *Too bad no one knows where I am.*

"What the heck is going on here?" a male voice shouted.

Lack of oxygen must be affecting my brain. The guy who asked the question sounded like my brother Matt, but that's impossible. He's not due to arrive back in the States till next week. Maybe it's the tow truck driver. I waited to hear more.

"Shut that machine off now," he commanded.

Whoa. This dude could definitely pass for Matt. He cuts to the chase, doesn't waste a single word.

"Not until this order is finished," Sharon screamed.

"Fine. I'll take care of it myself."

Pressed too tightly against the pickle jars and pallets, I couldn't witness the battle below, but I could hear it. Chairs and tools were being tossed about. Then nothing except the noise of the machine until it went dead too.

I couldn't believe it. I'd been saved. Whoever my hero was deserved a big smackeroo.

"Mary, are you okay?" my brother asked, as he tried to cut through the stretch wrap under my armpits with a utility knife.

"I feel woozy and itch all over. We gotta find out what Sharon added to the jar of pickles in her office. What did you do with her?"

"I knocked her unconscious."

"Well, at least she'll snap out of it."

Matt continued to cut through the tape. "Don't fret. Everything is under control. The cops are on their way. They'll get her to talk."

Now that my hands were free, I helped Matt tear away the tape from the lower half of my body. "I can't believe you're here. How did you know where to find me?"

"Call it a hunch."

"Uh-huh. What's so wrong with saying you had a premonition?"

"Stop talking," he ordered, "or I'll end up slicing you."

~58~

A few minutes after Matt had freed my body from its sticky prison, the police arrived on the scene anxious to bombard me with questions. Unfortunately, my behavior and the words I expressed didn't impress the men in blue.

Here I am, this crazy-looking broad, who can barely stand on two feet, rubbing off what appears to be imaginary substance from her clothing while blubbering on about Hickleman's HR Director who is slumped in a chair. If I'd been the main interrogation guy, I'd have escorted me to the nearest padded cell for a long rest. Thankfully Matt added excerpts along the way, which cut the questions down considerably, and I was finally told I could go home.

Frazzled from the events that took place within this past hour, I grabbed my brother's hand for support. "Get me out of here, Matt. I never want to step foot in this plant again as long as I live."

"I hear you, sis." He threw his arm around my shoulder and quickly steered me out of the distribution area and into the hallway near a window that overlooked the parking lot. "The wind is still whipping the snow around out there. You're going to need a jacket. Tell me where it's stashed and I'll get it."

My knees buckled. Matt caught me before I hit the floor. "That won't work," I said. "My purse and coat are up in Sharon's office with her belongings. It'll take too much time to describe them."

"Then I'm going with you. You're not too steady on your feet yet."

"If you insist." When I lifted an arm to point out the stairs to Matt, I noticed something different about him. "What's with the thin band of hair above your upper lip? Did you forget to shave?"

"No." He rubbed his mustache. "Don't' you like it?"

I walked into Sharon's office. "I'm not sure. Maybe it'll grow on me."

It's funny how one can miss certain things when you're focused on the conversation at hand, like my not noticing Matt's mustache right off the bat. The few times I'd been in Sharon's office I'd never noticed a small framed photo of Don Hickleman resting on a large oak bookcase that covered one whole wall. But I did now as I collected the stun gun off the floor and shoved it in my purse.

"What are you staring at?" Matt asked.

"That picture on the third shelf over there." I strolled over to the bookcase and picked it up.

"Do you recognize the photo?"

I nodded. "It's Don Hickleman, one of the men Sharon killed. He owned the plant." I studied the photo for a few more seconds, and then set it down. "How could I have missed it?"

He ran a hand through his red hair. "Missed what?"

"A piece of the puzzle has been sitting out in the open all this time. 'The eyes are the window to your soul,' according to Shakespeare, but in the case of Don Hickleman, they merely lead me to his illegitimate son."

Matt led me out of Sharon's office. "Then I'd say you hit the jackpot. That tidbit alone should be worth plenty, don't you think?"

"Not if he's who I'm thinking of."

By the time we returned to the main floor, my body felt a bit stronger, but the itching had increased due to the antihistamines Sharon had added to the pickles on her desk. A drug she learned I was allergic to. At least I knew I hadn't ingested poison and there was an immediate solution to my problem.

With all that happened, I hadn't given any regard to how my brother got out here until we were ready to walk out of the plant. "Who lent you their car, Matt?"

"No one. Rod Thompson happened to be home and offered to drive me. I told him to watch for the cops and tell them which door I'd gone in."

I zipped up my ski jacket and threw the hood over my head. I wasn't ready to face Rod Thompson. He'd have too much to say and I didn't want to hear it. "Matt, do you think you could convince Rod that I don't feel up to conversing with anyone on the way home?"

"Sure, leave it to me, sis."

~59~

Rod parked his car in his slot at the Foley, opened the back door, and stuck his head in, forcing me to remain seated. "Mary," he whispered, "there is something you should know before we go up to Matt's apartment—"

"Come on you two," Matt interrupted, "Aunt Zoe promised to have a delicious supper waiting for us and I haven't had a decent meal since early this morning."

I looked at Rod. "Should I warn him about her cooking?"

"Nah, let him be surprised."

As it turned out, I was the one surprised when we got to Matt's apartment, not only by the cooking but other developments as well.

Knowing how frantic Aunt Zoe must've been not hearing a peep out of me since I left for work, I expected her to throw herself at me the second we walked through the door. Instead, it was Gracie who flew at us at lightning speed in the narrow entryway, almost bowling the three of us over. "Wuff, wuff. Wuff, wuff."

I glanced at Rod standing behind me. He winked. So that's what he wanted to tell me. Gracie was back. I stooped down, rubbed her noggin, and hugged her. "I missed you too, but I bet you're even more excited to see your master." I couldn't get over how good the mutt looked considering she'd been missing for eighteen days. Someone had to have been feeding her. Even though I was dying to hear where she'd been found, I'd have to wait till I got Margaret or Aunt Zoe alone.

Gracie drew up alongside Matt and wagged her tail.

Eager to meet my brother's fiancée, I hung up our coats and then stepped into the living room. "What the heck?"

"Is something wrong?" Matt asked, coming up from behind.

I cleared my throat. "Ah, no." The living room was immaculate. The Vegas look had vanished. Margaret, Aunt Zoe, and Deirdre, Matt's fiancée, were sitting on the plain black sleeper couch. "I had ah, asked Aunt Zoe to dust and vacuum and I see she got it done. The room looks great, Auntie."

She smiled. "I thought you'd be pleased."

"I, ah, yeah I am."

Matt went over by Deirdre and plopped his 190-pound frame on the arm of the couch. "I can't remember when the living room looked this good."

Funny, I don't either.

Aunt Zoe stood. "Well, I tried to remember to put everything back the way we found it. As one grows older the brain cells tend to get foggier."

Not Margaret's.

Not wanting to hear any more about old age this evening, I quickly introduced myself to Deirdre, whose Caribbean-blue eyes looked straight into my soul. Perhaps she had a wee bit of gypsy in her. I hope she couldn't see much. "Congratulations, Deirdre. I've been looking forward to meeting you. I'm Mary, Matt's baby sister. Sorry I delayed supper so long. We had no idea you two would be arriving today. And wouldn't you know it when I finished work I discovered my car had two flat tires and my cell phone battery was dead." It had been a strenuous evening for everyone involved, and so that's where I left my tale for now. Besides, there were plenty of days ahead to share my close encounter with death.

Deirdre's appearance surprised me. I thought Matt would be steered towards a woman that reminded him of his ex-girlfriend Rita Sinclair, who was around five-four in height, had curves in all the right places, long curly dark hair, and emerald–green eyes. But Deirdre had short bobbed red hair that set her face on fire. She was much taller than Rita, thin as a stick, and flat chested. Her skinniness reminded me of Twiggy, a British model from the 1960s.

Margaret pushed herself off the couch. "Well, shall we go into dinner everyone?"

Rod begged off. "I really should get going," he said. "I've got a ton of paperwork sitting on my desk," and then he headed to the door.

"You're not going anywhere, young man," Margaret said. "You're included in this dinner as well. We're celebrating Matt's return with Shepherd pie and chocolate mint eclairs. Deirdre helped us with the preparations"

"And I've got good news to talk about too," Aunt Zoe shared. "Reed Griffin finally popped the question."

"What? When?" I said. "That means I'll be on my own?"

"Don't worry, sis. You can stay here. Mom and Dad said Deirdre and I could live with them until we find a house of our own."

"Hmm?" Rod looked at me and grinned. "This is turning out to be a very interesting evening? I guess I could forgo my dinner of Lutefisk. Come on, Gracie. I bet they've got a bowl of food for you too."

"Wuff, wuff.

Epilogue

Day 22

The Hoop and Holler Tavern in Spring Lake Park, where Matt and I chose to have a late lunch, was extremely busy for a Monday. It probably had something to do with people being cooped up in their homes all weekend due to the heavy snowstorm that cut a wide path across Minnesota.

After a twenty minute wait on barstools, in the dimly lit tavern with darkly- stained tongue and grove oak walls and no windows to speak of, the two of us were finally ensconced in the perfect spot, a booth near the back of the building, a good distance from the busyness of the bar area and much quieter; a place where one could actually have a decent conversation without shouting.

"I really appreciate Deirdre letting you spend time with me, Matt, especially since the police wanted to go over what happened one more time."

"Ah, that's what I love about her, sis. She's so laid back nothing gets to her. Besides, Mom offered to take her to the mall so she could buy a few Christmas presents."

"I hope you've got Deirdre's gift already. I know how you love to put off shopping till the last minute."

"Don't worry; I've got it taken care of. It's even wrapped."

"Whoa, Ireland has definitely changed you." I picked up my glass of Guinness the waitress just delivered and sampled it. "Not too bad. But I think I like 2 Gingers Irish Whiskey better."

Matt clinked his beer glass against mine. "*Sláinte*," he said and then took a couple sips of his drink before biting into a mustard-coated pretzel. "Did the folks ever tell you they thought about owning a bar like this?"

"Nope. I never heard that story. I wonder why they didn't go through with it."

"They probably thought they couldn't afford it with a third kid on the way."

I nibbled on a pretzel. "I've never liked being the fourth in line, but it does have its merits. At least I can't be blamed for Mom and Dad not taking on a business venture."

"Speaking of business, what on earth were you thinking of taking on a case at a pickle plant? You could've been seriously maimed or killed."

"But I'm still here," I said, brushing pretzel crumbs into the center of the table, "thanks to you."

"By the way, you never did tell me how the heck you got involved in the murder of Don Hickleman in the first place. Was it something you heard via the media?"

I held up a finger. "Just a minute. I want to flag the waitress down while she's looking our way."

The gal picked up the clue. She immediately rushed to our booth, bent her head slightly, and inquired what we needed. "Would you like another round of Guiness, Miss?"

"Not right now. However, I would like an order of Chicken Quesadilla please and an extra plate. Thanks."

"Got it," and she hustled off to the kitchen.

The minute our waitress was out of hearing range, I gave Matt a short explanation on how I wound up at Hickleman's Pickle Plant. "My taking on a case at the pickle plant had nothing to do with a news reports. Gertie Nash, at the Foley, had been bugging me since summer to help clear her Cousin Butch of a crime he supposedly hadn't committed, namely the theft of pickle recipes. Every time she approached me about his problem I refused to get involved. But then Butch got arrested towards the end of November for the murder of Don Hickleman and I knew I had to do something."

Matt pushed his fists into his cheeks. "That's when you got the idea to work undercover, right?" I nodded. "Nice idea, sis, but stupid move."

"Considering what almost happened to me I agree with you. I don't know why I thought I could handle this type of work. As a matter of fact, I'm thinking of going back to college to get another degree."

"It might be a good idea, but don't make any hasty decisions," he said. "Those cops you spoke with in the interrogation room today must've appreciated your input, Mary. They kept you long enough. Obviously, you told them more than you'd shared with me that day at the plant. Care to spill your guts now that we're alone?"

"Well—"

"Mary, there you are," Aunt Zoe said, squinting at us. "It's so dark in here I didn't think we'd find you." She set a package on the table. "Thanks for telling your dad where you two were stopping off for a bite to eat otherwise I'd still be sitting at the apartment."

"Matt must've texted him," I said, leaning sideways to see who stood behind her. I'd assumed she would be with Reed. She wasn't. "Trevor, what are you doing here? I didn't think you were coming down till the twenty-third."

"That was the plan," he said, "but then I caught the news that police arrested an employee from Hickleman's for the murder of Don Hickleman and Paul Mason so I decided to come to the cities a day early to help you celebrate." He squeezed my shoulder. "I'm so proud of you."

I would've told Trevor how much those few words meant to me, but with Matt having witnessed first-hand that I almost died I didn't dare express what I felt. "Matt, this is my friend Trevor Fitzwell. He works the beat for the Duluth Police."

"Yes," Aunt Zoe proudly exclaimed, acting as if she was Trevor's relative, "and his K9 partner Duke is out in the car."

Matt's hand shot out. "Nice to meet you, Trevor."

Trevor smiled and shook his hand. "You too. Your sister talks about you and your dog Gracie all the time."

Matt gave me a dirty look before scooting over to make room for Trevor on his bench.

"Don't worry," I said, "It's all good stuff," and then I slid over and Aunt Zoe sat next to me. What's in the package, Auntie? Been out Christmas shopping?"

She tapped her nails on the table. "Nope, but it's a gift to be revealed at the proper time."

"Good thing the chef cut your order into pie-shaped pieces," our waitress said as she set the quesadilla in the middle of the table. "Looks like you need two more plates."

"Yes," I replied, "and we could use a couple beverages as well: a Guiness and a Pinot Grigio."

"Coming right up," she said and went off to the bar.

"Zoe filled me in a bit on what happened at the plant on the way here," Trevor explained while keeping his gray-heavy-set eyes on me. "But I wouldn't mind hearing it from your lips, Mary, if you don't mind."

I shook my head. "I don't mind. Matt had just asked me the same thing right before you arrived. Taking a job at a place like the pickle plant offered plenty of opportunities for someone like me to pick up the latest gossip. Something I couldn't have done working the case from the outside. One rumor for instance led me to believe shift supervisor Paul Mason might have stolen company recipes years ago and possibly killed Don Hickleman to cover it up.

"Strange how things work out," I continued. "The morning of December sixth, Paul had asked me to meet him in the lunch room at noon. I didn't know why and thought perhaps he'd figured out what I was actually doing there. Unfortunately, I found Paul's body in the walk-in shortly before noon. While I waited for the cops to arrive, I searched his pockets for clues."

"Did you find anything," Matt asked.

"There was a note. Someone requested Paul meet up with them. I figured a woman. Roseanne Harsh, a trucker, came to mind. She had been delivering cucumbers to the plant for years and had a reputation with the men, including Don Hickleman."

I took a break, ate a slice of quesadilla, washed it down with the beer, and then continued. "Roseanne knew her way around the plant and could've easily stuffed cucumbers down Don and Paul's throat. Heck, maybe she'd killed other people using that same signature. But what motive did she have? If Roseanne stole the recipes and sold them, why was she still trucking all over the place?"

Aunt Zoe broke in. "Then someone attacked Chip O'Leary, the vat manager and Mary thought of Roseanne again."

"Yes. I'd witnessed her and Chip having a tiff over some secret they'd been keeping under wraps. So when she heard news of Chip being in the hospital, I didn't know how to read her reaction. Was Roseanne genuinely surprised or did she try to knock Chip off and fail?"

Trevor ran a hand through his thick hair. "I remember you telling me about that incident when I spoke with you on the eighth. However, you forgot to keep your promise you made to me."

I feigned forgetfulness. "What was that?"

"To keep me in the loop."

"Ah, well, nothing of significance came to light until Aunt Zoe and I attended Paul Mason's funeral on the twelfth."

Matt slipped his hands around his glass. "What was it, sis?"

"When Aunt Zoe mentioned what an expensive winter coat Sharon Sylvester had on, I immediately asked myself where she'd gotten the money to purchase it. That's when it dawned on me. Sharon had to have stolen the company's pickle recipes from the vault and sold them to a competitor. Mystery of recipe theft solved. But who killed Don and Paul? Had Roseanne played me like a fiddle?

"If she had, she wasn't going to get away with her crimes. In order to prove once and for all whether Roseanne was guilty or not, I decided to steal a cucumber from the next load she delivered and have Sgt.

Murchinak's lab compare it to the evidence found in the dead men's throats."

"Pretty much what I would've done too," Matt said.

I didn't know if my brother was being sarcastic or not. It had been a while since we'd had any kind of lengthy conversation.

Aunt Zoe sighed. "So that's why you wanted Sgt. Murchinak to know you'd be calling him."

I nodded. "I made a terrible mistake calling him from the plant. Every word I said was carried up through the heating vent to Sharon Sylvester's office. But it worked out in the long run. She confessed to everything: setting Butch up, stealing the recipes, killing Don and Paul, and injuring Chip." I picked up my beer and finished it.

"Wow, that's some story, Mary," Trevor said. "I don't know why I was ever worried about you being in danger. You did all right."

If he only knew.

Aunt Zoe turned to face me. "Mary, did Sharon ever say why she committed those crimes?"

"She didn't plan to kill anybody. All she wanted to do was get even with Don Hickleman for jilting her twice, once when she was sixteen and eight years ago. When the opportunity to steal the recipes came along, she went for it. Unfortunately, Don Hickleman finally figured out Butch hadn't stolen the recipes when he began to think about retiring and Sharon asked if he was still leaving the plant to her. He knew the only reason she'd ask that is if she'd read a copy of the will he kept in the safe. According to Sharon they had a late night confrontation that just got out of hand."

"What about Paul Mason?" Aunt Zoe inquired.

"Anyone care for another round of drinks?" Matt asked.

"No thanks," the three of us replied.

My stomach grumbled. Apparently the little I ate didn't help. I glanced at my watch: four more hours till supper. "Apparently Paul had put two and two together and Sharon was afraid he'd squeal." I slapped my forehead. "I'll be darn. Miss Marple warned a character in a story to watch out for the 'dyed blonde'. Guess what? Sharon Sylvester's real hair color is auburn."

"Really! How crazy is that?" Matt said, stretching his arms out over the table. "So who gets ownership of the pickle plant, sis?"

"Chip O'Leary, Don Hickleman's illegitimate son."

"Well, that ties everything up neatly, doesn't it," he said. "Aunt Zoe, I think it's time to show Mary what's in your package."

Aunt Zoe tore the envelope open and handed me huge eyelashes. "As soon as I saw these in a magazine, I knew I had to get them for your car. You attach them to your headlights. You're always saying how stressful driving can be. Now, everyone on the road will get a chuckle when you pass them by."

I gave her a hug. "You're the best."

"Hey if that's what it takes to get a hug," Matt said, "Wait till you hear what I have to say. I don't think you should go back to college, Mary. With all the work that'll be coming into my office, it's time for me to hire some help. What would you think of joining me?"

"Why… why would you want to hire me? You know the serious mistakes I made on this case."

Matt laughed. "You've proven that you've learned from your mistakes. Besides, I don't know anyone else who does as good a job of snooping."

I smiled back at my brother. He had no idea all the problems I had while he was gone, especially these past several weeks, but everything worked out in the end. Gracie was found on the steps of the police station, the living room was changed back to its original décor, I don't have to live with a roommate anymore, and I've got a new job. The only thing I haven't figured out is what to do with the two men in my life, David and Trevor. But that's a problem that'll keep for another day.

My Great Aunt Mame's Refrigerator Pickles

7 cups of unpeeled thick cut cucumbers (about 2 pounds)
1 chopped onion
2 Tablespoons of salt

Mix all together. Let stand for 2 hours. Then drain, but don't rinse.

Meanwhile, Mix 1 cup of white vinegar and 2 cups of sugar together before adding to cucumbers that have been drained. Fill sterilized canning jars. If you wish, add I teaspoon of pickling spice. Pickles last for several months in refrigerator.

■■■

Annette's Solar Pickles

Cut off ends of cucumbers and place in clean sterilized gallon jar.
Add:
Dill and garlic to taste
2 Tablespoons of salt
2 Tablespoons of honey
2 to 3 slices of Rye Bread
Boil:
2 quarts of water
3 cups of Apple Cider Vinegar
Cool until warm and then pour into jar. Put lid on tight. Set in full sun for 4 days and nights. **Refrigerate after opened.

■■■

Sweet Dommie Pickles

Buy 1 quart jar of small size dills--slice thinly
1 small onion thinly sliced
1 cup sugar
1 cup vinegar (if using dark vinegar need: ¾ cup of vinegar with ¼ cup of water) Boil vinegar and sugar for two minutes and

then pour immediately over sliced pickles and onions. Cool and store in a container in refrigerator.

■■■

Betty's Pickled Veggies

1 ½ -2lbs. vegetables cut into 4-5 spears such as peeled carrots, sweet onions, cucumbers, and yellow summer squash.

3 ½ - 4 cups fruit-flavored white balsamic vinegar. Can use mango, blood orange, apricot, or black currant for flavoring vinegar).

Directions for making flavored balsamic vinegar: Combine 3 cups of white balsamic vinegar with 1 cup of fruit or nectar mentioned above.

Wash vegetables. Place in two sterilized 1 quart glass canning jars. Add 1/8 tsp. pepper and a dill sprig to each jar. In medium saucepan bring vinegar to boil. Immediately pour over veggies in jars. Cover and chill 5 days in fridge.

■■■

Mike's Pickled Northern

Filet Northern and cut into bite size pieces—bones and all, except rib bones which will dissolve. Soak fish in salt water heavy enough to float an egg (Continue to add salt till egg definitely floats) Fish soaks in salt water for 24-48 hours. Then rinse pan and wash fish in cold water. Return fish to container used in first step. Cover with white vinegar and soak another 24 hours.

Drain. Use sterilized quart or gallon jar and layer fish and sliced onions in container.

Prepare Syrup: 1 cup water   2 cups white vinegar   ¾ cups sugar and

1 Tablespoon pickling spice. Boil for five minutes. Cool syrup and add

1 cup white wine. Pour over fish. Cover and Refrigerate 3-4 days before eating.

Bart's Pickled Brussels Sprouts

Need 4 Pint Jars
2 Teaspoons of dill
2 Teaspoons of garlic
1 Teaspoon of mustard seed
1 Teaspoon of sugar
2 ¼ cups of water
2 ¼ white vinegar
2 Tablespoons of salt
Stir all in pot and bring to boil for 5 minutes. While water boils, wash and prep 4-5 quarts of brussels sprouts (removing any brown leaves). Put in large bowl and then pour pickling broth over brussels sprouts. Cool to room temperature. Put sprouts in sterilized jars and ladle liquid over them, leaving ½ inch space between liquid and top of jar rim. Seal with lids. Wait at least 2-3 weeks to eat. Use within 3 months or so after opened.

■■

Suzie's Pickled Eggs

1 dozen hard boiled eggs
2 Cups of white vinegar
1 Teaspoon salt
1 Teaspoon pepper
1 Teaspoon of dry mustard or 1 Tablespoon of yellow mustard seeds
2 Tablespoons of Pickling Spice
½ of a medium onion thinly sliced
1 cup of water
Combine all, except hardboiled eggs, in large pot. Bring to boil and cook 5 minutes. Put hardboiled eggs in sterilized jars. Can use whatever size you want. Pour hot brine over eggs. Place lids on tight and refrigerate for at least 4 days. Uneaten chilled eggs can be kept up to a month.
***Easier version of pickled eggs-Take 6 hardboiled eggs and place in jar of pickle juice left from eating pickles. Make sure eggs are covered and fit that size jar. Leave in jar for 3 days.

Barbara's Crystal Pickles

Put 25 dill size cucumbers in brine strong enough to float an egg and cover cucumbers. Let cucumbers stand in brine 2 weeks.

Brine solution: 2 cups coarse salt to a gallon of water. To keep cucumbers covered in brine weigh down with a plate.

1. After 2 weeks take out of brine. Drain and wash. Cut into thin slices.
2. Put 2 Tablespoons of powdered alum (or piece size of walnut) in enough water to immerse slices completely in alum/water solution. Add enough ice cubes so water is icy and let stand overnight.
3. Next day drain and wash slices. Set slices aside in a container and proceed with the following: Place in a cloth sack: 2 sticks of cinnamon (broken) and 1 Tablespoon of whole cloves. Tie sack and add it to 1 quart of cider vinegar and 2 quarts of sugar. Bring to boil. Then pour boiling hot mixture over slices. Refrigerate overnight.
4. The next day take slices out of liquid, but save liquid. Wash slices and set aside as before. Then bring liquid to boil again, pour over slices and refrigerate. REPEAT this process 2 more days.
5. On the 4th day, put sliced pickles in sterilized jars and pour the hot vinegar solution on top of pickles. Seal jars.

▪▪

Jeanne's Dilled Green Beans

4 lbs. Fresh Whole Green Beans
½ Tsp. of Dill seed per pint jar
¼ Tsp. of crushed Hot Red Pepper per pint jar
½ Tsp. per pint jar-Whole Mustard Seed
1 clove of Garlic per pint jar
Fresh Dill Sprigs
5 cups of Vinegar
5 cups of Water
One-third cup of Canning Salt

1. Wash beans thoroughly; Drain: Remove stems. Cut into lengths to fit pint jars. Pack beans as tightly as possible in sterile jars. Then add pepper, mustard seed, dill seed, garlic, and fresh dill.
2. Combine vinegar, water, and salt. Heat to boiling. Pour boiling liquid over beans – filling to ½ inch from top of jar. Put jar lids on and screw on rings until tightened.
3. Process jars in boiling water for 5 minutes (start to count processing time as soon as water in canner returns to boiling). Remove jars. Set jars upright on wire rack to cool. Let sit at least a month before using.

Book Club Questions
Death of the Pickle King

1. What were the problems Mary needed to resolve before her brother Matt returned to the States? Did she succeed in resolving them?

2. Does Margaret Grimshaw offer sufficient advice to Mary whenever she seeks it?

3. Did you think Mary would ever decide to help Butch with his issues? Why or why not?

4. If you were Mary, an amateur sleuth, would you have taken on a job at the plant without some sort of backup?

5. When Mary first picked up gossip at work, who did you suspect might have killed Don Hickleman?

6. By the time this book draws to an end, has Mary's feelings in regards to her aunt's incompetence changed much?

7. Share some of the red herrings the author has sprinkled throughout the novel.

8. At any point in this novel did you feel Anita Crane might have killed Don Hickleman and Paul Mason? If so, what lead you to believe that?

9. Were you surprised to find out who actually murdered the two men and stole the company recipes?

10. Which character in this book was your favorite? Why?

11. What fact about the pickling process impressed you the most?

Made in the USA
Monee, IL
28 August 2020